The Chronicles of
ARAX

BOOK 1

OF WAR
AND
HEROES

BENJAMIN SANFORD

STENOX PUBLISHING
Clarksburg, MD

First originally published by Page Publishing 2021

Cover Art by Karl Moline

ISBN 979-8-9886249-0-5 (paperback)
ISBN 979-8-9886249-1-2(digital)

Printed in the United States of America

CHAPTER 1

A strong northern gale swept through the trees, drying the sweat building on his forehead. The solace of the early spring wind quickly waned as Terin urged the moglo beast onward, driving the double-bladed plow through the aqueous soil. Sweat ran down his back, soaking his brown tunic in wet patches. His bare legs and lower tunic were caked in black soil thrown up by the plow. The sun shone bright in the clear morning sky, bathing the land in warmth and light. This was Terin's last furrow, and he urged the beast forward despite the plow strap around his neck biting his flesh.

His dark-blue eyes lifted to his father's towering form waiting for him at the row's end. At sixty-eight inches, his father was the tallest man Terin had ever known. His taut muscled arms were crossed over his brown tunic as his eyes looked to his son with pride, smiling as the boy finished the last row. Terin ducked under the plow strap and stepped carefully through the soft furrow to unfasten the beast from the plow. Free of the plow, the beast lumbered forward, pulling the leather harness painfully from Terin's grip, burning his hand. Though wincing in pain, he did not cry out. He shook his right hand up and down, shaking off the pain.

"You have your mother's temperament. I would have kicked the beast and shouted a few choice words," Jonas said. Terin smiled at the thought, as he could clearly envision his father doing just that. Terin's mother, on the other hand, was slow to anger. Whenever pain or ill fortune visited her, she would respond with her soft voice and easy manner. "I'll have those," Jonas said, taking the lead ropes from Terin's hand, taking the beast in tow.

"Thank you, Father, but what about the plow?"

"I'll tend to it later. Your mother is waiting for you in the house. Your work is done here, son. Tomorrow, your new life begins."

Terin paused, stopping in the pasture, taking in the surroundings for the last time. All his father's fields were plowed. The dark, rich soil was turned over in long, even folds, awaiting the seeds that his father would bury along their furrows. Lupec and porian trees pressed close to the fields' northern edge while the southern edge bordered a meandering small stream.

Across the stream was the Jorgens' farm. They were friends and neighbors. Devlin Jorgen was a hardworking, hard-drinking man, who boasted four sons and three daughters in his brood. He and Jonas were close friends, and Devlin pledged his sons to help Jonas with his planting once Terin departed. Jonas had thanked them and would pay the boys a fair wage for their effort. Terin looked east and west along the stream with guilt as he beheld the work he was leaving his father to do alone.

"Perhaps I should stay, Father," he lamented.

Jonas grabbed his son's tunic sleeve with his free hand and dragged him along, leading the moglo beast with the other. "You're leaving tomorrow for Rego City, son. I'll hear no more about it."

*****

The house rested high off the stream. It was made with treated porian logs and ceramic-plated shingles over a steep, slanted roof. A graveled pathway separated the simple structure from the stable that rested just north of it. Unlike the stone, adobe, and brick structures that dotted the landscape of Arax's larger cities, rural dwellings were an assortment of whatever raw materials were locally available. Jonas Caleph had labored many years to build and perfect their log and stone home. It was comfortable, practical, and blended into their natural surroundings.

Terin entered the front door, stepping into the home's common area. The floor of this large, expansive room was made of flat, polished stones of various sizes melded together with stained mortar. A large stone hearth and chimney dominated the east wall, and a kitchen area the west wall. His parents' bedroom rested in the southeast corner while a wooden ladder led to the loft above where Terin slept. Near the back, his mother waited, standing beside the open rear door.

Terin's mother turned as her son entered the house, smiling, her eyes taking in his handsome face. He inherited her easy manner and golden hair and his father's face, but his dark-blue eyes were his own. Valera Caleph was still a beautiful woman despite years of country life and labor. An Araxan woman's skin kept its elasticity as she aged and her bone density as well. Only strands of silver hair denoted an Araxan's true age, and Valera could not stay the silver strands that began to shade her golden locks.

"You need a bath," Valera's soft voice said as her left hand directed him to the open doorway. "You need to wash the farm smell out of you before you track dirt over my clean floor!" she reprimanded before he could commit the crime.

"Close your eyes first."

"Terin Caleph, I've seen you naked since you were born and feeding off my bosom. Now strip and get in the tub!" she scolded him, her hands on her hips.

"Yes, ma'am," Terin conceded with a laugh. He stripped off his garments and crossed the floor and through the open door. Just outside, a metal tub rested over a stone circle surrounding a cluster of glowing coals, just warm enough to heat the water without boiling him once he stepped within. With trees edging the rear of the house, no one should see him bathing in the open air.

"Your undergarment too," she added.

He complied before stepping in one foot after the other. The warm water soothed his aching muscles as he sat down, the soapy lather lapping his chest as he closed his eyes. Valera retrieved a pot of heated water from the hearth and poured it over his head to wash his hair. She spent the morning bringing water from the stream, one bucket at a time, to fill the larger tub. Terin knew how much her back must have ached from the laborious task and would offer no more argument to anything she might ask of him. That was how mothers were, always pushing themselves to exhaustion for their child's benefit.

Terin was to journey to Rego City. Jonas's old friend Squid Antillius was the Torry ambassador to Rego. He offered Terin an appointment as his assistant and scribe, a rare opportunity for any lad, let alone one not born to privilege. For this position, Valera knew Terin needed to smell the part of an ambassador's assistant as well as look the part. She had taught him to read and write at an early age while Jonas taught him the sword and bow.

Valera went back in the house, returning after several minutes with a dry towel and fresh undergarment, tunic, and sandals, setting them nearby, leaving Terin to bathe.

*****

Valera prepared a meal of fish and wild tersk mixed with vegetables from her garden. They sat around the small table in the common room, eating the meal by candlelight as the sun passed to the west. Terin's last night with his parents was bittersweet. He lived there all his eighteen years and would miss them dearly, but the outside world beckoned.

Jonas took another bite of tersk meat while shifting a proud eye to his son. "Two days," he emphasized, raising the first two fingers of his left hand.

"I know, Father. Two days ride north, not one. I can make it in one, but Vonto will pull up lame."

"Don't forget that. If your ocran pulls up lame so far from home, you will be in dire need. Once you reach the main road—"

"I turn west. Four days later, I reach Central City. Then five days north from there, I reach Rego," Terin said, finishing his father's sentence.

"Good. Now don't get lost, because I'll not be there to find you." He slapped Terin's back.

"Terin will do fine." Valera touched his left shoulder warmly.

Jonas could see Terin finish his last bite. The boy must have been famished for how quickly he devoured his meal. Jonas finished his food, rapidly shoving the rest in his mouth. "Clean away these dishes and wipe your hands. I have some things to give you," he ordered before disappearing to his bedroom.

Valera began to rise to help him, but Terin put his hand on her shoulder to keep her seated. "Finish eating, Mother. I can do it." Terin cleared the table and wiped his hands as his father returned with an item in each hand. He set the object in his left hand upon the table. Terin stared at the sealed scroll before returning his eyes to his father.

"That is for you to deliver to the king's minister, Antillius, ambassador to the city state of Rego!" Jonas declared with an air of authority.

"What does it say?"

"I don't know. Squid sent it inside another scroll intended for me. He said for you to carry this with you as proof of your position. Open the seal only if necessary." The item in Jonas's right hand was long and masked in the room's shadow. Jonas swung his right arm forward, bringing forth the long-shaped item and holding it outstretched with both hands. Terin eyed the obvious shape curiously. It was a sword. Jonas removed the sheath from the blade and tossed it upon the table. "Take it!"

Terin reached out, retrieving the sword with his right hand. His eyes widened in childlike wonder as candlelight danced along the silver blade. The double-edged blade was more than half his body length but felt light in his grip, almost weightless. He felt a faint power emanating from the hilt into his hand, coursing up his arm, as a mysterious azure glow ran the length of the blade. Valera sat numbly, regarding her son with pitying eyes, as she dreaded this day and all that it meant.

Jonas's distinct purple eyes with specks of gold upon their irises fixed on Terin, his rigid jaw stretching the deep-olive skin of his face, framed by his short brown hair. "You must bond to the blade." Terin eyed the hilt melded of black metal and the bright-silver length of the blade. It was longer and lighter than any sword he had ever held. This was a sword of a king or a mighty lord. How did his father ever come to possess it? "You must bond to the blade!" Jonas's eyes narrowed harshly as he repeated the command.

"What does that mean? And how do I do it?"

"He is to be a scribe and aide to Ambassador Antillius. Can this not wait until he is ready?" Valera asked, her gray eyes filled with worry.

"The sword will keep him safe on his journey," Jonas said, addressing her plight while never taking his fierce eyes from his son. "Hold the hilt tightly, and swear a solemn vow to guard the sword with your life. Avow it!"

Terin didn't understand what his father was talking about, but he took the vow nonetheless. "I pledge to guard this sword with my life." His voice echoed weakly, drained by a power he did not comprehend. The power emanating from the hilt grew exponentially, coursing his right arm before filtering through his body with a heightened awareness.

"The sword shall not forsake you unless you will it as long as you keep it close," Jonas explained. "The longer you carry it, the stronger the bond between the sword and you shall grow."

"Where did you find this?" Terin marveled, his eyes trailing the length of the silver blade as the strange azure glow abated.

"I've had this for some time, since before you were born or Valera and I were wed. I found it among ancient ruins many leagues from here when I served the crown during the Sadden Wars. It served me well in battle and helped me win the hand of the most beautiful woman I've ever laid eyes upon."

Valera's face flushed red. "You did not need a sword to win my hand, Jonas." She fixed her eyes to his, her gentle smile warming his face.

"Your father thought otherwise," he answered. He left much unsaid, for Jonas told Terin little concerning his grandfather, not even his name. Terin had oft asked of his kin, though Jonas and Valera spoke nothing of them.

"You must go to bed, Terin. You'll need rest for your journey tomorrow," Valera said.

*****

Sleep did not come easy that night for Terin. Excitement and anxiety proved a restless mix, as it took hours for his consciousness to wane and sleep to overtake him. His dreams were rich in splendor as he beheld far-off lands, towering mountains, sprawling cities, and the white walls of Corell. Each was beyond his imagining, breathtakingly beautiful and perfect in the vague details that dreams projected.

There in that restless void between peaceful slumber and consciousness, Terin performed great deeds and won the hand of a fair lady. As the beautiful woman's lips drew nigh, a voice called him from his contented bliss. "Terin!" His mother's voice woke him as the vision faded painfully away.

*****

After a hearty breakfast, Terin found his father outside the house, tending to his ocran. The large-hooved beast stood five feet at the shoulder. It had a wide-set head with two horns protruding straight from its skull and a flush golden coat. The beast snorted as Jonas strapped the saddle to its back. "Easy, Vonto," Jonas said soothingly to calm the animal. He had already cleaned Vonto's hooves, inspected the iron shoes for bends or damage, combed Vonto's shiny coat, fixed the blanket and saddle, and packed two weeks of provisions, along with Terin's bedroll and shelter.

"Thank you, Father." Terin thanked him knowing his father must have risen early in order to beat him in completing the many tasks. Terin had a bundle of fresh clothes to add to his pack. He wore a knee-length brown leather tunic, booted sandals, and a sword belt loosely fixed around his waist. His father's sword rode upon his left hip. He tucked two knives in his belt and strapped his bow and quiver over his back.

"You're welcome, son," Jonas said, turning to face him.

Terin hugged him tightly. "I'll do my best, Father."

"I know, Terin," he said sadly as he stepped briefly away to fish something from his sack nearby. "I have one last thing for you if you desire it," Jonas said, pulling a leather strap with several items attached to it from his sack. He lifted the item reverently, indicating to Terin that it was precious to his father. It was a necklace with three pieces of bosa stone and two wooden carvings between them.

The stones were half the size of his fist with faces carved into them. All three stones were finely detailed, each depicting a different feminine face. Each was strikingly beautiful and finely crafted, the obvious work of a master artist. The wooden carvings between them were two ocran heads, each cut from pesal wood and as detailed as the female carvings. Small holes were carefully pierced behind the objects where the leather strap was woven through.

Terin reached out his hand, running his fingers over the contours of the stone faces. Two of the women he did not recognize, especially the most prominent one in the center, but the one to the left was clearly his mother. "Mother?" he asked knowing the answer as he tapped the stone gently.

"Yes, it is her."

"Who carved these? They are beautiful."

"I carved this one," Jonas said, touching the visage of Valera, but not claiming the work of the others.

"Who are the other women?"

"Two very special people, my son." Jonas said no more before lifting the necklace over Terin's head, gifting him the precious heirloom.

"Father, I can't. This belongs with you," he protested.

"It belongs to my son. When you are lonely and miss home, look to your mother's face and think of her and the man who carved it." Jonas touched a hand to his son's shoulder before embracing him.

As they separated, his mother came out the door and hugged him also. It was a tight, desperate embrace, the kind filled with uncertainty of what the future beheld. She wondered painfully when or if she would ever see him again. The outside world was fraught with peril, and no matter his profession, there were no guarantees from danger.

With no more ceremony than that, Terin put his foot in the stirrup, climbed atop Vonto, and rode away. Jonas put his arm around Valera as she sank her head into his shoulder to cry.

*****

Terin reached the crossroads in two days, as his father had said. The northbound road was barely wide enough for two wagons passing in opposite directions. The dusty dirt road contrasted sharply to the hard, rock-layered surface of the main east-west road that connected Corell to the northeast and Central City to the southwest. The main thoroughfare of Torry North was constructed hundreds of years ago by the founders of the Middle Kingdom. The road had seven different layers topped with smooth black stone. Four wagons could ride abreast along its length, and armies could move with haste from one border to the other.

Commerce was the most important function of the road, linking every corner of the northern Torry Kingdom. The tree line that pressed close to the north-running road receded near the crossroad. Waist-high grass replaced the tall porians nearest the road, pushing the broad-leafed trees farther off the path. Terin paused on a small rise just short of the main junction. A gentle gale swept in from the east, bending the grassy green reeds to their sides.

Terin longed to turn east, toward Corell. The fabled white walls of that ancient fortress were said to be the height of thirty men, and her inner towers could pierce the clouds, rising to heights where only giant eagles dared soar. His father visited the White Castle in his youth but spoke little of such things despite Terin's insistent begging. Much of his father's life was a mystery. Jonas Caleph seemed to live a contented life, seeking nothing more than what he possessed. The outside world held no allure to him as if he had partaken of its riches and found it lacking. But unlike his father, Terin felt adventure's seductive call, which played to his restless spirit.

"Someday," he whispered, vowing to visit Corell and see the mystery and splendor it beheld. "Come on, Vonto." He clicked his tongue and turned southwest.

*****

He set camp off the main road, amid a grove of porian trees. The skies were clear as the sun kissed the western horizon. Rain should not vex him this night. His archery skills proved their worth as he caught fresh game earlier that day, which he cooked over his small campfire. He removed the saddle, pack, and blanket from Vonto's back, then cleaned his hooves. He finished his meal before laying out his bedroll near the dying flames. The bath he had four days ago felt more like a year as the grime and sweat of the open road assaulted his senses. Terin hoped the next village he passed would have a bathhouse. For now, he made do with washing himself sparingly and not working up too much of a sweat.

Lying upon his bedroll, he stared up at the clear night sky and the wonder it beheld. Against the majestic lights spread across the depths of the heavens, he truly felt lonely and humble as sleep quickly took him. The endless road plagued his dreams, winding aimlessly beyond the horizon. The smooth black surface gave way to thick, high grass that slowed his progress, and then the road started to rise as he pushed Vonto up the grade of a hill.

After reaching the summit, another hill followed, then another. No matter how many hills he climbed, another would follow in an annoying repetition that tormented his sleep. Vonto grunted as he bore his young master up another hill. Vonto snorted again, but this time, it was much louder and out of place from the world around him. He snorted again, prolonged and forceful as thunder from the sky, jarring Terin from his restless slumber. Terin opened his eyes to the early morning of his campsite.

An alarm rang in the back of his head, alerting him that something was amiss. "Vonto!" Terin's brain screamed as he rolled to his knees, sprang to his feet, and stepped toward the edge of the tree line where Vonto was tied. There, he beheld a gangly fellow dressed in a knee-length black tunic and mask loitering near Vonto, trying to calm the brute while holding his reins. The man's form was illuminated by the early morning sun, which momentarily blinded him from Terin's presence. Before Terin knew what was happening, his father's sword was in his hand, and he found himself springing forth from the trees, closing in on the would-be thief with terrible swiftness.

The fellow's eyes drew wide as Terin emerged from the trees. He barely had time to draw his sword before Terin was upon him. Terin brought his silver blade down upon the thief's sword, shattering it into a dozen fragments. The thief cried out in utter torment, backed a step, and stumbled to the grass. He looked up with frightened eyes as Terin stood over him with his sword tip touching his throat. Terin needed only a weak thrust, and the man's throat would be split. "Please!" the thief said, pleading desperately. "Mercy."

A thousand thoughts ran through Terin's head. When he first spied the man trying to steal Yonto, he attacked without fear or thought. He simply acted, driven by an unfamiliar instinct. He felt fear now, however, as the sword trembled in his outstretched hand. How did he shatter the man's sword? The thief's weapon must have been forged with a flaw. More importantly was what was he going to do with the thief.

His first thought was that he did not want the man to see how nervous he was quickly becoming. "Roll over on your stomach!" The thief did as he commanded. "Spread your legs and arms far apart!" If the thief decided to rise to his feet, he would not do so quickly the farther his feet and arms were spread, Terin surmised.

Terin crept quietly away, retrieving the spare set of reins he stored in his saddle pack, before returning to the thief, who remained where Terin had ordered him. Terin cut the reins into two long straps. He hated ruining the precious item but couldn't think of a better solution. "If you move without me telling you, I will kill you," he warned before kneeling beside the thief.

Sheathing his sword, he grasped the thief's right wrist, manipulating the joint as his father had instructed him. He quickly bound the thief's wrists together behind his back. Taking the second leather strap, Terin tied one end around the thief's neck and the other to his pommel after saddling Vonto and packing up his gear. He would forgo breakfast until he knew what to do with his unwanted prisoner.

The thief had been busy that morning, as Terin discovered four other mounts tied to a porian some meters west along the road. "Where did you steal these?" Terin asked disgustedly while tearing the mask from the thief's head.

A narrow set of brown eyes stared at him from a freckled, thin-nosed face. "They are mine. I'm not a thief. I was only checking on your ocran because I thought he was abandoned. I meant no harm, friend."

"Abandoned ocran are not tied to trees," Terin answered, not believing anything the man said as they stood in the middle of the road amid the five ocran.

Something caught Terin's eye as he gazed past the thief's shoulder to the east. Two narrow forms appeared upon the road in the distance. The forms took the shape of men as they drew closer. The sun shone brightly behind the approaching men, obscuring Terin's vision. The hairs on the back of his neck rose in alarm as he descried the men running toward him. His hand reached for the hilt of his sword, gripping it tightly, ready to draw it forth if the strangers proved hostile. All Terin could make out was that one of the men was tall and that the other was equal to his own height.

The men stopped some ten paces before him. The taller of the two was taller than any man he had ever seen, even his father. He was seventy inches, Terin surmised. His coal-black hair dropped below a silver helm. His green eyes were even set upon a handsome square face. Dark-olive skin contrasted sharply with the white tunic he wore that stopped above the knee. His silver breastplate and shin guards marked him as a professional soldier in the service of the Torry king. Each of the men carried a three-foot longsword upon their left hip and an eighteen-inch shortsword upon their right, denoting them as men of rank. The second man was dressed the same but had light-brown hair and a smaller stature. Neither man drew a sword but was prepared to if they found the need.

"You have our ocran," the taller man declared in an even voice.

Before answering, an idea quickly formed in Terin's brain. "I shall return your mounts under one condition."

"And that is?" the tall man replied warily.

"You take my prisoner with you," he said, grabbing a fistful of the thief's tunic and thrusting him forth until the tether binding his neck to the pommel drew taught.

The tall man smiled. "I think we can arrange that." Terin quickly untied the knot at the thief's throat and pushed him stumbling forward into the waiting arms of the shorter of the two men. "It seems our thieving friend tried to steal one ocran too many." The tall man grinned.

"Greed is the bane of the foolish my father often says." Terin smiled in return.

The tall man stepped closer with an open hand. "I am Cronus Kenti, unit commander in the 9th Telnic of the 3rd Torry Army. My comrade is Arsenc Ottin. He is my second."

Terin's father had taught him the organization of the Torry army. Each unit consisted of ten flax, which numbered ten men apiece. A unit commander thus commanded one hundred men. His second meant his second-in-command. Arsenc was, therefore, a man of rank also. Ten units formed a telnic, which, therefore, numbered one thousand men. Twenty telnics formed the core of a Torry army, along with a compliment of archers and the logistical support such a force required.

Each commander wore braided cords about their shoulders of woven leather. The number of cords determined their rank. A single cord denoted a commander of a flax, two a commander of a unit, three a commander of a telnic, and four a commander of an army. A designated second was only assigned to a unit and wore two braided cords on their left shoulder only. Terin knew Cronus's rank by the double cords upon each shoulder and Arsenc's as his second by the double cord upon his left shoulder.

"I am Terin Caleph," he answered, grasping forearms with Cronus. "I am traveling to Rego. I was sleeping when I heard my ocran snorting loudly. That was when I found him trying to steal Vonto," he explained, pointing his finger at the thief.

"It is our good fortune that your ocran resented being stolen, or else we would all be walking to Central City. You said you are traveling to Rego. You seem quite young, Terin. What business have you in Rego?"

"I am to meet with Squid Antillius, the king's ambassador to Rego. My father has arranged an apprenticeship for me with Minister Antillius."

"An assistant to one of King Lore's ministers is quite an opportunity." Cronus's words were more admiration than disbelief.

"I owe my good fortune to my father and Ambassador Antillius. Nothing on my part warranted their benevolence. I am just lucky, I guess," he said humbly, embarrassed by the prestige of his unearned position.

Cronus smiled at his modesty. It told the Torry unit commander a great deal about Terin's character. He was honest. "Life often grants us opportunities, Terin. It's what we do with them that determines our success. You will do well." Cronus's attention momentarily shifted to Arsenc, who retrieved a pair of manacles from their saddle packs. He secured the thief's hands and then untied the leather strip that Terin had used. Terin shook his head, hating to have had to ruin his spare reins to secure his captive for so short a time.

"We also shall be traveling to Rego. You are welcome to ride with us if you choose. The road to Central City can be dangerous at times, but the road from Central City to Rego is fraught with peril, especially once we pass the border of Torry North into the untamed lands," Cronus offered.

Terin sensed the sincerity in the tall man's green eyes and a kindness that was difficult to miss. "I would like that very much."

"Very good." Cronus gifted him a smile that was genuine and reached his eyes. Terin's father taught him much about reading people's eyes. It oft revealed more than their words and actions, and Cronus's eyes put him at ease.

*****

That night, they set camp near a small stream not far off the main road. Their bedrolls circled the blazing fire they built from gathered kindling. The windless night allowed the smoke to drift freely vertical and not in the face of any downwind. Their captive was bound nearby. Terin brushed, fed, and cleaned their ocran's hooves while Cronus built the fire. Arsenc was the son of a fisherman, and he managed to snare a dozen pesto fish for their evening meal. Terin nearly had a wild tersk with his bow early in the day, but the fury critter bounded away with Terin's arrows missing left and right.

As dusk gave way to a clear, starry night, they sat cross-legged on their bedrolls, sharing stories. Terin felt at ease in the older men's presence. His best friends growing up were the Jorgen boys, who lived nearby. They would swim and fish and tease the Jorgens' sisters. Cronus and Arsenc were in their early twenties and had ventured far in their travels. Terin sat and listened to their tales. Cronus spoke of his brother Cordi, though when he spoke of him, sadness dampened his spirit. Terin later learned that Cordi was dead.

At last, the topic of Rego came up, and Terin asked why Cronus and Arsenc were venturing there as well. The two soldiers shared a look and stared at Terin as if he was touched. "If you are to be an ambassador's apprentice and scribe, you need to learn about the lands you travel." Cronus struck a mentor's tone with his young friend. "What do you know of Rego?"

Terin hooked his elbows around his knees and drew them together as he thought for a moment while gazing into the waning flames. "I know Rego is a foreign city state and that it lies north of our capital, Central City. The people there are merchants trading goods to the farmers in the region and then selling the farmers' crops to settlements along the Wid and Nila Rivers."

"That is all true, but the greater importance of Rego is that it stands at the mouth of the Wid River Valley. More than twenty years ago, the settlements along the Wid River drove the gargoyles, which plagued the region, from the valley. Since that time, human immigrants have poured into the Wid River Valley, building more settlements and taming the rich soil for farms and vineyards. Rego has grown wealthy in the process, rising from a small village into a powerful city state." Terin nodded his head in understanding, but he still did not answer why Cronus and Arsenc were going to Rego.

"All had been going well for the Regoans until recently. Gargoyle raiders have sprung attacks all along the Wid River. They have burned settlements and slaughtered people in gruesome fashion. Some claim that the Benotrist emperor is behind the attacks."

"The Benotrist emperor?" Terin asked.

"Tyro," Arsenc said.

Terin knew the name. His father had told him the story of the Benotrist people. The Benotrists were a collection of northern tribes that for centuries were subjugated by other nomadic tribes called Menotrists. Eventually, the Menotrists overthrew Old Northern Kingdom and overran the larger cities of northern Arax. The once nomadic Menotrists became landed overlords, who enslaved the Benotrists, forcing them to labor in their fields, mines, and cities.

After years of bondage and degradation, the Benotrist tribes revolted led by a rebel named Morca. Morca fell in battle, and the revolt seemed doomed until his second-in-command made a fateful decision that would bring doom to the world of men. The new rebel leader was the son of a Menotrist overlord and a Benotrist slave girl. His name was Tyro. To gain victory and dominion over his father's people, Tyro made a blood alliance with the gargoyle race.

Native to the Plate Mountains, the gargoyles had been vying with mankind for dominion of northern Arax for millennia. Their expansion was checked by the strong human kingdoms that ringed the Plate Mountains. The Torry Kingdoms blocked them to the south, and the Yatin Empire checked them in the west while in the old Northern Kingdom held them at bay in the north.

After the Northern Kingdom fell to the Menotrist tribes, the Menotrists, in turn, held the gargoyles in check. Despite their fierceness in battle and their ability to fly, the gargoyles were often defeated by the discipline of human soldiers. Once gargoyles reached a level of bloodlust, they could not be easily turned, redirected, withdrawn, or reasoned with. They were repeatedly devastated in battle by the sound tactics and discipline of seasoned human soldiers.

Hemmed in by enemies on all sides, the gargoyles could never multiply in great numbers to threaten any of their neighbors. The human kingdoms surrounding the gargoyles' ancestral home on the Plate Mountains shared an unspoken covenant to keep the gargoyle monster in its cage. Tyro changed that. He opened the cage door, freeing the monster and setting it loose upon our world.

Cronus explained how as leader of the Benotrist revolution, Tyro interceded to save the life of a gargoyle prince named Regula from the Menotrist overlord who held him prisoner and threatened to execute him. Tyro and Regula then swore in blood to bond their peoples for all time against their foes. With human allies as powerful and numerous as the Benotrist tribes, the gargoyles broke free of the Plate Mountains and bred in great numbers. Overwhelmed by the uprising Benotrist and gargoyle hordes flooding northward, the Menotrist Empire crumbled. Tyro forged the Benotrists and gargoyles into a vast empire that quickly spanned west and east across northern Arax.

In twenty-seven short years, he consolidated his power and conquered vast territories. Keeping an avaricious eye upon the Torry Northern Kingdom, he hungered to expand his empire into central Arax. If he could conquer Torry North, he would command all of Arax. Rego was central in his plan to move upon the Torry throne. Rego controlled the Wid River Valley. If he could annex the independent city state, he could strip away much of Torry North's natural defenses and sweep into the Torry heartland.

Still, the goings-on of the gargoyle raids were just conjecture. Nothing could be proven that linked Tyro to the marauding gargoyles that plagued the valley. Since Tyro laid no claim to the attacking bands, Rego was free to deal with the menace as they pleased. The Council of Rego called upon the Torry throne to intercede on their behalf. King Lore obliged, ordering the muster of the 3rd Torry Army commanded by General Bode to gather at Central City.

Terin listened as Cronus told of Tyro's rise and the threat he presented to the Torry Kingdoms. "If you journey to Rego and the army stops the gargoyle raiders in the Wid River Valley, will not Tyro declare war?" Terin asked, shaken to his core by such a prospect.

"War could be the end of us, but to do nothing would be the end of us," Arsenc reflected mournfully, his eyes fixed on the dying embers of their cookfire.

"Whether Tyro's invisible hand guides the raiders or not, we cannot allow the gargoyles to gain control of the Wid River Valley. With all of northern Arax under his sway, we cannot allow Rego to become a vassal of Tyro," Cronus added dejectedly, his voice carrying the burden of the task ahead. The sound of volu birds echoed through the night, their eerie love songs melding into a mournful discord.

"Have you seen a gargoyle before?" Terin asked.

"I have," Cronus answered in a quiet way, which conveyed he had slain many more than he would boast.

"What are they like?" Terin's voice reflected a youthful innocence just awakening to a darker world.

Cronus collected his thoughts, his eyes drifting out of focus over the burning embers. "You cannot appreciate the ferocity of a gargoyle until it stares into your eyes. Their eyes glow a blazing red with dark pupils that run vertically like narrow isthmuses dividing a crimson sea. Their skin is taut and shiny black, as if it could reflect the sun. Two prominent fangs curve down over their lower lip. I have seen them sink their fangs into human flesh. Once they latch on, they will not let go. Never let them get that close. They have a slight hunch to their back and clawed feet and hands. Their wings are leathery and clumsy but still strong enough to bear them into the sky, though not for long distances."

Just the thought of gargoyles filled Terin with apprehension. Would he have the courage to face such a threat if it arose before him? Rego would not be a safe assignment for an ambassador's apprentice. Perhaps that was why he was offered the position. Anyone formally trained for such a post would clearly have been placed above him, even with his father's friendship with the sitting ambassador.

"Staring into their eyes is akin to conjuring the phantoms of your darkest dreams. Pray you never meet their gaze or tarry there long if you do," Arsenc added.

Cronus sensed Terin's unease. "Don't let your thoughts linger on such things. There is much beauty in this world to counter the dark. Place your mind there before you sleep, and you shall rest more soundly."

As the others laid down to sleep, things of beauty were furthest from Terin's mind.

CHAPTER 2

Central City, the timeless capital of the old Middle Kingdom and the Torry realms that followed, was built on nine hills where the Stlen and Pelen rivers joined. Walls that reached the height of three men and made of thick baca stone circled the city. Much of the city had outgrown the sturdy ancient walls as dwellings sprawled along the Stlen and Pelen above and below the city proper.

The walls stopped at the river's edge and followed along the riverbanks some distance inside the city. The even-flowing Stlen cut a straight path through Central City, running northeast to southwest, with the narrower Pelen merging from the east, just south of the main road. More than a dozen gates lined the city's walls, but the grandest was the one upon the east wall, where the main road passed into the city. Archer towers the height of six men guarded each side of the east gate. The gate was made of seasoned lupec timber, which was unyielding to the strongest of blows, resistant to fire, and four feet thick. It had never been breached. In times of extended peace, it remained mostly open.

Terin craned his neck skyward as they passed under the gateway, his eyes wide with wonder as they beheld the archer platforms towering above. Misshapen white clouds drifted lazily overhead with sunlight breaking at their edges. Smooth gray walls ran endlessly in each direction, arcing north and south from the east gate. It was a warm spring day, and trickles of sweat ran under his black leather tunic.

"Hold, Commander!" a sentry guarding the gate commanded, regarding Cronus, who sat upon the lead mount.

Cronus saluted with a fist to his chest. "I am Unit Commander Kenti of the 9th Telnic, 3rd Army. I am accompanied by Arsenc Ottin, my second, and Terin Caleph, apprentice and scribe to Minister

Squid Antillius," Cronus declared with a deep, authoritative voice that boomed crisp and clear.

The sentry's dark eyes measured Cronus studiously before saluting in kind and waving him on. There were just the three of them in their party, as they had dispatched their prisoner the day before in the city of Actia, leaving him and his stolen mounts in the city magistrate's keeping. Losing their unwelcome burden speeded their journey, and now they entered Central City unhindered. The stream of wagons, ocran, and pedestrians flowed heavy nearest the gateway as the masses passed in both directions. The crowds thinned as they entered the city, breaking off in their appointed directions.

Terin was surprised by how close the dwellings were to the city walls. Structures made from simple wood to elaborate massive stone crowded within a stone's throw of the walls. Yet outside, no structure was nearer than two hundred paces, affording the city's defenders a clearer view. Terin's eyes took in the splendor around him. Never had he seen so many people gathered in one place, yet in each direction, he saw more people than all the people he had seen in his entire life.

The streets were filled with vendors trading their goods—from hand-drawn carts to full storefronts selling ever larger varieties of items. Merchants wearing felt caps and robes of gray and crimson sold their goods to women in long cotton gowns of red, green, and brown. Soldiers in shorter tunics of white and tan dotted the crowds, buying breads, wines, and dried meats before their musters were called in the coming days.

The road met the Carn-Ro, the main thoroughfare of Central City. The Carn-Ro was a wide stone avenue that ran the circumference of the city, within the outer walls, and connecting the three sections of the city, divided by the Stlen and Pelen rivers. The Carn-Ro narrowed at the three main bridges that connected the city. The largest bridge spanned two thousand feet across the Stlen, below the junction of the rivers. A masterpiece of engineering, it was constructed over a span of forty years, during the early days of the Middle Kingdom.

The Carn-Ro connected the main arteries of Central City, breaking off into primary and secondary avenues that led to all the gates exiting the city proper and the streets leading to the wharves along the riverbanks and the merchant districts near the rivers' convergence.

Cronus turned left onto the Carn-Ro. Wide enough for six wagons to ride abreast, the street allowed them to ride side by side without hindering the flow of opposing traffic. Large stonewalled warehouses lined each side of the street. Set back from the Ro's edge, they had high loading docks where wagons could pull close and load with ease. They were a series of massive structures, each running the length of a block and three levels in height.

While his comrades' eyes were fixed on where they were going, Terin's shifted with childlike discovery at each new wonder they beheld. "This is the Carn-Ro, Terin," Cronus said, answering Terin's unspoken question. "The street circles the city, crossing the Pelen and twice crossing the Stlen. You can travel on this avenue in an endless circle if you please."

"I never imagined the city to be so large, so..." Terin lacked the words to finish his thought.

"I know. But there are larger cities than Central City, my friend. Cagan Harbor, Laycrom, Barbaerio, and Tro are far larger."

The places Cronus rattled off were just points on a map to Terin. He knew so little of the world outside his father's farm. His mother had taught him to read and write. His father taught him swordplay, archery, and knives. After doing his chores, there was little time for anything else. Jonas Caleph instructed Terin on Torry history, the gargoyle wars, and the skills to survive in the wilds of Arax. In the few days since meeting Cronus, Terin had learned much more of the greater world. Cronus had taken him into his confidence like the older brother he never had, explaining each new experience in specific detail.

"You live here?" Terin asked, wondering what it was like to dwell among so many people.

"As agents of the crown, Arsenc and I don't spend much time in one place. But yes, I do live here."

Agents of the crown? Terin mused. Anyone holding rank of unit commander and above was a professional soldier. In times of peace, they acted as enforcers of law and conducted missions on behalf of the king. Whatever business they were conducting when they first met, Terin could only surmise. Knowing Cronus for so brief a time, Terin was quickly coming to know his character. Honor and duty defined the man. He would not betray his mission, even in casual conversation with his closest of friends, let alone a stranger he had known for mere days.

"Have you lived here your entire life?" Terin asked.

"Much of it, yes, but I've spent just as much elsewhere. My parents died when I was a child. My uncle raised my younger brother and I. He was a mercenary soldier and traveled far in his profession, taking us along when he could and teaching us all he knew. He was a rough man who rode with rough friends and lived a dangerous life. He drank hard and played hard but showed me nothing but kindness. He would strap our backsides when we deserved it, but only to instruct us to act better, not out of some cruelness in his nature."

Terin was taken aback by Cronus's openness. Though Cronus was often quick to smile and kind in his manner, Terin knew he did not share his past often or with many but his closest confidants. He should feel privileged to have Cronus share so much.

"Do your uncle and brother still live here?"

Cronus paused before answering. "They're dead," he said evenly, his eyes fixed forward as they rode. Terin would push no further. He suspected something amiss in Cronus whenever his past surfaced.

Before the quiet became uncomfortable, the Pelen river bridge came swiftly upon them. The Carn-Ro narrowed considerably at the end of the bridge, slowing the traffic in each direction. Pedestrians crowded closer to their mounts as they began to cross. The morning sun broke through the scattered clouds illuminating the gray-and-white stone of the bridge.

The bridge stretched endlessly in Terin's eye, spanning eight hundred feet across the Pelen. Generously spaced arches supported the structure, their massive forms rising from the Pelen like the arms of stone giants reaching from the gentle moving waters below. Terin's eyes widened at the bridge's apex, drifting downriver where the joining of the Stlen and Pelen was surrounded by towering structures to each bank. From high atop the bridge, he descried tall pillars covering the sides of several structures with slanting roofs with copper-colored tiles.

Arsenc grinned at Terin's reactions to all that he beheld. Having lived in Central City, Arsenc was accustomed to the wonders of the Torry capital. With Terin, he was seeing the city with new eyes. "You see the large structure on the north bank of the Stlen?" Arsenc extended his right arm and first finger straight down the Pelen where the rivers merged.

There above the far riverbank, a massive stone edifice dominated the surrounding structures. Tall white walls, the height of seven men, surrounded the lower half of the structure. Gleaming pillars of white stone circled the structure, set farther back and rising high above the outer walls. Before each pillar stood statues thrice the height of a man, each a king of old with his body facing outward as if standing post, guarding the structure from threats from each direction. Each statue had been the life's work of a master artist, yet they stood side by side, cut from marble and white stone, with such regularity as to seem pedestrian.

Even from this distance, Terin was awestruck by such magnificence. "I see it," he said, knowing his statement did not reflect the reverence the structure deserved.

"That is Leltic Palace—the Hall of Kings, as many refer to it. It is the royal residence of the king when he resides in the capital. Can you see the banner waving atop the palace?" Arsenc asked.

Terin narrowed his eyes as he searched the structure's apex. There, atop the palace summit, a small stone wall of a lookout post surrounded a flowing large banner of white with a gold crown centered on its alabaster field. "I see it."

"That means King Lore is in the palace," Arsenc explained.

"How often does the king visit?"

"He spends much of the year at Corell, but he splits the rest of his time between Cagan Harbor and here."

Cagan Harbor was the capital of Torry South. Long ago, King Torry wed the daughter of the regent of old Cagia, merging the coastal kingdom to the Middle Kingdom, thus renaming the lands

Torry North and South. As time passed, future Torry kings expanded the dominion of Torry South to its current borders. Despite their current borders, the Torry realms were still separated by an expanse of wild lands and independent small kingdoms that divided one from the other.

The Sadden Wars, during Terin's Father's time, achieved two objectives. It forced the gargoyles to the far side of the Plate Mountains and to the south, it expelled Yatin influence along the Nila and forced all the lands that separated the Torry Realms to acquiesce to the free travel of goods and troops along the Nila River. The Sadden Wars provided a secure link between the Torry Kingdoms. The royal residence in Cagan was every bit as grand as the Leltic Palace in Central City.

As Terin's thoughts linked one upon the other in an endless procession, they merged into one clear thought: Was King Lore in Central City because of the gargoyle threat upon Rego? The 3rd Torry Army was mobilizing. The calling up of citizen soldiers to fill their muster was no small matter. The Torry armies were mostly made up of free citizens. Most of these men were farmers who trained together a few times a year. The spring was plowing season. To call an entire army to muster proved the gravity of the situation. Yes, King Lore's visit to Central City was not a casual affair of state. It was for a council of war.

"We have much to do. Come along," Cronus reminded his slow-moving comrades as they crossed the far end of the bridge.

*****

Steam from the bathing pools drifted above the water in cloudy vapors. Closing his eyes, Terin leaned his head back, his arms resting on the pool's heated edge. Warm water had never felt so good. His legs ached from six days of hard riding. Before stepping into the water, he felt as if his legs would never straighten again. The knotted muscles of his back tingled in the soothing warm water, relieved at last of hunching forward in the saddle day after day. Terin had never ridden for so long a period. Cronus and Arsenc, though sore, were conditioned to days of hard riding.

"It has never felt so good to be clean." Terin sighed, reveling in his tranquil state.

"You look comfortable," Cronus observed, standing deeper in the pool's chest-high water.

"I am," Terin freely confessed. He didn't care if he ever got out of the water. Though the pool was presently shared by dozens of others, his body was so relaxed he thought of nothing but his own indulgence.

"Don't get too relaxed. We can't spend the whole day here," Cronus cautioned with hints of humor mixed with urgency.

"Where next?" Terin asked with an economy of words, lacking the enthusiasm to offer more than that. If he closed his eyes, he would surely fall asleep.

"You and Arsenc are going to Bungo Tavern to eat. Arsenc and I share a room at an inn nearby. You'll stay there tonight. I'll fetch you in the morn, and we'll be off to join the army. They're camped just north of here."

"Where are you going tonight?" Terin asked, a little more alert than a moment before.

"I have matters to attend," Cronus answered in a way that Terin knew not to inquire further.

Arsenc, who lingered a little further into the pool, was still close enough to overhear. "He's going to see a girl." He laughed, closing the distance between them as he waded near. Cronus threw him a dangerous look, though Terin could see it as insincere. "Not girl. A woman, actually, a very beautiful woman," Arsenc corrected himself. "She obviously has poor vision, and our friend has taken advantage."

"I cannot argue that point," Cronus conceded. "She is better than I deserve."

Terin laughed at his friend's self-mockery, though it was overplayed. Cronus was tall, handsome, and held a position of rank. He was the kind of man that women swooned over. If any woman claimed his heart, she must be beautiful indeed. Cronus was a very private person. After riding days together, he had not mentioned a girl, let alone her name.

"She is better than all of us," Arsenc added to Cronus's statement. "There is nary a man alive worthy of her hand. Cronus is the best of us, the best man I know. It might as well be him that the fates favor."

Terin wanted to meet this woman and see if she was as fetching as Arsenc boasted. He caught a look in Cronus's green eyes that told him the boast was true. "Enjoy your evening, Cronus. Savor every moment with your lady. After all you have done for me, I hope you have a good night."

Cronus placed a hand on his shoulder and smiled. "After all I have done for you? I believe you have it reversed. If not for you, Arsenc and I would be afoot, walking to Central City, while that thief made off with our mounts."

"You handled that thief like a seasoned warrior, Terin. Impressive work for a farmer no matter how much your father taught you of swordplay," Arsenc added.

Cronus knew there was more to Terin's breaking of the thief's sword than happenstance or the lessons of a doting father. No matter how honest Terin was, Cronus did not believe an ambassador as high-ranking as Squid Antillius would choose him as his scribe and apprentice. He believed Terin was telling the truth, for he could read his young friend's innocence in his eyes. No, the dishonesty resided with the ambassador. There was a reason why Terin was chosen, and he doubted even Terin knew why. The mystery surrounding his young friend would reveal itself in time.

Cronus climbed out of the bathing pool, his skin tingling with the change of temperature as the steamy air touched his flesh. He stepped carefully over the heated stone as an attendant brought him a towel. Lingering upon the heated stone without protected soles was ill-advised, so Cronus bade farewell.

The bathhouses of Central City were heated by vast furnaces built into their base levels. Tens of thousands of pounds of wood a day were imported to the city to operate the hundreds of bathhouses that dotted the urban landscape. Thousands of laborers loaded the furnaces, filled and emptied the pools daily, and catered to the varied clientele. The pools were fed by aqueducts that ran south from the foothills of the Plate Mountains, passing into Central City over their raised stone, clay, and wood conduits.

*****

He walked briskly through the wide avenues of Central City. Ancient structures cast in crafted stone soon gave way to modern two-level wooden buildings that lined the modest residential district of the merchant class. Cronus stabled his ocran on the Carn-Ro before working his way south and west to the home of Jarvis Celen, father of his betrothed, Leanna. Avenues of paved black turned into fitted brown brick, then cobbled gray. Wearing a simple tan tunic and brown leather sandals, he stored his armor and helm in a pack on his back along with the white tunics that denoted him a Torry soldier. This day, the only visible symbols of his profession were the shortsword and longsword riding upon each hip.

Anxious thoughts pushed to the fore, consuming his mind since the walls of Central City first came into view earlier in the day. His thoughts of Leanna drove him mad with longing. He remembered well his promise to her that upon his return, they would be wed. Despite her father's reluctant blessing, her family accepted his proposal. Poor in wealth but rich in honor, Cronus won them over with the strength of his character. Jarvis Celen knew that Cronus was not a slouch or a drunkard, and whatever fortune he might forswear for the modest salary of a commander of his rank, he would provide Leanna as comfortable a life as he could.

As Cronus cleared the corner of the last street, the tempo of his pounding heart quickened with each step. How he wanted to ride straight here upon his arrival and take her in his arms, but he needed to purge the stench of the trail. He also held no desire to present himself in the trappings of his rank. Around Leanna, he merely wished to be Cronus, and nothing more.

What weighed heaviest on his mind was his promise to wed. He had planned to fulfill his vow once he returned from Corell, but he hadn't expected to return so soon. With only this day to spend in her company, it was a vow he could not yet honor. Being married during peacetime, when he was tasked with enforcing the laws of the realm, was one thing. Doing so when the army was mustered for a campaign was something different altogether. As his thoughts circled endlessly on such matters, he found himself at her door. Standing alone before the wooden-framed home crafted with seasoned dark timber and stone, he took a deep breath and knocked.

Leanna greeted him, an infectious joy playing across her face. Her bright azure eyes danced with rapture as they fell on his masculine form filling the doorway. The golden strands of her sultry hair rolled below her shoulders, framing the delicate features of her face in feminine perfection. Flush olive skin radiated from her cheeks, stripping his defenses and melting any indifference that might have taken root in his mind. Her white dress clung perfectly to her womanly form, stirring his blood. She drank in the sight of him, her eyes unmoving from his handsome face for fear that he might be an apparition cruelly projected from her pounding heart and that once her eyes averted, the vision might cease.

Ardor swept away resistance and reason. Cronus took her into his arms, kissing her fiercely. She closed her eyes, feeling the heat of his breath upon her face as she breathed in his masculine scent. How she loved his smell. It tantalized with potential, promising erotic rewards limited only by what her mind could conjure. She ran her fingers through his hair as he stepped inside, carrying her with him. He kicked the door closed with his left foot while their lips never parted. They paused briefly, opening their eyes to stare one to the other. Exchanging their unspoken love, they kissed again and again with renewed vigor.

Passion ebbed and flowed like a shifting tide. As the heat of their embrace paused to renew itself, she took his large hand in hers and led him further into the house. Sitting him down beside her upon a settee in the center of the great room, she turned her nurturing gaze to him. She gently cupped his left cheek with her right palm, pressing her warmth to him.

"I did not expect you so soon." She smiled.

"I had to rush here from Corell once the muster was called. Leanna, I only have today and tonight to spend with you. I report in the morn. I promised that we would be joined upon my return, but I—"

"Shhh," she whispered, touching her fingers to his lips to quiet him. "I know. The army is waiting, and you must go. You needn't explain, my love. This is not the return you promised that we would wed. That promise I shall hold you to once this campaign is ended and not a day longer." Her soothing feminine voice set him at ease. He opened his mouth slightly when she placed a finger over his lips.

"Before you speak, grant me this moment to look at you." She smiled, taking in the sight of him. She wanted to look at him, to smell him, and to feel the warmth of his hand in hers. Holding his hand with her left, she returned her right hand to his cheek. "I love you, Cronus Kenti," she whispered. As their eyes locked, in his gaze she found his reply. He loved her too. His eyes revealed all. Her heart sang. She crossed her legs beneath the folds of her dress.

"I love you, Leanna Celen." He smiled in turn.

"You better," she warned with an eyebrow raised over her left blue eye.

"Where is your father?" he asked.

"Why do you ask? Are you planning to steal my virtue if he is absent?" she teased.

"I just might," he replied, challenging her taunt.

She smiled that he didn't take her bait. He was always quick to guard his honor, never one to accept teasing well. His skin was getting thicker. Perhaps his friend Raven was wearing off on him. "Father is off to Cagan on business, and Mother went with him. We are alone, my husband-to-be."

He had not seen her in weeks, and the temptation was overwhelming. Yet he had asked her father for her hand in this very room on his last visit. He could not betray the trust of his future father-in-law. "We've waited this long. We need only wait a brief time longer," he explained, not certain if her offer was sincere.

Her soft smile mirrored only a fraction of what she felt within. That was the man she fell in love with, always acting with honor, which had won her heart. "You are a good man, Commander Kenti."

"Not that good. I will be regretting my squandered opportunity all the way to Rego."

"Now you listen." Her eyes narrowed with her shifting mood. "I don't want you thinking of me when you are gone. I want you thinking of staying alive."

"I'll be fine," he answered to her admonishment. "We only have to kill off a few gargoyle raiders, make the good people of Rego feel secure, and then march home."

"And if Tyro takes our actions as acts of war?"

"I'll be safe. I will come back to you," he reassured her.

She moved her lips closer to his, her narrowed eyes searching his with the discernment of a predator. "I'll hold you to that promise."

"Yes, ma'am."

"Now tell me of your journey here. Did anything interesting transpire?" *Where to begin?* he thought. He told her of his trip to Corell, what he had done there, of his return once the muster was called, and of his ocran being stolen. Mostly, he told her of Terin. "I'm grateful you didn't have to walk here. Thank him for me," she said.

"I will."

"Things have not been boring here either."

"How so?" She piqued his interest.

"Raven was here."

"How long ago?" he asked.

"He left many days ago, maybe eleven or twelve. He was here on other business, but he was looking for you. He spent a great amount of time here, near half a day in our house. Father spoke with him at length."

"Your father and Raven in the same room?" Cronus winced.

"Father was civil, and Raven was a gentleman." Cronus shook his head in dismay. Her father was intolerable, and Raven was a barbarian. He couldn't imagine them sitting down together and discussing the weather. "Raven said he was going to Rego. That was before the muster of the 3rd Army was called. You might find him there if the army does not tarry on their march."

"Getting started is the slow part. The march itself should be fairly quick. How was Raven received in the city?"

"Not well. He creates a disturbance wherever he goes, I surmise. I feel sorry for him, Cronus." She spoke softly, her warm eyes fixed on his. "He really is a gentle soul." Cronus nearly burst with laughter at her appraisal. "Gentle soul" was the last description of Raven that he would render. "He still feels guilty over what happened to Cordi," she added.

"That wasn't his fault." Cronus sighed, reflecting on the loss of his younger brother.

"The absence of fault doesn't assuage guilt," she explained.

Cronus shook his head. "It wasn't his fault," he said again as if his statement of fact should be enough.

"Be sure to tell him that," she said as she moved closer to rest her head on his shoulder.

They spent the day together, sharing each other's company long after the sun retired to the west and stars dotted the sky above.

*****

Leltic Palace, the Hall of Kings, presided over Central City like a lone mountain looking over its surrounding foothills. The waning rays of the setting sun shone dimly upon its western wall. Deep in the inner sanctums of the ancient fortress, King Lore presided over a council of war. Purple robes draped his lean, muscled frame. Medium-cut black hair contrasted his taut square jaw. Even-set gray eyes scanned the elaborate map table, where the empires and kingdoms of Arax were displayed in fine detail.

The commanding generals of Torry North's three armies circled the table. The aged General Fonis of the 2nd Torry Army, the bold Tactician General Bode of the 3rd Torry Army, and the cautious Morton of the 5th Torry Army. The 1st and 4th Torry Armies were based in Torry South, thus too far away for their commanders to be called for a council of war on so short notice. Also attending was the silver-haired Torvin, commander of the garrison of Central City. Last in attendance was Eli Monsh, King Lore's chief minister.

Lore's eyes fixed on Rego with heavy reservation. From there, his eyes drifted northeast along the Wid River Valley, where human settlements dotted the riverbanks from Rego Minor and Costelin in the lower valley to Porticus and Vega in the upper valley. Should he stay his hand, those colonies would probably fall, and gargoyles would reclaim the valley. That would seal Rego's fate. If he acted to protect the valley settlements, that bold act might push Tyro to war, a war where his two Torry Kingdoms would be outnumbered ten to one.

Tyro did not claim the gargoyle raids upon the valley as his own, but to believe otherwise was the faith of fools. No, there was no mistake. The gargoyle raiders were directed by Tyro. If Lore put a stop to them, Tyro would view the act as an act of war.

"The day following the morrow, Commander Bode shall lead the 3rd Torry Army to Rego," Eli Monsh's clear voice began. "General Bode, what is your readiness?"

"Fourteen telnics have reported full. Three others are at 90 percent. I still have unit commanders that were far away on other missions when the muster was called, but they are filtering in by the day. In two days, I will be ready. I shall be sending the army north in groups two to three telnics in size per day so the stragglers have time to report," Bode explained.

"Very good," King Lore praised. He admired Bode's competence and professionalism. He was an aggressive commander whose men held him in the highest esteem. Of all his generals, Lore held Bode's judgment in the highest regard.

"May I protest, sire?" General Morton interrupted, looking at King Lore from the table's opposing side.

"Yes, General." Lore regarded him, eager to hear Morton's argument. "If each of us agreed beforehand, then I would doubt if we were thinking at all. Proceed." Lore liked to guard against groupthink, believing disasters occurred when all parties agreed in kind, blindly following one another into oblivion.

"Sire, if we move to Rego's defense, Tyro will declare war. Of that I am certain. I wish not to sound the coward or to cause you undue anguish, sire, but we cannot win this war. Tyro can field an army of 1 million men and gargoyles. We can muster 120,000 with both kingdoms combined, including reserves. At sea, his fleets have nearly five hundred galleys to our two hundred. Any direct confrontation at this time shall be the end of us. We must seek out allies before facing such odds." Morton hated the sound of his words. He felt like the mouthpiece of defeat and weakness. He was not. He was a man who examined the facts before him and based his opinion on what was, not what he wished it would be.

"What do you propose we do while we wait for a hoped-for alliance to materialize, give Rego City and the Wid River Valley over to Tyro?" Bode asked angrily. "Do you think that shall sate his thirst? Will he stop there? No. All of Arax is his true intention, and Torry North is the gateway to all of central Arax, and Rego is the gateway to Torry North. We must make our stand while we still have means to resist."

"I agree, Commander Bode, that we must move against Tyro immediately. But how we move will determine our success. I know the course you wish to lead us, and it will lead quickly to war, a war we are not in position to win. If we leave Rego be, it might fall to the gargoyles, but it will take time unless Tyro commits at least a legion to the task. I think he might be content to continue as he has, quietly moving upon our borders in a slow, methodical pace. It might be wise to allow him to continue while we move with haste in building an alliance strong enough to challenge him.

"The Yatins are no friends of ours, but they fear Tyro more than we. The Jenaii have often stood with us in the past. I don't think they shall stand aside while the fate of Arax hangs in doubt. If Rego can hold long enough for us to build an alliance that can stand against Tyro's might, then we can reveal our intentions at a time of our choosing from a position of strength, not desperation," Morton stated.

"Tyro has forged a formal alliance with the Naybin Empire. They shall occupy the kingdom of the birdmen, which limits any support we might obtain from our winged Jenaii allies," Eli Monsh stated in his diplomatic voice, void of emotion.

The news that King Lichu, the Naybin regent, made such an alliance was long rumored but not confirmed until recent days. The Naybins, in turn, had a defensive alliance with Mortus, king of the Macon Empire. A war with Tyro could trigger conflict with all three. Any allies General Morton hoped to rally to the Torry cause would be neutralized by these troublesome entanglements. Even Yatin proved problematic. They had been enemies of the two Torry Kingdoms for centuries, especially since the union of Cagan and Corell during the reign of King Torry. The only thing King Lore could offer them was the fear of Torry North falling to Tyro, who would then encircle them. Logic should prompt Emperor Yangu to their cause, but passion ruled the Yatin emperor.

The chamber quieted as King Lore's thoughtful silence permeated the air. Even the basin torches lighting the room seemed to bend in his direction. His generals and aides knew when his language changed from mediation to command. His eyes went out of focus as if drawn to a distant place.

"Many years have passed since we were lads no older than the boys mustering outside the city. Fonis was a telnic commander, and each of you were unit commanders or less when we marched off to fight in the Sadden Wars. Morton and Bode fought in the southern campaign against the Yatins. Fonis, Torvin, and I fought gargoyles in the north."

The others all nodded in agreement, each recalling those times in their youth. Those were the days of promise when the naivety of youth blended with invincibility. They were confident young men who went fearless into battle, seeking glory and adventure. How such dreams were quickly smashed when met with enemy steel and abject horror. But they were no fools, merely young men going to war as young men had since time began.

Lore continued. "I remember my detachment coming upon a burning village. I remember a peasant woman there among the survivors. Their village was attacked by gargoyles. Her husband had been slain, his entrails spilled upon the ground and his flesh chewed to the bone. We found him outside the village, where he was dragged and eaten throughout the previous night. That night, we secured our perimeter and sheltered the survivors, planning to march back to our command come the dawn. None of us then could have known the horror that would visit us that night.

"The peasant woman who suffered her husband's gruesome end cried out in the darkness for her children as gargoyles swept into our camp from above. They had spied her children's shadows passing in front of our campfires. Their black-winged forms dived into our midst. We raised our swords and rushed to meet the threat. Whether the days of my life are many or if they end tomorrow, I shall never forget that night. The red, feral eyes glowed in the darkness." His voice trailed in the thinnest of whispers.

"It was the first time I had seen a gargoyle. They pressed close with their savage eyes, eyes that penetrated the soul, stripping away the veil that shields your courage from your darkest fears, the veil that you spend a lifetime to construct when your childish imagination conjures those grim horrors that lurk in the shadows. One look into those savage red eyes and you are revisited by those fears that haunted you as a child. I shall never forget those red eyes and the white fangs that curved over blood-red lips like ghostly apparitions.

"Many boys froze, not even drawing their swords, gripped in abject terror or confused and slow to react. I remember my sword slashing and striking flesh. I remember the gargoyle's screams as I cut into him. Men were rushing around me in the faint light of the waning moon and the campfires farther back. The battle seemed endless and brief at the same time. Before I knew what had happened, I was straddling the creature with my sword in its chest. My men killed a score of gargoyles. Their bodies were strewn across our perimeter, but…" His voice stopped, stilled by painful memories.

"But the peasant woman's children were missing. Later, we heard the screams. We held the woman down lest she run out to find the source. The gargoyles risked many of their number in order to snatch the children. They killed few of my men, and we killed many of theirs, but they knew the effect of taking the children would have on us all. They feasted on the children, sending their innocent screams drifting to our camp.

"Holding the men in place proved difficult, but discipline held. Holding the woman down while her children were slaughtered rent the hearts of us all. Besides the red eyes and white fangs, the gargoyles were nearly invisible with their shiny, leathery black flesh. They wanted to bait us away from our perimeter and into an ambush. We did not oblige them. Instead, we stayed in place, listening to the children crying for their mother and her calling back their names in kind. We waited, we listened, and we felt our humanity withering with each helpless whimper." The others remained still, silenced by the grim tale.

"I believe you may be correct in your assessment, General." Lore spoke more firmly, his eyes locked with Morton's. "But I cannot sacrifice the people of the Wid River Valley to such a fate for the possible advancement of our greater strategic aims. I have pledged to the Council of Rego our support and the services of the 3rd Army. General Bode!"

"Yes, sire?"

"You shall proceed as planned. You shall lead your army north to Rego and rid the Wid River Valley of their gargoyles, every gargoyle. Tyro has made a pact with the greatest evil our world has ever known. We will defend humanity. Tyro be damned. If he declares war, then we will know that was his intention all along, and no measure would have stayed his hand."

The generals nodded, affirming his command, before stepping from the chamber one after the other. Morton was last. He paused at the entryway, craning his neck back to his monarch, who still stood before the map. "Whatever happened to the peasant woman, sire?"

Lore turned his steel-gray eyes to Morton. "She killed herself the next morning once we released her." His voice echoed the dead place in his heart where such memories resided.

CHAPTER 3

The late-afternoon sun filtered through the tree line that edged close to the road. It was a warm spring day, and the sun narrowed Terin's vision with its heated glare. The sparse foliage of the thin-leaved Lupecs afforded little protection. Large silhouettes swept overhead, briefly shading those below as they passed. Terin flinched, his eyes catching glimpses of brown-feathered wings beating smoothly through the air just above the treetops.

"They're magantors." Cronus answered his unspoken question, reassuring his uneasiness while leaning close.

"Giant eagles," Terin said, whispering the common name given magantor birds. His father had relayed many tales of their kind, yet Terin had never seen one in all his life. In ancient days, they ruled the skies as omnipotent lords, but now few roamed wild and free. Magantors were mostly tamed.

The great birds broke from the trees, coursing over the break in the road ahead as they soared northward. Terin stood awestruck, his eyes transfixed upon the fearsome war birds as they sped away, bearing their human riders to scout the lands ahead. Their wings stretched thirty feet tip to tip, their talons dangling below them like sharpened blades.

Each carried a Torry scout who guided their avian to reconnoiter the surrounding lands. The giant eagles' beaks curved downward, forming terrible points to strike at their prey. Their keen eyes could descry the slightest movement to the horizon. It took years to raise a magantor bird and bond it to its rider. Others could ride tamed magantors, but not with the skill and deftness of a bonded rider. Terin looked up at the empty blue sky as the birds became dots in the distance.

"Of all the wonders of our world, giant eagles are the most grand," Cronus said as they walked along, leading their ocran by the reins.

"Have you ever ridden one?" Terin asked.

"No." Cronus laughed. "Very few are trained to such a task. Riders are chosen at an early age. I was not that fortunate in my birth."

"You did well with the life you were born to," Arsenc admonished, walking upon his other flank.

"True. But I know each of us yearns to sit in a magantor saddle and soar through the heavens with the wind in our face," Cronus said. The others nodded their agreement.

They were six days out of Central City and found themselves amid the long columns of infantry moving north. They were four days out of Central City when the smooth road gave way to gravel and five days when the gravel turned to impacted soil. The army marched in elements two to four telnics in size. Cronus led his mount, reins in hand, at the head of his unit, who followed, marching five abreast. Arsenc and Terin walked beside him on either flank.

Some unit commanders preferred to stay mounted for much of the journey, using their mounts to move freely among their unit. Cronus believed that to build camaraderie with your men, a commander should share in the drudgery. His first five flax commanders followed next, each at the head of the nine men in their commands. Directly behind the last man marched the sixth through tenth flax commanders, leading their charges in disciplined straight lines.

They were making twenty leagues a day, a steady pace for an organized march. General Bode could push his men to thirty miles a day if need be but did not wish to tax his charges beyond necessity. Araxan humans were slender and swift of foot, though slight in stature. They could run fast or walk far at a brisk pace. Save for the native peoples of the lone hills, who had beards and were often portly, most Araxans were thin and had no facial hair and little hair upon their bodies except the top of their heads. They were of a singular racial makeup with varying shades of olive skin. Most had black hair, though some had red, brown, green, or gold. Their eyes spanned a broad spectrum from coal black to bright yellow. Their day was twenty-six hours, and their world circled their star every 329 days.

As they continued along the well-trodden road, Terin gave silent thanks that they were far enough past the raining season for the road to dry out. The thousands of soldiers marching over the ancient path were taking a heavy toll on the road linking Central City and Rego. Despite embankments and drainage ditches built alongside the route, many areas were still encumbered by standing water and erosion. Had they attempted this march several weeks earlier, the entire route of travel would have encumbered their advance. Terin was also thankful that their march was not conducted during high summer when the drier heat would have caused the long columns of troops to kick up storms of dust.

Despite the optimal conditions with which they marched, Terin bemoaned his aching limbs and back. The glare of the sun dimmed his vision, and sweat poured off his forehead, forming wet patches around his neck. Whenever he thought to complain, he regarded his comrades marching with helmets, breastplates, greaves, and vambraces protecting their forearms. Each carried a heavy pack filled with their gear. Atop their packs, they hung their shields. Wherever the road opened up on either side, the soldiers were allowed to remove their helms and cool their heads.

Terin knew the soldiers were haggard and spent, but they continued on without gripe or complaint. How could he belabor his discomforts if these tireless fellows endured far more than he? He was privileged to be allowed to march in their company. He was a guest of Cronus and marched in their company for no reason other than that. Cronus had to request permission from Telnic Commander Mastorn to allow Terin to join in their march. Terin's sealed scroll from Ambassador Antillius was opened for Mastorn's review. He allowed Terin to join them to ensure the safe arrival of Minister Antillius's new apprentice.

"When we reach Rego, Commander Mastorn shall allow me to escort you into the city and deliver you safely into the keeping of Minister Antillius," Cronus said.

Terin shook his head. "That won't be necessary, Cronus. I can find my way. I have troubled you enough. You're guiding me through the roughest terrain as it is. I thank you for that, but I do not wish to be a burden."

"You are no burden. and Commander Mastorn's liberties are not granted lightly. His suggestion is an implied order. You are the apprentice of King's Minister Antillius. Is your knowledge of his importance so dim? He has the king's ear on many matters. His ranking among King Lore's ministers is second only to Eli Monsh. Commander Mastorn shall not allow you to enter Rego alone after safeguarding your passage from Central City to the gates of Rego. I'm going with you."

"Don't argue with him, Terin. Cronus is stubborn and will not be moved when his mind is made up. Besides, if he escorts you into Rego, you might get to meet Raven." Arsenc laughed as they continued to walk along with their ocran in tow.

"Who is Raven?" Terin asked. He had overheard them mention the name at times but thought it rude to inquire on matters that were not directed to him. But now that they spoke of him, he was free to ask.

Arsenc nudged Cronus's arm. "You tell him."

Cronus released a measured breath. Describing Raven was easier shown than spoken. "Raven is…different."

"Different? Is he a human? A birdman? An Ape?"

"He's human," Cronus slowly answered. "He's just not human like we are."

Terin was even more confused than before. "He is a human, but not like us?" He cocked his head to his side while craning his neck to Cronus. "Huh?"

Cronus had the urge to stop in place to continue his explanation, but they were still marching in column. "Raven and his crew are Earthers."

"Earthers?"

"From a land called Earth."

"Where's Earth? Is it near Tro? Or Barbaerio?"

"No."

"Is it across the sea? My father said no human has crossed over the sea."

"No, they are not from across the sea. They aren't even from Arax," Cronus said, trying to explain while contorting his face, looking for words to explain what even he did not really understand.

"Then where?"

Cronus lifted his left forefinger and pointed skyward. Terin followed the direction with his nose, gazing at the lazy clouds above before looking back at Cronus. "Earth is in the clouds?" Terin made a face.

"Well, yes. Their home is far beyond the sky. The space between the stars we see at night is like our ocean, and they came across it."

"How?"

"I don't know. I don't understand it, and I cannot explain it. Raven and his comrades fell from the sky a few years ago and are stranded here, kind of like a shipwreck."

"Why don't they go home, then?"

"They can't."

"Why not?"

"The vessel that carried them here is broken. They used its remains to make a ship that can sail on our ocean, but it cannot sail on the ocean up there." Cronus again pointed skyward.

They walked in silence a ways while Terin tried to build an image in his brain of the things Cronus had spoken. After a while, the forest that ran close to the road angled farther back from both sides as if giant hands swept down from above and pushed the foliage away from the path. Cronus relayed the signal from the units ahead to his men to remove helmets. The men wasted little time lifting their helms and letting the air cool their brows.

Holding his helm in his left hand, Cronus raked his fingers through his thick black mane and rubbed his neck. Such was a soldier's life, Terin mused, observing his friend. Terin was raised on his father's farm, and his body was used to the heavy toil such work required. Though he worked hard, he set his own pace while soldiers worked at a pace set by others.

"Your helmets look very uncomfortable," Terin said.

"They are," Arsenc answered before Cronus could come up with a long explanation detailing how they were actually comfortable for the purpose they were intended.

"How did you become friends with Raven?" Terin asked.

Cronus thought for a moment, trying to recollect, when Arsenc interceded once again. "Raven is a mercenary, a soldier for hire. He did a job for the son of a wealthy merchant in Cagan. The man paid him half of what he promised, and Raven threatened to beat the other half out of him before he relented. Before Raven made it back to his ship, the merchant's son enlisted the aid of the harbor magistrate and gathered an angry mob. They cornered Raven in the streets, and he was prepared to go out fighting despite the dozens of arrows trained on him from all directions.

"Cronus and I were in Cagan on business for the crown when we heard the commotion. Cronus made his way through the mob and ordered the archers to hold while he spoke with Raven. Raven didn't trust him at first, but Cronus asked him what had transpired. Raven told him and offered a signed scroll detailing the arrangement he had with the merchant's son. Cronus called the young man out of the crowd, and he confirmed the details of the contract.

"Cronus admonished him and told the crowd to disperse. When they still threatened Raven, Cronus challenged the whole lot of them that if they wanted the Earther, they would taste his sword as well. The harbor magistrate's guards lowered their bows and blades, not wishing to defy a Torry unit commander. But the merchant's son was enraged and pulled a dagger, trying to stab Cronus when he faced the crowd and had his back turned." Cronus shook his head as Arsenc relayed the tale, scolding himself for violating a cardinal rule: do not turn your back on any potential adversary.

"What happened then?" Terin asked, captivated by the strange tale.

"Raven killed the man in the blink of an eye. The crowd drew back as a terrible blue light sprang from an object in Raven's hand. It was a weapon of some sort. Raven called it a pistol. The crowd regained their courage and stepped closer. Cronus backed them down, ordering the magistrate's guards to gather up the slain man's body and take it to the magistrate, and then we escorted Raven back to his ship.

"Cronus told Raven that it would be safer if he set sail immediately while he tried to sort out the mess. Raven told Cronus that he owed him and that he would see him again. The merchant who lost his son was a very powerful man and wielded great influence in the harbor council. He couldn't hurt Raven, but he caused Cronus nothing but grief. Cronus might have been a telnic commander by now had his name not been soiled by that incident."

"Justice was served." Cronus's voice reverberated with authority. "If promotion requires a blind eye to injustice, then I shall keep my current rank and, with it, my honor."

"You saved Raven's life," Terin stated, confirming what he knew of Cronus's character. Integrity and honor oozed from the man like juice from a tosi fruit.

"And Raven saved me from a knife in the back," Cronus answered.

Terin thought on that for a moment. "I guess one good turn leads to another. Had I not stopped that ocran thief and returned you your mounts, I would be traveling to Rego alone."

Cronus regarded him. "You don't need me to tell you to do what is right, Terin. You have done so since we met. When your heart speaks to you, listen. Doing what is right is rarely easy, but you will be better off for doing it."

*****

They set camp in a clearing several hours before dusk. The telnic commanders divided the perimeter and assigned their units accordingly. Soldiers immediately set about preparing the perimeter and building defensive positions. Others gathered wood for cookfires or erected tents for sleeping. While Cronus and Arsenc were busy issuing commands and overseeing their unit, Terin groomed and fed their ocran. He decided to gather wood for their cookfire and slipped away from camp.

Terin rode east, just beyond sight of the camp, where the clear knee-high grass gave way to higher grass, thicker forests, and rolling hills. Cronus warned him not to wander far, but as Terin spied the broad-leaved porians ahead, he noticed red tails bounding through chest-high green grass, running from his left to right. An idea sprang to mind, and he grabbed his bow from his saddle. They were a herd of douri bounding in his direction, probably spooked by soldiers foraging north of him. Sitting atop Vonto's broad back, he notched an arrow, waiting for the prey to draw close. Antlers swiftly appeared, standing above the deep grass like the dorsal fin of a dorun riding the surface of an emerald sea.

Before the lead douri could spot him and bound in another direction, Terin took aim where the creature's lungs should be behind the green-bladed foliage. He released the shaft as it sped to target. The antlers dropped from sight as the herd scattered. Terin notched a second arrow, holding it in one hand while urging Vonto forward. He found the douri thrashing timidly in the grass on its side. Delivering a second arrow to its heart, he dismounted and slit the animal's throat.

*****

The aroma floated in the air, teasing his nostrils with savory possibilities. Telnic Commander Mastorn followed the scent to its source: the cookfires of his 5th unit commander, Cronus Kenti. As the sun sank below the western forests, the glow of twilight mixed with the light of campfires that circled the inner rings of the perimeter. Mastorn spied a dozen shadowy forms lingering by Cronus's cookfire. He stopped several paces short, observing the activity until he was recognized.

"Commander Mastorn," Cronus said, his clear voice greeting Mastorn as he stepped away from the fire.

"Cronus." Mastorn clasped his forearm, his smile visible in the dim light. "I smelled your cookfire from the other side of the camp. What are you cooking?"

"Douri," Cronus quickly answered with no attempt to hide his glee.

"Douri?" Mastorn questioned. Armies on the march rarely ate more than dried meat and bread. Fresh meat was difficult to obtain. Soldiers simply had no time to hunt such game.

"Fresh douri."

"Where did you find fresh douri?" Mastorn asked.

"Terin killed it with his bow and brought it back to camp. He dressed it, skinned it, and cooked up the meat for all the men in my unit to share. He has made himself quite popular."

"Minister Antillius's new apprentice?"

"Yes."

Mastorn's eyes drifted to the fire where Terin stood with several soldiers of Cronus's command. "I thought him to be a dandy. I guess I was wrong." He shook his head.

"A dandy? I told you how I met him, did I not?" Cronus asked, shaking his head.

"I vaguely recall he caught a thief that stole your ocran."

Cronus leaned close, his eyes fixed on his commander. "He broke the thief's sword. He shattered the sword where the two blades touched. When Arsenc and I arrived, the thief looked a frightened animal caught in a snare. The thief was no simpleton or weakling. He was a dangerous subversive, and that boy brought him to heel."

Mastorn again shifted his eyes to Terin, spying Cronus's men slapping the boy's back and treating him as if he belonged among them. "You have the strangest friends, Cronus. First, that Earther friend of yours. Now a sword-wielding farmhand who happens to be an apprentice to King's Minister Antillius. I'm sure a band of Apes or a score of birdmen shall show themselves on our march, claiming to be good friends of Cronus Kenti and wishing to join us."

"You needn't fret, Commander. I don't know any birdmen personally, and I've never seen an Ape. Come. You best have some douri before it's gone." Cronus guided him to the fire.

"Careful. It's hot," Terin said after pulling the spit from the fire and sliding the impaled meat onto Flax Commander Tarlus's plate.

"Don't worry about that, son. Just pile it on." Tarlus grinned. In his fifth decade with strands of silver gracing his dark hair, Tarlus was Cronus's oldest flax commander.

"That's for all your men, Tarlus, not just you," Pomel Tonchas goaded. Pomel was Cronus's first flax commander. Brash and outspoken, he rarely let a moment to needle his comrade pass him by. Standing fifty-eight inches, Pomel was diminutive, even by Araxan standards.

"My boys will get their share, half soldier." Tarlus grinned, giving Pomel a shove while briskly walking back to his flax. "My thanks, Terin!" he shouted over his shoulder as he passed into the dark.

"You're welcome," Terin said, finally feeling at ease with the troops. In his own way, he contributed something to ease their journey.

"Make way," Marcus Criftus said as Mastorn and Cronus drew nigh. Marcus was Cronus's second flax commander. Nearing his fourth decade, he was well-spoken and respected among his fellows.

"Stay where you are, gentlemen. We are all soldiers here." Mastorn set them at ease. "I just came to test the douri you're cooking up, Terin. A good commander must test what his men are eating to ensure it's safe."

"I hope it meets your approval, Commander." Terin removed a second spit, offering Mastorn a generous helping. Mastorn wasted little time chewing off several pieces, savoring every morsel of the tender meat.

"Well?" Cronus asked, his eyebrows lifted, awaiting the obvious verdict.

"Very good." Mastorn could not mask the grin playing across his face. "You are quite skilled with the bow?"

"I understand the basics," Terin answered. His father had drilled him extensively on speed and accuracy.

"The basics?" Mastorn's eyebrow lifted, not believing a word of Terin's humble assessment. "Your father taught you to use the bow?"

"Yes, Commander."

"And the sword?"

"Yes, sir. He was a soldier during the Sadden Wars. He served with Ambassador Antillius. That was why I was chosen as his apprentice."

"You were chosen because of your father's friendship with Minister Antillius?"

"I believe so, Commander. There are many who must be far more qualified than I."

"Can you read and write?"

"Yes."

"Most cannot. That alone makes you very qualified, Terin. It's a shame to waste your skills as a scribe. You would make a good soldier." Mastorn gave the others an even look before stepping away and bidding them a good night. The others let out slow breaths as they huddled close to the fire as Mastorn disappeared into the dark.

"Feel privileged, Terin. Commander Mastorn likes you, and he is not an easy man to impress," Marcus said. "Let me take this to my men," he said, stepping away with a plate of douri. The others followed in kind, leaving Cronus and Arsenc alone with Terin.

"Commander Mastorn is right, you would make a good soldier," Arsenc said, sitting down, using his saddle pack for a seat.

"If Terin were a soldier, then he would not have had the freedom to hunt this game for us. No, Terin will do fine as Minister Antillius's apprentice." Cronus also took a seat on his saddle pack. He thought Terin's skills were wasted as a scribe and apprentice as well. He didn't know why, but a part of him sensed a different calling for Terin, and serving as a scribe was not it.

"Here." Terin offered his friends each a plate of douri as he removed the last spit from the fire.

"Thanks," Arsenc said.

"You better get some rest, Terin. We have another long march tomorrow," Cronus said, taking the offered plate. They were still several days from Rego.

*****

The 3rd Torry Army was camped just east of Rego. Telnics were arriving daily, adding their numbers to those already bivouacked within the hastily erected fortifications that the first telnics began constructing upon their arrival. The camp ran several miles along the south bank of the Wid River and bristled with activity. The Ninth Telnic marched through the gate centered along the southern barricade, following their guides to their appointed positions within the perimeter. The clear midday sky was fortuitous, affording the new arrivals fair weather to erect their campsites.

Cronus rode at the head of his unit with Arsenc and Terin riding upon either flank. Terin took in the sights around him with wide-eyed curiosity. The once knee-high grass that covered the campsite was well-trodden or displaced by entrenchments and barricades. They passed vast tents with dozens of smiths and armor masters plying their crafts with measured urgency. Women wearing long red robes of the healer castes hurried throughout the camp, tending to the minor injuries soldiers often incurred while setting camp. The smell of cookfires permeated the air, drifting in lazy streams from their sources. Each unit detailed five men apiece to cook their food and stir the pots hung over their fires.

Terin noted the vast specialization employed by the Torry Army. Tents filled with tailors to repair or make tunics followed leather binders that fixed sandals, belts, and helmet straps. Stacks of wooden shafts were piled near arrow-making tents. Saddle repair tents followed bit and rein makers. They passed corrals made from crossed timbers filled with ocran.

Passing through the camp's center, Terin's eyes were drawn to a large green pavilion fifteen meters in width. Stern-faced warriors with polished silver breastplates over gray tunics guarded its entrance. Men of rank loitered nearby, passing to and fro through the entrance. "General Bode's command tent." Arsenc leaned close, answering his unspoken question.

They next passed a large circled stockade where several magantor birds were tethered to posts driven into the ground. A few were brown, and others were gray, their shiny feathers reflecting the sun's light in flickering tiny rays. Their heads towered over the surrounding campsite, gazing keenly in each direction. Their riders busied themselves with the grooming and feeding of their giant war birds. They were on constant patrols, scouting lands in each direction. General Bode was most interested in the passes in the north and any movements from the Benotrist Empire proper.

"Once we set camp, I suggest you bathe in the river and change out of your leather riding gear and into a formal white tunic. Then I shall take you into the city," Cronus said.

"Thanks, Cronus," Terin said gratefully.

*****

The east gate of Rego was wide enough for three wagons to pass through abreast. The gate was made of heavy timber twenty-four inches thick. It was opened as traffic passed within and without at a steady pace. Terin's eyes were drawn to heavy eight-foot pikes driven into the ground on both sides of the gate. Atop each pike rested a head in varying degrees of decay with the freshest closer to the entrance. He descried the shiny black skin stretched over the harsh, angular features of a gargoyle.

Bold white fangs hung menacing from listless dark-crimson lips. Lifeless red eyes shrank within their sockets, staring sightless at everything and nothing. Sharp, pointed ears curved back from their skulls and forked blood-red tongues swung freely from their mouths. Terin's heart pounded emphatically as the ghastly sight sent waves of trepidation though his extremities. The Regoan soldiers displayed their trophies to drive fear into their gargoyle enemies, but Terin felt fear just gazing at their lifeless forms. If they manifested such fear in him when they were dead, how much worse would it be if they were alive?

They passed through the gate, riding under the stone archway that arched over the open gate. The soldiers at the gate acknowledged Cronus in his Torry uniform and let them pass. The Regoan suburbs on the south side of the Wid River ran far beyond the city's protective walls. Cronus and Terin passed hundreds of thatched huts and one-level timber structures before reaching the east gate, a testament to Rego's sudden expansion over the preceding years.

Rego was far younger than the ancient capitals of Arax's great kingdoms. The city was surrounded on both riverbanks by ten-foot mounds of hardened soil topped with a wooden wall of treated timber that ran the circumference of the city. Behind these fortifications were archer platforms liberally spaced and walkways that ran inside the walls where defenders could maneuver with ease. Soldiers clad in yellow tunics and bronze helms and breastplates guarded the walls. They kept a wary eye on Cronus and Terin as they approached the east gate.

The streets of Rego bristled with activity. Ocran-drawn wagons plodded along the busy intersections as goods of all sorts moved to and from the river, where ships loaded and off-loaded their cargos throughout the day. Cronus turned on the first northbound avenue he crossed, heading straight to the docks along the river. Much of Rego was built in the previous two decades. The streets were made of loose-fitting brick, and the buildings were more timber than crafted marble or stone. The structures were narrow two-level homes or small shops.

Patches of dark gray crept between the buildings ahead as they caught glimpses of the river. Passing several intersections, the riverfront opened up before them with hundreds of docks lining either bank. Half of the long wooden piers had ships or crafts of varying size and purpose tied off at their sides.

Cronus's eyes swept the river left to right, ignoring the vast flotillas passing in each direction with the sound of their oars slapping the water. Far to the west, Rego Bridge spanned the Wid River like a shallow rainbow arcing over the horizon. The bridge joined the halves of the city, and most traffic flowed over that one vital artery. Cronus clicked his tongue, turning his mount west along the avenue that paralleled the riverfront, his eyes scanning the ships as he rode apace.

"What does his ship look like?" Terin asked, pushing Vonto's gait to keep pace with his zealous friend.

"You'll know when you see it."

No sooner had the words escaped his lips than the object of his search caught his eye just ahead. There it rested, stern to pier and bow to the river, like a paradox that did not belong in their world. Terin's jaw slackened, and his eyes widened with wonder. The ship was nearly sixteen meters in length and six meters abreast. It was rectangular in shape with three levels. The stern section of the first deck was open with a low railing lining its sides and aft. The remainder of the first deck was concealed by a wall cutting across the ship, separating the forward three quarters of the deck from the exposed stern.

A single door was centered on this wall, an obvious entry point to the concealed section of the ship. A ladder was affixed beside the starboard side of the door. The ladder rose to the second deck, which also had an open stern section and a forward concealed section. The entire space of the second deck rested atop the covered section of the first deck. A wall divided the forward section of the second deck from its exposed aft section with another door centered upon it and with a ladder beside it rising to the third deck. The third deck was completely open with a low forward wall and no railing behind it. It obviously served as a lookout deck.

The entire vessel was made of a bluish-silver material, the likes of which Terin had never imagined. An unnatural power emanated from the ship, as if it could visit death to a vast host and sail away indifferent to the deed. There were no oar ports or sails affixed to the vessel, which caused Terin to wonder how it was powered. The ship was terrifying to gaze upon, and Terin stirred uncomfortably in his saddle as Cronus dismounted before stepping onto the pier. Terin followed, tying Vonto's reins to an ocran post at the pier's end.

The door on the first deck slid open as they neared the ship, and a man stepped out onto the stern. "Cronus!" the man said excitedly as he bound over the low railing of the ship onto the pier. He wrapped his arms around Cronus and lifted him off the dock as if he was made of feathers.

Terin stepped back at the sight of the man. He was immense. At seventy-three inches and two hundred pounds, he was larger than Cronus, and Cronus was the biggest man Terin had ever known. It was the man's other features that made Terin question if he was human at all. His skin was very dark, almost black. His hair was cropped close to his scalp. He had a broad nose and narrow eyes like a bird of prey. He wore the strangest clothes. He wore thick black boots, black trousers, black pullover shirt, and a thick black jacket. Across his waist hung a belt that had a strange object hanging from it upon the man's hip that was tied down upon his thigh.

"All right, Lorken, set me down before you break my ribs," Cronus pleaded helplessly. The large black man complied, still smiling at seeing his friend. Two other men then emerged from the first deck. They waited on the stern and were dressed like the first man, but their features were different from his and from each other.

One was as tall as the dark man that Cronus referred to as Lorken. One man's skin was very white. He had short brown hair and blue eyes. His bearing radiated a deep intelligence. He rested his left foot upon the low railing while his right hand rested on the object that hung from his hip. The other man was much shorter than his contemporaries, standing at sixty-five inches. His brown eyes slanted upward at their corners. His skin was closer to an Araxan hue, though not as flush.

"Brokov, Kato," Cronus said, acknowledging the other men. The taller white man was Brokov, and the shorter man with the strange eyes was Kato, Terin surmised.

"Cronus." Brokov smiled wryly. "Raven was wondering if you'd show up or not."

"I missed you by eleven or twelve days at Central City. I was hoping you would still be here when I arrived."

"We usually don't stay in one place for long, but our business here may take a while."

Cronus knew better than to ask what brought them to Rego. The Earthers were careful never to discuss who hired them or for what purpose. "Where is Raven?" Cronus asked, wondering why he had not exited the ship with the others.

"He and Zem are at the Uxel Tavern," Lorken said.

"The Uxel?" Cronus muttered, shaking his head. He knew of its poor reputation during a previous visit to Rego. It was a vile pit where the outcasts of civil society gathered to conduct their business.

"Not sure how long they'll be. How long can you wait here?" Brokov asked.

"Not long. I am escorting Terin to the council forum to meet Ambassador Antillius. The Uxel is along our route. I'll meet Raven there."

"You sure, Cronus?" Lorken asked. "The place can be a little rough. It's one thing for a lowlife like Raven to go there, but your friend and you look too respectable to be accepted there." Lorken eyed Terin, dressed in his clean white tunic, and thought him a little soft.

"We shall be fine." Cronus smiled. "Terin can take care of himself, and I've handled a few rough crowds in my time, if you remember."

*****

The Uxel Tavern rested two streets back from the river's south bank. Nestled in the heart of Rego's seedy west side, the one-level wood-framed structure was a poorly constructed den of iniquity. It was the sort of place where one needed a long, hot bath upon leaving.

"This is where your friend is?" Terin asked as they approached the long, windowless wooden structure. A crooked sign over the front read Uxel. He half expected a dozen vermin to scurry from the place once they entered the open front doorway.

"You should wait near the doorway when we go in while I find Raven."

They were nearly blind when they stepped inside, transitioning from the bright sunlight to the dim surroundings within. The dull glow of sparsely placed wall lanterns provided little light. They stretched some distance in each direction, outlining the immense size of the room. Terin sensed hundreds of eyes riveted to their exposed silhouettes in the doorway. The fetid stench of unkempt men permeated the air. He stepped aside, attempting to mask his presence in the shadows of the wall. "Stay here. I'll be right back."

Cronus disappeared in the shadows, leaving Terin alone near the entry. He made his way around the dozens of tables that separated the entrance from the main bar on the room's opposing wall. The tables were set in no particular configuration. He guarded himself, keeping his right hand gripped on the hilt of the shorter blade on his right hip. His longsword would be impractical in these close quarters.

The second table he passed had three men seated around it. Wearing a collection of fur and leather tunics or trousers and belts of knives across their chests, they eyed him contemptuously. "We hate the local soldiers enough, let alone the hired mercenaries of the Torry crown, boy," one of the three taunted as he passed. He had shaggy brown hair and several missing teeth in his lopsided grin. Cronus said nothing, weaving carefully through the gauntlet of tables.

Still adjusting to the dim light, Terin caught sight of the brief-skirted barmaid passing between tables nearby. He could not make out her face, only her curved form moving from table to table, avoiding the amorous advances, lewd remarks, and slaps to her posterior from some of the rowdy patrons.

"You lost, boy?" A harsh voice startled him. Turning to his left, he was met by foul breath upon his face. A man stood close, his fur vest open, revealing a leathery, scarred torso. His black hair was tied in braids, and his half tunic draped below his knees. The man's dull-yellow eyes stared through him, stripping Terin of any confidence he had entered the Uxel with.

He felt his father's sword heat his left thigh as if calling upon him to draw it forth, but he fought the urge of the blade, thus denying his gift as the man pushed Terin's chest with his left palm, driving him backward. His back struck two other men standing behind him, each catching his arms and gripping them tightly. They were obvious comrades of the man who stepped close with a sinister grin, which exposed stained yellow teeth and gunk-caked gums. "You don't belong here, boy. Perhaps we should escort you to a more fitting place for your kind. I know a man in Mosar who would pay a handsome price for a pretty lad like you."

Terin thought he might throw up from the man's putrid breath. He tried to wrest his arms free, but the effort seemed hardly worth it. They had him. His emotions raced faster than reason, numbing his ability to think this through. His eyes went wide as a dark shape rose behind the man. A large hand reached around the man's throat and threw him across the floor with a jerk of a hand.

Standing over Terin was a mountainous man. His black trousers, shirt, and jacket matched the Earthers he had met on the pier. This man was larger than the others. He was seventy-five inches and nearly 260 pounds. His jacket failed to hide his massive arms and thick chest. His skin had an olive-reddish hue. His black hair was cut close to his scalp, and dark-brown eyes peered through his narrow stare. The man hardly seemed human. He was the largest man Terin would ever see. This had to be Raven.

"I'd let the kid go," Raven growled, his right hand gripping the object hanging on his hip.

The man Raven had discarded like weightless trash slowly came to his feet. "What's the boy to you, Raven?"

"He's a friend of mine, Krixan. I suggest you stay put," Raven warned.

Krixan eyed Raven with contempt, his hand slowly playing along the handle of a knife sheathed in his belt. Despite the poor lighting, Terin's eyes made out what he was attempting. "Knife," he worded silently to Raven so as not to alert Krixan. He needn't bother. A towering form loomed behind Krixan.

Several inches taller than Raven and weighing hundreds of pounds, it was a creature made of metal. Its bulky frame was forged with a black-silver material that would not yield to the strongest of blows. Its eyes were two narrow lights of blue. It wore garb matching Raven's. The creature swung its left fist down upon the top of Krixan's head. The sound of cracking bone echoed dully as Krixan dropped to the floor, his head caved severely in an unnatural angle. The creature struggled briefly to dislodge its fist from the shattered skull.

Raven drew the object from the holster on his hip. A flash of blue light pierced the skull of the man holding Terin's left arm. Terin quickly turned as the man holding his right arm suddenly released it. He turned his head, his eyes catching the man's gaze. The man's eyes were wild with fright and then went slack. The man slipped to the floor as Cronus removed his shortsword from the man's back. The man fell on his face, exposing the wound in his lower back where Cronus had pierced his kidney. Blood poured across the floor, soaking the soles of Terin's sandals.

Cronus shifted his sword behind him, his eyes following in a quick scan. The Uxel's patrons stayed put. Men of this sort did not interfere in others' affairs unless there was a profit in it. There was never any profit in crossing Raven. Those who did found a quick death and a shallow grave.

"Out!" Cronus commanded as he backed to the door. Terin obeyed, still dazed by what he had seen.

"Come on, Zem," Raven said to his metallic comrade as they followed Terin out the door. They stepped carefully over the three corpses, first Zem, then Raven. Cronus still guarded the doorway with his sword drawn and facing the room. Raven paused before stepping outside, fixing his eyes upon Cronus. "Well, if it isn't the only human on this planet worth a damn." Raven smiled.

Cronus eyed him briefly, keeping his focus on the room. "You might find more of us to your liking if you didn't spend your time in places like this."

"This is where my customers are." They moved to the opposite side of the narrow street, putting a little distance between the Uxel and themselves. Cronus sheathed his shortsword. Their ocran were still tethered to posts in front of the Uxel. "Cronus Kenti." Raven shook his head. "It's never boring when you're around."

"I could make the same claim of you." Cronus smiled, offering Raven his right hand. Raven shook his hand, as Cronus was familiar with the gesture of a handshake. Terin thought the greeting odd, but next to Raven's and Zem's appearance, nothing else seemed odd at all. His eyes locked on Zem. The creature looked like death in physical form. Despite his smile, Raven looked as menacing a sight as Terin had ever beheld.

"We saw you come in the Uxel. We were sitting in the front corner where the shadows help us disappear. I was going to follow you to the bar, but then Zem noticed Krixan and his bunch moving toward the boy. I figured he must be a friend of yours, so we stayed close," Raven explained.

"I shouldn't have left him. Thanks, Raven."

"No problem. I owe you a few, if you remember." Raven slapped his shoulder, nearly knocking him over.

"It was my fault," Terin explained. "I should not have let them behind me."

"Think of it as a lesson learned. Terin, this is Raven and Zem." Cronus waved an open hand, introducing his friends."

"A pleasure, Captain Raven. Cronus holds you in high regard," Terin said.

"If you're Cronus's friend, then that's good enough for me." Raven offered his hand. Remembering how Cronus greeted Raven, Terin grabbed the big Earther's hand knowing that Raven could easily crush it.

"Terin." Zem's deep, metallic voice nearly startled him. The creature extended its hand as well.

"Z-Zem," Terin said, the name sounding strange on his lips.

"There's much I wish to discuss, Raven, but I think it wise if we wait. I think we have outworn our welcome at the Uxel."

"Yeah, I think you're right about that. Why don't you two leave? We'll cover your departure and then head back to the *Stenox*. We'll be in Rego for a while anyway," Raven said, his narrow eyes mainly focused on the front door of the Uxel. "Which direction are you going?"

Cronus lifted a finger to the east. "The Forum of Rego."

"The city forum? What for?"

"I'm escorting Terin. He is Ambassador Antillius's new apprentice."

Raven gave Terin a discerning look, perhaps reassessing his opinion of the boy. He did not hold politicians or their lackeys in high regard. He drew Cronus aside. "He's not one of those diplomat weenies, is he?" Raven made a face while keeping his voice low.

Cronus shook his head at his friend's bluntness. It was a quality that others found offensive but Cronus found endearing. "No. He's a fine young man. I think you'll like him." Cronus smiled, biting off a laugh.

"All right. Your word's good enough for me. You better get moving. We'll cover you."

Cronus and Terin bade their farewells, fetched their ocran, and headed east down the avenue.

*****

Terin's thoughts raced in a dozen directions. The sight of those men dying in the tavern conflicted with Raven and Cronus's indifference to their death. Should he feel guilt or sorrow or joy? Those men meant him great harm, and they were the dregs of society, the embodiment of vice, and the base of human nature. But he felt little joy at their demise. In fact, Terin didn't know what he felt. Everything happened so quickly that his mind was still working it out. Then he thought of Raven and Zem, and the questions that came to mind were too numerous to catalog. He wasn't sure if they were real or not. Often, when the brain saw things it could not comprehend, it rejected them out of hand.

"Are you all right?" Cronus's voice brought him back as they made their way through the streets of Rego.

"Oh, I'm fine." He collected himself.

"You don't look fine. You had never seen a man die before?"

"No."

"It's never easy. It is even harder when you are the one doing it."

"How many men have you killed, Cronus?"

"I've killed enough." Cronus sighed.

"I was also thinking about your friends." Terin changed the subject so as not to depress his friend.

"Raven?"

"Yes. He is quite large."

"Yes, he is that."

"He didn't like me when you told him that I am to be Minister Antillius's apprentice."

"Raven hates authority. Even in his world, he was a bit of a renegade. But Raven measures men one at a time on their own merit. If you come to know him as I have, he will see you as I do."

"Arsenc says your friendship with Raven has soiled your name in the Torry command."

"Listen, Terin, I would not trade Raven's friendship for any position of rank. He is a good man, just as you are. Never turn your back on good men. Their friendship is worth more than any worldly treasure."

"That is why I am sticking with you, Commander Kenti. You are a good man." Terin grinned.

"So I've been told."

Before long, they found themselves at the convergence of several broad avenues. Where the streets joined, they circled a massive stone structure. Tall columns the height of four men lined each side. Crafted from fitted stone and marble, they separated the inner structure from the broad steps that descended from each wall to the streets below. The roadway circled the structure, breaking off in many directions, each pathway a major thoroughfare of Rego. The bridge of Rego rested due north of the convergence.

The streets were thick with midday traffic. Carts of produce weaved their way through the crowds of pedestrians attending their hurried errands. City workers dotted the streets, cleaning up ocran feces left in their wake. Vendors peddled their goods from the valued storefronts that edged the circled junction. Terin spied a gang of young boys chasing one another through nearby alleyways, running barefoot and wearing well-soiled tunics. Soldiers dressed in yellow tunics and bronze breastplates guarded each side of the massive structure that was centered on the circled roadway.

"That is the Forum of Rego. Ambassador Antillius should be inside," Cronus said as they dismounted and tethered their ocran to a post near the base of the Forum. Cronus's Torry uniform stood out like a thumb in a field of fingers. The guard standing post atop the stair of the west face of the Forum spotted him immediately.

"Hold!" Cronus stood, holding his palms open to show he meant no threat. The guard descended the steps to the street level, attentive of any movement they might take. "State your purpose!" he said in a measured tone, standing several paces before them.

"I am Unit Commander Kenti of the Fifth Unit, Ninth Telnic of the Third Torry Army. I am escorting Terin Caleph to the Forum of Rego. He seeks the Torry ambassador, Minister Antillius."

The guard eyed Terin briefly before shifting his eyes back to Cronus. "What is his business with Minister Antillius?"

"He is to be the ambassador's apprentice and scribe."

The guard waited a moment, measuring their demeanor. Neither of them seemed nervous as he stared in silence. It was a method Cronus had told Terin that soldiers used to gauge truthfulness. Had they fidgeted or averted their eyes, the guard might have doubted their claim. "Remain here," the guard said as he ascended the steps and passed between the stone columns.

As they waited, Terin started to realize he might not see Cronus again once they parted. He doubted his duties would allow him much time to visit his friend. Cronus's duties would also provide little time to socialize. But events were fluid, and no one really knew what the future held or where the road might take you. He accepted Cronus's friendship for what it was, a friendship. If they never met again, he was better for having known him.

"Thank you, Cronus."

"For what?" Cronus eyed his young friend with a bemused look.

Terin shrugged his shoulders. "For everything. I don't know if I could have made this journey without you—at least not as easy as you made it."

"You would have been fine."

The guard emerged from the Forum, marching apace between the columns as the midday sun shone upon their alabaster surface. Two other men followed, one as tall as Cronus while the other was shorter than Terin. The taller man wore a dark-blue tunic and a wide belt with a longsword on each hip. His dark hair dropped below his shoulders, framing the hard features of his handsome face. Deep-blue eyes scanned their surroundings, suspicious of any anomaly and keen to any threat. The second man was diminutive and portly with short silver hair and trimmed beard. His eyes were steel gray, and he wore long burgundy robes edged in gold. Only Araxans native to the lone hills had beards or were portly. Jonas told Terin that Squid Antillius was born in the lone hills, so the shorter man must be him.

Squid Antillius's eyes locked on Terin as soon as they beheld the boy's face from atop the Forum steps. An infectious smile played across his lips as he descended the steps. "You must be Terin." He greeted him warmly, placing his hands on Terin's shoulders.

"Yes, Minister Antillius." Terin bowed his head, showing deference to Squid's authority.

"None of that, my boy. I am a humble servant of the crown. Save such formalities for official audiences. For now, call me Squid." The old man slapped his shoulders before lowering his arms.

"Thank you… Squid."

"Very good, Terin. Now who accompanies you?" Squid shifted his gaze to Cronus.

"This is my friend, Cronus Kenti. Cronus joined me for much of my journey. I owe him a great debt."

"My gratitude, Commander Kenti, for safeguarding my apprentice on his journey."

"I believe it was Terin who safeguarded me, Minister Antillius. We met east of Central City, where he disarmed an ocran thief who had stolen my mount. If not for his courage, I would have been afoot for much of my journey."

"Disarmed a thief? How so, Commander?" Squid asked, his brain fixed on that part of the story.

"He split the rogue's sword in two."

"Is that so?" Squid reflected quietly, his eyes shifting between Cronus and Terin, observing the boy curiously.

"I can't judge Terin's ability as a scribe, but I have measured his quality as a man. He will serve you well, Minister Antillius. My commander allowed me to escort Terin to your keeping. I must return now to my command."

"You have my leave and my gratitude, Commander Kenti," Squid said.

"Farewell, my friend." Cronus clasped Terin's forearm, then climbed aboard his white mount. Terin waved goodbye as his friend disappeared in the crowded street.

"Terin, this is my protector, King's High Elite Miles Standarn." Squid regarded his taller companion. Miles nodded his head, greeting Terin, his stoic face void of emotion. Terin regarded Miles with deference. Only a hundred men were named to the King's Elite, and only ten were named High Elite. They served as the personal bodyguards of the house of King Lore. They were also trusted agents of the crown. Such protection extended to the King's ministers. That one of King Lore's High Elite served as Squid's protector was proof of his high station. "See that Terin's ocran is stabled with mine," Squid asked the Forum guard.

"I will see it done," the guard stated and stepped away.

"Come, my boy. Let us begin." Squid placed a hand on his shoulder, guiding Terin into the Forum and to his new life.

CHAPTER 4

Three days had passed since Terin arrived at Rego. Squid Antillius invited him to share his lodging. Although uneasy about accepting such generosity, Terin eventually relented to Squid's insistence. A soft bed and his own room were far more than he expected. In his time with Minister Antillius, Terin had merely followed his mentor from place to place, meeting with the Regoan council and dignitaries in their homes or social gatherings. Terin had yet to demonstrate his abilities as a scribe. Squid only asked the simplest of questions, such as "How is your father? Your mother? Life on your farm?" It felt as if he was merely visiting a relative than learning a trade or vocation.

The evening of the third day found them in Squid's rented home, a single-level structure made of porian timber with stone supports. It was a humble abode for a king's minister, proving that Squid cared little for the trappings of his position. After a quiet dinner, Squid invited Terin to join him near the hearth. There, they sat in two cushioned large chairs half facing each other and half facing the warm fire. Squid discarded the robes of his profession for a simple gray tunic that fell below his knees.

"You have your mother's hair, but your face, that is your father's," Squid said, appraising his young ward. He stared into the crackling flames, a soft smile gracing his lips as he recalled the past. "Your mother was the most beautiful woman I had ever known. She and Jonas made a fitting couple. Those were grand days. Your father"— he returned his eyes to Terin—"your father was the bravest man I knew." Squid took notice of the necklace gracing Terin's neck. It was usually tucked within his tunic collar, but now it rested without, the flames of the hearth lighting its carvings. "Your father's necklace," he said.

Terin looked down at the object adorning his neck. "Yes. He gifted it to me when we parted. This one is of my mother," he said, touching one of the carvings off to the side. "But he did not say who these other women are." He lifted his eyes back to Squid, wondering if he knew.

"That one is your grandmother, Jonas's mother. Cordela was her name. I met her long ago. She was a fierce and beautiful woman, and he loved her very much," Squid said, indicating the carving opposite his mother's.

"Does she live?"

"No." Squid shook his head sadly. "She passed long ago. Did your father not speak of her?"

"No. He has never spoken of his family or my mother's. He guards the truth as if it might break me." He couldn't hide his frustration. "Do you know who this woman in the center is?" He touched the most prominent carving that rested on the center of the necklace.

"No," Squid said honestly. "I asked him once, as he oft wore that very necklace during our travels. It held only the two carvings of your grandmother and the mystery woman. Jonas must have added the one of your mother later. He has not spoken of your kin at all?"

"No. My father has told me little of his youth, kin, or the things he has done. When I ask my mother, she only smiles and says, 'Jonas is a humble man. It is for him to tell you, not I.'"

"Yes, he is humble. He told you little of our adventures, but he focused your thoughts on what was more important. He trained you."

"Trained me?"

"He taught you the sword and the bow?"

"Yes."

"He taught you discipline and honesty?"

"Yes."

"He taught you to hunt game, build a fire, and survive alone in the wild?"

"Yes," Terin answered, wondering why such skills were of use to a scribe or diplomat.

"You see, he taught you what you needed to know."

Terin was confused. "But he did not train me to be a scribe or your apprentice. It was my mother who taught me to read and write."

"Terin, do you know with whom you are speaking?" Squid asked in a harsher voice.

"I believe so," Terin said uneasily, a little taken aback.

"I am King's Minister Squid Antillius. I am second only to Chief Minister Eli Monsh. The Torry king defers to my guidance. Do you believe any training as a scribe on your part qualifies you as my apprentice?"

"No," Terin answered honestly.

"I chose you because you had a lifetime of training by Jonas Caleph, a lifetime for him to instill in you the values that he cherished. Character"—Squid raised a finger to emphasize the point—"character is the quality that is the ultimate measure of a man. Men may proclaim their self-worth or boast great deeds, but their character is what truly defines them. As a minister to the king, character is my greatest resource. If King Lore doubts my word, my counsel shall go unheeded. The king needs to hear our honest counsel, whether we offer good tiding or ill but especially when they are ill. Kings need to hear the truth, and only men of character will counsel truth when doing so casts them poorly in their sovereign's eyes.

"The highest trait I value in my apprentice is his character. Your father knows this. You were not chosen because you are merely his son. You were chosen because you were sired and reared by him. Even that was not enough until Jonas swore to me that your character and values reflected his own." Squid held up the scroll that Terin had returned to him, the very scroll that he was not to read.

"What is it you wish me to do, Squid?"

"Be honest. You are my eyes and ears wherever I send you. Use them. You have your father's sword?"

"Yes." He nodded.

"Give it here." Squid held out his hand. Terin drew the sword from its sheath, setting it carefully in Squid Antillius's open hands. Squid held it aloft, the dancing flames playing along its blade. The silver blade seemed to glow a bluish tinge in the firelight, just as it did when he first held it. Terin thought it an illusion, but the blade seemed alive with a cognizance of its own. Squid's gray eyes shaded a silver hue, mimicking the color of the sword. "What did your father tell you of this sword?"

"To keep it close. He said it would not forsake me if I did so."

"Remember that, Terin. Remember that above all else." He returned the sword to his young charge. Terin sheathed the blade, wondering why Squid placed such emphasis on the sword and his weapon-handling skills if his primary vocation was an ambassador's apprentice. "Your first assignment is at hand, Terin." Squid stroked his trimmed silver beard with his fingers, his eyes out of focus as they stared into the fire. "Your first assignment without me," he corrected.

"What do you wish me to do?" Terin asked, not expecting such independence so early in his service. He strongly desired to perform well in whatever was asked of him. He wanted Squid to be proud and pleased with the trust he had placed in him.

"In a few days, you are to travel upriver to the Costelin Colony. It is some days' ride from here. There, you shall stay until I call for you."

"What do you wish me to do there?" he asked, thinking it a strange task.

"I want you to observe. Nothing more." Squid shifted his eyes to Terin's, focusing his stare with a terrible intensity, the light of the fire playing frighteningly across his face. "I want you to remain within the colony. Do not wander afar, and keep your sword upon you at all times. All times," he said again to emphasize the point.

*****

The Costelin Colony rested at a sharp angle in the Wid River. The river's natural westerly flow jutted north, then south before angling west again, leaving a large section of riverbank surrounded by the Wid on three sides. The colony grew upon this parcel with the river bordering its north, west, and east sides. Narrow gravel streets converged in the village square where the open surface was made of layered stone. Single- and two-floored wooden structures lined the avenues. Strongly built stone barracks dominated the village square, housing scores of Regoan soldiers, though many had departed for settlements farther upriver.

Terin had been in Costelin for eight days, staying in one of the several inns at the center of the colony. The tedium of staying within Costelin dulled his senses. Squid had told him to observe, but what was there to observe? Eight days of staring at streets and buildings and villagers drove him to the brink of boredom. How much longer must he linger there, awaiting word from Squid to rejoin him at Rego? Perhaps this was a test by Squid to measure his discipline. That made sense, Terin thought as he trod the central avenue of Costelin.

He had made some observations, though they seemed trivial. The keeper of the inn where he stayed complained that his stocks of ale were running thin, but Terin saw several wagons laden with wooden casks enter the village daily. Perhaps they were bound for points farther east, but some should have been for local consumption. The locals also complained that the colony was poorly defended and that many of its defenders were detached for assignments elsewhere. The barracks were nearly empty.

The magistrate had requested that children not venture out of the colony, a monumental task considering children's inquisitive nature and need to play. Men often outnumbered women in the Wid River Valley, but there in Costelin, it was even more pronounced. Many of the locals wore heavy cloaks, covering themselves head to calf even on a warm spring day like this, Terin noted as sunlight bathed the village square. A few ships docked along the river's edge remained for days, their crews in no apparent hurry to unload their cargos.

Terin heard the soft pounding of footsteps behind him. He turned his head as a dozen young boys ran past. One bumped into him, the collision knocking the boy onto his back. He looked no older than six or seven years and stared up at Terin with wide eyes. "Uh, sorry, sir," he uttered before springing to his feet and continuing on after his friends.

"Wait, Conra! Wait! Mama said I could play with you!" a young girl shouted, chasing after the boys. She looked no older than four or five and held the skirt of her dress as she ran to catch up. Terin smiled, recalling times of his youth of running through the woods with the Jorgen boys and their sisters following them and pestering them wherever they went.

"You'll have to run faster if you want to keep up, Eppie!" the girl's brother shouted back to her without breaking stride.

The children ran through the streets and alleyways, snaking a route around barrels and wagons, making their way to the river. They were told not to wander from the colony's confines, but the children waited for a time when adults were otherwise occupied and slipped past the last row of buildings that edged the Wid River, just west of Costelin.

The older boys stripped their tunics and jumped into the slow-moving Wid, splashing cold water on one another. The late-spring temperatures were not warm enough to heat the water to a comfortable level, but young boys were undeterred by such things. They waited through the winter months for a day as warm as this to jump in the river, and they were not to be denied. Little Eppie stepped only a foot into the river, just enough for the water to lap her ankles. It was cold enough for her, but her brother followed the other boys farther into the water.

Conra swam back to his little sister and splashed water in her direction. She stepped back as uneven sheets of water swept the air before her. "Stop, Conra! It's cold!" she pleaded as her brother teased.

"You're never any fun, Eppie," he taunted.

Eppie retreated to the riverbank, holding her skirt high enough so it would not be soiled by the wet grass that lined the embankment. The river wound slowly around the colony behind them before passing west. She could see the snowcaps of the Plate Mountains in the distance and the lush green foothills that sloped into the valley below. Thick foliage pressed to the river's north bank, obscuring much of the Wid's far side. Eppie gazed at the wonders of the world around her—the boys playing in the water, the river, the foothills, the mountains, and the clear blue sky overhead.

The bold colors of springtime were magnified when seen through a child's eyes. Beauty was magnified when seen through a child's eyes. Imbued with innocence that saw the world for what it was but not why it was, children were the arbiters of obvious truth. But the wonder and merriment of the world around her quickly gave way to a new reality. Eppie's eyes shot wide open, staring at the opposing bank as dark forms sprang from the foliage and underbrush.

Eppie screamed. The sound escaped the narrows of her tiny throat, echoing the horror unfolding before her. Dark-winged forms took flight, pouring from the north like a pestilent swarm. "Gargoyles!" she screamed, the panic in her voice matching the pounding of her little heart. Some of the boys looked up, not cognizant of what she had said. Conra gazed at his sister's face, her eyes transfixed in utter terror. He craned his neck, his own eyes taking in their approaching doom.

"Kai!" the gargoyles screamed, sweeping over the Wid River like bats issuing from a cave. Their wings spread, flapping rapidly to carry them across. Their pounding wings filled the air, joining in a deafening chorus akin to the sound of rushing water. Black skin, shiny and leathery, stretched over taut-muscled limbs and sharp-angled faces. Some wore full tunics while others donned half tunics that revealed thin-muscled chests.

Their pointed ears curved back upon their skulls as if pressed by the wind. Bright-white fangs curved menacingly over blood-red lips. Split tongues slithered over fangs and lips, thick saliva dripping from their tips. Their eyes glowed a feral red as they fixed on the children's diminutive forms at the water's edge. Their terrible war cries raised their bloodlust, replacing reason with savagery.

Eppie turned to run but stumbled, her feet slipping in the aqueous soil. She fell facedown in the wet grass. She rose quickly to her feet but stumbled again, slipping in the grass as panic overtook her trembling heart. A small hand grasped her left arm, pulling her to her feet. "Run, Eppie!" Conra shouted. She gained her footing, running as fast as her little legs could carry her. Horrible screams echoed behind her, but she did not look back. Conra ran beside her, gripping her arm with uncanny strength as he pulled her to his pace. The cries of children being torn to pieces haunted their ears as their eyes fixed on the village ahead.

Conra suddenly released his hold upon her as a terrible weight struck his back, driving him into the ground. Eppie turned sharply to her left, her eyes wild with fright. There, a gargoyle straddled Conra's back with its fangs digging into his neck. The creature shook its head emphatically, jerking Conra's quivering form. The gargoyle raised its feral gaze to Eppie, its mouth soaked in dripping blood. Its crimson eyes blazed as they stared at her like an apparition conjured from her darkest dreams.

She turned and ran toward the colony, where the first structures were just steps away, but to no avail, for she could not outrun death. She fell short of the first building, her little body set upon by gargoyles, who swarmed over her, biting, ripping, and tearing before moving on.

*****

Terin stepped toward the door of the inn, his mind elsewhere as he wondered how many more days he would have to remain in Costelin. As his right hand reached out to open the door, a sensation coursed over his skin like a thousand bugs scurrying over his flesh. Something was amiss. Unconsciously, his right hand went to his sword hilt as he turned. Men came running his way with panicked eyes and swords drawn. "To arms!" they shouted.

Behind them came several gargoyles, running down their prey with short curved swords. Arrows arced from upper windows, striking down the gargoyles as they drew near. Though the gargoyles were dropped in quick succession, the fleeing men did not stop. Terin soon discovered why. Terrible screams echoed throughout the alleys and streets to the west. The first gargoyles were mere heralds of the vast host that followed. The west end of the village square filled with gargoyles, converging from all points west. Thousands of glowing eyes fixed to his direction.

The blood drained from Terin's face. His sword burned upon his left thigh, beckoning its master to draw it forth. Terin forced such action from his brain, struggling to think of a way out. He burst through the door of the inn. There was no one inside as he ran across the main hall of the inn, where the innkeeper's wife served the guests their meals. His room was on the opposing wall on the ground level. He opened the door, then barred it close behind him. He went to the window and barred it close as well. Terin closed his eyes.

"Breathe," he whispered to calm his nerves. He needed a better plan than hiding in his room. A locked door would not keep those creatures out for long, but what else could he do? He heard the clang of steel and the shouts of men outside in the street. The grating sounds of human and gargoyle screams melded in a morbid blend. A few moments passed before he heard the pounding of feet echoing off the stone floor in the outer hall. Then his door rattled. An angry hiss followed.

Thud. Thud. Thud. The sound of steel striking wood rang in his ears as splinters bowed inward with the door giving way. "Think!" he scolded himself. They were coming in, and he couldn't stop that from happening. He could escape through the window, but what chance did he have in the street, surrounded by their vast numbers? Something his father once said came to mind: "Often, a poor plan forcefully executed has a great chance for success."

He went to the side of the door and drew his father's sword. A strange sensation coursed through his blood, sending waves of euphoria rippling across his flesh. The sword felt weightless and heavy at the same time. It felt weightless in his arm but heavy in its power. He waited until the next blow fell, then he lifted the wooden block that barred the door and stepped to the side.

Upon the next blow, the door opened. A gargoyle stumbled forth, unbalanced, with its sword stuck in the swinging door. Terin's sword glided gracefully from the right, striking the back of the creature's neck. The black head separated where the blade struck, floating in the air as the winged body dropped to the floor. A second gargoyle stepped forth, eyes feral with rage, its curved sword swinging fiercely. Terin recovered, blocking the hasty blow. The creature's sword broke asunder upon touching Terin's blade.

Its eyes widened in disbelief, their red glow dulling with a new emotion: fear. Terin did not hesitate and drove his sword into the gargoyle's chest. The creature slid limply off the blade. Another gargoyle followed. Terin split its blade and hacked off an exposed wing. The creature stumbled back, tripping on the floor, as its clawed feet were tangled. Terin cut off its feet, then split its belly open. Thick red blood drained upon the gray stone.

The gargoyles gathering in the outer hall backed away, stayed by the silver blade that danced in his hand. Although torn between fear and hate, uncertainty gave the creatures pause. Their mouths hung agape, their fangs glistening over bright-red lips.

The power of the sword quelled his fear, banishing it to a whisper that could not be heard through the din of battle. A sane man would have surveyed the dozen gargoyles spread throughout the main hall with their feral eyes fixed on him and use their hesitation to flee, but Terin was overtaken by a madness, an urge, to follow the will of the sword. Was he its master, or was the blade his? He did not wait for them to move. He stepped to his right in smooth, forceful strides, closing on the gargoyle nearest him. The creature raised its blade, gripping the hilt forcefully with its two clawed hands. Terin swung quickly, the blow passing through the raised sword, the left arm that held it, and the gargoyle's midsection. A terrible shriek escaped its throat as it crumpled to the floor. A second gargoyle followed, meeting a similar fate.

The others, at first, stepped close, planning to set upon him from each direction, but they, too, were now afflicted with the sword's madness. They fled to the door, colliding clumsily one into the other as they attempted to reach the safety of the street outside. Terin came behind them, cutting them down one by one, piece by piece, a wing there, an arm there, a head if he could. The sword showed little discernment other than striking what was given, cutting through flesh, bone, and steel as if they were stale bread, an azure glow alighting its blade.

The gargoyles climbed atop one another, fleeing the slaughter as they poured through the door and into the street. Terin pursued, overcome by the sword's madness or the confidence with which it imbued. He caught one foe crawling over its comrades, clawing its way toward the entryway. His sword came swiftly, striking the center of its back where its wings fanned awkwardly from its spine. The sword passed through the rippling, taut muscles and angled bones as if they were parchment. The blade stopped after exiting the anus, leaving the creature nearly in half with its innards spilled upon its comrades beneath him.

Terin had never seen a living gargoyle before this day. Now he had felled half a dozen in as many moments. With euphoric energy coursing every vessel of his flesh, he charged his foes through the doorway and into the village square. Filled with the confidence to smite all that the heavens could throw against him or from the dark places from whence their foul race sprang, Terin stood alone. Unfolding before his eyes was the hellish metamorphosis of the village square.

The center of Costelin was serried with gargoyles flooding the street like a dark river. Many structures were set ablaze with flames dancing over the afflicted edifices, trapping those within to a morbid fate. The bodies of men and women were hung from the second levels of several dwellings by their feet, limply dangling as the gargoyles made sport of their suffering. Some were dead, and some were dying. The heads of other victims were raised on pikes and carried through the streets, trophies of the macabre slaughter.

Scores of gargoyles surrounded Costelin's barracks, ramming the door with a heavy log. Arrows arced overhead, finding fleshy targets wherever they fell, for the gargoyles were too numerous to miss. The sound of clanging steel rang dully from the streets to the east and south as the gargoyles swept forcefully in those directions.

Terin stood in the center of this storm, his eyes surveying the carnage, betraying his confidence to cold fear. The power of the sword waned as he stood alone. The gargoyles gathered in the square, slowed as their feral, glowing eyes took note of the lone human standing in their midst like a rock rising above the surf of raging sea. He stood alone, brazen and unmoved, defying their savagery with apparent indifference. Such a notion filled them with bloodlust and hatred. They could not abide his audacity to go unpunished. They stepped nigh, closing a circle about him, determined to tear him apart and bathe in his blood.

Terin betrayed no fear, his face as rigid as carved stone, but within his heart was a torrent of unfettered trepidation. What hope had he? The power invoked by the sword seemed distant now, and those who fled his deadly blade had turned back with courage rekindled by their reinforcements. Even his father's words of wisdom about forceful execution of a poor plan failed him at this moment. He had no poor plan left to execute.

Even if his father's sword still had the power to cut through its target, the gargoyles were unlikely to oblige him by coming one at a time. They closed now in unison. If he felled one to the fore, then the ones upon his flanks and rear would drive him through.

The smell of misty smoke teased his nostrils as he looked skyward at the sun shining bright over the snowcaps to the east. Wisps of darkening smoke failed to obscure the clear blue of the morning sky. At least he would die on a beautiful day.

Taking a fast breath like a diver before a deep plunge, he held his sword close as the enemy drew near. He spun, swift and true, spitting blades all around him in a deadly arc. Dark-red blood splattered his gray tunic as he hewed limbs, torsos, and wings. Gargoyle death screams rent the air as he surrendered himself to the sword's will once again, accepting whatever the fates ordained.

Terin had little time to note the heavy stream of arrows raining above or the sounds of clanging steel and battle cries drawing near from each direction. He spun as swiftly as his feet allowed, cutting indiscriminately and as quickly as he could. Time slowed as the blade danced in his hands, his eyes following the sword with each cut. The sword renewed his strength, masking the fatigue that taxed his muscles, spurring him beyond the limits of his endurance. He felt he could leap into the sky, transcending the bounds of his terrestrial limits. Suddenly, the gargoyles drew away like tall grass bowing before the wind. Then he heard a wondrous sound: the war cries of men, of men bringing battle, not fleeing in fright.

The savage faces of the gargoyles serried in the village square shone a great disquiet. Then he saw them in each direction, soldiers clad in white tunics and steel breastplates and helms, driving forth in close ranks with their shields interlocked and shortswords stabbing between them. They cut down gargoyles with methodical efficiency. Terin then noticed the archers, hundreds of them, lining the rooftops and raining their volleys into the enemy below.

There amid the fray, astride his tall white mount, rode Cronus, his silver helm resplendent in the morning light and issuing commands behind a wall of shields. "Forward!" he commanded, shifting his mount wherever the line looked weakest and ready to counter any incursion. Arsenc rode beside him, his brown mount guarding Cronus's flank.

Cronus's eyes shot north over the heads of his men and the gargoyles in their path. There, amid the enemy, stood a man not much more than a boy. He stood erect and proud and alone. He was staring at Cronus with a smile upon his face. *Why is he smiling?* Cronus wondered. The man stood alone, surrounded by the vilest creatures bent on his destruction. Recognition struck him suddenly. "Foolish boy," he mumbled distastefully. "Arsenc, take command!" he shouted over his shoulder as he raced his mount around the right flank of the formation.

"Marcus!" Arsenc commanded.

"Yes, Commander," Marcus answered over the sound of screams and clashing steel.

"Take command and drive onward." Arsenc kicked his heels into his ocran's flanks, speeding after Cronus.

Unsheathing his broad sword, Cronus cleared the right flank of his command and drove headlong into the gargoyle mass. Lacking the pikes to bring down the beast or the courage to meet the Torry's longsword at that speed, the gargoyles gave way to Cronus's bold charge. Several blades slashed as he passed, but their strokes were poorly measured and weakly cast. He found a neck for the taking and lopped off a gargoyle head.

This was the easy part, he reminded himself. Fetching Terin and riding back through the angry gargoyle crowd was the real challenge. He scowled as Arsenc came up upon his left. He hadn't the breath or time to vent his displeasure. As they drew near, their eyes marveled at the sight of Terin moving freely among the foe, chopping them down like finger-thin saplings. Gargoyles scattered at their approach, opening a clear path to Terin.

Terin's heart lightened when he first set eyes on his friends' familiar faces, shedding his worries like weighted stones lifted after a long journey. The enemy briefly drew away, allowing him enough time to savage any that lay between his rescuers and him.

Cronus's mount snorted loudly as he reared up beside Terin. "Come!" Cronus commanded, lowering a hand to pull his friend into the saddle.

"Argh!" Arsenc screamed painfully beside him. Cronus retrieved his open hand, turning to see his friend fall from his saddle.

Terin raced around Cronus's mount to aid their comrade. Arsenc lay sprawled upon the gray stone, nursing a viscous gash along his left thigh. His mount stumbled further ahead, set upon by gargoyles hacking away at the helpless beast. Several creatures converged on Arsenc with swords raised and eyes afire. Their swinging blades met Terin's sword as he blocked their path. Their swords broke apart ere touching his silver blade. He followed through, taking off whatever flesh his sword was offered.

Cronus quickly dismounted. Seeing Terin hold the enemy at bay, he wasted little time grabbing his fallen comrade under his arms and dragging him to the open doorway of the inn. "Terin! Come on!" He beckoned for him to follow. Terin retreated to the inn as Cronus greeted with his sword, ready for battle. Terin moved to close the door, but Cronus stopped him with a free hand upon his shoulder. "Let them in if they dare," he said, pushing Terin to one side of the entryway while he waited upon the other.

Some moments passed before a gargoyle tested them. Passing through the front door, he was set upon on both flanks. Terin took a wing while Cronus took an arm. Their second blows found more vital flesh, and the creature dropped to the floor between them, near the gargoyle corpses that Terin left there on his previous exit.

"You are a wondrous sight to behold." Terin smiled, locking eyes with Cronus across the doorway as they caught their breath.

"And you are a damned fool for standing in the middle of a village square filled with gargoyles. When we have time, perhaps you might explain yourself," Cronus admonished before a second gargoyle climbed over the corpse littering the entryway. They made quick work of that intruder as Terin nearly halved its torso while Cronus lopped its head.

Arsenc lay on his back, pressing his hands into his left thigh to slow the blood oozing through his fingers. "Keep up this pace and you two may win this battle by yourselves." He laughed over the pain.

"This will work till they test the windows or burn us out," Cronus answered sourly.

"They won't have time," Terin said as the sound of clanging steel and shouting men drew closer outside.

Converging from all points of Costelin, Torry soldiers drove into the village square, squeezing the gargoyles in a dozen deadly vices. Overhead, hundreds of archers lined the rooftops, dropping any gargoyles attempting to take flight and pouring their deadly volleys upon the serried ranks below. Gargoyles entered the inn now to escape the slaughter in the streets, not to pursue Terin and Cronus. Most were caught unawares as the two men cut them down. Before long, Torry soldiers swept past the inn.

"Stay with Arsenc and tend his wound!" Cronus commanded before marching out to join his men. Terin stood at the doorway, caught between his duty to his wounded friend and the sword in his hand that beckoned him to follow Cronus into battle. The longer the debate played in his mind, the quicker the power of the sword waned. Finally, he lowered his sword, his chest tightening as he tried to catch his breath. He sheathed his blade, nearly collapsing from exhaustion. The euphoria of battle must have masked the fatigue taxing his body.

"And Commander Mastorn thought you soft." Arsenc shook his head. "You slew more gargoyles than I've seen in my lifetime. How is that possible?"

"I... I don't know." Terin stumbled over the words. He really did not know. His father had taught him swordplay, but even he did not teach what he did this day. It was as if his hand was guided by a sentient force. In fact, all that his father taught him had escaped his memory when he first drew the sword. Panic always robbed men of their senses, their skills degenerating to their basest ability, but he remembered so little of what he had just done.

*****

Cronus stepped over the corpse-littered square. Carka birds circled lazily above, biding their time to feast on the fallen. The streets of Costelin were covered with the dead and the dying. Blood oozed in gelatinous pools throughout the avenues. Scores of men lay in foul heaps, their bodies twisted in unnatural angles with chunks of their flesh eaten off the bone. Dead eyes stared to the sky as if seeking mercy from an unknown omnipotence. Most of the fallen were gargoyles, their leathery black skin shining dully in the plain light of day. Hundreds died this day, perhaps two thousand, maybe three.

It was a trap. Torry soldiers had waited in ships, hiding in the hulls for days. Hundreds of bowmen had snuck into the colony two or three at a time, holding up on the second level of many structures. Many units were hidden on the village outskirts. Once the gargoyles took the bait, the invisible forces appeared on all sides and descended upon the enemy in force. A great victory it was, but the mothers of dead children would not see it as such. Spirals of black smoke twisted above as soldiers and villagers rushed water buckets to quell the flames. The bodies of the fallen would take days to clear, bury or burn.

*****

"Kenti!" Commander Mastorn greeted Cronus upon his return to the inn.

"Commander." Cronus greeted him with a fist to his heart.

"Give me your report as we walk." Mastorn was loathe to recall his unit commanders from their duties after a battle. Unless the enemy was nearby and ready to reform and attack, he preferred to track his unit commanders down one at a time to check their status.

"Two dead, six wounded. I ordered the wounded taken to the inn where I left Arsenc."

"Very good. How is your second?"

"His left thigh is badly cut. I don't know when or if he'll return to duty. The Matrons are tending him." As they neared the entrance to the inn, Cronus paused at the doorway. "Terin Caleph is inside." Cronus jabbed a finger through the entryway while giving Mastorn a knowing glance.

"Minister Antillius's apprentice? What is he doing here?"

"He was here when we arrived, surrounded by gargoyles in the center of the village square."

"And they didn't kill him?"

"They tried."

"What do you mean they tried?" Mastorn's voice raised another level.

"He killed more than I care to count."

"How?"

"With his sword."

"With his sw…" Mastorn scrubbed his hands over his face. "That boy is as much a scribe as you are one of Princess Corry's handmaids."

They entered the main hall of the inn, which was filled with the wounded. They lay stretched out side by side, some grievously wounded while others already dead. Matrons dressed in long red gowns and matching cloaks tended their wounds. Women had the healing touch, which matched their tender nature, or so custom decreed. Young girls began their apprenticeship at five years of age. They were schooled in herb lore, limb setting, and the cleansing of wounds. They knew that disease killed more than steel, and cleanliness was practiced above all else.

They were met by a comely Matron with a genteel smile. "Welcome, Commander of Telnic and Commander of Unit," she said, greeting them as they entered. She had bright-green eyes and dusty-brown hair. She seemed in her third decade but with the bearing of a much older Matron. Her hands were folded in the long, loose sleeves of her crimson gown.

"Matron Beasela." Cronus regarded her. "How is Arsenc?"

"His wound is very deep, Commander of Unit. He must remain here until we can remove him to Rego, then Central City. Your friend is waiting by his side." She waved them on with her right hand fanning to the opposite wall, to the doorway of Terin's room.

They found him upon the narrow bed in Terin's room. He could have been placed in the main hall with the others, but Terin had paid for the room and intended the bed for his friend before any other. Arsenc lay on his back, a blanket covering his pale form. He had lost much blood before the Matrons cleaned, sewed, and dressed his wound with herbs and tree moss. Terin sat upon a stool beside him and rose to his feet when Cronus and Mastorn entered.

"Cronus, you did well." Arsenc smiled weakly.

Cronus shook his head. He wanted to admonish his second for disobeying his order, but the blow he took would have been Cronus's if he had not ridden at his side. "You will heal soon, my friend. That is an order. I insist you obey," Cronus said.

"Yes, Commander Kenti." Arsenc smiled.

Commander Mastorn did not suffer commands to be disobeyed. Arsenc's disobedience was a grave matter, and he would think upon allowing his return to command once he healed. Mastorn also knew Cronus had acted rashly and left command to Arsenc for the sake of a civilian, a brave but dangerous act and not in his character. Yet in Cronus's eyes, Terin might have perished, and only his mount could have closed the distance to come to his aid. Add to the fact that Terin was no mere civilian. He was apprentice to Squid Antillius.

But what kind of apprentice? Mastorn wondered. His eyes shifted to Terin, who stood quietly to the side. The boy was not overly proud or full of himself for one who had slain so many of the enemy. There was something about the boy that did not fit. *Why was he placed here?* he mused. Yet Mastorn knew he would find him here. Minister Antillius had left instructions with him and the other telnic commanders placed near Costelin that if the enemy attacked, they were to send Terin back to Rego after such a battle. If Squid Antillius favored the boy, why did he place him in harm's way?

"Cronus!"

"Yes, Commander?" Cronus answered formally in response to Mastorn's stern voice, which always preceded an order he meant carried out with diligence.

"Take one flax of your unit and escort our young friend back to Rego. I will find you mounts for your detachment. I expect you gone within the hour," Mastorn said as his eyes bore into Terin's.

"Commander, Ambassador Antillius ordered that I remain here until he sends for me," Terin explained, fearing disobeying Squid's orders while obeying Mastorn's.

"I know" was all the commander said.

CHAPTER 5

They rode half a day before darkness closed from the east. Setting camp on the south bank of the Wid, they unfurled their bedrolls around a cookfire. Cronus would normally caution against lighting a fire in the night, but his men had fought all morning and rode the afternoon. Cold, hungry men would fare poorly in a fight, and he doubted any roving bands of gargoyles nearby had the stomach to test so obvious a target after their decimation at Costelin. In fact, they were probably safer with a fire. A fire in the night was either a sign of foolishness or of strength, and there were few foolish humans left in the Wid River Valley.

Commander Bode had set the trap at Costelin, weakening the garrison there while sneaking in fresh reserves a few at a time in wagons or many at a time in the hulls of ships. Costelin was not the only trap he had set. All along the Wid, he emptied the larger colonies of the Regoan garrisons while secretly slipping larger contingents of Torry troops into those colonies. Over the coming weeks, they would prove effective in draining the gargoyles' numbers. Once the creatures grew wary of such tactics, General Bode would send smaller patrols to hunt them down, ever adjusting to the fluidity of such warfare.

As the men settled near the fire, Cronus drew Terin away. They walked some distance downstream with the Wid lapping the riverbank to their right as they trod over dew-soaked grass. Trees covered the foothills to their south, spilling down to the river. Cronus left his helm upon his bedroll but still wore his breastplate and greaves. The closing darkness masked the bloodstains upon his white tunic, but not the weariness in his voice.

"We will reach Rego by tomorrow's end."

"I know you wished to remain at Costelin to see to your men, Cronus, but I am glad for your company. It is safer to travel this road with more swords than one. Twelve swords feel much safer."

"I feel safe as well with you as my twelfth."

Terin shook his head. "I am no soldier, Cronus."

"No, you're something else. What, I don't know. Might I see your sword?"

Terin unsheathed the blade, presenting Cronus the hilt in his outstretched arms. Cronus took the blade in hand, holding it aloft as the nearly full waxing moon shone along its length. The sword emitted a dull-bluish hue as the moonlight played upon it. Cronus had not noticed that before today. Was there something in the blade, or was it a queer effect of the moon that brought about such a manifestation?

"Where did your father find this?" Cronus asked, his eyes running the length of the blade.

"He only said that he found it and that it was long buried. He used it during the Sadden War."

Cronus returned the sword to Terin, the blade's glow strengthening as Terin touched it. There was more to the story than what Terin was saying. His father must have kept it to himself. It was no common blade, that much was certain. But what kind of blade was it? What mysteries were folded into it when it was forged? It was not steel or iron and certainly not bronze. Was Terin's appointment in part due to this sword? Did ambassador Antillius know of its nature? He also found Commander Mastorn's last order troubling. He told him that upon delivering Terin to Rego, he was to receive further orders from Minister Antillius. But why? And why would Mastorn send him when his unit lost his second as well?

*****

By late afternoon of the following day, they ascended the steps of the Forum of Rego. Leaving his men and his mount in the street below, Cronus escorted Terin between the stone pillars of the Forum's south face before passing into the inner sanctum. The pillars spaced at the entrance, giving way to a cavernous hall. Guards in yellow tunics ushered them through a maze of off-shooting passageways of gray stone, torches bracketed along the wall lighting their path. Their escort left them before an open doorway, then departed, the sound of his sandaled feet echoing weakly as he disappeared into the maze of corridors from whence they entered.

Cronus cleared his throat and stepped within the chamber as Terin followed. The room was small with a wooden table and chairs its only furnishing. Lanterns hung from each corner of the room and another from the center of the ceiling, just above the table. Miles Standarn stood off to the side, his left hand resting on his sword hilt, fixing them with his steel-blue eyes and guarded countenance. Squid Antillius stood behind the table, the lantern's light reflecting off his silver beard and gray eyes. He wore the burgundy robes edged in gold, the raiment of his station as a king's minister and ambassador to Rego.

"Terin," he said, greeting his young ward warmly. If he was relieved to see Terin alive, he betrayed nothing with his smile.

"Ambassador." Terin bowed his head courteously.

"Commander Kenti." Squid shifted his eyes to Cronus, acknowledging him as well.

"Minister Antillius," Cronus replied in kind.

"Our scouts reported of the attack upon Costelin. How bloody was the carnage?"

"I didn't receive a full account. We were dispatched just after the battle. I would guess a hundred or more settlers slain with a thousand or two gargoyles," Cronus surmised.

"A terrible thing, but such is the cost of war." Squid sighed. "I feared for your safety, Terin, and am most pleased that you survived your first encounter with the gargoyles. Many seasoned warriors cannot boast such a claim."

"I was fortunate," Terin said.

Cronus noted the timeless look on Squid's face, as if he knew fortune played a diminutive role in Terin's deliverance. *He knew,* Cronus mused. Squid knew that Costelin was a trap. He knew what he was sending Terin into, and he looked unsurprised to see that Terin had survived the ordeal. *But why? Why risk Terin's life for nothing?*

"I apologize for returning before you sent for me, Ambassador, but Commander Mastorn ordered me out of the colony."

"No need for apologies, my boy." Squid raised an open palm to quiet Terin. "Commander Mastorn did as he was instructed. I have little time and much to explain. For now, you are excused. Go to one of the city's bathhouses and clean the dust from the trail. Go to my home, don fresh garments, and return here by dusk. We have dignitaries to meet and many duties to attend."

"As you wish, Ambassador Antillius." Terin bowed before departing. Cronus turned to follow before Squid stopped him.

"Please stay, Commander Kenti. I have another task for you."

*****

Cronus led his companion through the bustling avenues of Rego's south side as the sun dipped in the western sky. Dressed in purple tunics and dark cloaks, they appeared to be merchants to the untrained eye. They stayed several streets south of the Wid River until they were well clear of the Uxel tavern before cutting north to the river. The waning sun cast hues of orange and gold over the rippling waters of the Wid as they made their way past the piers that lined the river.

They passed barges laden with salt, ore, and wool. Vendors lined the riverfront, hawking fruit, bread, wines, and garments of cotton and wool. Sailors dressed in leather tunics in groups of three and four passed by on their way to the central districts to visit taverns or brothels, paying them little heed.

Several empty piers followed a barge filled with salt before Cronus's trained eye fell on a lonely pier. They were fortunate, for Raven hardly stayed in one place for long, and his exit from Rego was long overdue. Cronus paused several pier lengths short of the vessel. No one appeared topside, and he wondered if Raven was aboard.

"Is it safe to proceed?" his companion asked.

"If we approach slowly, yes. Just follow my lead, and let me do the talking until you are properly introduced."

"Very well. Lead on."

They moved closer, stepping onto the pier and closing upon the stern with careful, measured steps. Cronus stopped short of the vessel as the door centered on the back wall of the second deck opened and a man stepped out, casting a long shadow as the sun lighted his right flank. The man's gaze fixed on Cronus's slender silhouette.

"Raven?" Cronus squinted in the sunlight.

"Cronus?" Raven said, recognizing his voice.

"Yes." Cronus let out a breath. "Can we come aboard?"

"If you can vouch for your friend," Raven answered, resting his heavy forearms on the low railing that lined the stern of the second deck.

"I can."

"Then come aboard."

Cronus's companion marveled at the ship's construction as they stepped onto the stern of the first deck. The *Stenox*'s silver-blue hull resembled the surface of a dark sea as their sandaled feet echoed dully as they stepped. A louder thud followed as Raven descended from the second deck, forgoing the last several rungs of the ladder and landing loudly before them.

Raven's narrow dark eyes found Cronus's. He slapped his friend on the shoulder, jerking Cronus with the heavy blow. "Good to see you, buddy. I thought you were campaigning upriver with the rest of your people."

"I was upriver, but things have changed. Can we come in?" Cronus asked, placing his right hand upon Raven's shoulder. Cronus's companion noted the gesture, indicating the depth of their friendship.

"Sure, but who's your friend?" Raven eyed the other man warily. The fellow had a moderate build with even-set brown eyes and short dark hair mixed with thickening bands of silver. He was clearly older, but Araxans aged slowly, and he was never really sure how old any of them truly were.

"My companion's name is best not spoken out here."

"All right." Raven shrugged. "Come on in." The door slid open, and they followed Raven's towering form into the heart of the vessel. Entering the first deck of the *Stenox*, they found themselves at the end of a narrow hallway with three doors along either side and a seventh at the end of the hall. Raven led them through the first door on the right. "Have a seat, fellas," Raven said.

The cabin had reflective black flooring and silver walls. Light emitted from the ceiling, powered by the Earthers' sorcery, no doubt. A storage cabinet covered half of the far wall. In the cabin's center was an oval-shaped table made of the same material that was in the flooring. It had a glossy black texture that mirrored your reflection when looking down upon it. Though small, the table was large enough to place eight chairs around it. Before taking their seats, they removed their dark cloaks, revealing their deep-purple tunics,

"You don't make very convincing merchants. If you put a tutu on a pit bull, it's still a pit bull," Raven said, commenting on their attire.

"What's a pit bull?" Cronus asked.

"What's a tutu?" the other asked.

"Never mind." Raven knew it was pointless to explain such references from his world.

"Raven, this is General Bode, commander of the Torry 3rd Army. General, this is my good friend Raven, captain of the *Stenox*," Cronus stated, introducing them.

"General Bode." Raven offered his hand. "I am honored. Usually, men in your position send a lackey to speak with me. They never come in person."

Bode smiled, shaking the Earthman's hand, as Cronus had informed him of the Earth greeting of a handshake. "What I have to say is of grave importance, and I prefer to say it face-to-face. Having you come to me would be noted by those that I wished not to know of our meeting. I had a better chance of approaching you undetected than you had of approaching me."

"You got me there, General. We don't exactly blend in," Raven said, casually resting his right hand on his holstered pistol. "So why are you here?"

"Do you remember your dealing with a wine merchant named Lorious Sarga?"

"Yeah," Raven answered warily.

"I've heard only rumors of your dealings with him and how he refused payment for a task he had contracted with you."

"Yeah, he tried to stiff me. What of it, General?" Raven couldn't figure what Commander Bode was getting at.

"The facts, as were told to me, were that you forced him to pay his debt by afflicting a portion of his vineyard. They claimed you dried out the vines with your magical tools before they burst into flames."

"It's science, not magic. Yes, I did that and threatened to do the same to his entire vineyard if he didn't pay up. I can't imagine you came all this way to see me over such a dispute."

"The improprieties of Merchant Sarga do not concern me. The question I have is, can you repeat such magic with wet grass?"

"Yeah. Grass is easier to dehydrate than a vineyard. How much grass are we talking about?"

"Twelve to fifteen miles," Bode said bluntly. "I don't want it set on fire. I want it ripe to set afire."

"Fifteen square miles?" Raven's voice rose in disbelief. "What are you trying to do, burn down half the region?"

"If need be. Can you do it?"

"I don't know. Lorken and Brokov are the experts on this, and I use the term loosely." Raven lifted a small device to his lips and spoke into it. "Lorken!"

General Bode marveled as another man's voice broke from the device in reply. "Go ahead, Rav."

"You still in the engineering room with Brokov?"

"Yes."

"Come to the dining cabin, both of you."

General Bode had never actually seen the Earthers before. He had heard what they looked like from others' recollections, but such interpretations never matched the picture for oneself. Raven was very large, far larger than any man Bode had ever seen. His skin's reddish hue was unique. His narrow dark eyes matched the firmness of his square jaw. If a man could kill with a look, then Raven would have struck him dead several times with those penetrating eyes.

As odd as Raven appeared, his comrades were even more so. Lorken's skin was so dark that it was nearly black. Brokov's was nearly as white as a cloud. They each had narrow eyes and wore the same black trousers, shirts, jackets, and boots with holsters around their hips. After everyone seated themselves at the table, General Bode relayed what he wanted them to do.

"Where do you want this done?" Brokov asked skeptically, doubting their ability to replicate the procedure on such a grand scale.

"North of Rego. Between the rolling foothills of Tuft's Mountain and the western forests lies a gap. The area is many miles long and three miles wide at its greatest width. It is the main avenue of advance that the enemy will most likely take."

"Which enemy?" Raven asked, his eyes shifting between Cronus and the general as they sat across from him.

General Bode paused, unsure how much he should reveal to the Earthers. He also felt Cronus's eyes upon him, for his unit commander was unaware of what he was about to reveal. "Our magantor scouts have spotted legions marching south from the Benotrist border. It seems Emperor Tyro will not sit idle while we secure the Wid River Valley. We are at war." The realization struck Cronus in his stomach, though his face was stone. It seemed he would not see Leanna for a long time.

"What type of legions?" Brokov asked.

"Three or four. All Gargoyle, no human," Bode answered.

Gargoyle legions moved rapidly unlike their more heavily armed Benotrist human comrades. Carrying small circular shields and curved shortswords, gargoyles wore no breastplates, helms, or greaves, for such weight hindered their ability in flight. Unlike humans, gargoyles could feed off the land, devouring flesh or vegetation indiscriminately.

Tyro organized his legions, whether human or gargoyle, into elements fifty thousand strong. His Benotrist legions required thousands of supporting elements, including smiths, foragers, quartermasters, and healers. Gargoyles were able to move unencumbered by such logistics. Gargoyles were limited in other ways. Though swift, they were lightly armed, making them vulnerable to arrows and disciplined defenses. Their savage bloodlust, once released, was nearly impossible to call back in battle. Once set in motion, their advance could not easily adapt to the fluidity of battle. This forced their commanders to keep them in tight ranks until the battle was joined.

"General, we don't take part in wars between nations. It's bad for business," Raven said.

"I am not asking you to join our cause. I merely wish to extend a contract for specific services. Your obligation would be complete before any battle takes place. You would not be asked to kill anyone."

"Not directly," Brokov said. "But they'll be dead all the same. As far as our business goes, if Tyro conquers Arax, we will be out of business."

Raven bristled at the notion. "If Tyro wants war with us, we'll kick his ass."

"Tyro's army has over one million men and gargoyles under arms. There are only five of us!" Brokov emphasized the word *million*.

"That's only two hundred thousand apiece. Don't sell yourself short," Raven said. Brokov rolled his eyes while Lorken chuckled. Bode wondered if Raven's boasts were serious until the look in his dark eyes confirmed that they were.

"Will you do it?" Bode decided to push forward.

"I have my reservations, General, but Cronus brought you here. That's enough for me. We'll do it if Brokov thinks it's possible." Raven shifted his eyes to his comrade, who nodded affirm.

"All right. That settles it. Now let's talk payment. Ten thousand certras."

Bode released a slow breath at the sum. He knew it was not worth haggling to bring down the price, so he relented, but he acquiesced slowly enough for Raven to think it a difficult decision. "Very well."

"Also, I want any bounties placed on our heads by any Torry merchants revoked by royal decree," Raven added.

"Anything else?" Bode asked, half expecting him to ask for the hand of Princess Corry.

"I want all future contracts with your merchants reinforced by the magistrates of Central City and Cagan."

"Agreed. Anything else?"

"One last thing." Raven smiled with that cocky half grin of his. "I know Cronus has taken a few hits over his friendship with me. That ends today. The next telnic commander opening goes to him."

Cronus looked at his friend, touched by his sincerity, but he did not want what was unearned. "Thank you, Raven, but I don't want what I have not earned. There are better men than I who have served longer and deserve—"

"Done!" Bode cut him off.

"Then it's a deal." Raven shook his hand across the table.

"When can you begin?" Bode asked, coming to his feet.

Raven turned to Brokov. "We'll gather our equipment tonight and be ready at first light. We will need a sizable escort, though."

"I'll have two units of cavalry and one of foot meet you downriver near Hatis Point. I would like fewer eyes upon you."

"We'll be there," Raven said.

*****

The news broke upon the Council of Rego like a club to a beehive. They gathered that evening in the inner sanctum of the city forum. The chamber's center was a ten-meter circle of polished brown marble. A stone bench curved around the center floor with three breaks where stairs descended from rows above as the chamber rose higher in concentric rings so those seated farther back could see the activity below as if perched atop a giant bowl. This night, only nine members of the Regoan council were in session so the higher rows of the assembly were barren, with guards posted at each entrance.

"The people must be warned!" Council Targarus declared.

"Nay! The populace will riot once the news breaks," warned Council Greaboss.

"We must flee. Evacuate the City and take refuge elsewhere!" Argued Council Varanus.

"There is nowhere to run in so short a time lest we leave all we own to be plundered," said Council Marios.

The Torry delegation waited to the side as the Council debated. Some argued to flee, others to fight. One member suggested beseeching Emperor Tyro to plea for peace. He was shouted down as the others knew it would be a useless endeavor. Tyro had chosen war and would not be turned. The Council at last called for the Torry delegation to state their intent.

"Ambassador Antillius, if you would address the Council," Chairman Pontus waved an open hand toward his counterparts seated upon the stone bench on the Forum's lowest level that surrounded the stone circle.

Terin looked on as Squid rose from the bench and smoothed his burgundy robes before stepping forth. He scanned the nervous faces of the Regoan council, cognizant of their plight. His words would not assuage their fears—no words could—but he had to stiffen their resolve. This was not the time for flowery speeches that bespoke the glories of a just cause. This was a time for cold facts, upon which hard decisions must be made.

"Gentlemen, King Lore offers you the full support of the Torry Kingdoms. When we moved against the threat in the Wid River Valley, we knew that such a show of force would either stay Tyro's hand or provoke him further. His threats upon the river settlements were meant to undermine the sovereignty of Rego. Tyro means to have Rego, whether through the methodical assault upon Rego's river settlements or a direct strike upon the city itself. Denied the former, he has chosen the latter. Preparations are underway to meet this invasion north of the city. Before I give the floor to my military counterpart, I must emphasize that our mutual survival depends on your cooperation. Anything less and we shall be undone. General Bode!"

General Bode strode forth, his armored sandals slapping the polished stone like thunderclaps. He wore a dark tunic and polished silver breastplate, shin armor, and helm, presenting the image for which he was renowned. His cold brown eyes surveyed the faces waiting upon his words with bated breath. He let them take in his dominant presence, hoping to instill in them a greater confidence and respect for his person than the enemy fast approaching.

"The enemy marches south from the Benotrist border 150,000 to 250,000 strong, all gargoyles," he began. "I will meet them north of Rego at a site of my choosing. Your garrison and auxiliary forces shall be joined to our own. General Fonis and the Torry 2nd Army have already mustered at Central City and shall be marching post-haste to our aid. No persons shall flee Rego upon the southbound roads. Those routes must be clear for Fonis's advance.

"Further, no traffic is to venture upriver until we recall all our forces positioned there. No persons shall, under pain of death, venture north of Rego. What plans I lay there shall be kept secret. Anyone wishing to escape the city will have to follow the river downstream. How you evacuate your populace is your concern, the exception being every able-bodied male fifteen to sixty years of age. They shall be armed and complement our forces in the field."

"General Bode, how can you hope to face four legions with only fifty thousand men?" Council Varanus asked.

Bode gazed into Varanus's eyes with a dead, cold stare. "The same way we have fought the gargoyles throughout the ages—with courage, discipline, and the battlefield of our choosing."

*****

"Packawww! Packawww!" Two magantor birds screeched overhead. Terin gazed skyward as the giant eagles beat their wings in slow, powerful thrusts. Their gray feathers blended into the scattered clouds above as they sped northwest. His gaze then swept the western horizon from north to south, overlooking the gap some two thousand feet below. The view from the lower western slopes of Tuft's Mountain was breathtaking. Tuft's was set at the far-western edge of the Plate Mountains' range. Its snowcap dominated the surrounding region, especially the grassy gap that skirted its western face. Terin carefully watched his footing along the rock-strewn slope, wary of the loose stone and soft soil that doomed better climbers than he.

"Ready?" Lorken's deep voice echoed behind him.

"As ready as we're likely to get," Brokov answered him.

"Terin, you might want to step aside," Lorken warned.

Craning his neck over his left shoulder, Terin descried the tall Earthers crouched behind a long, tubular black object with three stick legs sprouting from its base. Terin quickly stepped aside. In his short time knowing the Earthers, Terin knew even their slightest suggestion was best quickly heeded. Their mysterious tools and weapons were often dangerous to extremes, but they spoke of their use in casual passing, without the reverence or awe such things inspired in their Araxan host.

No sooner had he stepped aside when a wide beam of purple-and-red light sprang from the end of the tube. The beam continued in an unbroken stream from their perch on Tuft's western slope to the high green grass below in the gap. Brokov and Lorken slowly shifted the beam over the grass, moving east to west, then west to east. The process was slow and measured.

Terin could do little but observe and stay out of the way. Ambassador Antillius ordered him to act as the Torry liaison with the Earthers. He wasn't sure if it was his role as Squid's apprentice or his friendship with Cronus that made him the most suitable candidate for such a task. Either way, he preferred the Earthers' company to the pomp and ceremony of accompanying Squid in his meetings with Regoan dignitaries. Deep in his heart, he never desired the post of minister's apprentice. He felt a greater calling to the sword and a life of action. He had never confessed such misgivings to his parents, for their plans for his future always centered on him becoming a king's minister one day.

"Ready?" Lorken's voice echoed.

"Yes!" Brokov answered.

The conversation caught Terin's attention as he observed Lorken adjust their device while Brokov aimed the beam on the higher grass below. Lorken then stepped back, standing beside Terin. "What did you do?" Terin inquired.

"We increased the width, see." He pointed his finger to the beam of light as it nearly doubled to thirty inches in diameter. That would hurry the process along, but a sudden thought pushed to the fore of Terin's brain.

"Lorken, what if it rains? Will not that undo all your labor?"

Lorken laughed. "It would take a flood. Besides, there will be no rain for the next twelve days."

"How do you know?"

"We have our methods. You'll have nice weather. Bank on it."

"Bank?"

"Never mind." Lorken shook his head. "It won't rain. That's all that matters."

Somehow, Terin believed him. Truly, the Earthers were sorcerers of vast power even though their demeanor more resembled barbarians. They were not awed by any Araxan authority. They hated the idea of a monarchy and thought it repugnant for men to kneel to other men. Despite the power they wielded, they did not take themselves very seriously.

In his short time knowing them, he noted how they ridiculed one another mercilessly; but instead of taking offense, they would simply laugh and respond in kind. They spoke despairingly of one another's mothers, eyesight, intellect, sexual prowess, and especially the size of their sexual organs. He heard them use words he dared not repeat and words he dared not ask them to interpret. Whenever they used terms or phrases unique to their native tongue, he would ask their meaning. They would always respond with, "Never mind," Lorken especially. Kato was the only one who spoke carefully and explained any question Terin had with clarity and in terms he understood. Kato also took little pleasure in throwing about insults with his fellow Earthers.

Araxans who had heard of the Earthers grouped them as a monolithic entity, but the Earthers were so diverse in their appearance that they had more physical differences between them then they had with the Araxans, at least on the surface. Lorken's skin was very brown, almost black. His nose was broader than his comrades'. His hair, though cut close to his scalp, was very curled. Brokov was the opposite. He was very pale, almost white. Terin had never seen a man as white as Brokov or as dark as Lorken. Kato and Raven had complexions closer to Araxans, but they were still whiter than any Araxan.

From what the others said, he knew Raven was sired by parents of divergent racial lines. His mother was partly white, like Brokov, and partly Tejano while his father was a Native Alaskan, whatever those terms meant. When he inquired what a Native Alaskan was, Lorken said, "Never mind," as if explaining it would have been exhausting and pointless.

Kato's unique feature was his eyes. They slanted sharply upward at their outside corners. He was also much smaller than his comrades. Zem was the strangest of all. He spoke very little, and his immense size dominated any company in his proximity. When he did speak, his voice boomed with authority. The others claimed that Zem was a created life-form with his own personality. Their explanation was very strange, and Terin understood little of it.

Another odd thing about the Earthers was the fact that Raven was their leader, yet they reserved their most vicious taunts for him. He would respond in kind or strike them in their upper arms, leaving them bruised and sore from his blows. Such joking didn't seem to undermine his authority, as he was the largest and strongest of them other than Zem and was probably selected as their leader for his fierceness and intellect.

"Lorken?" Terin asked.

"Yeah," Lorken answered distractedly, his gaze remaining fixed on the tubular device.

"Why hasn't Raven assisted with this process?"

"Why would he?" He snorted.

"I assumed since he was your captain, his knowledge of such things would be greater."

Lorken nearly choked with laughter. "Raven? Raven doesn't know anything about this. He doesn't know much about anything except shooting, drinking, and flying."

"He can fly?" Terin zeroed in on that word, his eyes wide with wonder.

"Not that kind of flying. We had giant machines that could fly, and we piloted them."

"Oh!" Terin said disappointedly. "If he lacks knowledge or wisdom, then why was he chosen as your leader?"

"Because the rest of us were lieutenants before we crashed on your planet while Raven was a captain."

"What is a lieutenant?"

"Well, a lieutenant is similar to your unit—oh, never mind. Look, Raven held a higher rank before we crashed, so we let him be in charge until we are rescued. Raven might be a goofball, but he's our goofball. Besides, no one else wants to be in charge anyway."

"Except Zem," Brokov added.

"Yes, the one who would be worse than Raven." Lorken laughed.

"He would?" Terin knew there was more to that story.

"Zem has an unhealthy high opinion of himself." Brokov rolled his eyes.

"Nothing worse than a stuck-up robot," Lorken said.

"Don't use that word around him." Brokov laughed.

"Oh, sorry. Advanced humanoid life-form." Lorken shook his head.

*****

General Bode surveyed the activity as he rode across the southern end of the gap. Soldiers armed with spades prepared defensive works from the rocky foothills in the east to the edge of the thick, forested underbrush to the west. He shifted his gaze northward, where others were depositing layers of oil that were extracted from oozing pools west of Rego. The highly flammable, gelatinous material was methodically moved and placed. The Earthers were helpful in this regard as well, as they treated the oozing liquid, altering its properties, making it more flammable.

Regoan soldiers prepared defensive positions upon the rocky foothills of Tuft's western slope. To the south, General Fonis's 2nd Torry Army was nearing Rego with twenty telnics of infantry and three thousand bowmen. Commander Meborn's Third Torry Cavalry to complement Connly's Second Torry Cavalry was already there.

"General Bode!" Cronus's voice carried through the breeze, riding forth to meet the commander of the 3rd Army.

"Commander Kenti, how goes the training of your men?"

"They are nearly ready. We've scouted the areas north of the gap and found several staging areas that meet our specifications," Cronus explained. For his aid in enlisting the services of the Earthers, Cronus was afforded a special mission that was pivotal in the coming campaign but fraught with peril.

"Very well, Commander. I need not remind you the importance of the task given you."

"I understand, General," Cronus said, humbled by the trust the general placed in him.

"Commander Mastorn speaks highly of you, Cronus. Your friendship with the Earthers has proven a boon to our efforts here. Your integrity is beyond the reproach afflicting lesser men. Those are the reasons I have chosen you for this task."

"I am honored," Cronus said.

"I wish I could afford you the time to bid your friend Raven farewell, but when his comrades finish their work up there, they will be leaving. Since Raven is back in Rego with his ship, you shall have to give any message for him to Lorken and Brokov. Raven said when they return to the *Stenox* that they will be departing for Central City."

"I will say my farewells to Lorken and Brokov, then. My thanks, General," Cronus said.

"Be sure to speak not a word of your special assignment. I wish as few people to know of it as possible."

"I will not speak of it, General."

CHAPTER 6

The north wind whipped the snowcap of Tuft's Mountain, swirling around its summit in deafening howls that echoed to the foothills below. The jagged peak projected a tranquil image from afar. General Tanius, commander of the 17th Gargoyle Legion, eyed the mountain from far north of Tuft's Gap. Tanius rubbed his clawed digits over his chin, his dull-red eyes surveying the lay of the land like slender crimson slits peering from a dark abyss. His skinny, sharp nose and curved, pointed ears jutted rigidly from his skull. Thick slaver oozed over his fangs, dripping from their tips. He wiped his fangs with the back of his right hand and then wiped it on the skirt of his red tunic. A northern gale rippled through the high grass, their blades bending like a grassy sea.

"Your orders, Commander?" his aid hissed beside him. The legions commanded by Vicon, Marcisis, and Tombin were subordinate to his command and awaited his orders. His magantor scouts skirmished with their Torry counterparts over the skies above for much of the campaign. As his legions neared the gap, his magantors finally drove them off. The Torries had prepared their defense of Rego at the southern end of the gap. If he led his legions over the mountains to the east or the forests to the west, they would come through the other side separated. If the Torries pounced before he could consolidate his legions, they could destroy him in detail. He had the strength of numbers, and he planned to use them with blunt force.

"Forward!" Tanius commanded. Gargoyle horns sounded their advance, echoing their macabre melody o'er the battlefield. The legions were formed up side by side, miles wide and miles deep. They lumbered forth like a vast pestilence, devouring the land wherever they passed. Sunlight flickered off their curved swords like the twinkling of thousands of clustered stars.

General Vicon's 15th Gargoyle Legion was deployed to the east, nearest the foothills of Tuft's Mountain. General Tombin commanded the 16th Gargoyle Legion, which aligned farthest west, skirting the forested underbrush on their march south. Tanius's 17th Gargoyle Legion and Marcisis's 18th Gargoyle Legion aligned between the other legions with the 17th to the east of the 18th. Standard legion formation in march was one hundred abreast and five hundred deep. The gap of Tuft's Mountain was the only place where Tanius could fully deploy his legions, making the choice a logical one.

*****

He watched them pass in their endless columns, chanting in their guttural tongue. The lush foliage of the forest concealed his position as he counted. His men were well-placed far to his rear as he scouted the gargoyles' advance. He trusted no one else to make an accurate count, as so much depended on the timing of his raid. The rustling of branches and leaves caught his ear as something large approached from his left. Cronus crouched down and withdrew quietly several paces, shielded by the thick, overhanging vines of a topac tree. He felt his heart pounding in his stillness.

The approaching form emerging some meters before him was black with a red half tunic and wings wrapped to its sides, a gargoyle scout. Two others emerged in his line of sight, making little effort to hide their number or mask their sounds. They hissed curses over the task assigned them, paying little heed to any signs Cronus might have left behind. Gargoyles were creatures of open spaces and night air, not the thick forests where their wings were of little use.

The careful approach and attention to detail they employed farther north at the start of their patrol quickly waned as they struggled to keep pace with the legions that marched over open grass. Fortunately for Cronus, the place he had been was hard soil, and only careful inspection would have revealed that he had been there. The gargoyle scouts passed quickly by as Cronus released a breath.

*****

Terin stood behind the large palisade in the center of the Torry line. Men armed in breastplates and helms aligned forward of him in lines stretching endlessly in each direction. Shoulder to shoulder they stood with large rectangular shields in their left arms, interlocked with their shortswords in their right hands, ready to jab between them. Men filled in behind them with shields ready to lift overhead to further protect their fellows in the fore ranks. The palisade was built atop the forward slope of a raised mound of soil with protruding stakes jutting sharply forward. Waist-high grass pushed near the base of the mound and stretched endlessly north through the gap.

Terin could see the men placed high upon the rocky foothills and sharp slopes of Tuft's Mountain to his east. Others were placed in the forested underbrush to his west but could not be seen from his vantage point. Not far to his west, General Bode placed his pavilion behind the extreme center of the Torry line. Arrayed in their white tunics and steel helms and breastplates, the army appeared as a rocky shore awaiting the tide with Torry and Regoan cavalry patrolling the rear and flanks.

The sound of horns and drums echoed dully over the horizon, their disjointed melodies merging in a ghastly chorus, unnerving even the bravest of men. Here Terin stood among his countrymen and Regoan allies, wearing borrowed helm and breastplate of ill-fitted iron. The helm was far too large for his head and shifted loosely about his crown. Armor was scarce in Rego, as every able-bodied man was put in the field with whatever arms they could find. Many were rounded up in the streets and given only pikes with a path of ground to defend.

Every archer had an aide who held out arrows for them to snatch and fire without wasting motion. Each archer had dozens of arrow bundles piled behind them. Terin noted how few archers were placed in the Torry center. Most congregated on the flanks and upon the slopes of Tuft's Mountain.

Magantor birds soared overhead, their Benotrist and Torry riders parrying the others' probes and exchanging crossbow bolts through the crisp air. Neither gained a decided advantage. Two Benotrist war birds received enough darts and withdrew. One giant Torry eagle received a mortal blow, a dart penetrating its heart. It fell listless through the air, its young rider's eyes wild with panic, riding his felled war bird through its rapid descent.

The grassy field in the gap came swiftly upon him. He was thrown from his saddle, his body breaking upon impact. He lay helpless in the tall grass with his back, legs, ribs, and right arm broken in several places. As the young Torry opened his eyes with the deafening sound of war drums drawing near, he could only see the high grass around him, but the hissing voices of gargoyles drifted perilously close.

His left hand ran across his sword belt, searching for the dagger upon his right hip. He panicked, finding the sheath empty. He tried his sword hilt on his left hip, prying emphatically, as it was pinned to the ground by the weight of his crippled body. If he could only free the blade and slash his throat, his pain would be ended. Alas, it was not to be.

The enemy fell quickly upon him. The forward scouts of their approaching formations quickly hacked his good arm, and each in turn bit into his helpless flesh, his piercing screams drowned in the sea of drums, shouts, and horns as the gargoyle columns moved into battle formations across the gap. Their dark mass covered the land from the foothills to the forest with nary a patch of green visible in their midst.

*****

They burst from the forest, their ocran's hooves slapping the ground like pounding thunder. The few gargoyles left to guard the north end of the gap stared awestruck as the Torry cavalry swept over the gap, bearing torches. "Fan out!" Cronus commanded as his flax commanders sped off to their appointed destinations. Cronus led the first flax with Pomel Tonchas at his side. They raced south, angling toward the center of the gap over the matted grass. The legions had trampled much of the grass flat, but the green stems were still brittle and laced with oil. Cronus dipped his torch to the grass in a low arc, the flames kissing the green blades as the battered stems burst into flame.

Across the north end of Tuft's Gap, hundreds of fires quickly dotted the landscape. They burned independently at first before joining one to the other and slowly touching the deeper trenches of oil that ran north and south. Soon, columns of fire shot southward, racing along the gap like comets through a jade sea.

*****

Approaching the southern end of the gap, the gargoyle legions formed into their line of battle. General Tanius kept his ranks tight and disciplined, but once he released them, they would not be easily recalled. Gargoyle discipline often gave way to bloodlust and savagery. Drummers pounded in monotonous tones, driving their ranks ever southward, toward the awaiting Torry armies. General Vicon released five telnics to ascend the foothills to the east to skirt their advance. General Tombin, likewise, dispatched three telnics into the forested underbrush to the west.

Arrows spewed from the left and right flanks of the Torry line of battle, riddling the fore ranks of Tombin's and Vicon's legions. Thousands of shafts filled the late-morning air, striking unprotected gargoyle flesh that was massed wingtip to wingtip. "Kai-Shorum!" General Tanius shouted the gargoyle battle cry, ordering his legions forth.

The fore ranks charged afoot through the high grass that separated them from their human foes. Balls of flame flew overhead, falling in their midst like meteors from the sky. Each ball exploded into swirling flames when they struck the ground, fanning out along the dry, brittle grass. Torry catapults delivered a deadly volley with their archers riddling the charging ranks.

Positioned behind protruding pikes and atop a raised mound of earth, the Torries awaited the dark tide flowing southward in an unbroken stream. "Light the fires!" The command went out along the Torry line. Soldiers with torches set them to shallow trenches that ran vertically northward and were filled with oil. Flames sped northward, fanning out east and west across the gap and through the gargoyle legions. Panicked by the flames swirling amid their serried ranks and lapping their exposed flesh, the gargoyles pounded their wings to raise themselves onto the air.

The fore ranks had ample space to sprint away from their fellows and glide into the air and over the Torry palisades. Those congregated farther back had little room to maneuver, as the southern end of the gap was narrower than the middle where they first moved into battle formation. The narrowing of the gap drew their ranks in tighter, preventing those in the middle and rear from unfolding their wings to take flight.

Those in the fore ranks broke formation, speeding toward the Torry line, their wings pounding emphatically in taxing desperation. They drove forth through the hail of arrows whizzing to meet them. Terrible death screams rent the air as gargoyles dropped in the hundreds, Torry shafts riddling their unarmored flesh. Wearing only cone-shaped helms for armor, the gargoyles had arrows slide off their heads, striking shoulders, chests, and wings. Many dropped, crashing helplessly into the flames below, far shy of the Torry line. Others passed over the palisades, only to be met by walls of shields with swords slashing between them.

Fires erupted along the forested underbrush to the west, driving General Tombin's legion further into the gap. The left flank of General Vicon's legion broke toward the foothills, skirting the east side of the gap. There, atop the rocky slopes, Regoan archers poured volley after volley into the serried mass of gargoyle flesh rising from the valley floor.

General Bode concentrated his archers upon his flanks and the foothills, leaving his center mostly bereft of their protective cover. Gargoyles flooded toward the Torry center, converging from east and west and squeezing their own troops between them.

Scores of Torry magantor birds coursed overhead, sweeping their foes from the sky while dropping balls of fire into the dark mass below. General Tanius cursed the heavens, as his tenuous hold of the air was but fool's gold, for the Torry magantors now ruled the aeries above. The Torries were holding upon the flanks but giving way in their middle, where Tanius's 17th Legion and Marcisis's 18th Legion pushed emphatically to the fore. The fire died quickly in front of the Torry center while burning intensely to the east and west. "Fires to the north!" The hissing cries of gargoyles lamented as they descried the encroaching flames speeding upon their rear.

*****

Terin gazed awestruck, entranced by the carnage wrought around him. Clouds of foul smoke choked the air as fires burned unabated northward through Tuft's Gap. Torry infantry to his front kept their ranks tight, their discipline matching gargoyle fury. They stood shoulder to shoulder with shields interlocked while their right arms jabbed their shortswords between their shields, never extending their exposed limbs beyond their wall of shields. The enemy flew at them over the heated ground, reaching the wall of steel exhausted from their harried flight.

The Torries made quick work of the first gargoyles that reached their line, but they came again like water breaking from a dam. They slammed into the Torry line with slaver dripping from their fangs, snapping and biting and hacking like demons conjured from a foul abyss. The lightly armored creatures were easily dispatched by the methodical Torry infantry, who struck at them from the safety of their shield wall. When the piles of dead festered before them, the Torres fell back several paces, freeing their feet from the corpse-littered ground.

Terin beheld the darkening storm as the enemy host filled the northern sky, screaming over the din of battle and pouring into the Torry center. Hundreds coursed over the Torry line, dropping onto their human foes like weighted stones. The Torries held their shields overhead while jabbing the creatures with dozens of quick stabs before tilting their shields, allowing the slain creatures to drop into their midst. But every foe they slew left another cumbersome obstacle at their feet. Some would glide completely over the Torry ranks, landing behind their lines exhausted and spent.

Terin raced along the Torry rear, his eyes fixed on a gargoyle that had set down upon the matted grass. With sword raised, he swung as the foul creature turned its feral gaze upon him. Fearing for its life, the creature summoned all its strength and raised its blade to block Terin's blow. Terin gazed into those terrible red eyes, which glowed like embers, while bringing his blade down upon his foe's. The creature's hateful crimson eyes dulled as Terin split its sword upon touching it, passing through steel and flesh. Blood sprayed his face as the creature fell before him, its body rent in half. Fear gripped his mind, but his arm followed the will of the sword. A second cut separated the creature from its head as Terin moved quickly on.

Thousands of gargoyles set down beyond the Torry line, but Torry cavalry closed quickly upon them, felling them in twos and threes. Never did they reach the Torry rear in force. The weight of the legions bowed the Torry center as general Bode gave the order to withdraw. The shield wall was riddled with punctures, but the rear ranks filled the breaks, denying the enemy any fissures to exploit. The center of the line where the 2nd and 3rd Torry Armies joined slowly gave ground.

Fires raged unchecked through the gap, spreading miles north, the entire gap turning into a flaming sea. The gargoyles had marched miles through the oil-soaked grass, coating their legs with the slick fluid. Once the flames touched their flesh, thousands burst into living torches. They beat their wings emphatically, trying to flee wherever chance might take them. Many soared through the gap like shooting stars, screaming their death cries with fire lapping their flesh. Most could not take to the air, as they were squeezed into the center where the flames were mostly absent.

*****

General Vicon observed the madness with a cunning eye. Fires coursed through the center of his legion, sending most of his troops toward the west. To follow them into the center was folly, for the Torries could roll their flank. Staying put meant certain death, and he lacked the numbers to threaten the Torry right.

With fifteen telnics at his disposal, he led them due east and up the foothills. "Kai-Shorum!" he shouted. The gargoyle battle cry echoed through his diminished ranks as they assailed the Regoan pikemen and archers positioned along those rocky slopes.

*****

Squid Antillius brought his sword down upon a gargoyle blade, driving the creature back a step. The creature's bright tongue slid across its pink lips, its glowing crimson eyes fixing Squid with a terrible gaze. Its eyes drew slack as Terin's blade pierced its back. Squid's eyes widened in awe as the glowing blue sword tip emerged from his opponent's chest. He was struck by a memory from long ago on a different battlefield. The man was different, but the sword was the same.

With every swing, Terin was mastering the blade, just as the blade was mastering him, its azure glow strengthening with its use. Few noticed Terin moving freely across the battlefield, felling gargoyles one after the other. "Well done, lad!" Squid grinned as Terin withdrew his sword from the creature's back. Terin regarded him briefly before spotting another foe setting down beyond Squid and ran to meet him.

*****

Driven by fire, panic, and desperation, the four gargoyle legions pressed into the Torry center. The Torries gave way as Tanius's legions bowed the Torry line. Generals Bode and Fonis ordered more men from the flanks to the center, as their line was thinning in retreat.

Bode needed to limit the breaks in his line, as he had his center withdraw.

*****

"What do we do now, Commander?" Pomel asked.

"We wait for the field to cool," Cronus answered as they rode across the north end of Tuft's Gap. They had set the field ablaze and cut down any stragglers they encountered. There was little else for them to do but wait. Cronus wondered how his countrymen were faring to the south. He was surprised by how few gargoyles followed the main host. Had this been a human army, their baggage and logistical lines would have been spread out for miles. His men moved with the shifting wind, ever dodging the thickening smoke blowing northward. The orange glow in the southern sky bespoke the effect of their handiwork. They now only had to wait.

*****

Several parts of the Torry line broke at once. Gargoyles poured through the fissures, hacking at their tired foes with vengeful fury. Most had not eaten in a day and quickly fell on wounded Torries, sinking their fangs into living flesh. Torry cavalry filled the breeches until foot reinforcements could be mustered. They slowed the breaks enough for men aligned to either side to close ranks. The late-afternoon sky was a maelstrom of smoke and towering flames, lamentations haunting the poisoned air.

*****

The gap was a sea of flames as fires ranged its width and length. The most intense fires erupted across the southern end of the gap, wreaking havoc within the gargoyle legions. With their legs caked in slicks of oil, flames shooting through their formations found easy victims as their legs burst into flames. All their ranks flowing to the center pinched the gargoyles close together. None could free their wings to gain lift, and few could raise a sword, as their comrades squeezed from all sides. Many would catch fire, unable to flee as the flames shot up their legs.

The gargoyle mass pushed on the growing bulge in the Torry center, pouring into the safe ground outside the flames. They overran Bode's pavilion as the Torry ranks carefully withdrew, keeping their lines as tight as possible. Once tens of thousands of gargoyles filled the bulge, Torry war horns sounded, giving the signal to advance. The Torry lines drove forward, squeezing the gargoyles in the gap on all sides. They marched forth in slow, methodical steps, pushing on their shields while stabbing any flesh they could with their shortswords.

Squeezed by the Torries to their front and their comrades on their flanks and rear, the gargoyles had little space to maneuver. Barely able to lift their swords in defense, they were easy prey for the opportunistic Torries, who slashed at their exposed flesh. It was a slow, methodical slaughter. The Torries cut the enemy down one by one, then stepped over the corpses to push the survivors into an ever-shrinking bulge. Each step shortened the Torry line and strengthened their ranks.

General Tanius was trapped in the bulge, pressed within a sea of flesh squeezing upon him from all sides. Through the smoke-filled air, he descried the walls of shields drawing nigh. He stood helpless as Torry swords cut down his soldiers layer by layer. Those outside the bulge fared little better, caught amid flames, smoke, and withering arrow fire until their ranks rapidly thinned.

*****

As general Vicon's gargoyles assailed the Regoan ranks upon the foothills of Tuft's Mountain, he gazed into the gap below with knowing dread. What at first glance appeared to be a break in the Torry center manifested into a death vice. The legions were caught in a ring of Torry swords to their front and flanks and a wall of flame to their rear. Vicon was cognizant of the larger meaning: the battle was lost.

Vicon's gargoyles swarmed up the steep, rocky slopes in scattered formations. Regoan soldiers met their charge with shield and blade, holding back the tide as their archers took aim. Volley after volley thinned the gargoyle ranks, but their multitude eventually overran the Regoan foot soldiers in many places. The Regoan commanders pushed their reserves forward, but the rocky ground hindered their progress as it did likewise their gargoyle foes.

The battle along the foothills degenerated into a hundred small engagements, disjointed and disorganized. Vicon ordered a full retreat, but his soldiers were slow to respond. It took hours to turn them back northward to escape along the foothills and away from the heated grounds in the gap.

*****

Terin eyed another winged form emerge through the smoke-filled air. It flew gauche and disoriented like a bird with a broken wing. The creature set down some meters away as Terin ran forth, dispatching his exhausted foe. One swing split the gargoyle across the breast, dropping it in a crumpled mass at his feet. A second blow hewed its head from skull to neck. Terin noticed Miles Standarn fighting at Minister Antillius's side. They were separated earlier in the battle but now were joined. Fewer gargoyles were escaping the slaughter at the front, as General Bode's plan to force them into the center seemed to have worked.

The cool evening air brought a welcome respite as the battle continued. The Torry fore ranks surrounding the bulge grunted as they pushed the enemy in upon themselves. Sword tips jabbed out between their protective shield walls, stabbing whatever gargoyle flesh that was freely offered. As the enemy dropped, the Torries stepped over the fallen foe, slashing the fallen corpse to pieces before pressing on.

General Tanius hissed futilely as the Torries drew near. He had stood amid his serried ranks for hours, helpless as his gargoyles were slaughtered row by row like the peels of an onion, barely able to raise a sword in defense, as they were squeezed on all sides. Tanius's eyes glowed crimson as he slithered his split tongue over his parched lips. Blood oozed from the corners of his mouth as Torry sword tips punctured his lungs, stomach, wings, and thighs. Tanius slipped to the ground before being hacked and dismembered. The Torries pressed on. Thousands of gargoyles in the center died of asphyxiation as their comrades pressed on all sides.

The bulge closed by late day, leaving the salient littered with corpses. Tens of thousands more were strewn across the scorched fields north of the bulge, felled by smoke, flame, and arrows. Hundreds of thousands of arrows covered the burnt fields, forming a forest of shafts jutting from the blackened soil. The smell of burning flesh and smoke mixed in a putrid cocktail. The scorched bodies of thousands of wounded gargoyles flopped across the gap like fish cast up from a foul sea. Fires swept through the forested underbrush to the west, checked only by its moist vegetation.

General Bode surveyed the carnage from the palisade of the Torry center, where his men had retaken the ground that they earlier surrendered. His maneuver was successful. The weakening of his center and the strengthening of his flanks allowed the gargoyles to bulge his line but not break it. Once the enemy was concentrated and pushing upon their own troops, their fate was sealed. Only remnants of Vicon's legion escaped north along the foothills.

"Commander Connly!" Bode ordered his cavalry commander forward.

Connly stepped nigh, his white tunic, gray breastplate, and helm stained with blood. "General Bode." He slapped his fist to his heart.

"If the ground is cool enough, send a sizable force north through the gap. I wish to retrieve Commander Kenti's detachment."

"As you command." Connly hurried off to obey the command. The setting sun and rising moon provided ample light as three hundred Torry mounts sped north over the scorched fields.

*****

Cronus led his men along the gap, skirting the foothills. Gargoyle stragglers had retreated across the gap in small numbers. To remain where they were was folly if the enemy retreated in force. He had no way of knowing if the battle went well or ill for his comrades to the south. If the enemy came up the gap in force, he thought it best to abandon their mounts and hide among the rocky slopes. Wisps of smoke choked the air as the veil of night closed from the east like a canvass drawn across the sky.

Cronus had doubts to the wisdom of his line of march. Perhaps it was wiser to ride west into the wilds, eventually circling west and south and return to Rego in a long arc. But those lands were filled with unknowns. This entire mission was fraught with peril at every turn. This was the final test, returning to the safety of their own army with four legions placed between them.

The lead scout in the column sat wary in his saddle, a strange sensation coursing his flesh. He turned his head to the left, where glowing pairs of red eyes met his cautious glance. Gargoyles sprang from the foothills, gliding from the rocky slopes, their wings spreading like birds of prey. The lead scout was knocked from his saddle, his neck snapping as his head hit the rocky ground. Dozens were swept from their mounts, tumbling from their saddles as scores of gargoyles swarmed over them, biting and slashing with Torry blood spraying from their fangs.

"They're coming from the east. The foothills are filled with them!" Marcus shouted over the din of battle.

"Curse the night!" Cronus swore. The risen moon provided ample light to see short distances but not far enough to direct his troops. "Into the gap!" Cronus commanded. The order echoed down the column. Torry riders broke ranks, spurring their ocran through the gap as thousands of gargoyles swept down from the foothills, chasing them onto open ground.

The cries of the men being eaten alive rent the air. The clang of swords and the panting of ocran mixed with gargoyle war cries as Cronus rode forth. He saw men tumbling from their mounts to either flank, their bodies dropping into the growing dark as if lost in a tumultuous sea. Winged forms cast weak-shadowed silhouettes below, moonlight playing through the smoky air.

Cronus felt a great weight press upon his back. He pulled back upon his reins, crouching to his left. The sudden halt caused the gargoyle to lose its hold. It fell from the saddle as Cronus sprang from his mount. A quick blow struck the creature across its back, snapping its spine. Before he could catch his breath, dozens of winged forms swarmed over him.

"Don't kill himsssss!" he heard one give command as fangs snapped near his ear. He was pinned to the scorched soil with several holding him down.

"Whyssss?" one hissed in reply with blood-red eyes.

"He isss their commander. Look at hisss rank! Bringsss himsss!"

*****

Torry and Regoan soldiers swept the battlefield throughout the night, killing stragglers and finishing the enemy wounded who were strewn across the scorched killing zones. The battle was decided, but the fighting would continue well into the next morning. General Bode's pavilion was destroyed when the gargoyles caved his center and overran his position. His plan was designed to draw the enemy into his center, then squeeze them from the flanks, so the loss of his pavilion was not unexpected. A second command pavilion was erected south and east of the first. Fifteen meters abreast with bold stripes of red and white, it illuminated the nearby ground so all could find it amid the chaos of night. Tall torch posts circled the surrounding grounds. Runners hurried to and fro, relaying messages throughout the command.

Terin followed Squid and Miles through the encampment, their sandaled feet caked in dirt and blood. The cries of wounded men rent the night air as they passed vast pavilions set aside as field hospitals. Matrons in their scarlet robes hurried through the entrance of the vast tent to treat their charges to the best of their limited abilities. There was only so much they could do for amputated limbs except to cleanse the stump and treat it with herbs to prevent rot. They were completely helpless with mortal wounds, where they could only try to ease the suffering before death made its claim.

Thousands were hobbling nearby, gathered in cloisters about the pavilions to wait their turn. The chill night air seemed a cruel torment for helpless men who laid upon any ground they might find, waiting for hope that might never come. Terin stepped past a wounded soldier not much older than he. The lad lay upon his back with his hands gripping his stomach, trying to hold in his innards that spilled out around his fingers. Terin saw the soldier's face clearly in the moonlight. The haunted eyes of the dying man stared into Terin's soul, beseeching him for aid that Terin could not render. He continued on, following Minister Antillius through the serried encampment until stopping before the large red-and-white pavilion. Passing between posted sentries, they came swiftly upon the entrance.

Squid drew Terin aside. "Remain out here, lad, whilst I speak with the generals."

"As you command," Terin answered.

"You did well this day, Terin. I could not be prouder of you." Squid squeezed his shoulder.

"Thank you, Minister."

"Nay, it is I who thank you for keeping me alive." Squid smiled warmly.

"Well done, Terin," Miles Standarn added. As a member of the King's High Elite, Miles never granted unearned praise. From his lips, there could be no higher honor.

The two men disappeared into the pavilion as Terin released a slow breath. He was spent. He had lost count of the enemy he had slain this day. Being at the army's rear, few noticed his fell deeds. His tunic was soaked in gargoyle blood. His ill-fitting helm was twisted and bent, and his shield was cloven in half. Every muscle ached, especially his sword arm. He was more than himself this day, for his father's sword had guided his hand and masked his fatigue.

He felt the blade call to him, and he drew it forth in the cool night air. The light of the waxing moon cast luminous blue light along the glowing blade as Terin held it aloft. "What powers do you possess?" he mused, contemplating the strange properties folded into the ancient metal. The sentries posted and those passing by shifted their eyes to the mysterious weapon and the boy who wielded it. Terin quickly sheathed the sword to avoid the curiosity of watching eyes.

*****

"We have withdrawn our troops from the western forest," Telnic Commander Vortonus said, indicating the location on the map placed upon the table.

"Good. Pull them back to our left flank until the fires die out. Keep your lines tight, for we do not know how many of the enemy escaped the gap. They could reemerge anywhere along this line in force." Bode swept his hand over the western forest and the open lands south and west of Tuft's Mountain.

"Our patrols have found nothing south of us, General," Cordan Torhiz said, commander of the Torry magantor contingent.

"Your birds can't see through the thick foliage that goes on for miles all along that front. We must be vigilant," Bode explained.

"General, Ambassador Antillius and King's Elite Standarn," Bode's aide declared, announcing their arrival as he stood post at the pavilion's entrance.

"Minister Antillius, Miles, welcome." Bode waved them forth as the half dozen commanders circling the map table slapped fists to chests and backed a step.

Squid stepped near, his tunic caked in blood, soot, and mud. His breastplate was dented, and his hair disheveled. His eyes weighed heavy, reflecting the weariness of his exhausted mind. He hadn't fought in battle in nearly twenty years, and every muscle ached. "What is our status, General?" Squid asked as his weary eyes swept the banners dotting the map. Basin torches illuminated the table, casting their shadows upon the pavilion's circling wall.

"Our lines have held," Bode said dryly.

"There is no need for modesty, General Bode. You have won a great victory," an older voice said, echoing from the shadows of the pavilion's far wall. General Fonis, commander of the 2nd Torry Army, stepped forth as he came to Bode's side and placed a hand upon his friend's shoulder.

"General Fonis." Squid regarded him with the deep respect he held for the elder field commander. Fonis was leading armies when Squid and Bode were young men. He refused promotion beyond command of the Second Torry Army. King Lore repeatedly offered to make him the realm's first supreme commander since the reign of King Torry, but Fonis refused, stating that was the king's function.

"You asked our status. Squid and I'll have to tell you because our beloved general is too modest to speak of it. We slaughtered them, Squid. Four legions smashed to bits. The stench of burning flesh and rotting corpses will stink the air for months. Bode lured them into our center over my misgivings. By strengthening our flanks and lighting the fields ablaze, they flowed like water along the venue of least resistance.

"Once congregated in our middle, they basically killed themselves. Thousands were crushed by their own lines pressing upon them. Thousands more died of asphyxiation. Only their fore ranks could lift a sword or spread a wing while the rest stood helplessly, shoulder pressing upon shoulder. Once we cut down their foremost ranks and drove into those behind them, it was merely a matter of exhaustion. I surmise their loses to exceed one hundred and fifty thousand. Our loses are around nine thousand dead, wounded, and missing," Fonis said.

"One hundred and fifty thousand?" Miles asked in disbelief.

"That count may go higher, much higher," Fonis added. "The only enemy troops we have confirmed escaping are approximately fifteen telnics of General Vicon's legion. They fled north along the foothills."

"What of Unit Commander Kenti's contingent?" Squid asked. "Have you received any word on their return?"

"Commander Connly's cavalry just returned from the north end of the gap. They found most of Commander Kenti's men slaughtered near the foothills. They appeared to have collided with Vicon's retreating contingent. One of Kenti's men was still alive when they arrived and told that some of his comrades were taken prisoner. Cronus Kenti was among them," Bode said somberly.

"Did the soldier say anything else?" Miles asked.

"No. He died shortly after."

"I see." Squid sighed. Terin would not receive the news well. "See to your men, Generals. I must return to Central City at first light. The king must hear of this posthaste. A new ambassador will be sent to Rego as soon as I reach our capital. You have done well, gentlemen. Our kingdoms owe you a great debt."

"The debt is owed to the nine thousand," Bode answered. "Give our regards to King Lore, Minister Antillius."

"I shall."

"And, Squid?" Bode said.

"Yes?"

"It was an honor to have our king's high minister fight beside us this day," he said fondly.

Squid smiled. "It was my honor, General," he said before stepping without.

CHAPTER 7

Terin drew his cloak about his shoulders as the evening wind blew through their campsite. They were midway between Rego and Central City, just within the Torry border. Thickening clouds darkened the sky, dimming the moon and shielding the starlight above. He huddled near the campfire beside Squid Antillius. They had ridden dawn to dusk for two days, pushing their weary mounts at a reckless pace. Terin hoped Vonto would not pull up lame, but his trusty mount met the challenge thus far.

Commander Connly had dispatched a score of riders to escort them back to the Torry capital. Despite their company, the soldiers kept to themselves, affording Squid and Miles proper deference. Terin would have preferred friendlier company but understood the disciplined professionalism of the Torry soldiers. The needled branches of torbin trees pressed close about them, their strong odor vying for dominion with the smoke drifting from the fire.

Terin stared into the crackling flames, stricken with a profound loneliness. Squid told him that morning of Cronus's fate. Though he was a prisoner, he might as well be dead. Nay, he would have been better served if he were dead. Life as a gargoyle captive would be measured by the lash, toil, and torture.

"I know you mourn your friend, Terin, but take heart in the magnitude of his service to the Torry cause. The name Cronus Kenti shall be immortalized and whispered with awe and gratitude from the lips of our people," Squid assured him.

"Why did you not tell me of his capture sooner?" Terin asked numbly.

"For fear that you might go after him, lad." Squid pursed his lips as he, too, stared into the crackling flames. Terin hadn't thought of that, but such a move would have been irrational to an extreme. "Why do I think so, you might ask. I will tell you. That sword you carry makes you do things a sane man would never think of. The madness of the blade your father once called it."

"You know the power of my father's sword?" Terin shifted his gaze to Squid's aged face lighted by the fire.

"Aye. Even a blind man could see the mysteries folded into that blade. Had you fought in the fore ranks of our armies at Tuft's Mountain instead of the rear, every soldier would have now known of the wonder you carry on your hip."

"Is that why you chose me for your scribe?"

"You are no scribe, Terin, and I doubt you wish to be one. Nor shall you ever be a king's minister."

Terin was taken aback. "Then what am I?"

"Time will reveal your true calling, my son. Do as you feel yourself led. I know what you would have done had I told you of Cronus's fate two days ago. There may be a time to go after your friend, but not now."

"If not now, then Cronus has no hope. How long do gargoyles keep their prisoners alive?"

Squid released a slow, measured breath. "If they keep their captives alive for long periods, they usually impair them in some way."

"Impair them?" Terin's heart raced.

"Cutting off certain limbs or gouging of their eyes, sometimes both. But Cronus might be different. They may take him before their emperor to pass judgment upon him. He was instrumental in their ruination at Tuft's Mountain."

If Cronus was taken to Fera, the Black Castle, the seat of power of Tyro, then there was no hope. Terin pondered his friend's fate and wondered why he was here among these men. Why did Squid and his father arrange an apprenticeship that neither man thought suited him?

Terin eyed Miles's return from one of the short patrols he conducted around their campsite each night. His face was stone, betraying little of the man behind the constant scowl. Since the battle, Miles looked upon Terin differently. Terin could sense that the warrior held him in a higher regard, cognizant of the enemy slain by his sword arm in battle. Terin noted the twin swords that Miles wore on each hip. They were moderate in length, strong yet light. They were handcrafted by Torg Vantel, the king's master of arms and commander of the Torry Elite.

Miles rarely spoke to him, often nodding his regards and passing on. This night was no different, as he regarded Terin briefly, spoke with Squid sparingly, then retired for the evening. Terin followed in kind, lying upon his bedroll and drifting slowly off to sleep as visions of Cronus's suffering plagued his dreams.

*****

Cronus stumbled forth, the sting of the lash biting his flesh. His hands were bound behind him, and a chain around his neck connected him to his comrades in the coffle. His legs were free, but there was nowhere to run, bound as they were. His armor was stripped away, and his tunic was ragged from the abuse administered to him by his zealous captors. "Movesss Torry scumsss!" spat the gargoyle brandishing the lash. Cronus struggled to keep his feet without his arms to balance his stride.

Lazy clouds drifted above, shielding the glare of the morning sun for brief moments as the cool air whipped through the rolling grassland around them. Like black marks dotting a jasmine sea, the gargoyle host swept through the plain. Cronus counted eighteen of his men in the coffle. Of his flax commanders, only Marcus remained, chained two places in front of him. No one spoke, for to do so, the gargoyles would cut out their tongues.

He wept for his men. They fought bravely and conducted themselves with the skill of professional soldiers. They were only citizen soldiers, called to only train in arms when their kingdom needed them. When the call went out, they answered, filling the muster without gripe or complaint. They marched to Rego, fought at Costelin, and joined Cronus on his mission to set the north end of the gap afire.

The task was dangerous to the extreme, yet they volunteered to a man and followed their commander far behind the enemy line of battle. They completed their task and then fought bravely against the enemy host that sprang upon them from the foothills. Cronus remembered seeing Tarlus fall under his mount, set upon by a dozen foes, who ripped the flesh from his bones. He could still hear his maddened screams renting the air. He thought the same fate awaited him, but he was not as fortunate. If he only had the means to kill himself, then he needed not fear the torture to come. *But how?* he mused.

"Getsss upsss!" a gargoyle screeched farther ahead. Cronus saw the creature's shiny black skin move amid his comrades, striking at one of his men who had fallen. The lash fell again and again, saliva dripping from the gargoyle's foaming mouth, running the length of his bright curved fangs. Cronus closed his eyes as a dozen creatures set upon the lad. Piercing screams issued from the Torry's throat as gargoyle fangs tore his flesh.

The terrible sounds of ripping flesh and crunching bones continued long after the dying soldier fell silent. The whistle of whips continued anew after the short respite, driving the coffle onward. As Cronus stumbled past the spot where his young soldier fell, he descried the ghastly sight. The meat of his limbs was eaten to the bone. The head was torn off and discarded with the tongue torn out and cheeks chewed away. Blood stained the matted grass where the neck lay, forming dark pools on either side. Several ribs poked through tattered flesh like shafts of ivory rising from a sea of twisted flesh. The vision imprinted in his brain, haunting his memories to his dying day.

*****

The sky was clad in gray as they rode through the streets of Central City. They looked the part of road-weary travelers at the end of a taxing journey. Their escort bade them farewell once Leltic Hall rose imperiously before them. When Terin last approached the massive structure, he crossed the bridge over the Pelen. This time, he came from the north, crossing over the busy Carn-Ro. They were spotted by the keen eyes of the palace guards long before they passed under the shadow of the massive outer walls. A golden crown on a field of white blew proudly in the evening breeze atop the lookout post upon the highest citadel. It was the sigil of King Lore, giving proof of his presence at the palace.

"I'll have no need of you this night, Terin. I know you wish to seek out Arsenc to relay the news of Cronus and his comrades. Most of the wounded men from the Wid River campaign have been garrisoned over there." Squid regarded a long structure across the avenue from the palace. Made of gray block stone, it ran the length of the street, and Matrons in red-dyed robes passed freely through the crafted stone archway centered on the building proper.

"My audience with the king and Chief Minister Monsh shall take quite a while. When you finish with your friend, come to the palace. I shall leave word with the commander of the gate to let you pass."

*****

The Matron was a comely woman in her fourth decade. Her dark hair was covered in the folds of her red cloak as she led Terin through the chambers filled with wounded men. Some suffered from mortal wounds, lying upon narrow cots, awaiting the relief of death to ease their suffering. Some were unconscious, their lives drifting further afield to that nether place of eternal rest. Others were alert, fully aware of the fate appointed them and the pain that racked their broken bodies, cursing the minutes and hours left to them with bitter agony. Most of the soldiers suffered far less, many with severed limbs or missing eyes.

When he last saw Arsenc, he suffered a severe gash in his thigh. Such a wound could go either way. If the Matrons cleaned the wound properly and stitched it closed, then he might regain its full measure. If infection took hold, however, the limb would have to go and might take his life with it. Of the sixty-nine wounded men, only a handful were commanders of unit or of flax. Arsenc shared a chamber with a unit commander of the Sixth Telnic.

The Matron led Terin to the open doorway and waved an open hand to the entrance. "You will find Commander Ottin within." She smiled warmly, then continued on with her appointed tasks.

"Thank you, Matron." He bowed his head, paying her the respect her profession warranted. Terin heard a woman's voice echoing softly from within the chamber as he quietly entered.

"You look much better, Arsenc," the woman said. She sat at his bedside, dressed in a long sun-colored gown that matched the golden hue of her hair.

"If I'm well, it is your porridge that has restored me. My leg is well enough to stand on, Leanna," Arsenc said as he spooned another mouthful of her homemade delight into his mouth before catching sight of Terin standing behind her at the doorway. "Terin?" he asked.

Leanna turned at the name, her eyes taking in the handsome boy at the entryway. She knew his name well, first from Cronus, then Arsenc. Each successive story about the fair-haired youth built upon the other, growing in wonder at their telling with his fell deeds. If this was the Terin she had heard so much about, he seemed boyishly young and very tired. His eyes were older than his age, as if the sights they beheld already filled a lifetime.

Terin was, in turn, struck by the woman's beauty as her azure eyes swept the room, stopping as they met his. She had impossibly beautiful eyes that sparkled like starlight. The light in her eyes and the ease of her smile bespoke a tenderness mirroring the feminine symmetry of her face.

"Arsenc." Terin smiled, happy to see his friend alive and whole. "I… I can come back later if you would like to spend time with your friend."

"Come sit beside us, Terin. This friend is Leanna Celen, Cronus's betrothed." At the utterance of her name, Terin's face grew ashen. His heart sank, dreading to tell her what must be shared.

"Terin, I am pleased to meet you." Leanna struggled to keep her smile, which was feeling more out of place with the queer look upon his face.

"What troubles you, Terin?" Arsenc's tone shifted with Terin's dour mood. "We heard that our armies smashed four gargoyle legions at Tuft's Mountain, but we know little else."

"I've just returned, Arsenc. We have won a great victory, but…"

"But what?" Arsenc asked, feeling his throat tighten.

Terin gave Leanna a pained look that sent her heart racing. "Cronus's unit was overtaken by the enemy. Most were slain, but one survived long enough to tell of his capture."

"Capture?" Leanna's voice rang in alarm. She held her arms across her chest as if struck by a sword.

"How?" Arsenc asked.

*****

She rushed out into the avenue, oblivious to the cool evening air, tears forming rivers running the length of her face. As Terin finished the tale of Cronus's demise, she could hear no more and ran from the chamber clutching her breast, desperate to hold in her breaking heart. Leanna didn't remember how long she ran. She only remembered panting, standing atop the Tarelian Bridge that spanned the lower Stlen.

The massive structure equaled the other works of man that dotted the great cities of Arax save for the seven-towered castles that dwarfed the citadels of the lesser palaces. The great Tarelian Bridge might as well have been a plank over a ditch for as little as Leanna regarded its significance. She paid little heed to the wagons passing behind her or the ocran hooves slapping the dark stone of the bridge. She stared downriver as the setting sun broke through the darkening stormy sky, flickering over the water's surface.

What hope was there for her beloved Cronus? The thought of him captive to those foul creatures conjured the darkest possibilities of her imagination. Terin said that Minister Antillius believed that the gargoyles would take Cronus before their emperor for judgment for the significance he played in their ruination at Tuft's Mountain. A chill touched her shoulders as she pondered what cruel end Emperor Tyro might devise for him. There was still time before that end, but if she had a thousand years to plan and prepare, she still could not save him. As if drowning in a sea of despair, she clung to any hope that might deliver her from the watery depths.

Then it struck her. She stood upright, a new hope sparking as her eyes beheld that glorious ship anchored downstream with its silver-blue hull shining resplendent before the waning sun. "Raven!" she shouted joyously, running across the bridge as fast as her feet could carry her.

*****

"Four legions? Are you certain?" Eli Monsh asked as the basin torchlight played across his face.

"Yes," Squid answered, surveying the map table before them. To his left stood Torbin, commander of the city garrison. Eli Monsh, the king's chief minister, stood to his right. Across the large table stood King Lore, his gray eyes distant, as if he hadn't heard a word Squid had spoken. Something was amiss, but what the king left unsaid would wait until his report was finished.

"General Bode believes our total casualties are nine thousand dead, severely wounded, and missing. The Regoan contingent suffered two thousand dead and missing. At least ten telnics of Vicon's legion escaped northward, but not before slaughtering the unit Bode had placed north of the gap. A few were taken captive, including the commander of the unit."

"They'd be better off dead," Torbin thought aloud.

"Other than Vicon's ten telnics, the bulk of the four legions were slaughtered in Tuft's Gap. Any other survivors are scattered to the winds. Commander Connly's cavalries are hunting stragglers east and south."

"General Bode did it," Torbin marveled.

Such news should have been received joyously, heralded from the rooftops of the city with thunderous merriment and relief, yet Squid found no such sentiment in the king's council. "I bring news of a victory beyond our imagining, yet it is ill received. Might I ask what other news has dampened your spirits so profoundly?" he asked the chief minister. The others shared a look.

"Tell him," King Lore commanded with a tired voice.

Eli Monsh fixed Squid with a stern gaze, smoothing his burgundy robes as he placed a scrolled parchment upon the table. "Vintor Ornovis received this from a pirate envoy. He passed the message to us posthaste, reaching this council yesterday morn." The chief minister pushed the scroll across the table.

Squid unrolled the parchment, reading the details in disbelief. He finished, setting the unrolled parchment upon the table before addressing the king. "What are your intentions, Your Majesty?" Squid asked softly. Lore was not only his king but also his friend, and he empathized with the conflict twisting his heart.

"I'll pay their demands."

"I see." Squid sighed. "To act or acquiesce, either path is fraught with peril."

Lore knew Squid well enough to know he had more to say. "Share your thoughts, my friend."

"Perhaps we could take action in a way they would not expect."

"How so?"

"Is the *Stenox* still in Central City?"

"The Earthers?" Torbin asked.

"Yes," Squid said.

"They are," Eli Monsh confirmed.

"They arrived some time ago, brandishing a scroll with General Bode's seal. It seems Bode was quite generous with their demands. Now they sit moored along our docks, treating with every unsavory character that dwells in the city. Two days past, an envoy from the Ape Empire joined them. He remains aboard their strange vessel even now, hatching plots, no doubt," Torbin said in disgust.

"The Earthers are an uncivilized band of ruffians, but they provide a unique service that no others can offer," Squid said.

"You mean to hire mercenaries?" Torbin argued. "They are no better than the pirates."

"The integrity of Captain Raven can be weighed favorably against that of a pirate to keep his word if we meet his demands," Squid countered.

"Enough!" the king declared. "Do you trust this Earther, Squid?" He fixed Squid with a terrible gaze.

"I trust him to honor his contract. If he takes the job, he will see it through. Of course, he may refuse us. We've only dealt with him through his friendship with a unit commander in the 3ʳᵈ Army named Cronus Kenti."

"Can we send for Commander Kenti to treat with him?" Eli asked.

"No. Cronus Kenti is the unit commander taken prisoner by the gargoyles that escaped Tuft's Gap."

"Of the handful of men taken prisoner, one is the friend of the Earthers? That is unfortunate," Eli lamented.

"He was taken captive because he was far behind the enemy front. He was entrusted to the task appointed him because of his ability to enlist the aid of his Earth friends in preparing the battlefield for General Bode." The look on their collective faces told Squid that they were unaware of the extent the Earthers played in their victory at Tuft's Mountain. "If Your Majesty wishes to proceed with my proposal, I can visit with Captain Raven and enlist his aid in this endeavor. My apprentice and scribe is an acquaintance of the Earthers, and they share a mutual fondness for Cronus Kenti. He would be instrumental in securing Raven's services."

"We move on the appeal of a scribe to win over the most dangerous mercenary on Arax?" Torbin asked, shaking his head.

"A wise man measures the metal of a man on the strength of his character over the weight of his title," Squid answered.

"True. My father often said to judge no one in ignorance. The great war of our time is upon us, the age of war and heroes, where even a scribe may be more than he appears." King Lore gave Squid a knowing look. "You have until morning to secure Raven's services, Squid. If not, then I must meet the pirates' demands."

"As you wish, sire. I'll have Miles accompany us unless you have other need of him."

"His sword is yours."

"Then I best be off." Squid regarded the others and stepped without. He hadn't even had time to bathe or change his clothes before embarking on his next task. He would leave it to Eli and the king to send his replacement to Rego while he oversaw the matter at hand.

*****

Raven stepped onto the bridge of the *Stenox* as droplets of rain splattered upon the slanted viewport that overlooked the Stlen River. The bridge was on the second deck, in the covered area forward of the exposed rear section of the deck. Raven set his wet black jacket over the arm of the captain's chair beside him, his thick arms bulging from his short-sleeved black shirt. His right hand rested on his holstered pistol as he turned his eye toward his comrade who stood near the helm to his left. "Well, this weather sucks," he complained, wiping the rain from his forehead.

"You are protected from the weather on this ship," Argos's rough voice answered.

"Except when I have to go to the first deck. We need to cut a hole in the floor so we can access the first deck without stepping outside."

The sections of the first and second decks of the *Stenox* were covered with the entire area of the second deck resting above the covered section of the first deck. The open third deck rested atop the covered section of the second deck. Each lower deck was accessed by a door centered on the back wall of the covered sections of the deck. A single ladder was placed beside each door, providing access to the deck above. To reach either of the other levels, one had to step upon the exposed stern section of their deck, then either climb or descend a ladder to access the other level.

Since each deck rested upon the covered deck below, each upper level was far smaller than the one below. The covered section of the second deck contained a crew cabin upon its port side and the bridge upon its starboard side. The captain's chair was centered upon the bridge with the helm to port and a lookout area to starboard. The second deck was metallic gray in color with a soft, gripping texture, which prevented slippage. The walls and ceiling were made of the bluish-silver material that lined the outer hull. The captain's and helmsman's chairs were black with silver sides and low arms. They were fixed to the deck and swiveled 360 degrees.

"Where would you like the hole?" Argos drew his laser pistol from his holster, aiming it on the floor.

"Don't do that, Arg!" Raven cautioned, forgetting that Argos took what he said literally. "I was just joking, big fella. We can't go cutting holes in our ship."

Argos snorted his disappointment. He wanted to use the pistol they had given him. Since his arrival two days ago, they had given him a set of clothes and weapons to match their own. Argos found the black trousers, boots, shirt, and jacket to his liking. The pistol belt was lengthened to fit around his girth. Argos was large, even by Ape standards. Araxan Apes stood erect and were similar in build and strength to the humans of Earth, but Argos was one of the largest Apes, standing six feet and weighing 380 pounds. He was General Matuzak's champion.

His gruff and humorless disposition intimidated most Apes and Araxans, but the Earthers counted him among their few friends. He ventured across the continent to seek them out on behalf of the Ape general Matuzak, the leader of the Ape Empire. The Ape Empire was not an empire in the true sense but a collection of thirty-three tribes loosely united for mutual protection.

After arriving on Arax, the Earthers befriended General Matuzak and aided him in overthrowing the rule of the Casian Federation that occupied much of the Ape Coast at that time. Raven and Matuzak shared a great fondness for each other, and the general had need of him once again for a purpose only known to the general.

"How do your clothes fit, Arg?" Raven asked.

"The trousers are similar to my own, but the shirt is far lighter than my heavy mail."

"Lucky for you, you're the same size as Zem."

The Apes' clothing was similar to the Earthers' unlike the tunic-clad humans, gargoyles, and birdmen of Arax. Raven never had the heart to tell Cronus that only women wore skirted garments on Earth. Perhaps their mutual style of clothing was another reason for the Earthers and the Apes' mutual fondness. They also shared a love of freedom and disdain for aristocracy. Like the Earthers, the Apes knelt to no one. They selected the strongest among them to be their chieftains. If the chief was ineffectual, they were replaced.

The door separating the bridge from the stern section of the deck opened. Lorken stepped within, accompanying a woman whose soaking yellow gown clung to her body, revealing the feminine perfection of her curves. Rain dripped from her wet golden hair, her moist blue eyes looking hopefully to Raven's towering form, captive to the desperation gripping her heart.

"Leanna." Raven smiled as she rushed into his arms, hugging him fiercely. He was taken aback by her boldness, quickly surmising that something was amiss.

"Raven, they have him! They shall kill him. I didn't know where else to turn. If any can find a way, it is you."

"Whoa, slow down a minute." He forced her back a step and lifted her chin with his left hand so he might see her face. "Say it again slowly. Who has who?"

"The gargoyles captured Cronus!" she cried.

"What?" Raven's eyes narrowed darkly.

"At Tuft's Mountain. The enemy captured him as they fled the battle. Cronus's friend Terin told us of what transpired—"

"Us?"

"I was visiting with Arsenc when he came to us, relaying the awful tale. He said Minister Antillius believes they will take Cronus before their emperor for judgment."

"Their Emperor?"

"Tyro," Lorken answered.

"Tyro," Raven said, repeating the name to himself, his gaze shifting toward the viewport, scanning the north bank of the Stlen. He did not note the passing of ships or the massive structures lining the far embankment. Instead, his mind collected all that it knew of the Benotrist emperor. Tyro's seat of power was at Fera, the Black Castle.

Fera was the largest of the great castles, built ages ago. Its outer walls rose two hundred feet high with high, jagged ramparts that oversaw its barren plain like sentinels overlooking a hellish landscape. Its inner citadels towered higher still like black spearpoints aimed at the aeries above. It was a forlorn, hopeless place and wholly unassailable. It was hundreds of miles from the coastal waterways that the *Stenox* required. What could he possibly do to free his friend? It didn't matter if he lacked the answer. He would not let his friend die without trying. He would find a way.

Raven's dark eyes returned to hers. "We'll get him," he assured her.

"How?" Her expectant blue eyes pleaded.

"We'll work out the details as we go. I want you to gather your things if you wish to come along. We leave as soon as you return."

Leanna threw her arms around his large shoulders and hugged him tightly. "Thank you, Raven. Oh, thank you."

"All right. I haven't done anything yet."

She pulled back a step, staring up into his eyes with a soft smile playing along her lips. "You have given me what no other could, Raven. You have given me hope."

"Lorken, have Kato escort Leanna to her home to fetch her things. Here, take my jacket." He put his coat over her shivering shoulders, engulfing her slender form.

"Thank you," she whispered, kissing his cheek.

"Fetch Arsenc on your way back. I'll need him. He may be charged with desertion, but he'll kill more of the enemy with us than lying on his backside."

"He'll come. I am certain," she said, stepping without.

After several minutes, Lorken, Brokov, and Zem joined them on the Bridge. Zem stood beside Argos with his large metallic arms crossed. The massive android and the large gorilla shared a mutual fondness. Zem often spoke of his physical and intellectual superiority, for which his fellow Earthers took offense for some unknown reason that only a human could attest. Argos agreed with Zem's honest self-appraisal, often complimenting the android on his prowess. Zem, in kind, thought Argos smarter than his human friends for demonstrating such obvious insight that they apparently lacked. Raven just called Zem a snob. Zem simply replied that a snob was one who thought themselves better than their peers, whereas Zem truly was better.

"So what's your plan, Rav?" Brokov asked skeptically.

"I plan on sailing into Tinsay Harbor and demand Cronus's release. If they don't hand him over, we destroy the harbor."

"That's your plan?" Brokov asked, Raven's idiocy never failing to surprise him.

"That's the plan until you guys come up with a better one."

"Though Raven has displayed questionable decision-making in the past, his plan is logical. Tyro would be wise to trade one human life-form in exchange for the hundreds of ships and thousands of men he would be certain to lose," Zem stated.

"Thanks, Zem." Raven shook his head at the android's back-handed compliment.

"Your gratitude is acknowledged."

"And if Cronus is dead before we get there?" Brokov asked.

"Then we sink Tyro's entire navy," Raven said grimly.

*****

Raven sat in the captain's chair on the bridge, scanning a holographic image projected before him. The image was a map of the Benotrist coastline with each harbor, inlet, and river mouth displayed in wondrous detail. Adjusting the console on the arm of his chair, Raven expanded or contracted various parts of the map as he searched for the place with the shortest route to Fera.

Time was of the essence, for he needed to contact the nearest Benotrist authority, issue his demands, and have that potentate relay the demand for Cronus's release all the way to Fera. Each step would take precious time, and Cronus could die at any time, if he was not dead already.

"Rav!" Lorken's voice broke through the comm on his chair.

"What do you need, Lorken?"

"We have visitors."

*****

Raven entered the narrow hall of the first deck, stepping through the first door on his right. The room had silver walls and reflective black flooring with an oval-shaped table centered in the cabin with metallic-blue chairs surrounding it. A food processor lined the starboard side of the cabin, opposite the doorway. The cabin acted as a dining and conference room.

Besides Lorken and Argos, three others were seated at the table. They wore soiled dark cloaks over well-worn travel tunics. They were seated opposite the doorway, facing him as he entered. One was quite old with a silver beard. Only Araxans native to the lone hills had beards, revealing the man's origin. The second man looked to be in his third decade. His square jaw and discerning eyes matched those of a warrior of some sorts. He reminded Raven of Cronus, but the man lacked Cronus's warmth. The third man was…

"You I know." Raven pointed at Terin. "Who are these two, Terin?"

"Raven, this is Minister Antillius and King's Elite Miles Standarn," Terin said, introducing them.

"It is an honor to finally meet with you, Captain Raven," Squid said.

"First, General Bode, and now Minister Antillius. I hope I don't soil your reputation by you visiting me, Ambassador."

"Quite the opposite, Captain Raven."

"Just Raven. Exchanging tittles is a waste of time, and I have little to spare."

"Very well, Raven," Squid continued. "Treating with you is indeed an honor that I shall only deny to keep our affairs secret. Your aid to General Bode at Rego is acknowledged with gratitude by King Lore."

"What brings you here, Squid? It's not to say thank you." Raven's mood was souring as he eyed them.

"We are here on behalf of King Lore. The matter which brings us to you in this dreadful weather is most urgent. Before I speak of it, Terin wishes to share information that you may find unsettling."

"I already know, Squid. Cronus was captured at Tuft's Mountain." Raven stood with his left foot upon a chair, resting his forearm upon his knee while he leaned forward, staring down at them from across the table. "What I want to know is, why was he captured?"

"He was—" Terin began to explain.

"Not you, Terin. I want to hear it from him!" Raven pointed at Squid.

"Commander Kenti was given a special task. His unit was placed north of the battlefield. When the enemy passed them, they set the north end of Tuft's Gap ablaze. The enemy was mostly destroyed. However, a few telnics escaped and discovered Commander Kenti's men during their retreat. They were overwhelmed, and a few were taken prisoner," Squid answered with his trained diplomatic tone.

"I help you win a battle, and you thank me by sending my friend on a suicide mission?" Raven growled. "I should shoot you right now!"

"Commander Kenti was given a place of honor on the battlefield. His heroism dealt the enemy a crippling blow," Miles said, defending Squid.

"Honor? Heroism? The graveyards are filled with heroes."

"Cronus Kenti followed his orders and did his duty!" Miles replied heatedly.

"Every soldier does his duty, but suicide? A man deserves a fighting chance. You didn't give one to Cronus!" Raven snarled.

"Commander Kenti was offered his place in battle as an award for his service to the realm. He could have declined the offer," Squid explained.

"No good soldier declines his commander's suggestions. Declining such an offer was not an option for an honorable man like Cronus. It was your job to protect him from himself. That offer should never have been made. Now I'm gonna have to get him out, and I got news for you, pal, so you better listen well. If Cronus is dead before I can get to him, we're going to sink Tyro's navy, every last ship. And when we're done with Tyro, we're coming for you!"

Terin's heart was racing. This was a side of Raven he had not yet seen. He felt he might reach across the table and snap their necks like twigs. If Squid was unnerved, he did not reveal it. He stared at Raven with calm, expressive eyes that sympathized rather than admonished.

"My dear Captain Raven, the loss of Cronus Kenti pains us deeply. We lost many precious sons at Tuft's Mountain. To their families, each of those men is as precious as Cronus is to you and Terin. Please understand, we are hopelessly outnumbered, and every engagement is fraught with great risk. But if you can secure Cronus's freedom, we would be most grateful."

Squid's words assuaged Raven's anger, but not his tongue. "All right, Squid. We'll leave it at that. But I have to say, I don't like diplomats."

"I'm not asking for your friendship, Raven. I only wish that you hear what I have come to say."

"Go ahead and spit it out."

"King Lore has received grievous news. His daughter, the princess Corry, has been taken hostage by a pirate named Monsoon." Raven's eyes narrowed firmly at the mention of that name. "You know this pirate?" Squid asked.

"I know him," Raven grunted distastefully.

"The princess was taken at the Harbor of Bansoch on the Isle of the Sisterhood. From there, she was taken to Molten Isle."

"What was she doing in a foreign land when you were on the brink of war?" Brokov asked.

"Every six years, the queen of the Sisterhood invites the females of the royal houses of Arax to partake in certain festivities known only to them. We are asking for your assistance. Can you rescue her from Molten Isle without raising their suspicion?"

Molten Isle was a little-used, sparsely populated isle far off the coast of Cagan. The pirates must have overrun the indigenous people and seized the isle. The pirate Lord Monsoon was from the east, so Molten Isle was far off his range. "Pay the bastard what he wants, Squid. I don't have time to waste on your princess, not even a day." Even if Cronus lived, his life was measured in hours and days, and Raven would not trade away precious time for the handsome reward the Torry crown would surely pay.

"I fear if you refuse us, then the princess will meet a terrible end, Raven," Squid lamented.

"That's possible considering Monsoon's reputation," Raven said. "But that's if you're only dealing with Monsoon. I find this whole abduction story a little hokey. How do you know the Sisterhood wasn't behind it or Tyro or the Yatins?"

"That is unlikely considering…" Squid started to explain.

"Considering what?" Raven asked.

"That Princess Corry was not the only princess taken. Princess Deliea, daughter of King Mortus, regent of the Macon Empire, Princess Felicia, daughter of King Lichu of Naybin, and Princess Tosha—"

"Tosha?" Raven cut him off. Tosha was the daughter of Queen Letha, first guardian of the Federation of the Sisterhood. The Isle of the Sisterhood was a matriarchy, resting off the northwestern coast of Arax. Tosha was also the daughter of Tyro. When Tyro came to power, conquering much of northern Arax, he wooed the young queen of the Sisterhood. From their union came one daughter, the princess Tosha.

The queen soon discovered that Tyro planned to undermine her federation and absorb her isle into his greater empire. She dissolved their marital union, casting him from her isle. The queen did not deny him his daughter, however, allowing the princess to visit at length with her father throughout the years. How Monsoon managed to seize all four princesses, even Raven couldn't guess.

"Monsoon states that only the first monarch to agree to his terms can be assured of their princess's safety. The others may be disposed of as he sees fit. We dare not tarry lest the princess meet an ill end," Squid explained.

"Thirty thousand certras!" Raven said bluntly. The certra was the common coin of exchange among the coastal regions and sea lanes of Arax.

"Thirty thousand?" A queer expression crossed Squid's face. "I do not understand. Are you accepting—"

"We'll rescue your princess. I expect to be paid when we return her safely to Cagan Harbor," Raven said.

"When shall we depart?" Squid asked.

"We?" Brokov asked.

"Yes. We three shall accompany you on this quest," Squid said tiredly.

"We're leaving within the hour, so fetch whatever you plan on bringing," Raven said.

"Tonight?" Squid asked, surprised by the rapidity of events.

"Time is precious, Squid. We're not wasting time we don't have. You have one hour to be back here, or we leave without you."

"Why the sudden change?" Miles asked suspiciously. "A moment ago, you stated that you were too busy to rescue Princess Corry. Now you are—"

"Enough." Squid placed his hand upon Miles's shoulder. If Raven was willing to help, then they had to accept no matter his motive.

CHAPTER 8

The *Stenox* sped downriver at breakneck speed. No sooner had they collected Leanna, Arsenc, Miles, Squid, and Terin that they set off. Traveling throughout the night, they put three hundred miles behind them, racing down the Stlen as it merged into the wider Nila. Never had the Earthers pushed the *Stenox* to such speeds while traversing the river. Araxans standing along the riverbanks stared in awe as the strange bluish-silver object sped past, leaving trails of rippling waves in its wake. The Earthers took turns at the helm, using their radar to scan the river far enough ahead to maintain their speed.

Terin awoke late in the morning, his body taxed by the battle and the long journey from Rego. He found the cabin that he shared with Squid, Arsenc, and Miles empty when he woke. Their cabin was on the port side of the first deck and had two sets of stacked bunks on opposite sides of the cabin. Donning a dry tan wool tunic, sword belt, and sandals, he stepped out into the corridor and then into the open air of the stern.

Stepping upon the uncovered stern, he nearly lost his feet, taken aback by the speed of the vessel. Tall porians lined the north bank, their broad leaves catching the morning sun, while scrag and morla grass ran along the south bank. Terin shaded his eyes from the bright glare of the sun reflecting off the river.

Leanna stood at the stern, looking over the low wall railing that circled the uncovered section as she watched the river pass swiftly away. She still wore her golden gown. Her hair was matted with dark circles surrounding her watered eyes. Terin approached her carefully, unsure of her reception. He came beside her, sharing her forlorn view of the rippled water left in their wake. She turned at his approach, sharing a smile as he stepped near.

"Good morning, Terin."

"Good morning." He smiled in turn.

"Did you sleep well?"

"Yes. I could sleep for days if I am truthful."

"You must be very tired. You traveled so far. Cronus…" His name caught in her throat, a painful reminder of how much she missed him. "Cronus often complained of the long journeys he traveled. You fought in a battle, then traveled to Central City. Before you could rest, you find yourself with us, sailing south," she said.

"It is no burden, my lady. I wish only…" He caught himself wishing that Cronus were there but didn't wish to upset her.

"Wish what?" she asked.

"Cronus," he said sheepishly.

"I know." She sighed. "I am sorry that I ran away when you spoke with us last night. It was ill-mannered."

"I understand," Terin said.

"You told me the truth. I appreciate that, Terin. Other men would have attempted to spare my feelings. I prefer the truth. The truth will find you eventually, so I might as well face it today. Besides, the truth drove my desperation, leading me to Raven."

"Can he free Cronus?"

"I don't know." She sighed. "There is much we don't know. Cronus might already be dead, or he might be taken elsewhere. But if anyone can do the impossible, it is Raven."

"You are fond of him." Terin smiled.

"Yes." She smiled. "I can see how some are frightened of him. He is so large and feral at times, but he has always treated me with kindness." Terin stifled a laugh. "Something humors you?" She lifted a brow.

"He did not appear so kind to Minister Antillius last night."

"How so?"

"Raven said if Cronus dies, then he would destroy Tyro's navy before he destroys ours. He said he should kill Squid anyway."

"Why would he do so?"

"He claims that Cronus should not have been given the task they assigned him. Raven said that it was a suicide mission and that it was no way to treat his friend after they helped prepare the battlefield."

"But Cronus accepted the task," Leanna said.

"Raven said they should have protected Cronus by not offering it. He said no good soldier would refuse such a task. He said Cronus was too honorable and had to be protected from himself."

"He said that?"

"He did." Leanna turned away, wiping a lonely tear so Terin could not see. "Are you well?" he asked.

"Cronus never spoke ill of a friend, either for his own betterment or for the amusement of others. He said true friends are worth more than mountains of gold," she said.

"He was right."

"He was, and he spoke well of you, Terin."

"Me? I've done nothing to warrant such praise, especially from a man like Cronus."

"You are humble. That is rare in a scribe appointed to serve a king's minister. I know your true quality, Terin. If Cronus spoke well of you, that is all I need know. Arsenc, however, relayed a fanciful tale of your swordsmanship at Costelin. He said they found you surrounded by hundreds of gargoyles, fighting alone and slaying them in great numbers. Very strange, don't you think, for a scribe?" she asked with a timeless look on her face.

"Arsenc is generous in his telling. I was surrounded and faced certain death had Cronus not come to my aid. I was fortunate to stay alive until he could rescue me. That is the extent of my greatness, my lady."

She shook her head, not believing his interpretation. "You need not address me as your lady, Terin. I am a merchant's daughter. Call me Leanna." She smiled.

*****

"So what's your new plan, Rav?" Lorken asked as he manned the helm. They were alone on the bridge, the river spanning endlessly before them. Lorken and the others were taken aback by their friend's sudden change of heart the night before. He was adamant about freeing Cronus and would not entertain any offer that diverted them from that task. He even refused to rescue the Torry princess before abruptly changing his mind amid Minister Antillius's plea. Now they found themselves sailing for Molten Isle.

"If we're gonna free Cronus, we might need a carrot to go along with our stick," Raven said, standing at his side with his right thumb hooked into his holster.

"Are you suggesting we trade the Torry princess for Cronus?"

"No, though that's not a bad idea. I plan on trading Tyro's daughter for Cronus."

"Princess Tosha?"

"That's the one."

"So we now have to rescue two of the pirates' hostages." Lorken rolled his eyes.

"No. We'll rescue all four. The others we give to their fathers. Tosha we exchange for Cronus. It's simple, really."

"Yeah, I see how simple it is." Lorken shook his head. "And do we tell the Torry ambassador?"

"He's paying us to recue Corry. The others are ours to do with as we please."

"He won't like it."

"Who cares?" Raven shrugged.

*****

The *Stenox* reached Cagan Harbor in two days. They traversed the calm waters of the bay, sailing between towers of gray and alabaster spiraling above either shore, their lighted beacons atop their highest peaks guiding approaching ships to port. Several rocky islands dotted the mouth of the Nila. The Torries had built stone forts on four of them with heavy ballista lining their ramparts. The Nila cut westward to the sea, dividing the city into Cagan North and Cagan South.

Thick thirty-foot walls protected the land side approaches of the city while a series of fortifications lined the seashore. Most of the Torry fleet was moored on the north side of the bay, housed in circular docks that jutted from the shoreline. Several Torry galleys traversed the waves, their triple-oared rows cutting the waves.

Terin stood at the starboard stern, gazing in wonder at the world around him. He had never seen so much water in his eighteen years. The expansive bay was a visual feast for the virgin eye with towering beacons, long piers, and the covered docking chambers of the Torry Navy spread across the shoreline.

"Come, Terin." Squid took him by the arm, guiding him to the port side of the first deck. "Look there, along the southern shore." Terin narrowed his eyes, focusing on the distant southern shore of Cagan Bay. There he beheld massive columns rising above an expansive fortress. They were centered atop the structure in a half circle facing the bay. The base of the structure spread far along the shoreline with granite walls the height of three men. Terin descried the lush green foregrounds that followed from the base of the structure to the shore's edge. Statues spread across the palace greens, but from a distance, they appeared simple slivers of white and gray.

"That, my young friend, is Soren Palace, the seat of power of the kings and queens of old Cagia. When the Yatins besieged the harbor, King Torry led a great host down the Nila and saved the city. King Gorena rewarded King Torry with the hand of his daughter and only child, the princess Galena. Since that day, we have been one throne but two kingdoms."

"Which banner graces the palace?" Terin asked as he descried a blue banner blowing fiercely above the palace.

"That is the banner of Vintor Ornovis, regent of Cagan and cousin of the king. A closer eye would discern the gray fish centered on the field of blue, the signet of House Ornovis," Squid explained.

Once the *Stenox* passed the mouth of the Nila, Terin ascended the third deck, overlooking the ocean from atop the ship. He stared in wonder as water stretched endlessly to the horizon. The sight was humbling. How could one not feel insignificant before such majesty?

*****

Lorken, Kato, and Miles climbed through the hatch in the diving room, entering the mini sub *Atlantis*, which was docked below the first deck. Kato descended first, climbing forward into the driver's seat, forward on the port side of the submersible. Lorken followed, taking his place in the weapon control seat, forward starboard. Miles stared through the open hatch, wary of the strange vessel. "Go on in, King's Elite. It won't sink," Raven chided him, standing at the doorway of the cabin. Miles gave Raven a look before descending, taking his place in the seat centered below the hatch.

Kato pressed the hatch seal switch on his console, and the hatch slid into place. Raven closed the hatch of the *Stenox* as Kato released the *Atlantis* from its docking lock. Miles's eyes drew wide with wonder as the darkened vessel came alive with subdued lighting emitting from the console built into the arm of his chair.

"You have a rare privilege, Miles," Kato said over his shoulder.

"And that is?"

"You are sitting in the sub commander's chair. Only one other Araxan human has ever set foot in one of our submersibles. You are the second." Miles knew the first was Cordi Kenti, brother of Cronus Kenti. The Earthers spoke of him fondly, and he couldn't help but sense there was more to his death than they had revealed. "Next stop, Molten Isle," Kato said as the *Atlantis* slipped beneath the hull of the *Stenox*, speeding off toward the southwest.

*****

"I hope your friend isn't claustrophobic," Raven said after stepping into the corridor of the first deck.

"What is claustrophobic?" Squid asked.

"It means frightened of tight-fitting places."

"Miles Standarn is a good soldier. He will do his duty," Squid answered, following Raven across the hall and into the dining cabin.

Raven poured himself a cup of juice from the food processor on the opposite wall, then offered Squid a cup. Squid received it graciously. After several days aboard the *Stenox*, the ambassador was still in awe of the wonders of the strange vessel. The alien technology that the Earthmen brought with them was beyond imagining. Yet the Earthers had little understanding of the construction of their devices. Their civilization was thousands of years beyond Arax. All their knowledge was built upon the advances of past civilizations, as discovery builds upon discovery like the blocks of a structure.

"How many days until they return?" Squid asked.

"Now that we're free of the river, the *Atlantis* can go at top speed. They'll reach the isle in several hours. Once ashore, Lorken and Miles will need time to scout the isle and find where the princesses are being held. By the time they finish, we'll catch up with them."

"Then we rescue the princess," Squid said.

"Yeah." Raven shrugged.

Something in Raven's response raised Squid's suspicion. "Is there something you wish to add, Raven?"

"You might as well know, Squid, that I plan on rescuing all four hostages," he said, placing one foot upon a chair as he leaned forward, resting his forearms on his leg.

"That would be preferable to the pirates despoiling them should we only rescue the Torry princess," Squid reasoned. "Of course, the crown is not paying for the others."

"That's fine, because I have plans for Tosha anyway."

"You mean Princess Tosha?" Squid corrected his informal reference.

"She's not my princess."

"I see. And what are your plans for her?"

"I'm trading her to her father in exchange for Cronus."

Squid's face paled. "Rav-Raven, you must not do this. Queen Letha is a dear ally to the Torry throne. If you attempt this—"

"I don't care about your throne, your allies, or your precious honor, Squid. I mean to free Cronus, and I will do it any way I can."

*****

"These control our starboard lasers," Brokov said. Leanna and Arsenc listened attentively as he explained the workings of the large consoles that they were each seated in, in the starboard bow section of the first deck. Brokov stood over their shoulders, instructing them on the operation of the ship's weapon and communication systems.

"What about these?" Arsenc pointed to similar controls on the opposite side of his console.

"Those are the port side lasers." Brokov pointed out each grouping. "We'll practice operating them later. Leanna, those are the controls for the upper deck and bow lasers, and those are for our subsurface weapons systems."

Since Arsenc's leg still hobbled his movement, he would remain on the *Stenox* with Leanna and Minister Antillius. At times, Brokov or Zem would be the only Earthers on board, so they needed to familiarize their temporary crewmates on the workings of the ship. There were many controls on the console, covering a myriad of uses, one of which connected to a person's mind to teach them a new language in a short time, which explained the Earthers' ability to learn their language with little accent.

*****

Terin drew his cloak tight as the cool sea air swept over the bow of the third deck. Sea surf sprayed his face as the swirling winds kissed his bare legs and hands. He hoped to see the sun set upon the ocean, but the graying sky dimmed his hopes. He had always longed to see the ocean, but now he stared at the endless sea with profound loneliness. He remembered his last moments at home, bidding his parents farewell as he rode off for Rego. It seemed as if it was yesterday and so long ago at the same time.

His mind was a whirlwind as if adrift on a swift-flowing stream, captive to the current's course. He had no control of where the road took him, merely following its path. The Costelin Colony, the battle at Tuft's Mountain, the endless trek, and the wonders of the *Stenox* overwhelmed his simple comprehension, but the loneliness of that endless sea quieted his mind.

"You might want to get below before the weather turns to crap." Terin turned as Raven cleared the ladder and stepped onto the third deck. Raven rested his forearms on the low wall that stood fifty inches in height and lined the starboard, bow, and port sides of the deck. Terin smiled at Raven's comments. They were crude and blunt but lightened his dour mood.

"I'll only be a moment," Terin said, returning his eyes to the sea.

"What are you looking at?" the big Earther asked.

"The ocean. I have never seen it before."

"Well, there it is. Now let's get below."

"Raven, Minister Antillius told me what you are planning to do with the Benotrist princess. I just want to say that I agree with you. I am willing to risk war with the Sisterhood if that is the price to free Cronus."

"That's not the kind of thing a diplomat is supposed to say." Raven smiled.

"I'm not a diplomat, nor am I a scribe," he said quietly, his eyes distant as he stared ahead.

"Then what are you?"

"I do not know." Terin turned his tired eyes to Raven. "A wise friend said I must venture where I feel myself led. My heart screams out that I must save my friend, so that is what I shall do. After we rescue the princess, I wish to go with you if you'll have me."

"I thought you were too nice of a kid to be one of those diplomatic weenie types anyway. We'd be glad to have you." Raven slapped him on the back, nearly knocking him off his feet.

*****

They gathered in the dining cabin, crowding around the small table, as Lorken, Kato, and Miles reported their findings. The others listened as they pointed out key features on the map that lay across the table depicting Molten Isle and the surrounding sea in rich detail. The isle was twenty miles in length, running northwest to southeast. It was five miles abreast at its widest. North and east of the island was a deadly reef that blocked Araxan ships from sailing directly to the isle. The seafloor was littered with wrecks, a graveyard of fools who tested those deadly waters. The pirate Lord Monsoon knew no enemy could approach the isle directly. The only way was to circumvent the reef and approach from the south or west. Either course was fraught with peril, as poor navigation could lead a ship to overshoot and be lost far out to sea.

"The pirates have repaired much of the old fort that overlooks the sea cliffs here," Lorken said, pointing to the middle of the southwest shore of the isle. "We believe some of the hostages are being held there."

"Which hostages?" Squid asked.

"Which ones would you like them to be?" Lorken said sarcastically.

"We do not know which are held there," Miles answered, giving Lorken a dark look, reproaching the Earther's lack of respect for Minister Antillius and the Torry throne.

"Take it easy, King's Elite. Lorken was just having a little fun with Squid," Raven said.

"I do not find it humorous!" Miles gritted his teeth. "His title is King's Minister Antillius, not Squid."

"We're not much into fancy titles on this ship, Miles. Just be thankful we decided to take this job, or you'd still be paddling your way down the Nila with no chance of rescuing your little princess," Raven shot back.

Miles's cheeks flushed with indignation. "You assume much, Captain Raven."

"No, I only assume the worst. And on this planet, I'm usually right. Either way, it doesn't matter which princess is held at the fort, because we are rescuing all four of them anyway."

"All four?" Miles asked.

"Yeah," Raven replied, "all four."

"Why?"

"Miles." Squid gave him a look telling him to cease before addressing Lorken. "Please continue with your assessment, Lorken."

"All right. The stone fort has been much repaired," Lorken continued. "We estimate a garrison of forty to fifty men there. The princesses, if they are there, are probably being held on the lowest level of the sea-facing wall. With a thirty-foot vertical plunge and swirling currents below, no Araxan ship could affect a rescue escape that way."

"But we have no such limitation," Brokov added.

"Three miles northwest of the fort is the island's only harbor." Lorken ran his finger over the map, indicating the point of interest. "There are no less than a dozen pirate galleys docked there. The harbor is crawling with hundreds of pirates. They are expecting any negotiations to take place there."

"Are the other hostages being held there?" Brokov asked.

"No. We think they are being held in a small village here." Lorken's finger indicated a place near the northeast coast. "It is a simple village with several huts. We estimate a garrison of twenty men, probably handpicked by Monsoon for their loyalty and discipline. The village is some one thousand meters from the shoreline. A narrow road connects the village to the fort, which is four miles due west of the village on the opposing shore. Monsoon also has amassed a dozen magantor scouts. We spotted a pair of the giant eagles passing overhead when we were ashore. They are patrolling the sea lanes south and west of the isle. We believe Monsoon used the magantors to bring the hostages to the isle."

"If they spot us, they might kill their captives and flee," Brokov said.

"That is a possibility," Kato answered.

"If they spot us, we'll shoot them out of the sky. Monsoon won't kill his hostages if a few magantors go missing. Besides, the weather is gonna be lousy for the next day and a half. That will keep those birds grounded. That will also catch them off guard, as no Araxan fleet should approach the isle under those conditions," Raven said.

"If what Brokov says is true, then we must take every precaution to avoid detection until we are in position to affect the rescue." Miles fixed his eyes on Raven. "We cannot risk the princess's life."

"We're past the point of no risk, Miles. You passed that point when your princess was kidnapped. But don't worry, King's Elite. We'll do everything we can to keep your little princess safe," Raven said. Miles threw up his hands in disgust. "Let's go over our plan, then we best get some sleep. I want us to be ashore at first light," Raven said.

CHAPTER 9

He stared at the waves lapping the hull of the submersible with misgivings. Raven stood beside the open hatch atop the mini sub *Spectre*, looking down at the murky water as dark gray clouded the morning sky. He eyed the beach some thirty yards away, calculating the length of his swim. Resting his right hand on his holstered pistol and scratching his head with his left, he looked down the open hatch of the sub.

"Brokov, are you sure you can't get us closer to the shore?" he shouted through the hatch.

"No! This is as close as I dare go without running aground," Brokov shouted over his shoulder as he sat in the pilot's seat of the *Spectre* with Argos and Kato waiting their turn to exit the sub. Raven shook his head, wondering how long it would take for his clothes to dry out once he went ashore. "Go on!" Brokov said.

"I'm going, but the water looks pretty cold."

"Cold? I thought you were an Eskimo or Inupiat or whatever you call yourselves," Brokov chided.

"Half Inupiat. My mother is a Texan, and right now, my Texan half says it's cold." Raven recalled using the Eskimo moniker when he was a child visiting his paternal grandmother in Anaktuvuk Pass when she whacked him on the head with a ladle. His brothers put him up to it, laughing at his expense when she hit him. She was fiercely proud of her tribal heritage, tracing her people back to the Nunamiut, who dwelled in Far North Alaska.

"Well, quit your complaining and jump in. That wagon is approaching the intercept point, so hurry up!"

"Aw, hell." Raven relented and slipped off into the frigid sea. His breath caught in the narrows of his throat, the cold constricting his chest. He wasted little time adjusting to the temperature before swimming ashore. Brokov piloted the *Spectre* around Raven, moving fifteen yards closer. Argos and Kato climbed through the hatch and followed Raven into the water, though their march through the water was half as far. "Why, that son of a b…" Raven growled as seawater filled his mouth.

Kato and Argos waded easily ashore with the water reaching their upper thighs. They could hear Raven's cursing as he finally found his feet and stormed up the beach, throwing a scowl over his shoulder as the bluish-silver shape of the *Spectre* slipped below the surface. Raven closed on Kato with long, powerful strides, his feet squeezing water from his boots as he marched. Raven scooped Kato into the air and marched back into the water, dropping him in the surf.

"What was that for?" Kato spat the salty water from his mouth.

"Because you knew he was gonna do that!" Raven growled.

"Well, he might have mentioned something about giving you a longer swim." Kato grinned.

"Yeah, I bet he did."

"Argos heard him also. Why don't you throw him in too?" Kato asked, gaining his feet before wading back up the beach.

"Because Arg's three hundred and eighty pounds, and you're one hundred and thirty."

"If you two are done taking your bath, we should be moving along!" Argos shouted from the tree line that pressed upon the beach.

*****

The north side of Molten Isle was an endless stretch of rocky shore with jagged reefs stretching far out to sea. Tropical frolog trees mixed with thick foliage pressed close to the barren, rocky beaches that lined the northern shoreline. The center of the isle was flat with rolling, windswept hillsides at either end. Zem set them ashore, piloting the mini sub *Atlantis* through the twisting maze of jagged coral. Lorken, Miles, and Terin waded ashore, stepping rock to rock as they moved along the beach to mask their sign.

The inhospitable nature of the north side of the isle reduced the possibility of any fool landing there, so the pirate patrols were likely infrequent. Nonetheless, Lorken and Miles preferred not to chance their discovery, so they entered the tree line without stepping in sand. Terin and Miles had tied their sandal boots about their necks before entering the water, donning them once passing within the tree line. Only the hems of their tunics were wet, but the warm air would quickly dry them. Lorken was another matter. His thick black trousers and boots were laden with water. He sat down after entering the tree line, taking off his boots and emptying them one at a time.

"I told Raven we should've worn our wet suits," he complained as Miles and Terin stood nearby.

"I doubt your Captain Raven ever heeds wise counsel," Miles said, loosening his swords from their scabbards, testing their ease of being drawn if the need should arise. He and Terin wore simple brown tunics and cloaks. Miles shifted his belt around his waist, positioning his twin swords on opposing hips. He had a pair of daggers sheathed behind each sword. Terin was only armed with his father's sword upon his left hip.

Lorken stood, removing a flat fist-sized device from his jacket pocket. Sweeping the object through the foliage south and west, he descried the bold-crimson images on the device's green field. "That way," Lorken said, indicating the route of travel. Miles and Terin drew their cloaks over their heads and followed the large Earther through the vegetation.

*****

The old man's tongue clicked, urging his ocran onward as it pulled the lumbering wagon along the coastal road. He lifted his tired green eyes to the gray overcast above, wondering if he would reach the stone fort before it rained. The coastal road snaked along the southern coast, running from the harbor southeast toward the fort. The route led through patches of trees and foliage, but mostly, the path was barren unlike the fierce jungle on the isle's northeast side. He stared off to the south, where rough waves pounded the shore.

A steep, rocky embankment dropped off his right, some seven meters to the beach below. The slope continued off the left side of the road, rising another six meters before tapering. Flocks of lumar birds skimmed along the rolling surf below, diving for fish when they dared swim near the surface. The white-feathered lumars would spot their prey, then climb before descending through the surf, grasping the fish in their deep beaks.

The coastal road was barely wide enough for his wagon, so he was careful not to crowd the road's southern edge. He passed within a large swath of trollas that swept over the embankment like an emerald waterfall. Halfway through the broad-leafed grove, the old wagon driver descried a felled trolla straddling the road. Bringing his ocran to an abrupt stop, he flinched as a towering stranger stepped from behind a trolla on his right. His hand moved thoughtless to the blade on his hip.

"I wouldn't do that!" Raven cautioned, freezing the man's hand at the hilt. The old man released his bladder, soling his gray tunic as Argos and Kato emerged from his left. He stared saucer-eyed as his gaze moved from one to the other. Despite the silver strands sweeping the dark from his hair, the old man looked not much different from his youth like most Araxans.

"We should kill him!" Argos growled, his black nostrils flaring and gray eyes fixed on the driver.

"We will if he doesn't do what we ask." Raven fixed his dark eyes on the trembling driver.

"Wha-what do you…want of me?"

"It's real simple, old-timer. All you have to do is hide us in the back of your wagon and sneak us into the fort," Raven explained.

"What if we are discovered?" the man said, pleading to Raven's sanity, hoping he would reconsider.

"Then a lot of people are going to die, but we're not. The last one to die will be you. I'll bury you up to your neck in the sand down there during low tide, then I'll sit on a fat rock and eat my lunch while you hold your breath when the high tide rolls in. How's that sound?" Raven said, jerking his thumb over his shoulder toward the beach.

*****

"What is that?" Leanna asked as a bright-red shape emerged on the radar. She sat at the communications console on the first deck as Brokov looked over her shoulder.

"That's the *Spectre*. Zem should be returning from dropping off Lorken's team. Push that." He directed her to a luminous blue button on the console's right side. She complied. "Go ahead. Talk," he said.

"*Stenox* calling *Spectre*," she said into the comm.

"*Spectre* here. Approaching south by southwest of your position," Zem's deep metallic voice echoed in return.

"ETA?" Brokov mouthed wordlessly to her.

"What is your ETA, *Spectre*?" Leanna asked as she looked to Brokov for guidance.

"Six minutes, thirty-seven seconds," Zem responded.

"Received. We await your return. Out," Leanna finished.

"Well done." Brokov smiled kindly as he patted her shoulder. "We'll make a crewman out of you yet." She gave him a knowing smile. The Earthers had shown her great kindness and had given her a sense that she was accomplishing something toward the goal of freeing Cronus. She put the thought of him suffering and dying from her mind, as it would only cause her pain. If he was dead or maimed, she would know soon enough. She reserved that time to grieve, but not now. Now she had a job to do.

"Any word?" Ambassador Antillius asked, standing in the doorway.

"Not yet, Ambassador. Zem just dropped off Lorken's team. They have two hours to get into position. Raven's team should be approaching the fort about now."

"We must wait, then," Squid said.

"Wait and hope," Brokov added.

"Yes," Squid agreed, pensively stroking the silver in his trimmed beard.

"Something else on your mind, Ambassador?" Brokov asked.

"Hmm," Squid mused, shifting his gray eyes back to Brokov. "I was curious, Brokov. You and your companions hail from a civilization far beyond our limited comprehension, yet I am struck by your temperament and articulation in comparison to your Captain Raven."

"What's your point?" Brokov asked as Leanna observed their curios exchange.

"Why did your superiors choose Raven for command over you?"

"I don't know, but it's obvious they didn't base their decision on charm, wisdom, or good looks."

*****

The moisture melded his tunic to his back as they crept carefully through the dense foliage. The unseasonably cool ocean water contrasted with the humid air of the tropical isle. Terin followed Miles as Miles followed Lorken, their pace easing as they drew close to the village. Terin pondered what strange fate brought him to this place. Was it mere happenstance or the design of providence? From the mysterious power of his father's sword to the sweeping battle at Tuft's Mountain and then to this pirate stronghold, these were tales no one would believe.

He no longer marveled at the strangeness of these events but began to accept them as the norm. He suddenly realized that he wasn't thinking of rescuing a princess or storming a village. He was merely focused on moving quietly from tree to vine. Suddenly cognizant of their larger objective, Terin's heart quickened.

He moved his right hand to his sword. Gripping his fingers around the hilt, he felt the blade's calming aura cleansing his body of apprehension. His senses quickly heightened as the air felt lighter, bringing the world around him boldly into focus. Every blade of grass, every leaf, and every insect was magnified in rich detail.

Miles paused, freezing Terin where he stood. Up ahead, Lorken placed the flat of his palm toward them, signaling them to halt. Lorken eyed the device in his left hand carefully, sweeping the forest before them. Several red dots emerged in the device's green field. Fixing the dots' location, he looked back at Miles with four raised fingers.

*****

"Why are we always on patrol?" the pirate complained, ambling behind his three comrades. They were all dressed in black tunics with shortswords sheathed on their belts. The complainer, in his third decade, was diminutive, even for an Araxan, with dark braids and narrow-set eyes and a missing ear. His three comrades walked several paces in front and side by side. The one in the center turned swiftly upon the complainer. He was gangly and tall, and he bore a terrible scar running the length of his face.

"We patrol because Monsoon tells Torgan, Torgan tells Chutzan, and Chutzan tells me. If I hear you complain again, I'll whelp you across your good ear, Virguns!" His foul breath backed the complainer a step. Virgun wanted to ask who Monsoon might be worried about considering that no one could approach the isle from the north or east. The only way to reach the village was from the narrow road that ran west to the stone fort on the isle's other side.

They stood on a narrow trail that circled the village with thick foliage to either side. The clicking of insects and the singing of birds mixed in disjointed unison as the fetid smell of a dead carcass tortured their nostrils. The trail was only two meters wide and was little more than matted grass with patches of mud.

No sooner had the taller pirate turned his back upon Virgun than a blue beam sped from the outer tree line, striking the gangly fellow's skull before passing through. His listless body crumpled to the ground, blood flooding the cavity that ran the length of his brain. Hands went to hilts as a second blue beam pierced the right breast of another pirate.

Virgun stepped back as he descried a black-haired man rush from the dense foliage dressed in a brown tunic. His sword slashed quicker than thought, striking a third pirate with repeated blows, before Virgun had freed his blade from its sheath. He turned to flee, oblivious to the silver blade passing behind him. He unwittingly turned into the arc of the approaching blade.

Terin caught the last pirate unaware as his father's blade met the man's face between lip and nose. The blow passed through bone, brain, and tissue like crumpled parchment before exiting the back of the skull. The speed of the blade barely registered a dull, audible crunch as Terin's breath held with the fell deed. His eyes averted from the form of his beaten foe crumpling to the ground, his upper skull falling away as he dropped. Terin's gaze swept to his left, where Miles stood in the middle of the trail with sword at the ready, standing amid the other slain pirates.

Lorken's dark face emerged from the foliage with rifle in hand. Neither had time to witness the swiftness of Terin's arm or the devastation wrought by his terrible blade. "Let's move these into the tree line," Lorken said, slinging his rifle over his shoulder as he reached down and grasped a pirate by the ankle, dragging the corpse into the foliage. Miles thought it useless to conceal their handiwork since they could not remove the blood that soaked the ground in matted red pools, but to argue the point would take more time than helping Lorken with the task.

Terin released his breath, slowly cognizant of what he had done. It all happened so quickly. When he saw his friends engage, he felt his hand draw the sword, independent of his will. He killed gargoyles at Costelin and Tuft's Mountain, but this was a man. He killed a man. Shouldn't he feel a greater remorse? Oddly, he felt little. The man was a pirate. He was the enemy. What choice had he?

Following his comrades' lead, Terin sheathed his sword, then reached down, grasping the dead pirate's legs and pulling him into the dense foliage. He, too, thought Lorken's idea foolish, as any poorly trained eye could see the blood trail on the grass leading to the cluster of corpses that they stacked together. No matter, he did as his friend suggested. He nearly lost his footing, his sandaled foot catching on a vine, but managed to stay erect as he dragged the body to where the others were gathered. He moved as swiftly as his strength allowed, keeping his eyes fixed away from the dead.

"You cut this guy's head in half!" Lorken observed in disbelief, eyeing the corpse Terin had deposited beside the others.

"A fortunate blow," Terin answered quietly.

Miles finished with the last body, overhearing Lorken's assessment. He knew only a very powerful blow could have inflicted such damage. *A scribe indeed,* he mused as he shook his head, disbelieving Squid's claim of the boy's purpose.

"Lucky or not, it was a good swing of your sword, Terin." Lorken slapped him on the back. "You'll need to fetch the rest of him, though."

Terin swallowed past the lump in his throat knowing he would have to now look closer at what he had done. He stepped back onto the trail, finding the gooey bottom of the skull facing him. Closing his eyes, he reached down, seizing the crown by the hair. Lifting it in his left hand, he returned swiftly to the others, depositing the severed crown beside its master. Terin backed away, turned, and deposited the contents of his stomach on the ground.

Neither Lorken nor Miles spoke of it. For them, it was enough that Terin had done what was required. He faced an enemy and slew him without respite. Lorken drew his laser pistol, adjusting the setting, and fired at the pile of corpses. A wide beam of green light bathed the pile of dead flesh, melting it away into a mound of charred debris. With a lower setting, he swept the beam over the trails and pools of blood left in the corpses' wake. "That's four less we have to worry about," Lorken said, holstering his pistol. "We best get moving."

*****

Arsenc sat at the helmsman's post on the bridge of the *Stenox*. He outstretched his left leg, as it stiffened if left unused for any length of time. Brokov schooled him on the operation of the helm. He guided the ship carefully through the slight chop of the surf as the graying skies portended poorer weather to come. Brokov thought Arsenc had adjusted to the alien technology surprisingly well for an

Araxan. It often struck him how the Araxans' demeanor and civility exceeded their own.

"Brokov, what is that?" Arsenc asked, his eyes fixed on the green-lighted field of the radar screen on the helm's right console. Brokov stood from the captain's chair and stepped toward Arsenc's right shoulder, eyeing the eight scores of red dots clustered together in the corner of the screen. He touched the corner of the screen, expanding the dots into a larger image. They were clustered in a long, narrow oval shape.

"Looks like one ship, one hundred and sixty-three crew. Let's get a closer look. Twenty degrees starboard full ahead, thirty knots."

"Aye, aye, Captain."

Arsenc surprised Brokov with the Earther response. Obviously, he had picked up enough of the Earthers' jargon to mimic such a response. "Who taught you that term? Raven?" Brokov snorted.

"Lorken. He said to respond with 'Aye, aye' to every command."

"Did he mention the Jolly Roger and buried treasure as well?"

"Buried treasure? Where?" Arsenc's interest piqued.

"Never mind. Let's see whose ship that is."

*****

Lorken peered north through the dense foliage, examining the small village in detail. He counted seven makeshift structures with thatched roofs divided by a pathway running east-west. Four huts were on the north side of the pathway, and three on the south. The village was surrounded by a six-foot-high barricade made of trolla wood. The wall's only opening was on the west side of the village, where the pathway led several miles west toward the stone fort on the isle's opposing shore.

Sweeping his imaging device from one end of the village to the other, he spotted twenty-one pirates spread throughout. In the center structure on the south side of the village, he spotted two human forms bound to poles driven into the ground. Two pirates stood guard on the inside and two outside at the hut's north-facing entrance. The village would be expecting their patrol to return shortly, forcing them to hasten the rescue before the pirates grew suspicious.

*****

Arsenc transferred the magnified image onto the bridge viewport. The rain slapping the clear slanted glass was replaced by the image of a galley traversing the choppy sea. Brokov observed the double row of oars along its sides and the three square masts extending from the deck. Increasing the image magnification revealed no kingdom of origin, only a dark-gray banner atop its forward mast.

"Pirates," Brokov snorted. "They must be late to the party."

"What do you plan to do?"

"Sink 'em. But we have to be quick about it, because Raven's team is moving into position, and Zem will need to depart shortly for the rendezvous."

*****

The pirate galley followed the westerly current that flowed south of Molten Isle. The lookout atop the forward mast descried the rocky shore of the southeastern tip of the isle, north and west in the far distance. "Land!" he shouted over the gusty wind and choppy waves to his crewmates below. Sailors in leather tunics and skullcaps relayed the announcement as they rushed to the starboard side to see for themselves.

By midday, they hoped to be in the safety of the harbor and escape the coming storm. Every sailor feared being caught in open water amid a raging sea. The elated pirates were slow to discover the bluish-silver object bearing down from the north until a beam of blue light spewed from the object, striking the forward hull of the galley. Every eye drew wide, transfixed by the terrible beam sweeping along their hull from bow to stern at the waterline.

The sea poured into the lower hold as the ship listed severely to starboard. The screams of drowning men issued from the bowels of the dying vessel. Those above deck jumped into the choppy waves lest the sea claim them with their fated ship. The terrible azure beam swept the top deck of the listing vessel, ripping the deck asunder from stern to bow. Several sailors were caught in the laser's path, their flesh splitting where the beam passed. One lad who held tight to the center mast straddled the path of the beam. The carnage wrought around him drowned his dying screams as the laser passed through his chest with his lower half falling away.

Within minutes, the ship was gone, swallowed by the unforgiving sea. The few survivors bobbed in the mounting waves, helpless against the current's path. Any faint hope of reaching the shore was extinguished as the beam of blue light separated into smaller streams, each striking the survivors one by one, caving their skulls with deadly accuracy. None survived to tell their tale as the *Stenox* passed over their watery grave.

*****

The stone fort rested atop a vertical face of jagged rock that dropped ten meters into a maelstrom of swirling currents. Above the seawall, the fort rose another six meters of fitted stone and mortar. It was a simple four-sided structure with circled turrets to each corner that were two meters abreast. With the sea to the west, the fortress gate was centered on the east wall. Guards in gray mail and armed with crossbows patrolled the ramparts above and stood post at each turret. The fortress was built for protection from brigands, pirates, and petty thieves, but it was ill-suited for organized siege craft or armies of any sorts.

The pirates manning the gate paid little regard to the old man's wagon lumbering along the harbor road. Old Torz drove his wagon to the fort every morning and returned to the harbor every night, ferrying supplies to the fort and messages in each direction. With little vegetation atop the sea cliff surrounding the small fort, Torz's wagon was spotted far afield from the castle gate. The guards at the gate raised the portcullis as one stepped without to treat with the old wagon master.

"Did you bring the rum we asked for, Torz?" The guard's foul breath blasted from his mouth. He had a bent nose, broken teeth, and a face that even his mother might not have loved.

"I've got your rum, and I have salted moglo and fresh bread as well. Phew! When are you going to bathe, Gorlis? I could smell you a hundred paces off." Torz wrinkled his nose.

"I'll bathe when there are women about—women we can touch, that is," the guard said as he circled the stopped wagon, lifting the tarps that covered it. A cursory peek showed nothing out of sorts, but Gorlis wanted to confirm the rum in the inventory. After a brief inspection, he waved Torz on.

The wagon rumbled on, passing through the gate and across the small courtyard of the fort. The fort's walls were forty meters abreast. Barrack houses lined the east wall, one to each side of the gate. A small stable was built on the base of the south wall, and a larger structure lined the sea-facing wall with two guarded entryways at the ground level. Torz turned his wagon toward the storehouse on the north wall, where he unloaded his cargo every day. He backed his wagon into the alcove of the deep stone chamber as a slave wearing a brief brown tunic and an iron collar hammered about his throat rushed from the stable to help unload.

Once in the recess of the chamber, the slave was stunned by laser fire from the wagon. Raven, Argos, and Kato climbed out, shielded from prying eyes by the stone walls of the storehouse. Kato swept the stone structure on the west wall with the thermal imaging on the small device he drew from his jacket. "There!" He pointed out toward a subterranean chamber dug into the seawall.

Raven bound the slave's hands behind him and then tied his legs to his hands, leaving him trussed in the storehouse. "San Jacinto, this is Alamo," Raven said, speaking into his comm, which he drew from his jacket pocket.

"Alamo, this is San Jacinto. State your position," Zem's deep, metallic voice echoed in reply.

"We're in the fort, big fella. Ready for stage three. How far out are you?" Raven asked.

"I am at 72.4 meters from the seawall of the fortress. Will surface on your command."

"Can you be more specific on your location?" Raven asked.

"I am at 72.4169 meters. Is that specific enough for your human mind to comprehend?" Zem said, returning Raven's sarcasm in kind.

"That'll do. Alamo out." He closed the comm. "Boy, Zem is getting a little thin-skinned."

"He's figured out your sarcasm and is responding with the proper put-downs. Now he's just like the rest of us. That's pretty impressive for an artificial life-form." Kato grinned.

"I liked him better before," Raven lamented, turning off his comm.

*****

Lorken lifted his comm as it vibrated in his hand. A luminous green light filtered from the device, and he responded in kind by pressing his thumb to the base of the comm.

"What is that?" Miles asked, standing at his side under the shade of the trolla.

"That's our signal. Let's go."

Miles and Terin crept to the edge of the tree line that bordered the south side of the village as Lorken climbed the trolla to see clearly over the short wall circling the village. Terin carefully drew his father's sword, his breath holding as his pulse raced. He stared through the dense foliage across the open grass that separated the tree line from the wall. It was five meters from the wall to where they stood. No sentries were posted upon the wall to spy their approach.

He released a measured breath into the humid air as blue laser struck the base of the wall in a thick, heavy beam, buckling the timber and blasting a meter-wide hole in its perimeter. The strange power of his father's sword coursed his flesh, driving him forth with an intense desire to sate its thirst. The sword hungered for action as it stripped away Terin's inhibitions. He broke from the foliage, closing on the wall, with Miles hurrying to keep pace.

*****

She sat upon the hut's dirt floor with her hands bound painfully behind the pole at her back. Her long emerald gown was torn, ragged, and soiled. Her once golden hair was matted and clung to her sweat-drenched face. Two guards stood post at the doorway, each fixing a lecherous eye upon her and Princess Felicia. They boasted often of their sexual prowess and warned that if the ransom was not quickly paid, they would claim her maidenhood. Her abduction and her long trek to this forsaken isle taxed her strength. The misery of each passing day surpassed the day preceding.

Her tired blue eyes widened as a thin blue ray of light passed through the rear wall, striking one of her guards in the forehead. His eyes went out of focus as the beam burned a hole through his skull. His body went slack. Before he crumpled to the ground, a second beam struck the second guard below his left eye, melting his face where it struck. Before the second guard's body started to fall, she heard a powerful crash behind her.

A single blow of Terin's sword tore a wide hole in the hut's wall. The blade came quickly back to the ready as he broke through. Daylight bathed the dimly lit structure as his eyes quickly found the two slain guards and the girls tied to opposing poles, one to his left and the other to his right. The girl to his right brought her desperate blue eyes to his, taking his measure. The briefest of looks that passed between them seemed an eternal moment. She was breathtakingly beautiful. He failed to note her torn garments, matted hair, or the grime and filth of that wretched place. Her bright azure eyes were as deep as the ocean and seemed to pass through his mind as if his thoughts were translucent.

Her sudden apprehension abated as she met his eyes. Despite the savageness of his entrance, she quickly noted the grace with which he carried the dull-glowing sword that emitted faint hues of blue that matched the beam of light that felled her guards. She noted the handsome symmetry of his boyish face and the smooth, flawless contours of his arms and legs. *Who is he? Another pirate? No.* She could tell by his bearing that he was not of that nature.

With dizzying speed, he cut her bonds with a single stroke, careful not to break the supporting pole that kept the roof from collapsing upon them. Before she could bring her hands forward, he had freed her companion from the opposite pole. She then regarded a second man as he burst through the hole in the wall. Recognition lighted her smile as she beheld the familiar face. "Miles!"

"Princess Corry." He regarded her with a slight bow of his head. "Pardon my informality, but we dare not tarry. Come." No sooner had he spoken than the guards posted outside the hut entered with short curved swords drawn. Blue laser passed over Miles's left shoulder, striking one in his right breast. Terin's sword came swiftly upon the other, splitting his blade at the hilt before passing through his torso. The pirate's upper half slipped from his blade, falling to the ground in a sound akin to a sickly, gelatinous thud. The other pirate staggered forth despite his mortal wound, but Terin's blade took his left arm, then his head.

"Move!" Lorken swore as he watched the action through his rifle's scope. He told them to enter the hut and take a knee so as not to obstruct his view. They were on their own with the two guards that entered. "Aw, shi——" Lorken swore again as a dozen pirates converged on the hut from all directions north. With maddened cries, they sprinted toward the hut with curved swords, axes, or spears. Lorken had no time to aim. He simply pulled the trigger, pouring a steady stream of laser all around the structure.

Within the hut, the second girl came to her feet. Her reddish-black hair framed her sweetly rounded face and thin nose. She stared in awe first at Terin, then at Miles with her expressive green eyes. "Thank you," she said.

"You are most welcome, Princess."

"Felicia," she said, offering her name. She was the daughter of King Lichu, the Naybin regent.

"Princess Felicia." Terin regarded her. "We must hasten our…" A half dozen pirates burst through the entryway. Terin's sword danced in his hand, striking down the first to enter with a single blow. He moved to the second as the others swarmed past him. Felicia turned to flee as a pirate struck the back of her head with the flat of his blade, driving her into the dirt.

Miles sprang to her defense, striking the pirate's exposed left knee. The blow crushed the joint, crumpling the pirate to the ground as his leg gave out. Miles finished him with a thrust to the heart. Two others were quickly upon him. He parried one blade, moving to that pirate's side and keeping the other stacked behind his comrade. Miles's breath caught in the narrows of his throat, his eyes bulging in desperation. He was slowly cognizant of the arrow piercing the left side of his neck. He staggered a step before his opponents pressed their attack, striking him down with several repeated thrusts to his chest and stomach.

"Miles!" Princess Corry screamed. She reached for the nearest sword that lay upon the dirt floor. Lifting the curved blade, she struck one pirate from behind at the knees. He stumbled forward, reeling in pain. Terin finished the archer who struck Miles his fatal blow before turning back to slay the last pirate standing. The man raised his sword arm, but Terin's blow took the sword and the arm. He finished him in quick order, then spun about, searching for more foes.

The power of the sword began to wane, and his breath finally matched the pounding of his heart. The scene suddenly struck him as he beheld the mangled pile of human flesh littering the dirt floor. His breath eased as he discovered that no one else would follow. He turned at the sound of tearful sobbing as Princess Corry knelt over Miles's body. He quickly came to his friend's side, opposite the princess, as he stared into Miles's lifeless eyes.

"Who are you?" she asked kindly, lifting her watery eyes to his.

"I am Terin, Highness."

"Thank you, Terin. You are very brave."

"So are you, Highness, by the look of it." He smiled as he regarded the sword she wielded tightly in her right hand.

"I'm not brave. I just want to live," she answered. He thought her voice was the most beautiful thing he had ever heard. It matched the intelligence and understanding he saw in her eyes. She lowered her lips to Miles's face, pressing them to his forehead to honor his sacrifice. She then crawled over to Princess Felicia, who lay unconscious.

"Is she alive?" Terin asked, coming to his feet.

"Yes," she answered, turning her over.

Terin's brain was spinning, struggling to assuage the gambit of conflicting emotions with the loss of his friend, the beauty of the princess, and the peril that surrounded them, each vying for prominence. It was surreal, as if he was in a waking dream.

"We need to move. Now!" Lorken's deep voice barked as he crashed through the hole on the south wall. Corry craned her neck at the sound of his voice, her eyes wide with apprehension as they beheld the black-skinned giant towering over her. She quickly surmised by the strangeness of his clothing and the long object slung over his shoulder that he was the source of the blue light that felled her guards.

"Miles is dead," Terin said.

Lorken looked down upon their fallen comrade. "He deserves better than to be left to rot, but we can't take him. What about her?" He pointed to Felicia's prone form.

"She's alive but was struck on the back of her head," Terin explained.

"Who are you? Did my father send you?" Corry asked, not able to take her eyes off him.

"Lorken, and yes, if you are the Torry princess," he answered as he scooped Felicia into his arms and threw her over his shoulder. "If you want to take a sword, ditch that piece of junk you're holding and bring Miles's twin blades."

"What about the rest of the village?" Terin asked warily as Lorken walked toward the entrance.

"They're dead," Lorken said as he stepped without with Terin and Corry trailing behind. As they stepped into the clear, Terin spied a dozen corpses littering the narrow pathway that ran the length of the village, each a victim of Lorken's deadly aim.

"You can wield magic," Corry said, awed by Terin's sword and Lorken's strange weapons.

"Not hardly," Lorken said while leading them out of the village.

*****

"They're set," Kato said, stepping into the stone storehouse with the heavy cloak and hood concealing his Earth garb.

"Good. Let's move," Raven said as he and Argos drew cloaks over their heads. They stepped without, walking briskly across the courtyard and toward a locked iron door on the northern end of the structure that lined the west wall. They left the wagon driver bound within the storehouse.

Guards patrolling the walkways above paid mild interest to the three hooded figures moving below. It was a brief ten meters from the storehouse to the iron door. As they drew near, Raven leveled his pistol on the door's lock and fired. His boot followed, kicking the door ajar, and they quickly passed within. Discarding their cloaks, they narrowed their eyes in the dim light of the stone corridor that ran the length of the wall. Torches lined the inner corridor, bracketed into the wall and liberally spaced. They found no guards in the corridor. As Kato swept the area with the imaging device, he observed the two occupied cells in the floor below. Raven blasted a hole in the floor. The laser buckled the stone, caving a two-meter circle of rubble, littering the corridor below. "Who wants to go first?" he asked.

*****

A moment before. She sat upon the stone bed built into the wall with a shackle fastening her right ankle to an iron ring in the wall. Her hands were bound in front of her with close-fitting fetters biting painfully into her wrists. Her once lustrous ebony hair was knotted and disheveled. Her brief white tunic rested far above her knees, contrasting sharply with her olive skin. Her garments were soiled and stank. A bucket by her bedside reeked of her filth. But if she found her condition intolerable, she would not reveal it to the likes of him.

He stood at the entryway, appraising her with devil eyes that drank in the vision of her flesh. He was modest in height, standing sixty-four inches. His dark-reddish hair yielded to tints of silver gracing his temples. He wore a black leather tunic and a simple sword belt. He visited thrice a day, staring at her with lecherous eyes that made her want to gouge them out.

"It would be unfortunate if your father is not first to pay your ransom. If he fails to do so, I shall, of course, pluck your virtue before I claim your life, Princess," the pirate lord sneered.

"Any harm visited upon my person shall be returned a thousandfold, Monsoon. My father shall hunt you to the ends of Arax. He shall flay your flesh one tender morsel at a time, savoring your torments everlasting. As for my maidenhood, you are ill-equipped for such an undertaking!" Tosha admonished with upturned nose and dismissive golden eyes.

"I have been hunted for years, Princess, from the ruling families of Tro to the city states of the Casian League. None has found me, just as your father's net shall come up empty as..." His voice ceased at the sound of falling rock, the thunderous echo of crashing stone shaking the outer corridor. Monsoon gathered his bearings as he drew his sword, stepping toward the door before it burst open.

Tosha's eyes drew wide as a towering man with feral black eyes entered. A flash of blinding blue light sprang from a strange weapon in his right hand, striking Monsoon's sword arm. The pirate lord winced in pain, his sword slipping from his grasp. Recognition lit the big man's face as he beheld Monsoon. He stepped forth, his heavy boots pounding on the gray stone floor. He struck Monsoon about the head with his free left hand, knocking Monsoon to the floor as if he was a doll.

"Monsoon!" Raven growled, holstering his pistol as he knelt over him. Twisting Monsoon's neck with his right hand, he forced his face to the floor as he fetched a pair of binders from his jacket pocket and bound his hands behind his back.

"Raven!" Monsoon coughed. "Please, Raven. I...will pay you handsomely if you just leave me be."

"You don't have enough coin to buy back Cordi Kenti's life!"

"Who are you?" Tosha asked, taking in his full measure with her bright golden eyes. He shifted his terrible gaze to her, nearly taking her breath in the exchange. He was larger than any man she had ever known. He had a handsome square jaw and penetrating dark eyes that undressed her. His reddish-hued skin was unlike any she had ever seen. His strange clothes and weapons denoted him as an

Earther. She had never met one but had heard of their telling. "He called you Raven. Is that your name?" she asked as if speaking to an insolent child. Her voice was sultry and haughty, stirring his lust and anger in equal measure.

"Never mind my name. What's yours, girl?"

"Mind your tongue, savage. I am Princess Tosha, second guardian of the Federation of the Sisterhood and daughter of Tyro, emperor of the Benotrist Empire."

"You're Tosha?"

"Princess Tosha!" she corrected him.

"Well, Tosha, you're just the one I was hoping to find." Raven drew his pistol. She covered her face with her chained hands as he blasted the iron ring from the wall, freeing her leg.

"What…what are you doing, knave? You could have killed me!"

"If I want to kill you, all I have to do is snap your neck." He fired again, blasting the loose chain near her ankle, freeing her further from its length. He holstered his pistol and took the short chain connecting her wrists and snapped them with his bare hands. "A little gratitude wouldn't kill you, you know."

She glared at him. Was she angry at him or at herself for having been captured in the first place? Or was she angry for being so helpless when she first set eyes on him? She stood slowly, rising to her full sixty-five inches as she looked up into his penetrating dark eyes. Though she towered over most Araxans, she felt small and frail standing before him. She was a warrior born and reared and would never reveal her insecurities to one such as him. She walked past him to fetch Monsoon's sword from the floor, feeling her confidence return with steel in her hand.

"You don't need that, kid," Raven said, not unkindly.

"I'll not be denied the means to protect myself, and do not address my person so familiarly."

"I'll call you what I damn well please, little girl!" Raven growled.

"When my father enlisted your aid to rescue me, he did not intend for you to stain my honor with such insult!" she snarled.

"I'm not working for your father."

"My mother, then?"

"Her neither," he said, taking a step toward her as uncertainty played across her face. She looked nervously at the entryway, trying to work out an escape in her mind. Raven saw what she intended. "Go ahead. Run. I won't stop you, but if you really want to live, you'll have to come with me."

"What are your intentions?" She leveled the sword toward him.

"I need your help."

"My help?" She raised a suspicious brow.

"Raven! We're coming in!" Argos's deep voice boomed from the outer hall.

"Come on in," Raven answered, not taking his eyes from her.

Tosha shifted her eyes nervously to the entryway as Argos's massive frame passed within. Apes were a rare sight on the western shores of Arax. The fact that the Earthers were in league with the Apes was unsettling. She quickly noted a second Earther pass within. He was much smaller than Raven and with golden skin. His eyes were very strange with their corners arcing up at their edges. Tosha's attention quickly shifted to the woman who followed the two. It was her fellow captive, Princess Deliea, daughter of the Macon king. "Deliea," she whispered audibly.

"Tosha!" Deliea ran into her arms. "Oh, how I feared for you."

Tosha held her friend while still gripping the sword, pointing it toward the others while glaring at them with a distrustful eye over her friend's shoulder. "Have you seen the others?" Tosha asked as they briefly parted. Deliea nodded sadly.

"The others aren't here," Raven said bluntly. "Do it!" he commanded Kato. Kato squeezed a fist-sized oval-shaped object in his left hand. The ground shook violently, reverberating through the fort in deafening thunder. The women cringed, frightful of the thick stone that was surely to fall upon them.

"What have you done?" Monsoon shrieked as he lay bound upon the floor.

"We just destroyed your barracks," Kato answered dryly as the sea-facing wall of the chamber buckled outward before crumbling into the sea, leaving a three-meter hole in the wall. Tosha stared dumbfounded as daylight filtered through the hole. The smell of fresh sea air cleansed the noxious odor of her broken prison.

Raven stepped toward the wall, looking through the hole at the swirling currents below. The surf crashed violently into the vertical seawall ten meters below. Five meters from the cliff, he spotted the familiar bluish-silver shape of the *Spectre* rise to the surface.

In a moment's time, Zem opened the top hatch, and his imposing form straddled the open portal. Raven's heavy boots pounded the chamber's floor as he crossed the room and snatched Monsoon with both hands as if he was made of straw. Raven carried him back to the wall and tossed him through the hole. Monsoon screamed through his descent until he was swallowed by the surf. "You better go get him, Arg." Raven jerked a thumb toward the hole.

Argos mumbled incoherently, mimicking some complaint about getting wet. He tied down his pistol and slung his rifle across his back, then jumped through the wall. He quickly surfaced before snatching Monsoon's tunic collar as the pirate lord struggled to stay above the water with his hands bound. Argos towed him toward the submersible, and Zem pulled them aboard. Zem stowed the prisoner in the stern before climbing back into the pilot's seat while Argos remained topside to help the others.

Deliea came next, pausing at the precipice and casting a wary eye on the long drop. Raven grasped her arm, drawing her attention from the frightful plunge. She turned her expectant green eyes to his. "How far can you jump wearing that?" He regarded her tight-fitting gown of scarlet with golden folds pleated in its skirt, doubting if it was far enough to clear the cliff face without hitting the sheer cliff wall below.

"I don't kno—" Her words were cut off as he lifted her off her feet and tossed her clear of the wall. She screamed through her descent, her rich black hair billowing above through her fall.

"Go help her," Raven told Kato, who wasted little time following her through the hole.

Tosha stepped back with sword leveled at his throat. "You dare treat royal blood thusly?" she snapped. Her heart was racing, emotion overtaking reason as she stared at him intensely. Why was she so angry with him? His rough handling of Deliea was an affront upon her high birth, but time was pressed, and her hesitation at the wall required his decisive hand. But an inner voice warned Tosha to reveal no weakness to such a man.

"You're next," Raven said, eyeing the sword in her outstretched hand with amusement. She stood unmoved. He noted the swell of her bosom pressing taut against the white of her tunic and the fire in her yellow eyes.

"Are you gonna stab me, girl, or do you want to escape?" He held out his hand to her.

"Argh!" Cries rent the air as several pirates rushed into the chamber. Raven cleared his holster with lightning speed, blue laser cutting the fetid air. Tosha shifted, stepping into a guarding stance to meet the lead foe, but Raven cut him down. The pirate stumbled as the laser burned a finger-sized hole from his right breast to his left lung before passing through. Tosha thrust her sword tip through his throat, then kicked his gasping chest, freeing her blade as he fell backward. She withdrew a step, bringing her sword back into a guard stance, and assessed the remaining foes.

The others were piled at the entryway, their bodies riddled with laser fire, their blood pooling on the gray stone floor. Raven spun his pistol back to his holster. Quick as a thought, he closed on Tosha, snatched her arm, and twisted the blade free, tossing it aside. She struggled to free herself from his iron grip.

"Unhand me!" she snarled, regarding him darkly.

"Come on!" He dragged her toward the wall, ignoring her protest.

"You dare—"

"Jump, or I'll throw you like the other girl!" he growled, pushing her toward the hole.

She glared at him with dagger eyes, incensed by his roguish manner. She was not one to be pushed or browbeat. "Do not touch me!" she hissed, standing defiantly before him. Raven snatched her into his arms and attempted to throw her clear of the wall, but she wrapped her limbs around him as he tried to dislodge her. Voices sounded in the outer corridor, as the entire garrison was now alerted to their presence.

"Ow!" he howled as she bit his arm. Raven stepped toward the gaping hole in the seawall and jumped through with Tosha wrapped around him and arrows passing overhead as he dropped to the swirling surface. His legs pulled up before him as he fell, slamming him into the water on his back with Tosha clinging to his chest. He struck the surface emphatically, the blow taking his breath with its force.

Tosha broke free of him as they resurfaced. She swam toward the *Spectre*, where Kato awaited with outstretched arms to pull her aboard. Raven struggled to breathe as he slowly made his way toward the submersible. Arrows struck the surface around him as pirate archers took aim from the hole they had made in Tosha's cell. After pulling Tosha aboard, Kato drew his pistol, spraying the hole in the seawall above with laser fire. Raven struggled to climb aboard, his lungs gasping with shallow breaths. Within moments, they were inside the sub and away.

*****

"We'll stop here," Lorken said, setting Felicia upon the ground to catch his breath. They stood near the rock-strewn beach, just inside the thinning tree line. Tall frologs bowed toward the sea like devout worshippers. The green foliage contrasted sharply with the tortured gray sky and the rolling dark waves lapping the shore. Lorken removed the scanner from his jacket pocket, sweeping 360 degrees. "All clear. Now we just wait," he said.

"Wait? Wait for what?" Corry asked, her eyes shifting between Lorken and Terin.

"The Earthers are sending a ship for us, Highness." Terin threw a glance toward Lorken.

"When?" she asked.

"Soon," Terin answered.

"Thank you, Lorken," she said.

"You're welcome," Lorken said, his eyes scanning the sea as his shoulder leaned against a bending frolog.

"And I thank you, Terin." She offered a smile that nearly took his breath.

"It is my honor, Princess." Terin bowed his head with reverence.

"You are Torry?" she asked.

"Yes, Highness."

"You are new to the Torry Elite, for I do not know your face," she observed, her eyes running the length of him.

"I am not of the King's Elite, Princess," he said, lifting his blue eyes to hers.

"A mercenary, then?" she asked warily.

"No, Highness. I am sworn to the Torry throne. My sword and life are yours."

"How is a warrior of your skill overlooked for service in the King's Elite? In what role do you serve, Terin?"

"I…" He paused.

"Tell her, Terin," Lorken goaded, eager to see her expression when he revealed his true vocation.

"I am a scribe and apprentice to Minister Antillius, Highness."

"A scribe?" She nearly burst in laughter. "Surely you jest."

"It's true, Princess." Lorken laughed. "It's apparently a new form of diplomacy where you slice up the opposition before you negotiate. Terin's getting very good at that."

"A warrior-scribe. How unusual." The words rolled off Corry's lips lasciviously.

"Just a scribe, Highness, and not a very good one at that," Terin answered.

"A humble warrior-scribe. Even more interesting." She smirked.

*****

The *Spectre* glided neath the hull of the *Stenox*, slowing as it neared its docking latch above. Once the magnetic field was engaged, the submersible ascended into the hull of the *Stenox*. Within seconds, Raven had opened the top hatch of the sub and had climbed into the weapons room of the *Stenox*, Leanna and Brokov greeting them as they boarded. Leanna noted Raven's foul mood the moment he emerged through the hatchway.

Within moments, the others climbed out with Zem coming last, pushing the bound Monsoon ahead of him. They had called ahead, alerting Brokov of the identities of their passengers. Leanna noted the soiled garments of the two princesses. Their hair was matted and filthy, and their eyes bespoke the weary road they had traveled, but their disheveled appearance could not dim their natural beauty and proud carriage.

"Leanna, take these girls, clean them up, and see if you can find some better-smelling clothes for them," Raven said. Tosha stepped forth, standing her ground before Raven, her yellow eyes glaring up at him. She swung her right hand to slap his face, but he caught it in his own, squeezing her wrist painfully. "I wouldn't do that, Tosha," he warned.

"You soil my name on your tongue, savage. You will not address me so informally again. Am I understood?" she snarled.

"What are you gonna do, beat me up?" he mocked, pushing her away.

"I demand an audience with your captain!" she declared.

"Leanna, clean her up and escort her to the bridge. The captain will meet her there." The others exchanged a look as Tosha received the remark with a measure of satisfaction. "Zem, secure Monsoon. You better get going." Raven shifted his eyes to Brokov, who nodded and stepped without.

*****

Brokov guided the *Atlantis* as close to shore as possible as Lorken waded through the surf with Felicia over his shoulder. Terin followed, guiding the Torry princess and keeping her from losing her footing. The gray sky slightly opened, droplets of rain sprinkling around them. Within moments, they had climbed aboard the submersible and were underway.

*****

Raven stood alone on the bridge of the *Stenox*. Taking off his heavy jacket, he tossed it over the arm of his chair. He lifted his thick right arm to his face, examining the deep bite marks that Tosha had given him. If not for the thickness of his jacket, she would've torn right through his skin. Nonetheless, she left deep indentations on his forearm. "That little witch!" he growled to himself, turning as the door slid open behind him.

"Raven," Leanna's soft voice echoed as she stepped onto the bridge. She waved Tosha forth. "Come, Highness. The captain awaits." The rain was coming down at a steady pace, as Leanna's soaking hair paid tribute.

Tosha quickly entered as Leanna stepped without, leaving them alone on the bridge. The golden pools of Tosha's eyes narrowed at the sight of him. "You are the captain?" she said, visibly disappointed. He nodded affirm, taking her measure as her breasts swelled neath the fabric of her blue gown. Her black hair sparkled like obsidian. Leanna had tied it in a tail behind her. Her deep-olive skin shone smooth and glossy despite the rough treatment she had endured.

She was tall for a woman and Araxan. Her nose was narrow, and her high cheekbones bespoke her royal lineage. She stood bravely before him, the daughter of a queen and an emperor. Most men would have trembled in trepidation before Raven's towering form. His arms bulged from his shirtsleeves, nearly making her swallow a lump in her throat. She steeled her nerves, fixing her eyes to his.

"You said you needed my help," she said with her shoulders back and chin lifted.

"Yes, I do."

"If you require my assistance, then you should demonstrate the proper appellation of my title and deep respect for my station. I am of royal blood and demand—"

"Well, la-di-da. I don't give a damn what title you have, girl. On this ship, I'm the captain. If I give you an order, you do it. Is that understood?" he growled, staring down at her.

"If a male spoke to me with that tone in my mother's realm, I would castrate him!" she snapped back.

"If you think you can cut 'em off, go ahead and try!"

"They're probably so small that it would take a fortnight to find them."

"Keep pressing me, girl, and you'll get to know them personally." She slapped his face. Raven seized her hands, twisting them behind her back and holding them there with one hand. His other hand retrieved a pair of wrist binders tucked into the pocket of his trousers and fastened them on her.

"You dare—"

"I suggest you behave yourself." Raven pressed his right forefinger to her nose, warning her. Tosha bit his finger, and he pulled it away. He dragged her back to the captain's chair and sat down, pulling her over his knee and spanking her very hard. She refused to cry out from his stinging blows. She simply glared at him over her shoulder with consuming dark thoughts. Once finished, he brought her back to her feet.

"I will never help you," she hissed.

"I don't need your cooperation, girl. All I need is you."

"For what purpose?" she asked warily.

"Your father has my friend. I intend to trade you for him. Pray he is still alive, or you'll never see your home again."

"You kill me and my father shall hunt you down to the ends of the world."

"Don't worry your pretty head, Tosha. I don't kill girls."

"Then what fate would I suffer?"

"I'll have you stand where you are now and witness me sinking every ship in your father's navy and destroy every port in his realm."

"And then?"

"Then I return you to your mother."

"After you take my maidenhood, no doubt!" she sneered.

"And leave you begging for more? No, your maidenhood is safe from me."

"Why, you conceited—"

"Conceited? Humble ole me? You're the one making assumptions, girl."

"Would you stop calling me that?" she pleaded after a deep breath.

"All right. I'll call you Tosha, and you can call me Raven. Fair enough?"

She wasn't accustomed to any man treating with her as an equal. "Fair enough, Raven." His name came strangely to her lips.

"Turn around." She complied, and he freed her hands. "Behave yourself, or I'll put these back on you."

"You have my word as second guardian of the Sisterhood that I shall not attempt to do you harm or try to escape." As the only daughter of Queen Letha, Tosha was next in succession to the throne of the Sisterhood, which placed her as the second guardian of the realm.

"*Stenox*, this is *Atlantis*," Lorken's voice echoed over the comm.

Raven touched the console in the arm of his chair. "Go ahead, Lorken."

"ETA, three minutes."

"Received. Approach confirmed," Raven said, keeping his eyes trained on her. She felt his gaze upon her as she examined the rich detail of the bridge. She noted the bluish-silver walls, gray floor, and black chairs with silver arms. The slanted viewport provided a clear view of the ocean stretching endlessly before them as the stormy skies raged overhead.

"Your ship is impressive, but do you truly believe that you can destroy my father's entire navy if he fails to conjure your friend?"

"That's a fact."

"Who is this friend of yours? Is he an Earther like you or a mercenary?" She returned his stare with her arms folded under her breasts.

"He's a Torry soldier."

"A Torry? Why would my father have a Torry captive?"

"He was captured at the battle of Tuft's Mountain. The only detail I know is that he was taken north, probably to Fera."

"My father is at war with the Torry Kingdoms?" she asked, her eyes narrowing suspiciously.

"Yes."

"The Torry minister aboard this ship, did he hire you to capture me?"

"He contracted us to rescue the Torry princess. I decided to rescue all of you and use you to set my friend free."

"Then the Torries have declared war on my mother's realm as well?"

"No. My actions stand alone. The Torry minister wants me to set you free rather than piss off your mother."

"Must you be so crass?"

"They didn't hire me for flowery speeches."

"They didn't hire you to take me hostage either."

"No. They want me to set you free."

"Then why don't you?"

"I told you, I want my friend released."

"He must be quite a friend. You realize your life is forfeit if you do this? My father does not suffer such insults lightly."

"And neither do I. I owe Cronus my life. I'll be damned if I let him suffer at your father's hands. I always pay my debts."

"So do I, Raven," she said, not able to take her eyes off him. He was the most dangerous man she had ever known, even more than her father. For some strange reason, she felt safe in his company.

"I know you pay your debts by the teeth marks you left on my arm." He lifted his forearm for her inspection. She had forgotten. The marks looked painful, but she would not confess guilt.

"You will do well to remember that, Raven."

"Oh, I'll remember it, just like you'll remember the sting on your backside when you sit down."

She pursed her lips, blushing with indignation, recalling his abuse. She had never felt weak in her life until she was captured by Monsoon, but even then, she did not fear the pirate lord. She saw him for the weakling he was. With Raven, it was different. She felt helplessly weak before him. She was the second guardian of the Sisterhood. Men trembled at the mention of her name. Two realms bent their knees to her, yet in his presence, she felt she was a peasant. It was a feeling she did not like. He was handsome in a frightening sort of way, igniting emotions that she struggled to tame.

*****

The top hatch of the *Atlantis* opened as Lorken climbed out, emerging in the diving room on the port side of the *Stenox*. The others followed as Lorken lifted Princess Felicia's unconscious body from Brokov's outstretched arms below, Squid and Leanna greeting them as they emerged. Squid's eyes alit as Princess Corry stepped onto the firm deck with Terin beside her. "Welcome, Highness." Squid could not swallow his smile, bowing his head in reverence.

Corry placed her palm upon Squid's cheek, the warmth of her hand passing through his silver beard, warming his flesh. "My dear Antillius, thank you."

He lifted his gray eyes to hers, his smile widening further. "I did nothing to aid in your rescue, Highness."

"You are a poor liar, Antillius. Your scribe"—she turned a flirtatious blue eye to Terin, who stood beside her—"provided a far different telling. He spoke of the counsel you provided my father. The manner of my rescue was your endeavor. Any other course would have been folly. I regret the loss of Miles, though. He sacrificed his life in my rescue," she reflected sadly.

Squid's eyes moistened. Lorken had relayed Miles's misfortune once they were aboard the *Atlantis*. The Torry High Elite had been his guardian for many seasons. He was a brave and loyal soldier, and the realm was much weaker with his passing.

"These were his. Perhaps they should be returned to his kin." She handed him Miles's twin swords.

"Of course. They were handcrafted by Master Vantel." Squid sighed. The fabled Torg Vantel was King Lore's master of arms and commander of the King's Elite. He personally forged all the swords of the King's High Elite.

"Your Highness," Leanna said with a deep curtsy and with her head bowed. "Would you care to wash? I have fresh clothing if you like."

"Of course, Leanna. That would be lovely," Corry answered kindly. Leanna returned a strange look, wondering how the princess knew her name. "Terin speaks well of you," she said, answering her unspoken question. "He also spoke of Commander Kenti. May the fates watch over him and return him safely to you."

"Thank you, Highness." Leanna was touched by her kind words. "Come," she offered with her left arm extended toward the open door. Corry stepped forth. Turning back at the door, she fixed her sea-blue eyes at Terin. "I believe your apprentice is miscast, Antillius. I think we must find a more appropriate role for his unique skills." She stepped without with Leanna hurrying after.

Lorken followed Brokov, carrying Felicia in his arms. She still had not awoken since the blow to her head. Lorken carried her to the second crew cabin and placed her upon a lower bunk while Brokov examined her. Lorken left to join Raven on the bridge, leaving Brokov to attend to her. Arsenc and Zem were positioned in the engineering cabin while the others were eating or resting.

*****

Raven sat in the captain's chair with his fist in his chin, scanning the endless sea. The tortured skies above foretold the coming storm. The calm surface masked the coming tumult as the *Stenox* sped across the wine-dark sea.

"We may beat the storm back to Cagan," Kato said as he manned the helm.

"We'll make it with time to spare," Raven said.

"Are you certain?" Tosha asked, standing to his right, as she watched the white caps and black skies far off to the south.

"The storm's moving northward at a snail's pace."

"What's a snail?" she asked.

"It's a…a snail." He struggled to put words to the picture in his mind. "Ugh, never mind."

The door slid open as Lorken stepped onto the bridge, rain dripping from his hair and face as the door closed behind him. "Are we going to beat the storm?" he asked.

"Yeah. We'll be in Cagan by morning," Raven said.

Tosha was taken aback by Lorken's appearance. First, Raven, then Kato and Brokov and now Lorken. Lorken was as dark as Brokov was light. It seemed each Earther bore a distinct look that was as alien to one another as they were to Arax.

"Kato, escort Tosha safely below. Get her some food, and show her to bed," Raven said.

"I can see to my person, Raven," she countered. "I don't think I can sleep anyway."

"That wasn't a suggestion, Tosha. Go eat, and go to bed." She clamped her mouth shut, her eyes shooting him daggers. "Either move, or I'll carry you below over my shoulder!" After a time, she relented, following Kato off the bridge. "The helm's yours," Raven said to Lorken, waving an open hand toward the helmsman's chair.

"We lost Miles," Lorken said.

"I heard."

"And the Naybin princess is still unconscious."

"I heard that too."

"What was Tosha doing up here?"

"What any woman does: making my life difficult."

"She is a princess, you know. Did you expect any less?"

"She doesn't act like a princess!" he growled, thinking of the bite marks on his finger and arm.

"We got three more princesses down below."

"Wonderful," he moaned. "Step on it, will you? The sooner we reach Cagan, the sooner we can dump off three of them and their creepy ambassador too."

CHAPTER 10

Raven sat in the captain's chair with his fist in his chin, surveying the choppy sea with disinterest, his mind drifting elsewhere. Time was slipping away like a ship passing in the distance, ignorant of your pleas to slow or turn. With each passing day, Cronus's odds of survival waned. The *Stenox* glided over the chop, escaping the stormy seas that closed on Molten Isle. Cagan Harbor was one hour away at their steady pace as the sun crept over the horizon, bouncing off the rippling surface of the dark sea.

"Raven, check your radar forty degrees off port," Lorken said from the helm. Raven depressed the radar switch on his chair, raising the radar screen from the seat's left arm. Twelve miles north and east, he viewed the heat images on his screen. Tapping the radar, he expanded the image, revealing thirty clusters of heated images forming narrow oval shapes upon the surface.

"Looks like thirty warships by the number of crew," Raven observed.

"But whose?"

"What's their heading?"

"From the direction they're pointed, it looks like they're following the trade winds to Molten Isle."

"Hard to port, Lorken. Let's see who they are and what they want at Molten Isle."

*****

"Argh!" Princess Felicia moaned, slowly awaking.

"Rest easy, Your Highness," Leanna cautioned as she sat at her side upon the lower bunk of the second crew cabin. The Naybin princess had been washed and dressed in a simple gray shift, as her tattered gown was thrown away. Her green eyes fluttered open, struggling to take in her strange surroundings. Leanna's image was mirrored in her vision.

"Who—"

"I am Leanna Celen, Highness. You are aboard the *Stenox*. You were rescued by the Earthers. They are returning you to Cagan Harbor, where transport to your homeland shall be arranged."

"Why are there two of you?" she asked fearfully. Leanna fetched Brokov, who examined the Naybin princess at length. "What is wrong with my eyes?" She nearly burst into tears.

"Just relax, Felicia. You were hit on the back of the head. You might have had bleeding in the occipital region of your brain. That is why you are having double vision. Let's see if this corrects itself over the next hour. If not, I can attach a cerebral scanner to your cranium and relieve the pressure of any bleeding. Leanna will fetch you some food, and then you should continue to rest," Brokov said, placating her with his soothing tone.

*****

Princess Corry stood at the starboard railing of the first deck, staring out at the endless sea with the fresh spring air swirling her golden hair about her face. Her heart sang joyously at her liberation. She swore to never wear chains or fall captive ever again. She thought that she would perish on the isle or suffer unbearable ignominy, but fate intervened.

"Your Highness," Terin said, greeting her.

Corry turned to see Terin standing before her upon the deck. "Come stand beside me," she ordered.

Terin lifted his blue eyes to hers, matching the slight smile twisting the corners of her lips. He noted the swell of her bosom pressing upon the fabric of her white tunic and her slender-muscled thighs peeking below the skirt of her garment. Her beauty was disarming, and he was nearly struck dumb in her presence. "Minister

Antillius wishes to know if you are hungry, Highness. Kato has prepared breakfast for the crew if you would like to partake."

"In a moment, perhaps." She ran her eyes over him, head to foot and back again. "I would like to thank you again, Terin, for my freedom and my life."

"It was my honor, Princess, but it is to the Earthers we owe the greater debt. Without them, we—"

"Their intervention was fortuitous, but they were driven by monetary reward. You were driven by honor."

"I merely followed the course set before me, Highness. Honor was furthest from my thoughts."

"Your thoughts, perhaps, but not your heart. You are a fascinating person, Terin Caleph. I spoke with Arsenc about you. He tells a marvelous tale of you at Costelin, facing a host of gargoyles and felling them in great numbers. Minister Antillius spoke of your exploits at Tuft's Mountain, where you slew many more. Just months ago, you were a simple farmer. I wonder what adventure awaits you next."

"I told Raven that I will aid him in rescuing Cronus," he said, his eyes drifting over the rail to the open sea.

"And how does Captain Raven plan to free your friend?"

"He intends to use Princess Tosha to affect his rescue."

"Minister Antillius has approved of your absence from your duties to partake in such a venture?" she asked in an icy tone.

"Minister Antillius knows that I must follow my heart. He—"

"If it were my choice, I would forbid it!" she reproached him sternly. "But you have given your word to Raven, so you are bound to it. Antillius has told me that you must be allowed to follow where you feel yourself led. When you return from this next adventure, you are to come to Corell. My personal guards were slain during the pirate raid at Bansoch. I shall request your reassignment from Minister Antillius's service to my personal guard."

"Princess, I am not a warrior. You would be better served…"

She placed a finger to his lips, quieting him. "I was not asking. I was telling. You shall serve as my personal guard. I may choose whomever I wish from any Torry save the King's High Elite. Since they place no such claim on you, then I am free to choose. I have already spoken with Antillius on this matter, and he has acquiesced. You can save your friend, then return to me."

*****

The Benotrist fleet traversed the waters of the Cagian coast, their narrow bows slicing the white caps as the sun hung in the eastern sky. Admiral Kruson surveyed the sea ahead, his eye fixed intently on the horizon, hoping to reach Molten Isle two days hence. They had sailed without respite since the messenger arrived from Tinsay instructing them to sail with all haste to Molten Isle to affect the rescue of Princess Tosha. Most of his heavier galleys he left behind, taking only his swiftest vessels.

They skirted the southern Yatin coastline, sped by the wind and lash. The oar slaves suffered the cruel ministrations of their overseers, who drove their charges to keep pace. Large crossbows lined the outer edges of the ships' main decks, each capable of hurling large flaming arrows into enemy vessels. Heavier ballistae were set farther back, capable of hurling balls of gelatinous fire from afar. Rams the length of a man were affixed to the prow of each ship just below the waterline.

Admiral Kruson was a thin, weathered man in his sixth decade. He served fifty years at sea, first as a deckhand for his Menotrist overlords, then as a revolutionary in Morca's revolt, rising through the ranks to become admiral of the Benotrist 2nd Fleet. The spray of the ocean slapped his thick leather tunic as he nervously scanned the sea to his south and east. He feared the Torry Navy awaiting him in these perilous waters, catching him without his heavier galleys in a full engagement.

The Torries had enough magantors to spy every approach to Cagan. The prospect of avoiding their fleets and reaching Molten Isle before them seemed fated. His own magantor carrier was too cumbersome to bring along, as he was forced to sacrifice reconnaissance and power for speed. Only the magantor used by the emperor's agent was available to him. The giant bird was perched on the deck behind him.

"Admiral! Look!" a scout perched upon the crow's nest above shouted below. Kruson gazed south and west from the port side of his flagship. There in the distance, a small bluish-silver object sped across the surface, its hull blending with the hue of the sea.

*****

"A catapult on a field of gray." Lorken observed the banner blowing fiercely above the mast on the lead ship.

"The Benotrist 2nd Fleet," Raven said, standing beside him at the helm, both looking at the magnified image on Lorken's screen.

"How did Tyro get a fleet here so quickly?" Lorken wondered aloud.

"I don't know, but we seem to have beaten them by a whisker. Send a warning shot across the lead ship's bow and pull to within three hundred meters. I'll call below and have Tosha come to the bridge."

*****

The narrow beam streamed from the bow of the *Stenox*, slicing the misty morning air, impacting the surface, shy of the lead ship's bow. A wall of vaporized seawater sprayed the fore deck of the ship, the Benotrist sailors staring in wonder at the beguiling sight. Admiral Kruson ordered several ships to break ranks, sending them toward the strange vessel. He would attack quickly while his men still had the nerve and before their bewilderment turned to panic. "Prepare to attack!" The rally cry went out to the fleet.

*****

Arsenc escorted Tosha to the bridge as the Benotrist warships closed on the *Stenox*. Her eyes were immediately drawn to the familiar ships in the viewport as the crews readied flaming ballistae.

"Your father's fleet," Raven said from the captain's chair to her right as she stepped onto the bridge.

"Wh…" She struggled to put her question to words.

"They're headed to Molten Isle, apparently to rescue you."

"What are your intentions?" she asked warily.

"That depends on them." Raven returned his eyes to the sea ahead as flaming balls hurled from the nearest vessel yet falling short of the *Stenox* and swallowed by the sea. "And there's the answer. Light 'em up, Zem!" he commanded into the comm.

"Affirm," Zem acknowledged from the weapons room of the first deck.

Blue laser streamed from the bow in thick bands, sweeping the length of the offending vessel's bow at the water level. The ship buckled as if run aground on a jagged rock. Water flooded the fore section of the galley, the sound of snapping timbers mixing with rushing waves and screaming oar slaves. The laser lifted, running over the fore deck and masts with devastating effect. Heated braziers broke asunder, spreading flames over the deck as the ship started to list.

"Stop!" Tosha pleaded, staring desperately into his dark eyes.

"Hold your fire, Zem," he spoke into the comm.

Tosha returned her eyes to the sea, watching desperately as the crippled vessel listed severely with its bow sticking profoundly into the sea and stern lifting above the surface. The other Benotrist war galleys slowed, their oars lifting above the waves, their captains uncertain of direction and wary of the *Stenox*'s terrible power.

"We can sink every ship in this fleet with little effort, Tosha. I won't do it unless they keep shooting at us. The choice is theirs," Raven said, hoping this demonstration would make her mindful that his boasts were not hollow. She now knew that he would sink her father's entire navy if they did not give Cronus over.

*****

The sound of Nels Draken's soft-soled boots echoed dully as he strode across the wooden deck of the Benotrist flagship. He wore brown leather trousers with crisscrossed leather folds running from hip to boot. Thick leather mail overlapped a black tunic. Studded guards graced each forearm and elbow, and a black cape billowed behind him. Twin swords hung from each hip. He was well into his fourth decade with a wind-worn face, even-set gray eyes, and sand-colored hair. A vicious scar ran the length of his left cheek.

A mercenary by trade, he was a renowned swordsman and cunning warrior. He had cast aside his independence and taken up the cause of the Benotrist emperor. He now ranked seventh among Tyro's High Elite, a position of unprecedented prestige and a future full of possibilities. He stepped to Admiral Kruson's side, surveying the carnage wrought by the *Stenox* with an air of feigned disinterest. "I warned you, Admiral, that dealing with the Earthers must be undertaken with great care."

"My ship!" Kruson threw up his palms toward the sinking vessel. He clenched his jaw tightly, his eyes burning with fury.

"Raise the blue flag, Admiral, before you lose another."

"You counsel me to treat with them?" He gritted his teeth, pointing his left forefinger toward the *Stenox*.

"I know their captain well. I will treat with him. He might be pliable."

"And if he is working with the pirates?"

"Raven hates Monsoon. He would never work with him. In fact, he desires the pirate lord's head. Nay, our Earth friend has more likely been contracted to rescue one of the other princesses."

"And if he does, it means certain death for Princess Tosha. Monsoon was adamant that only the first to deliver the ransom would be spared!"

"If Raven is in another's employ, he will beat us to Molten Isle. Perhaps we can outbid the contract or offer a joint rescue attempt. I'm certain he has little desire to offend our emperor."

"So be it, Draken. Raise the blue flag and lower the skiff!" he ordered his crew.

*****

Tosha stared helplessly as the Benotrist galley slipped beneath the waves. The heads of the surviving crew bobbed amid the surf, as no galley rushed quickly to their aid.

"They're raising a blue flag," Lorken said.

"What does that mean?" Raven wondered.

"It is a sign of truce. Are you truly so ignorant?" Tosha shot him an incredulous look.

"Yeah, he is." Lorken shrugged.

"Who won Super Bowl 236?" Raven asked her.

"What?" She lifted a curious brow over a golden eye.

"The Detroit Lions beat the Moscow Bears 46 to 24. I guess you're as ignorant as I."

"What are you babbling about?" she asked.

"I asked you a question about my world, and you couldn't answer. I guess that makes you a moron." She just stared at him as if he had grown a second head.

"Their flagship lowered a smaller craft into the water," Lorken said, relaying his observation. "It likely means they intend a parlay."

"Don't tell me they're gonna try to row all the way here?" Raven asked, shaking his head.

Lorken eyed the small craft as the dozen crew dipped oars. "It appears they are."

"We don't have time for this. Close the distance."

"If I do, we will be surrounded by their fleet, Rav. You really want to get that close?"

"What are they gonna do, throw fireballs and little arrows at us? Let's just hurry this along and hear what these clowns have to say," he said, dismissive of the threat they posed.

"Is there no limit to your arrogance?" Tosha reproached, her arms folded neath her breasts.

"I'm sorry if I lack your humility," he said, rising from his chair to stand beside her. "But it's hard to be humble when you're me." She rolled her eyes. "Arsenc, go below and have your people stay out of sight while we talk with the Benotrists," Raven said. Arsenc nodded his agreement, then stepped without.

"Rav, take a look at who's on that boat," Lorken said, expanding the image on his view screen.

Raven stepped to Lorken's shoulder, his curious eyes quickly hardening as he spied the familiar face with the scar running the length of its left cheek. "Draken!" he mumbled under his breath. "What's he doing aboard a Benotrist warship?"

"Perhaps they contracted him to help rescue Tosha. He is familiar with Monsoon," Lorken said.

"No." Raven shook his head. "They didn't have time to fetch him from the east. He must've been in their company before Monsoon's raid."

"For what purpose?" Lorken asked. "Nels Draken is a free sword. What reason has he to be with Tyro?"

"Do you know, Tosha?" Raven craned his neck to her.

"I do not know this man."

Raven was struck with a notion. "Tosha, I have an offer for you."

"You desire a parlay before your parley?" She lifted an eyebrow.

He turned completely to her, stepping close, placing his large hands on her shoulders, staring deeply into her golden eyes. The intensity of his gaze made her chew her lower lip as she tucked it between her teeth. "If we release you at Tinsay Harbor, will you go to Fera and free my friend? If you do, then I will give you Monsoon to do with as you please. This way, you and your father save face. All I want is my friend's freedom. Can you do this?"

The gentleness of his voice disarmed her. She gazed up into his dark eyes that penetrated her soul, tearing through her mental veils as if they were translucent. "I will save your friend, Raven."

"On your word?"

"I avow," she answered.

He studied her countenance, confirming her sincerity. If she was lying, she hid it well. It didn't really matter. If she did not free Cronus, he would still destroy her father's navy and coastal cities. Her acquiescence was the only peaceful way to achieve Cronus's freedom and perhaps the only way, peaceful or otherwise. "All right. Stay here." He stepped toward the entryway. "Lorken, have Argos join me at the stern."

*****

The *Stenox* glided over the surface of the sea like a block of ice along a wet, smooth stone. The small skiff was a mere two hundred yards from the Benotrist flagship as the *Stenox* drew up alongside it, port side to port side. A dozen Benotrist sailors with brown leather tunics and caps lifted and retracted their oars as Nels Draken stood in the skiff's center with an open palm facing the *Stenox* to show he bore no threat. A dozen war galleys surrounded them at a fair distance, wary to engage the unknown power of the Earthers' vessel. The Benotrist sailors stared with slackened jaws at the wonder of the *Stenox*.

"The one with the scar on his face may board. No others!" Argos's rough voice echoed, his rifle leveled on the skiff. Hands went to hilts at the sight of the large gorilla.

"Tell your boys to not even flinch!" Raven warned.

Nels Draken's eyes shifted to Raven's towering form standing at the stern of the second deck with his pistol aimed at his head. "No one move!" he commanded his crew. "Stay your hand, Raven. These men are under the banner of truce. Might I come aboard?"

"I'll have words with the Benotrist admiral, not his hired lackey."

"My authority exceeds the admiral's, old friend. It is I with whom you should speak."

"What authority?"

Draken slowly turned, revealing the back of his black cloak for Raven's purview. Across the billowing black folds were sewn a sword and whip intertwined, dividing a sun and moon in gold stitching. Draken completed his turn, facing Raven, craning his neck up to see the large Earther standing on the deck above. "I stand seventh among Emperor Tyro's Elite. I have set aside the path of a free sword and have sworn my oath to my emperor."

"Tyro must have low standards."

"You are still angry with me I see, old friend."

"I haven't been on this planet long enough to have any old friends, and if I did, you wouldn't be one of them."

"You wound me, Raven." Nels smiled falsely. "Permission to come aboard?"

"Come aboard, but only you." Nels went to the bow of his small skiff, tying the bow to the *Stenox*'s port railing, and then climbed aboard. "Drop your weapons on the deck!" Raven commanded from above as Argos backed a step, keeping his rifle trained on Draken's chest. Draken unsheathed his twin blades, setting them carefully on the deck. "Your daggers you keep on your back and boots," Raven reminded him.

Nels shook his head with a smirk. "You don't trust me very much, do you, Raven?"

"Trust gets you dead dealing with the likes of you, Nels. Go ahead and search him, Arg." Argos slung his rifle over his back and stepped forth, placing his massive, furry hands on Draken's shoulders, nearly jerking him from his feet. He quickly found a blade hidden within Draken's cloak and discarded it on the deck. After searching him head to boot, he shoved him toward the ladder.

"What are you doing?" Draken stopped at the ladder as Argos gathered up his weapons and tossed them over the starboard side of the ship.

"You should've left them behind." Raven smiled. "Don't worry about it, Nels. I'm sure your new master will pay for their replacement. Come on up, and we can talk about your princess."

Nels quickly climbed the ladder to the second deck, his eyes warily fixed on Raven, who stood at the door of the bridge with his right hand resting on his holstered pistol. "By your words, I am led to believe that you have been contracted by a rival kingdom. Have you been asked to carry the ransom demands or to affect a rescue? Emperor Tyro will surely double whatever you have been offered if you would—"

"Save your breath, Nels. I already rescued your little princess. She's inside."

"Princess Tosha is aboard this vessel?" Draken's eyes drew wide, taking a step forward.

Raven's eyes grew suddenly feral as Draken drew close. His right fist jabbed Nels in the chest, knocking him from his feet. Raven towered over him. "That was for Cordi Kenti. Don't think I've forgotten!"

"I didn't kill him, Raven." Nels coughed.

"You enabled his killers. That amounts to the same."

"I was deceived. That doesn't make me culpable." Nels came to his feet, wary that Raven might strike him again.

"Deceived? I warned you about taking prisoners. You ignored that advice, and Cordi paid for the mistake." Had any Araxan struck Nels Draken, Nels would have beaten them senseless, but fighting Raven was futile. "Come on in. She's inside." Raven waved him on.

Nels stepped carefully past Raven as he entered the bridge. He had never met the Benotrist princess, but the young woman standing beside Lorken bore some resemblance to the emperor. Her hair was as black as a starless sky and rolled thickly to her shoulders. Her skin was flawless olive, and bright golden eyes stared intently through him. "Princess Tosha?" he inquired.

"Lorken says you are Nels Draken. Is this so?"

"Yes. And you?"

"I am Princess Tosha, daughter of Tyro and second guardian of the Sisterhood."

Nels knelt at her declaration. "Your Highness, I am seventh among your father's Elite. I have been so named to this high post since your last visit to your father's court."

"If you are so named, then you must bear a symbol of your station."

"A signet, Highness." Nels drew a golden coin from his pouch that bore the symbol of Tyro's Elite: a sword and whip intertwined dividing a sun and moon. "My apologies, Highness, but I must verify that you are indeed who you claim. Do you know who stands highest among your father's Elite?"

"Morac, son of Morca, is first among my father's Elite. The gargoyle champion Kriton is second—"

"He is now third, Highness, but you would not have known since a recent addition has supplanted him."

"And who would that be, Elite Draken?"

"A name I dare not say in present company." He eyed Raven and Lorken warily. Raven found the comment out of place, suspicious of what he meant. "Fortune lights our journey, Highness, as our dear Earth friends have affected your rescue. If you would accompany me to our flagship, we can—"

"I shall remain with Captain Raven, Elite Draken. He shall accompany me to Tinsay. From there, he shall serve as my escort to Fera, where he shall be my most honored guest at my father's court and be aptly rewarded for his brave deed." Lorken and Raven shared a look but held their tongues.

"Are you certain, Your Highness?" Nels came to his feet as she bade him rise.

"Yes. I shall reach my father's court with greater haste in Raven's company than on our slower-moving galleys."

"I have a magantor saddled and ready upon our flagship—"

"Nay, Draken. Raven shall escort me to the palace. If you wish, you may join us there. Return to Admiral Kruson and convey my wishes and gratitude for his timely intervention."

"As you wish, Highness." Draken bowed and withdrew. Raven signaled Lorken to follow Nels and see him off the ship.

"What was that?" Raven growled.

"Something vexes you, Raven?"

"Who said anything about escorting you all the way to the Black Castle? How stupid do you think I am?"

She stepped nigh, placing her right palm upon his heart. "My father shall reward you for my rescue, Raven. If you do not accompany me, he shall think your efforts of less worth and little regard. You are brave and bold, and it befits your nature to declare your great deed before the black throne. My father respects power above all else. If you deliver me safely to him in person, your demands shall have a stronger claim."

"And what assurance do I have that I won't wake up with a dagger in my back?"

"I avow that no harm shall befall you in my father's court, Raven. You saved me from that accursed fortress. I was angry when I first saw you, for I was ashamed to be seen so helpless by one such as you. I am a proud woman, Raven, and I do not suffer such weakness lightly. I haven't truly thanked you." She gazed intently into his dark eyes. She then did what she had wanted to do when her eyes first beheld him.

She reached up and pressed her lips to his, closing her eyes as they joined in an emollient embrace. He lifted her off the floor while she wrapped her legs around his hips as he returned the fervor of her kiss. Their emotions raged in a maelstrom of lust, anger, and passion, forging an unchecked tempest sweeping over them like a raging sea. "No," Tosha whispered, pushing him back a step as her feet touched the floor, catching her breath. "I..." She struggled to convey her thoughts, wondering just what her true thoughts were.

"I don't understand," he said. "All I know, Tosha, is that I trust you even less than I trust Draken."

"If you escort me to Fera, I promise to protect your friend from all harm. He will be safe."

Raven thought for a long, quiet moment. "All right. I'll come." He sighed.

"It is for the best."

"I warn you, Tosha. If this is a trick, I promise that I won't die alone."

*****

Cronus knelt in the muddy soil. His shoulders ached from his hands being bound behind him, the unforgiving metal biting painfully into his wrists. The muscles of his legs trembled from misuse, as they marched countless miles each day, crossing the rugged wilds that separated the Benotrist realm from the northern approaches to Rego. They passed countless villages that were once vibrant but now desolate and lifeless.

The gargoyles returned whence they came, passing through the desolation they had wrought on their journey south. The gargoyle legions swept over the land like a malignancy, devouring all in their wake. They ate livestock, trees, crops, grass, and people. Black-crusted soil and debris covered the landscape as far as the eye could see. Hills of mud rolled one into the other. Forests of scorched trees twisted like tortured spirits.

Village after village lay barren with only lonely chimneys protruding from the ground like gravestones for dead homesteads. Carka birds circled lazily above, ever searching for bones to pick, yet every skeleton Cronus had seen was bleached. They stood out among the ashes like white beacons upon a dark sea. His men now numbered ten besides himself. Some had succumbed to gargoyle abuse while others succeeded in taking their own lives.

Those who had killed themselves had found sharp-edged stones and cut into their wrists during their brief rest periods. Since then, the gargoyles chained their wrists together with their palms facing outward. The gargoyles were desperate to return their captives to their emperor alive, hopeful that they would take the brunt of his fury, sparing them his full ire. They constantly struck their captives' hands, ensuring they were empty. They caught one soldier named Vorin Kleftus trying to cut his wrist with the sharp edge of a flat stone. They dragged him before his fellows and cut off his fingers one at a time as the others looked on with forlorn faces. There was no escaping their fate, for even death was beyond them now.

Cronus shifted painfully as he knelt in the muddy soil with its small stones digging into his knees. His men knelt in a line to his right, connected by the chain around their necks. Their tunics were ragged and stank of piss, feces, and grime. Ten thousand gargoyles surrounded them, the last vestiges of the four legions sent to Rego. General Vicon stood some distance before them, his blood-red tunic contrasting with his shiny, taut black flesh. His eyes blazed feral as scores of Benotrist cavalry flooded into their midst. These were the gargoyles' human allies, traitors to the human race. They wore gray breastplates over red tunics with iron greaves and black helms, dark eyes peering through their narrow slits.

"General Vicon!" the Benotrist commander hailed.

"Commander Corg!" Vicon hissed.

"I shall take you and a small contingent of your troops on ahead of your main force. I will take you to a temporary magantor base north of here, where your journey to Fera can be expedited."

"I have eleven prisoners I mean to deliver to the emperor. They are responsible for the ruination of our legions, and I shall see them suffer as humans have never suffered before!" Vicon's eyes blazed like the midday sun.

"Then let us not keep the emperor waiting."

CHAPTER 11

The *Stenox* caused an uproar when it stopped on the south bank of Cagan Harbor, beside the palace grounds. Hundreds of garrison soldiers flooded the palace green that ran from the massive structure to the river's edge. A hundred archers lowered their bows once Minister Antillius disembarked, stepping away from the *Stenox* and identifying himself to the palace garrison commander. Lorken navigated the dangerous waters near the palace, guiding the vessel between jagged stones that jutted away from the bank but below the waterline. The massive stones were placed to rip the hulls of any ship attempting to approach the palace outside of authorized areas. The *Stenox* had little difficulty passing between such impediments and stopped relatively close to shore with its starboard side facing the palace green and its port facing the bay.

Raven stood on the starboard side of the second deck with his forearms resting on the low wall that circled the exposed stern half of the deck. He observed the Torry minister conversing at length with a commander dressed in a sky-blue tunic and silver breastplate and greaves. The fellow wore a bright helm that covered his head above his eyes. Squid kept pointing behind him toward the *Stenox* as he explained the situation to the commander.

"Hurry it up, old man. We don't have all day!" Raven grumbled to himself.

"Must you always be so irreverent?" Tosha scolded, standing to his right.

"All he has to do is tell them we've returned their little princess, have her run out and join them, give us our money, and we can be on our merry way," he explained, annoyed with the whole thing.

"Are you truly so ignorant of royal protocol?" she asked incredulously. "Corry is the princess of the Torry realms. She cannot merely climb off this ship and run into the palace. That would be an affront to her father's house. She must be properly received."

"Properly received?" He made a face.

"Yes. The commander of the palace guard shall have to inform the highest-ranking official in the palace of Princess Corry's arrival. That will most likely be Vintor Ornovis, the regent of Cagan. He will then formally acknowledge the princess as his superior regent and invite her to the palace."

"Sounds like a big waste of time," Raven argued.

"Are royalty treated so disrespectfully in your homeland?" she inquired.

"We don't have royalty where I come from, Tosha."

"Truly?" she asked, astonished.

"Yeah, truly."

"Then how could your people have developed such wondrous technology without the guiding hand of monarchy?"

"Guiding hand of monarchy?" He nearly burst in laughter. "What good are monarchs? Royals are like leeches sucking on the public treasury."

She was ill amused by his remark. "Then how, pray tell, do you organize your society if not by monarchy?" she asked darkly.

"We choose our leaders by popular vote."

"So you determine the wisest of your people to lead you?"

"No. The wisest don't want the job. We usually choose between two idiots who cater to the masses with lavish promises that are never fulfilled. Then after a six-year term, we replace them with another idiot. It's a wonderful system."

"I can never tell when you jest or when you speak true." She half smiled.

"Most humor is grounded in truth, Tosha."

They both returned their gaze to Squid, who was returning to the *Stenox*. The commander of the palace garrison hurried off in the opposite direction—to fetch the palace regent, most likely. He quickly emerged from the palace accompanying a silver-haired dignitary wearing golden robes. A small army of advisers and courtesans surrounded the richly dressed fellow. The man stopped mid distance between the *Stenox* and the pillars that surrounded the base of the palace. Soldiers lined the palace green, forming two lines facing each other from where the dignitary waited before the *Stenox*. Squid then emerged from the first deck, accompanying the Torry princess.

Corry paused at the stern of the ship to address Minister Antillius. "Fetch Terin. He shall serve as my escort to the palace."

"As you wish, Highness." Squid bowed, then withdrew to the inside of the ship. He reemerged after a short respite with his apprentice in tow. Squid examined him head to foot, brushing lint from the shoulder of his tunic and straightening his sword belt properly above his waist. "Not exactly formal attire, my boy, but it shall suffice." Squid regarded his sand-colored garment. "I know I have not explained the protocols of court, Terin, or the expectations of a royal escort. For now, just follow the princess at three paces. When she stops to treat with Regent Ornovis, you are expected to kneel. After the official greetings are exchanged, you shall follow her into the palace and do as she bids. Do you understand?"

"Yes," Terin said, feeling a little awkward with such formality.

"This is a great honor, Terin. Royal escorts are usually high-placed ministers or members of the King's High Elite, of which several are present in the palace. The princess has passed them over for you."

*****

Terin helped Princess Corry step ashore, following her between the two columns of Torry soldiers, who knelt as she passed. Trailing the Torry princess was Princess Felicia, escorted by Minister Antillius, and Princess Deliea, escorted by Kato. Corry wore a simple tunic with Miles's twin sword upon either hip. Her cross-laced sandals stepped deftly over the aqueous grass field, stopping short of Regent Ornovis, who greeted her warmly as Terin knelt.

"Welcome to Soren Palace, Your Highness. I stand as second during your visit," Vintor Ornovis greeted as he knelt while the assemblage surrounding them knelt in kind.

"Rise, Regent Ornovis. I am grateful for your courtesy. We have journeyed far and suffered great privations before our deliverance."

"The news of your capture was ill received, Highness. Our fair city mourned your plight and rejoices that you are returned to us unharmed."

"The House of Lore is grateful for your kind words. I wish to welcome our esteemed guests to Cagan, Princess Deliea and Princess Felicia. They were my fellow captives on Molten Isle." At this pronouncement, Felicia and Deliea stepped forth, coming to Corry's side, as Vintor Ornovis bowed in kind, kissing their proffered hands. Squid and Kato drew up beside Terin and knelt.

Raven shook his head at his comrade's deference. "You don't approve?" Tosha asked him, observing the proceedings from the second deck of the *Stenox*.

"Kato can do as he pleases, but I wouldn't bend my knee for anyone." He snorted.

"You would if you were my escort. I would insist upon it." She smiled, the breeze blowing her hair across her face. She smoothed the ebony folds of her hair behind her ear, her eyes narrowed against the sun.

"Then I suggest you pick a different escort. I don't care for formalities."

"Actually, this ceremony is quite informal in compare to my mother's or father's realms. It is customary in Bansoch for all to kneel with both knees before royalty. In my mother's queendom, men are further required to place their heads upon the ground in her esteemed presence."

"Sounds like a lovely place. Remind me never to go there."

"Once we free your friend from my father, perhaps you could visit my mother's realm. You could be my honored guest." She smiled.

"The only way you could bring me to your mother's kingdom is if I'm a corpse. And why are men required to further abase themselves in your mother's presence?"

"In the Sisterhood, women hold the power, and men serve. We honor the sacredness of life and those who bring life into the world. The bearing of children is a sacrifice that men can never know or appreciate."

"So the stories are true about women ruling your island?"

"Of course," she said as if he just said the sun brought light.

"Women in charge? That's a dumb idea."

She gave him a dark look before returning her eyes to the proceedings afar. "Your arrogance is without peer," she icily said.

"You're not so humble yourself, Princess."

"You have much to learn before I can present you to my father. The formalities of the Benotrist court are intricate and—"

"Save it, Tosha. I don't give a damn about the formalities and customs of your father's realm."

"Do you wish to free Cronus or not?"

"That's the general idea," he conceded.

"Then you must swallow your pride and conduct yourself in the same manner as any other guest of Fera."

"I'm not kneeling, Tosha, not to your father or anyone else. I'll speak to your father man to man and eye to eye. I'm going there under your counsel by offering him the carrot instead of the stick. If he refuses to see reason, then I'll use the stick, and I know just where to put it."

"Carrot? What is a carrot?"

"It's a—well, it looks like. Never mind." Tosha cringed at the thought of Raven defying her father in his court. Surely he must not think such an act would in any way achieve his objective.

*****

Princess Corry turned, slightly lifting the fingers of her left hand. Squid rose on her signal, motioning Terin and Kato to do likewise. "Here are three of my brave rescuers, Regent." Corry waved them forth.

"I am honored to receive them," Vintor Ornovis said.

"Regent Ornovis." Squid bowed his head briefly.

"Minister Antillius." Vintor smiled at the sight of his old friend. "I see you have added rescue missions to the duties of the ministers' council."

"No, my friend, I merely counseled our king to consider his alternatives. He wisely chose to employ the services of our Earth friends. It was they, along with King's Elite Miles Standarn and my apprentice, Terin Caleph, who planned and conducted the rescue," he explained.

Vintor shook his head in wonder, for only Squid would have thought to employ such an odd assortment of characters. "Come, my friends. Let us enter the palace and retire to a more comfortable setting."

*****

After watching Terin and Kato disappear into the palace, Raven stormed onto the bridge, disgusted with the pace of the needless proceedings. Neither Kato nor Terin was supposed to go ashore. He asked Tosha to remain as well so they could get underway as quickly as possible. Minister Antillius had insisted that Tosha join the other princesses to be formally received at the palace, but Raven had resisted such an undue delay. Tosha acquiesced to Raven's concerns and agreed to stay aboard, only to have Terin and Kato ruin Raven's plan for a hasty departure.

"So much for a quick exit," Lorken said with his arms crossed as he leaned against the helm.

"How long will this take?" growled Argos.

Tosha followed Raven onto the bridge, stopping at his side. "Hell, I don't know. Do you?" he asked her.

"It could take several moments or half a day. Time is often immaterial in such affairs."

"It's not immaterial to me!" Raven growled. He lifted his comm to his mouth. "Kato!"

"Go ahead, Rav," Kato answered after a long pause.

"Tell Squid to hurry this along."

"Well…" He paused.

"Well, what?"

"We have another complication."

"What complication?"

"It seems a representative of the Sisterhood was visiting the palace when we arrived. She and the harbor regent were discussing the princesses' abduction as we pulled into port. Since we arrived with all the princesses except Tosha, the representative insists that we present her so that she can be assured of her safety."

Raven let out a slow, impatient breath as he looked at Tosha. "Tell her if she wants to see Tosha, then she can walk down here and have a look, but tell her to make it quick."

"That's not how they do things here, Rav. Tosha has to come ashore to be properly received. Then we can be on our way."

Tosha snatched the comm from his hand before he could curse and growl in reply. "I'll be ashore momentarily, Kato. Inform Regent Ornovis to send the proper delegation to the *Stenox*, and my escort and I shall follow them to the palace." She stared mischievously at Raven.

"All right." Kato closed his comm.

"Make it quick!" Raven glared at her.

"Of course." She smiled. "I did warn you that these matters have to be handled with diplomacy and—"

"I remember what you said, Tosha. Now go!"

"All right," she said lasciviously. "Come along."

"What do you mean come along?" he growled.

"I need a proper escort, and I choose you."

"Tosha, that might not be a good idea," Lorken warned, unfolding his arms.

"You want me to be your escort? Fine." Raven frowned, taking a step closer, looking down into her golden eyes.

"Yes," she said slowly before chewing her lower lip as she met his terrible gaze. She could hear her heart pounding in her ears, an unfamiliar tingling sensation coursing her flesh. Raven snatched her wrist in his hand and pulled her after him, exiting the bridge. "Raven, wait!" Tosha shouted as she ran to keep up as he stormed across the palace green. He didn't slow his brisk pace or wait for the formal delegation to usher them into the palace.

The columns of soldiers on either side put their hands to hilts, ready to draw their swords, but Raven's fierce countenance took them aback. Tosha reached for his right arm, attempting to stop him, but he pulled his arm free of her grasp. "Raven, as my escort, you must follow and not lead," she snapped.

"If you want to lead, Tosha, I suggest you run ahead."

"You're impossible!" she fumed, walking at his side. "You're the most stubborn, unreasonable, bombastic…"

He turned swiftly, gripping her arm as he spun her to him, their faces inches apart. "If you don't like the way I dance, then you shouldn't have invited me to the party. We're wasting time I don't have. Come along."

*****

The sound of flutes and mandolins echoed gaily through the central hall of the palace as Princess Corry greeted scores of dignitaries, courtesans, and harbor officials. The open vast hall was a cavernous chamber with massive marble pillars to each wall, spiraling to the vaulted ceiling above. The floor was mirrored black stone, which contrasted with the hues of alabaster and sand-colored walls, pillars, and archways. The musicians occupied a raised platform in the chamber's southwest corner.

Princess Corry took her place upon a silver throne that rested upon a dais along the hall's east wall. The throne sat lower than a larger golden throne that towered behind it. The golden throne was reserved for the Torry king, whereas the silver throne represented the ranking member of the royal family present in the city. On most occasions, this honor was the purview of Vintor Ornovis, cousin of the king and regent of Cagan Harbor.

As the official escort of the Torry princess, Terin stood at the base of the dais and off to the left. He was torn between his duty to the princess and Raven's desire for a hasty departure. As a subject of the Torry kingdoms, he was bound to obey Corry until she released him, so he stood where he was instructed to observe the affairs of the princess and guard and attend her as she desired.

"Your Highness, I present Crown Princess Deliea, daughter of King Mortus and vice regent of the Macon Empire!" Vintor Ornovis bowed at the waist. He stood opposite Terin, upon the right side of the throne at the base of the dais, with his right arm extended to the Macon princess. Deliea stepped forth with Kato trailing her. Kato knelt as she approached the dais. Deliea slowly knelt and bowed her head, paying tribute to the host royalty, as was custom in Arax.

"Rise, Princess Deliea." Corry lifted an open palm, signaling her friend to stand. "You are welcome in Soren Palace. May you find rest and comfort in the House of Lore."

"My gratitude, Princess Corry. The House of Mortus accepts your invitation." Deliea stepped away, and Kato rose and followed her into the gathered dignitaries, who lined the other walls, as servants dressed in shimmering calnesian tunics drifted among the congregants with platters of food and drink.

Regent Ornovis continued with the proper introduction of Princess Felicia, then the ambassadors of Yatin and the Jenaii minister representing the birdmen. Various heads of wealthy merchant families were greeted in proper succession. Leila Torvana, ambassador of the Federation of the Sisterhood, waived her place in the introductions, as she awaited the promised arrival of her crown princess.

Terin felt unease standing below the throne as men and women of high station paraded before him to greet the princess. He felt the condescending stares of richly dressed courtesans, each wondering why a poorly dressed peasant was given such a place of honor in the palace court. He wished nothing more than to disappear into the crowd and return to the *Stenox*, but Corry insisted he serve as her escort. He enjoyed her company when they were alone and couldn't help but imagine a world where they could be together, but such fancies were mere fantasies, as he could now see the life she was born to.

He understood so little of life at a royal court, having grown up far in the country and away from such things. His father taught him how to fight, hunt, and survive in the wild. His mother taught him to read and write. Neither explained the protocols of palace life or how to interact in such settings. All he knew was that he didn't belong there.

He should have been in awe of the wondrous splendor of the palace. The craftsmanship of every angle and pillar represented the highest achievement of hundreds of master craftsmen. The stone carvings of kings and queens of old Cagia were displayed throughout the vast chamber, each cast in uncanny detail. They were so lifelike that Terin thought they might come alive and speak of their glorious past.

Terin should have been awed by such splendor, but he found the palace cold and uninviting. Perhaps it was the formality the palace engendered that he found off-putting. He was coming to realize how important his friends were and preferred their company to the fake smiles and feigned courtesies of high-born strangers. He felt out of place, wondering why the princess chose him for this task.

"Surely Minister Antillius could have selected a more appropriate apprentice," Valen Croftus sneered, observing Terin from afar. Valen was apprentice to King's Minister Gregor Vors, counsel to Regent Ornovis, and steward of the palace. Valen was two years Terin's elder and had served Minister Vors since his twelfth year. He was slender of build with shoulder-length buttercup hair and narrow-set features that bespoke a feminine quality. He wore the formal ankle-length golden tunic of his office. He was slightly shorter than Terin, and his diminutive build reflected the soft life of a palace courtesan.

"Antillius holds the king's favor, Valen. He could select his ocran to the post of minister's apprentice, and the king would no doubt applaud the choice," sneered Minister Vors, who stood beside his assistant. Minister Vors was of similar build and stature as his apprentice but wore floor-length calnesian robes of burgundy with gold hem.

"I would be surprised if the boy can even read, let alone transcribe official parchment," Valen choroused.

"Making such a poor choice for his apprentice is damaging enough to the Torry Council of Ministers, but to ask the boy to accompany the princess as her escort is the apex of audacity. It shames me as a king's minister."

"I concur, Minister. I can sense the ambassadors of Macon, Naybin, and Yatin snickering behind their false smiles."

The two men quickly noted the quieting of the central hall as their eyes drifted to the chamber's arched entryway. Princess Tosha passed under the archway, entering the great hall with Raven walking beside her. The congregants gasped at his presence, let alone his audacity to walk beside her so disrespectfully as they approached the throne.

"The beast belongs in a cage," Valen whispered, and Vors chuckled at the remark.

The crowd gasped as Raven placed a hand on Tosha's shoulder, whispering in her ear. "I'll hang back as you deal with these people. Just be quick about it." Tosha shook her head, giving him a look before stepping toward the dais.

"Your Highness, I present Princess Tosha, second guardian of the Sisterhood and crown empress of the Benotrist Empire." Vintor Ornovis bowed. Tosha advanced a step and knelt just as Regent Ornovis caught sight of Raven standing several paces back.

"Kneel, you fool!" Vintor whispered harshly, but Raven ignored him. Raven stood with his right hand resting on the grip of his holstered pistol, disregarding the heated glares of the people surrounding him.

The captain of the guard stepped forth with a dozen soldiers, forming a half circle facing him, stepping between him and Tosha. The soldiers wore silver breastplates over sea-blue tunics. Their hands went to their hilts, awaiting their captain's command. "You will kneel or be knelt!" the captain declared.

"Step away, boy, before I stomp you in the ground," Raven said dismissively.

"Captain Colza, stand down and withdraw your men!" Princess Corry ordered.

The Torry captain bit his tongue, glaring at Raven. "Yes, Your Highness." He withdrew his men.

"Rise, Princess Tosha. Welcome to Soren Palace. May you find rest and comfort in the House of Lore," Corry said, greeting her formally.

"I am honored by your invite, Princess Corry. The House of Letha is grateful for your hospitality," Tosha answered, coming to her feet. "I apologize for my escort's rudeness, Your Highness." She craned her neck, making her annoyance known to Raven.

"You are not accountable for Raven's lack of decency, Princess Tosha. Only he is responsible," Corry said.

"You wanted Tosha's company, well, here she is. If you girls will quit your yapping, maybe you can do whatever you're supposed to do so we can get the hell out of here," Raven growled impatiently.

"You are expected to kneel in my presence, Captain Raven. Were you not told?" Corry asked with a raised brow.

"I don't kneel to anyone, Corry. You should have figured that out by now." Terin winced at Raven's words, wondering how this could end peacefully.

"Must we suffer this barbarian's insults any further, Highness?" Minister Vors declared, stepping forth from the crowd.

"I'm sorry, miss. I didn't catch your name," Raven asked him.

Gregor Vors's olive skin flushed indignantly at this insult. He puffed his thin chest, trying to hold his ground as the large Earther's eyes locked dangerously on his. Gregor found Raven's stare unnerving and shifted his accusatory gaze to Squid. "Perhaps the fault lies not with this Earther but with the man who enlisted his services to begin with."

"Minister Antillius asked Raven to rescue our princess. Had he not done so, she would have perished for certain!" Terin spoke in Squid's defense, overstepping his bounds as a minister's apprentice.

"Another example of Minister Antillius's questionable judgment!" Minister Vors waved an open hand toward Terin. "To appoint an unfit boy to the post of a minister's apprentice is one thing, but to offer him up as a suitable escort for the princess is the height of presumption! And now he speaks out of turn, proving his unsuitability to the post appointed him." Squid's heart swelled with pride at Terin's defense of him even if he spoke out of place.

"You talk a lot of smack for someone who wasn't even there when we rescued your princess, pal. Terin was there, along with another of your countrymen who gave his life in the rescue. You can criticize Squid all you want, but what else would you have suggested? Do you think you and your little sister over there could've raided Molten

Isle?" Raven said, pointing toward Valen. Minister Vols backed a step from Raven, realizing that he was a man who could and would kill him if he desired. There was no wall of shields or swords that could protect him from such a man.

"Minister Vols!" Corry said firmly.

"Yes, Your Highness," Vols answered, thankful to shift his eyes from Raven.

"Minister Antillius and Terin Caleph are honored sons of the Torry realm. You shall apologize to them both, for I owe them my life!" she said icily.

Vols paled. "My apologies, Your Highness," he groveled as he went to Squid and Terin to offer them apologies in turn.

"Since my presence offends you to no end, I'm returning to my ship. Tosha should be able to find a suitable escort from this cheerful bunch to take her back," Raven said, turning to leave. After one step, he thought of one thing to add as he turned back, facing Corry. "Keep in mind, Princess, that my friend's life is at stake, and time is essential. So maybe you can understand my anger while we're farting around here with your useless ceremony." He turned again and left.

A collective sigh of relief could be heard throughout the chamber as Raven disappeared through the arched entryway. Tosha noted the tension ease on every face she beheld. She found it amusing that Raven had that effect on nearly everyone but her. Oh, he made her angry unlike anyone she had ever known, but she knew that she had a similar effect on him. The prospect of traveling all the way to Fera with the large Earther made her smile. *It is going to be such fun,* she mused wickedly. She only wondered how she was going to keep Raven and her father from killing each other. She shrugged, figuring she had time to work out that little detail.

"Your Highness, I present Minister Leila Torvana, ambassador from the Federation of the Sisterhood!" Vintor Ornovis formally introduced the minister to Corry and Tosha. Leila Torvana stepped forth and kneeled, half facing the Torry princess and half facing her own.

"Rise, Minister Torvana. You may treat with your crown princess." Corry waved an open hand toward Tosha.

"Come. Let us talk." Tosha guided Leila away from the throne.

"Your Highness! Surely you do not intend to remain in that… that man's company? Let me arrange safe passage to Bansoch. The queen would insist upon it," Leila Torvana pleaded as they stood in a secluded corner of the vast hall.

"I am in safe hands, Leila," Tosha assured her. "As you can see, I am free of the pirates, and Raven shall escort me safely to Fera."

"Raven is dangerous, Highness. You must not go with him!" Leila's green eyes were wide with fright.

"Pfft! Raven is harmless." Tosha dismissed her concern with a wave of her hand.

"But the queen—"

"My mother shall be fine. Inform her that I am safe and that I shall be visiting with my father for a time."

"She will not be pleased, Highness," Leila warned.

"Tell her not to worry and that I shall be returning to Bansoch with a wondrous gift. Now fetch me proper clothing. This tunic is far too brief for my taste."

*****

With the formal greetings concluded, Terin was free of his duties. Tosha and Kato started making their way back to the *Stenox* while Squid held Terin back, allowing the others to go on ahead. Standing at the palace entrance, Squid placed his hand on Terin's shoulder, his gray eyes staring into Terin's blue.

"I would be remiss if I do not share with you the apprehension that rends my heart. This is a dangerous journey for both you and our realm."

"Do you wish me not to go?" Terin asked, finding Squid's manner unnerving.

"This choice is not mine, Terin. It is yours. You must follow as you feel yourself led. Your instinct told you to aid Raven in freeing Cronus. You must obey the leaning of your heart. To do otherwise just for the purpose of pleasing me would be the greater folly. There is a reason that you must undertake this journey. Just be mindful to keep your sword with you at all times."

"I will," Terin assured him.

"Very well. Do not think that you shall be neglecting your duties while on this quest, my boy. You are to deliver this to Emperor Tyro." Squid raised a sealed scroll in his left hand, placing it in Terin's right.

"What is it?"

"It is best if you do not know."

"As you wish." Terin smiled, bidding him farewell as Princess Corry's shapely form emerged from the shadow of the palace entrance.

"Walk with me, Terin," she commanded softly, extending her hand to his.

Squid regarded the princess with a bow of his head and stepped back as Terin offered her his arm. They descended the steps to the palace green, walking slowly over the low-cut grass toward the *Stenox*. A dozen palace guards fanned out to either side, guarding their princess.

"I still do not approve of your decision to embark on this journey," she admonished.

"I am sorry if it displeases you, Highness." He sighed.

"It displeases me greatly, Terin. But you have given your word, and you intend to help a captive son of the Torry realm, so I can forgive you."

"Your forgiveness is warmly accepted, Highness," Terin answered, choosing his words carefully.

"I fear for your safety on this journey. Only the foolish and brave dare venture to the perilous lands of the north, and you are no fool."

"It is kind of you to say so, but I am not brave either, Highness."

She regarded him with a timeless look as she shook her head. "A humble warrior-scribe," she stated in disbelief. To hear her speak fondly of him made his heart race. "I do not approve of your association with Raven, however. He is an offensive, bombastic oaf who lacks the barest shreds of civility. I fear the consequences of his roguish manner when he treats with the Benotrist emperor."

"His manners may be unconventional, but he has shown me nothing but kindness, Highness. He is the only hope we have of rescuing Cronus."

Corry released a measured breath as she contemplated his words. "Then let us hope he knows what he is doing not only for your sake but also for Lady Leanna's as well."

Terin recalled Leanna's tearstained face that morning as she cried through the night, lamenting her lost love. "Thank you for understanding why I must go, Highness."

She turned, facing him. He mirrored her stance as she placed her hand upon his cheek. "I only ask that you take care and return safely to Torry North. I shall expect you at Corell upon your return. There you shall enter my service."

"I shall return, Princess."

"Very well. Now be off, for Raven grows impatient."

*****

Squid Antillius greeted the Torry princess at the palace steps as the *Stenox* pulled away from the shore. She regarded Miles's twin blades sheathed upon his hip.

"I wore these this day in honor of Miles's sacrifice," Squid explained.

"When you deliver them to his father's house, please extend the condolences of the House of Lore," she said.

"I shall see it done, Highness," Squid answered, moved by her sincerity. Miles's family lived on the southwestern border of Torry North. He would visit them on his return to Central City.

"Antillius, you will now tell me everything you know about Terin," she commanded.

"Your Highness?" he asked, taken aback by her forcefulness.

"Who is he really, Squid? Surely he is more than a farmer's son."

"His mother was once promised to your father, and there was not a fairer maid in all the land." Squid smiled at the memory of those long-ago days.

"Who was she?" Corry's interest was piqued. "And why did she marry another?"

"Her name was Valera. Though she was promised to your father, her heart belonged to another, a young warrior and member of the King's Elite named Jonas Caleph. I served with Jonas in those days and shared in his many adventures during the Sadden Wars. He loved the lady Valera very much but never acted upon his feelings out of loyalty to his king. She acted the same as he, willing to do her duty to the realm and honor your father."

"How sad," she thought aloud. "What transpired to bring them together?"

"Jonas won much renown during the war, turning many defeats into victories and saving your father's life on more than one occasion," Squid said without mentioning the sword he had found among the ruins of Celti that carried him to many of those victories, the same sword that Terin carried now. "Once the war ended, King Lore chose to bestow upon Jonas the highest honor available to him: naming him Prime among his Elite." The Prime was first of the King's Elite, answerable only to the commander of the Elite and Corell's master of arms, Torg Vantel.

"What happened then?"

Squid sighed at the memory as he continued. "Jonas Caleph is an honorable man, but he was mindful of the failings of his human heart. He asked your father for a private audience, where he confessed the leanings of his heart and why he could no longer serve in such proximity to the future queen. He offered King Lore his life for betraying him, if he only did so in thought. The king placed his heavy hand upon Jonas's head, touched by his honesty and empathetic of his inner turmoil. He summoned the lady Valera and asked of her the truth of her heart. She confessed her love for Jonas."

"What did Father do?"

"He asked Jonas, if he was allowed to wed the lady Valera, where would he take her? Jonas answered that he would live a simple life as a farmer in the Torry heartland. Jonas also offered his wondrous sword to the king. King Lore returned the sword to Jonas and had him kneel beside Lady Valera. King Lore then placed Valera's hand in Jonas's. He told them that they were forever joined, but there were three conditions."

"What conditions?"

"The first was that they had to follow through on living a simple life away from the palace. To this they heartily agreed. His second was that if either violated their fidelity to each other, they would be put to death for offending the love for which fate had ordained." Squid paused before telling the last condition.

"And the third? What was it?"

"The third…the third was their firstborn child."

Corry's eyes drew wide. "Their child? How? Why?"

"Your father demanded that when their eldest child came of age, they were to be sent to his service. Terin is their only child, and the debt falls to him. Had he been born a girl, your father would have wed her to your brother, Lore II. Since Terin is a boy, he was trained as a warrior by Jonas and given his father's sword. It was agreed that he would enter your father's service under the guise of my apprentice."

"Why did my father ask for their child?"

"I asked that of him one time, and he said it was destiny, that there was a reason that he didn't fully understand. Any other monarch would have slain any subject who made a confession like Jonas's, but your father felt there was a reason why Jonas confessed the deepest inclination of his heart. King Lore cared deeply for the lady Valera and did not surrender her up lightly. He understood that if fate ordained their union, then it must be for the significance of their offspring. For that reason, Terin is my apprentice."

"His service has already been a boon to the Torry realm." Corry smiled. "Perhaps my father's wisdom will bear greater fruit than his vision foretold."

"Yes, your father's mercy for Jonas has been rewarded with the deeds of the son," Squid said fondly.

"You are proud of Terin, are you not?"

"I am not alone in that regard it seems." He smiled inquisitively.

"No, you are not alone in that." She smiled.

"You must never tell anyone what I told you, especially Terin."

"My lips are forever closed, but there will come a day when he must know the truth."

"When that day arises, I will tell him."

CHAPTER 12

Ten days before. The Yatin Border.

Smoke, black and gray, twisted in tortured spirals above the aged fortress. The bodies of hundreds of Yatin soldiers littered the battlefield; most were entombed within the battered gray walls. A token force that could have only offered token resistance, the Yatin border garrison was overwhelmed by three gargoyle legions. Dead Yatins hung from the battlements while the severed crowns of others were impaled on stakes surrounding the ruins.

General Yonig surveyed the carnage with his dull-crimson eyes. He was studious and cunning, rare traits for a gargoyle, and as such, this allowed him to rise rapidly through the ranks. His tactical brilliance equaled that of the Torry general Bode. With three gargoyle legions at his command, he was tasked with the conquest of the Yatin Empire. Two Benotrist fleets under the command of Admiral Mulsen would shadow his advance, destroy the Yatin Navy, and envelop Tenin Harbor while one of Yonig's legions completed the land side of the encirclement. He would delegate that task to Commander Torab while he led another legion to a far more significant objective.

He sat astride a gray ocran as the long columns of troops passed before him in lines stretching to the horizon, marching through the forest vale. The late-morning sun broke through the gray-clad sky, illuminating the darkened ruins of the Yatin fortress. Yonig narrowed his eye slits, observing the macabre handiwork wrought by his legions. First blood was the sweetest of nectars, and they bathed in it this day. They had caught the Yatin border forces completely by surprise.

Yonig shifted his keen eye south, where the Yatin heartland lay open before them. The Yatin emperor foolishly depended on the fortresses of Tenin Harbor and Telfer Castle to hold his northern flank while he concentrated his forces to guard Torry South. Yonig would have smiled if it were in his nature, though even his glee could not encroach upon his permanent scowl.

He regarded a dozen prisoners shuffling north, locked in their coffle. Their haggard faces and torn garments belied little of their true suffering. Yonig found a dozen captives not worth the effort to bring back alive, but the greedy Benotrist slavers charged with securing such contraband disagreed. They gladly clapped the prisoners in irons and collars, driving them north to the slave markets of Laycrom and Tinsay.

Yonig thought enemy soldiers made poor slave stock and should be destroyed. The only work suitable to such warlike captives was pulling an oar on a galley, and for that, they had no need for eyes. If it were his decision, he would have blinded these prisoners before dragging them to Tinsay Harbor and selling the lot of them to the galleys. Male slaves had no need of their testicles either. He would have gelded them all if the choice were his. Most slavers agreed with the latter assessment and gelded all male chattel.

Yonig reflected on the time when the Benotrists and gargoyles overthrew their Menotrist overlords. Many Benotrists castrated all their Menotrist slaves, using other Benotrists to bed their female slaves. Even then, some would still slay any males born of such unions. The practice was prevalent throughout the western half of the empire. Within several generations, the Menotrist bloodlines in those regions would be negligible. Yonig could envision a similar fate for Yatin—new lands filled with Benotrist humans and mountain ranges where gargoyles could establish new nesting grounds.

Unlike other gargoyle legions, half of Yonig's troops wore iron breastplates and greaves and carried heavier rectangular shields strapped to their backs, along with other gear. Such added weight impeded their ability to fly but enabled them to better engage human armies head-on. Any of his troops caught complaining of the added load was dragged out of formation and impaled along the route of march. Every mile throughout their trek, the gargoyle soldiers would find at least one of their brethren hanging upon a shaft, a grim warning for their disobedience.

*****

"My prince, I must caution against this. Let us fully garrison Telfer rather than meet the enemy upon open ground," General Morue said, pleading with Yanku, the crown prince of the Yatin Empire. The young prince refused his counsel, observing the columns of soldiers parading before them. They sat astride their tall dark mounts as the army passed below them. Their magantor scouts had reported for weeks upon the gargoyles concentrating north of the border, forcing the Yatins to call their banners.

The garrison of Telfer completed its muster—forty thousand men clad in purple tunics that matched the hue of Telfer Palace's dark stone walls. They wore bronze mail, helms, greaves, and leather sandals. They had been marching for two days, advancing north and west through the winding vales and rolling hills of north Yatin.

General Morue commanded the garrison of Telfer. He was medium of height with nondescript features and cropped brown hair. He sighed in hopeless exasperation. To his great misfortune, the Yatin crown prince was visiting the palace when this border crisis erupted. Though only a boy of fifteen years, the prince was granted certain liberties by the emperor. As the crown prince of Yatin, Yanku's commands could only be countered by his father, who happened to be in the capital city of Mosar, leaving Morue helpless to counter Yanku's decrees.

Once the muster of Telfer was complete, the boy prince immediately ordered thirty of the garrison's forty telnics to follow him into battle. He also brought with him Telfer's entire cavalry contingent of seven hundred mounts. Morue's suggestion to leave one full unit of cavalry at the palace was overruled by Prince Yanku. He pressed such counsel when their last magantor scout failed to return. The cavalry would be the castle's eyes and ears should the enemy outflank them or if Morue's greater fear manifested and their army met with misfortune.

Prince Yanku sat astride a dusty-gray mount with his fur-lined cloak drawn tight. He had dark-brown hair that rolled freely to his shoulders, framing his narrow nose and high cheekbones. His tunic was a deeper purple than his men's. A golden ocran rearing into the air was emblazoned upon his cloak, the signet of the Royal House of Yatin. Yanku envisioned himself as a Yatin ocran lord of long ago, when his ancestors first emerged from the western steppes of the Cress Mountains and conquered the kingdoms along the Muva.

"Something vexes you, General?" the prince asked, his adolescent voice laced with condescension.

"Your Highness, we are marching blind into unknown peril. Our magantor scouts have not returned and are days overdue. Our cavalry has only provided sporadic patrols at best. Please release two full units to patrol deeper north and west and additional patrols south and east," Morue pleaded.

"Reconnaissance is a secondary function for my cavalry. If we meet the enemy, I want all of my cavalry to be recalled in time for such an engagement. When the enemy comes, they will not stand against heavy ocran slamming their front."

*****

Four days out of Telfer, the Yatins met the gargoyle host at Salamin Valley. General Morue deployed his telnics across the valley heights with five telnics guarding each ridgeline and the remaining twenty holding the center. Prince Yanku placed his cavalry in the Yatin center, anxious for the battle to commence. Salamin Valley ran southeast to northwest in an angular yet gradual grade. The valley narrowed at its apex with sporadic clumps of underbrush mixed with open grasslands that lined either bank of the Salamin stream, which meandered the vale.

Prince Yanku paraded before his men, galloping along the front with sword drawn and blue eyes staring through the gray slits in his helm. "To me, men of yatin! The blood of ocran lords courses our veins. This day will attest our metal in the lands of our ancient kin. The enemy awaits us below. They have come to steal our land and slaughter our children. Let us bleed them upon these sacred grounds. To me!" he shouted, kicking his ocran's flanks as he charged.

The Yatin cavalry lumbered forth, their heavy hooves clapping the soil like thunder. The leading gargoyle telnics were spread out in a loose formation, moving methodically up the vale. Yanku could see the advent of their thousands flooding the valley along either side of the stream as he led his cavalry along the northeastern side of the stream before planning to cross the ford several miles downstream and wreaking havoc on the opposite bank upon his return.

The leading cohorts of Yonig's legion stared stupefied into the face of the advancing cavalry. Haggard and weary after their ascent up the vale, the gargoyles' faces alit with fright as the Yatin riders lowered their lances in unison. The Yatin riders dressed to their left, keeping their line straight as they galloped forth with little space between them.

Prince Yanku's eyes flashed with abandon, the wind lifting his dark mane, trailing his helm freely in the breeze. "Forward!" he commanded aloud over the din, his men relaying the command along the line. Beside him rode his standard bearer, bearing the golden ocran on a field of black, which the riders to his left and right fixed their position to.

The gargoyles in the leading cohorts where lightly armed with only thin helms and small circular shields. Those who could took to flight, their wings struggling to gain lift as the bladed lances drew nigh. Others threw themselves upon the ground, hoping to avoid being crushed by the heavy hooves clapping the ground, with swords raised to meet their foe.

The Yatin cavalry smashed the loose wall of infantry like mailed fists striking clay. Their lances skewered the gargoyle fore ranks, their bladed tips slicing through soft flesh. The Yatin riders were greeted with gargoyle screams as lances ripped wings from backs or heads from necks. Many were sliced nearly in half, disemboweled before they were cognizant of their wound. Many lances failed to slice completely through their opponent's flesh, weighing their tips with the dying wretches, forcing riders to discard their lances for longswords.

The Yatin cavalry thundered on, leaving hundreds of gargoyle carcasses in their wake, their dark blood staining the grassy vale.

Many gargoyles took to flight, just missing lance tips slicing the air neath their wings. Some dropped upon the riders below, knocking them from their saddles with the weight of their descent. Gargoyle archers released their volleys upon the charging ocran, their feathered shafts imbedding into their thick hides, but the cavalry advance could not be stayed by such tactics. They sped onward, smashing another line of gargoyle infantry like shattered twigs. The ocran trampled smaller vegetation while sweeping around thicker foliage. Several riders dropped from sight, slipping helpless into a sinkage or tripping on uneven ground, but such losses were negligible. A third line of gargoyle infantry crumbled as quickly as the second as Prince Yanku led his charges through their panicked ranks.

*****

A westerly gale contorted General Morue's weathered face as he observed the cavalry charge from the valley heights. The prince was rapidly slipping from sight, his riders obscured by foliage and distance. He had urged Prince Yanku to allow the enemy to consolidate before striking in force. The enemy was stretched out five miles along the valley floor, and his ocran would tire before reaching the ford. Where, then, could they regroup with tired mounts and gargoyles all around them? The cavalry needed the Yatin infantry to advance in order to destroy the disordered gargoyles in their wake. But to do so would mean to surrender the high ground, and the infantry could not hope to keep pace with the cavalry, which had disappeared from sight. Morue would hold his position and trust the fates to safeguard his crown prince.

*****

Drunk with glory and brimming with euphoria, Prince Yanku dispatched a fourth line of gargoyles and drove headlong into a fifth. As the Yatin riders drew nigh, they discovered the fifth line of gar-

223

goyles arrayed in splendid ranks and equipped with breastplates, thick rectangular shields, and heavy iron helms resplendent in the midday sun. They made no attempt to scatter, fly, or flee. They simply stood their ground with dull, lifeless eyes fixed blankly ahead as the Yatin cavalry leveled their lances.

Suddenly, the entire gargoyle line bent down and lifted pikes the length of three men. They hoisted them aloft with the aid of their comrades behind them, sticking the butt ends into the soil with the sharpened ends jutting forth to greet the cavalry. The Yatins did not believe the gargoyles capable of such tactics. At a dozen paces, the cavalry had no time to turn or slow, facing the forest of pikes with knowing dread, driving headlong into those wooden fangs.

A dozen members of the Yatin Elite guarded Prince Yanku's flanks. The two closest to him swept around him into the pikes meant for their prince. Their ocran jolted to a halt, throwing them afar as gargoyle pikes impaled the beasts' breasts. Yanku swerved to miss the dying beasts that thrashed painfully on their sides. His mount bounded over the gargoyle line as arrows pierced its flanks and throat.

Hundreds of Yatin ocran slammed into the unforgiving wall of pikes, losing half their number upon contact. Others slowed enough to be dragged from their mounts and set upon by gargoyle blades. A third of the Yatin cavalry remained mounted, continuing apace with spears and arrows, further thinning their ranks.

Most of Prince Yanku's personal guard lay broken upon the battlefield, their bodies torn asunder as gargoyles fixed upon their royal sigil. Others of the Yatin Elite became separated from their royal charge, lost amid the chaos of battle. Some stumbled forth, eventually overcome by withering rains of arrows and spears. A few shadowed their liege prince, surrendering their lives to save his, until none remained to guard him.

Prince Yanku was dragged from his saddle, his body hitting the ground emphatically as the wretched screams of his dying men tortured his ears. He felt his sword stripped away with his helm and breastplate. He was thrown on his stomach and bound hand and foot.

Only one of the Yatin prince's royal guardians survived the day. Yeltor, son of Yelton, was ninth among the Yatin Elite. He was tall and dark of hair with dark-brown eyes. Separated from his liege amid the wall of pikes that greeted their host so terribly, he found himself skirting the narrow stream that bisected the vale, passing amid thick foliage that cut his bare legs and arms. He felt darkness close about his eyes as he slipped from the saddle amid the thick underbrush, the sounds of battle echoing faintly in the distance.

*****

General Morue awaited the gargoyle host atop the valley heights with disquieting forebode. The late-day sun shone brightly in their eyes as the enemy drew nigh. The ill-advised cavalry charge was hours past, and they were still blind to the prince's fate. A few stragglers returned, and Morue ordered them to strip their mounts of armor and convert them to scouts. Prince Yanku had left Morue with no mounts to reconnoiter their flanks and rear, insistent to deploy every ocran they possessed to his ill-fated charge.

Morue found the gargoyles' tactics unnerving. They attacked throughout the day in small waves, testing his line for weakness before withdrawing. Their sporadic attacks lacked the typical frenzied gargoyle bloodlust. Instead, they seemed controlled and calculating, yet they could strike in mass at any time.

Yonig's more heavily armed gargoyles paraded before their Yatin foes in ordered ranks, marching forth to engage with dull-red eyes as if their savageness had been beaten out of them. Twenty-five heavily armed gargoyle telnics mirrored their Yatin foes before slamming into their wall of shields. The more heavily laden gargoyles carried short, straight swords rather than the curved blades of their lightly armed brothers. The shortsword was more effective, stabbing in quick thrusts between shields. The two armies bled each other sparingly as the day progressed. The high ground strengthened the Yatins' position, but the uneven ground prevented them from exploiting breaks that manifested in the gargoyle line.

As daylight waned, little had changed until Morue's scouts returned with ill tidings.

*****

Twenty gargoyle telnics swept around Salamin Valley, ten to the south and ten to the north, each driving far to the Yatin rear before joining and closing the gap between them. General Morue abandoned the valley heights, leaving five telnics to guard his retreat lest his entire army fall into Yonig's closing trap. Morue cursed his misfortune. Had the crown prince not ordered a mindless advance blindly into the unknown, he could have maintained his army behind the thick ramparts of Telfer. Now he had to outrace the gargoyles closing behind him and then outpace them all the way back to Telfer. Even if he were successful, how many men might he have left after such a journey?

*****

Yeltor, son of Yelton, awoke, greeted by a starlit sky painted across the heavens above. The sound of water gently lapping the north bank of the Salamin stream echoed off his left. His body ached from head to foot, and his dented helm explained his lengthy sleep. He rolled on his side as nausea tortured his stomach till he emptied its content in the thick reeds pressing all around him.

"Movesss!" The guttural voice echoed in the distance, followed by the high whistle of a lash. The moans of tortured souls followed, rising high in the night air, feeding the sadism of their gargoyle captors. Yeltor froze, fearfully cognizant of the danger perilously close. He slowly stripped his armor, setting his breastplate, greaves, and helm quietly aside, then he drew his dagger and crept through the thick reeds and underbrush that scraped his arms and legs.

The glow of torches flickered in the distance as coffles of chained Yatins were herded westward. He could make out their pitiful forms in the dim light, chains connecting collars fastened about their necks with hands bound behind them. The battle must have gone ill for his countrymen. General Morue, if he did survive, would be withdrawing to Telfer. Yeltor had little hope of evading the gargoyles that lay between them. He remembered his prince being dragged from his mount before he was lost in the underbrush. If his prince still lived, he had to free him or die in the attempt.

He froze at the sound of clawed feet drawing near. He withdrew deeper into the brush line as a lone gargoyle passed before him, its winged silhouette clearly defined, even in the dark of night. Yeltor let the creature pass before stepping from the foliage and closing upon his prey. "Make a sound and I cut your throat!" he whispered as the creature felt the steel blade pressed to its neck. Yeltor backed the gargoyle into the underbrush with his head pressed tightly to the base of its skull. "Answer my questions and I'll let you live," he whispered in its ear.

"Asksss yoursss questionsss."

"Where is the Yatin Army?"

"Theysss runsss awaysss."

"Where?"

"Eastsss."

"Where is the Yatin prince? He was captured during the cavalry charge."

"Westsss, towardsss thesss bordersss, withsss thesss othersss slavesss. Argh." Yeltor slit its throat, easing the carcass to the ground.

*****

Yatin soldiers plodded along through the dark of night, not daring to stop to rest lest the enemy fall upon them. They continued on in long columns, making for Telfer with haste. General Morue pushed his men to the brink, knowing their fate if they failed to reach the safety of the palace. They failed to slip the flanking elements of the gargoyle legion, forcing them to fight through their vast numbers in hasty formations. There was no ordered battle plan, only a savage instinct to survive.

The Yatin Army disintegrated into a mob after breaking through the gargoyles that blocked their way. The enemy harried them throughout the night, dragging off whomever they could. The troops in column could hear the gut-wrenching screams of their fellows as gargoyles made sport of them in the distance. The sound of clanging steel echoed throughout the night as the enemy attacked in ones and twos without cease. Arrows withered their ranks with sporadic fire. The Yatins would respond in kind, releasing volleys blindly into the dark in the direction of the enemy fire.

*****

He retained his sword and dagger, discarding his armor and any symbol of his rank or loyalties. He slew a dozen stray gargoyles throughout his trek, relieving the second of his victims of a bow and quiver. His purple tunic was torn and bloody, and his sandals were failing with misuse. Yeltor had made his way north and west since the battle, tracking the caravan that held his prince captive.

Keeping to the thick foliage wherever it was available, he shadowed the brightly visible sign left by the plodding caravan. The tracks left by chained men locked in coffles were impossible to miss. He surmised sixty to eighty men in the coffle. He spotted three sets of wagon tracks and several free riders. The day was growing old, and every moment, the prince was being taken farther away. Yeltor had to close the distance and free him before he reached the Benotrist border.

He knelt in the dirt pathway, examining the recent tracks. The sparse vegetation yielded to the open, rocky terrain of the lower plateau, losing him its protective cover. Even the thick, wet grasslands of the Salamin Valley gave way to the windswept, barren ground that stretched to the western horizon. The wagon tracks left deep ruts. The footprints left by the coffle seemed just hours old. He might catch them afoot, but he would have to quicken his pace.

Pressing his left palm upon the ground, he felt a distant vibrance. Craning his neck, he descried a lone rider bearing down from the east. He withdrew to the little foliage left to him, notching an arrow and drawing back on the string. The lone rider drew near, oblivious to the Yatin's presence in the thickets to his left till the shaft sped to meet him. It struck his left breast before his eyes discerned the danger.

He stumbled, his grip loosening on his reins as a second shaft struck above his hip. The human rider slumped forward in the saddle before a strong hand dragged him from his mount. The rider was little more than a boy, a youth in his seventeenth year, with saucer-wide brown eyes that pleaded mercy as they beheld Yeltor's fierce countenance.

"Who are you?" Yeltor whispered harshly. The boy lay speechless. "Answer me!"

"Kill me. I won't answer," the boy said through gritted teeth.

"Kill you? No, I'll let you live after I cut the tendons in your arms and legs and leave you for the carka birds."

The boy swallowed past the lump in his throat. "I am…a royal messenger. I carry a scroll with General Yonig's seal for the emperor."

A royal messenger, mused Yeltor. That explained the boy's lack of breastplate, helm, or mail. Messengers rode swift Torlin-bred mounts and no armor to slow their pace. Messengers carried no sword or shield, only a pair of dual-bladed daggers. Yeltor slit his throat.

*****

He hated discarding his sword and bow, but he needed to play the part of a royal messenger. He stitched and cleaned the boy's white tunic in the nearest stream. It cost him time, but by the next morning, he was well on his way with a swift mount.

CHAPTER 13

The dungeon of Fera, the Black Castle, rested five levels below the surface, carved from bedrock over the centuries. Sunlight was alien to the dark cells and torch-lit corridors of the subterranean holdfast. The fetid smell of human waste and rotting flesh assailed the nostrils of the dungeon's newest guests. They were led hooded and chained while led through the palace, shuffling blindly into these cavernous bowels of Fera.

They completed the last leg of their arduous journey tied to the backs of magantors. One had come loose of his bonds and fell from the bird in flight. Several others had succumbed to their ill treatment, leaving only ten survivors, who stood chained in the coffle. Their hoods were removed, their eyes squinting in the dim torchlight.

The garrison of Fera was almost entirely Benotrist humans, but the dungeon was guarded by gargoyles. A dozen of their winged forms surrounded the captives, their crimson eyes always teetering between dull red and glowing scarlet. They each wore blood-red tunics with a sword and whip divided by the sun and moon emblazoned upon their chests in gold stitching, a sigil of Tyro's Elite.

A cold dread washed over Cronus as those fiery eyes undressed him with unveiled malice. What fate awaited his brave fellows in this evil place he could only fatally surmise. They were unshackled from the coffle two at a time and placed in their cells. Marcus and Cronus were thrown together in a cold, dark chamber, their only light filtering through their grated door.

Marcus immediately collapsed, his weak, famished body crumpling to the rocky, uneven floor. Marcus Elien was Cronus's only surviving commander of flax, his once proud carriage reduced to a shivering, ragged, and famished skeleton with flesh drawn over it.

Marcus moaned, his body racked with fever, as he forced a shallow cough. It was sickly and weak, and he dared not breathe deeply into his lungs, for it hurt to do so.

"What shall be-become of us, Cronus?" Marcus coughed, the words coming with great duress as he lay curled on his side.

"We saved our people, Marcus. We delivered the death blow to a terrible host. Our captors shall not overlook our role in that. Take solace in our fell deeds, my friend, for children shall sing of our valor long after our bones turn to dust. Nothing the enemy does to us can diminish our glory or stain our honor. No matter how we meet our end or how loudly we beg for mercy can undo that," he said kindly, placing his hand on Marcus's shoulder. His friend was shivering in the cold, damp cell. Their tunics were ragged, torn, and filthy. Their undergarments were tossed away during their trek north, soiled with feces and piss. They were unable to wash and were forced to relieve themselves while en route.

Cronus's words were a kindness, a balm, for a heart forlorn of hope. Marcus knew they were fated. There was no recourse but death, but Cronus's words were true. They had done a great service for the realm, and their families were safer because of it. His family was safer, he reminded himself. Marcus dreamed of his beautiful wife and two young girls, who would never see him again, but through them, he would live on. He would suffer a thousand deaths for their sake if such a price was demanded. How he longed to hold them one last time and feel the warmth of their arms around his neck.

He fixed his dark-brown eyes on Cronus's green. "Thank you, Commander." He smiled weakly. "It was an honor to serve as one of your commanders of flax."

"Was?" Cronus shook his head. "Nay, my friend, you still are my commander of flax."

No, Marcus thought. *We are merely corpses waiting to be burned or buried.* "So be it." He smiled before falling fast asleep.

*****

His clawed feet scraped the dark stone floor of the cavernous corridor. The ceiling, the height of three men, rose imperiously above with a series of even-placed arches of black stone running the length of the passageway. The waning afternoon sun shone through the tall windows that lined the opposing faces of the long corridor. Human guards dressed in knee-length black tunics with copper-hued breastplates, helms, and greaves stood post at each archway, their eyes following him as he entered their periphery. Each guard wore a longsword upon their left and a short blade upon their right with a shield upon their back and spear in their hands. As he passed, they presented their spears vertically before them, offering respect for his rank. He wore a clean blood-colored tunic with four golden cords around each shoulder of his tunic, a symbol of his rank as a commander of a legion.

He continued apace, driving the hateful weakness of fear from his mind lest it consume him. Of all the range of emotions that afflicted the gargoyle race, fear was the most loathsome. They fed rapaciously off the fear of their foes, but once similarly afflicted, their power waned exponentially.

At last, the corridor expanded, spanning the width of a score of men laid head to foot, where it met adjoining concourses that formed a T before the throne room. Centered upon the mirrored black stone floor of this vast mergence stood a statue that rose imperiously above in horrific splendor. 'Twas a man and a gargoyle standing apart at their legs before merging into one form at the waist.

It had a man's torso with gargoyle wings sprouting from its back. Human shoulders transformed into gargoyle hands through the arms' transition. The head itself was an amalgamation of the two halves of the Benotrist-Gargoyle Empire. Human lips and nose contrasted with gargoyle eyes and sharp, curved ears that swept back from its skull. The human and gargoyle portions were cast in white and black marble respectively.

General Vicon skirted the massive sculpture, his head barely reaching the knees of the towering symbol. On the back side of the sculpture were the twin doors of the throne room. Half a dozen guards were posted at the entrance, halting Vicon in place. They slowly opened the heavy doors, which were as tall as four men lying head to foot. As he faced the throne room, the corridor breaking toward his left dropped into a broad stair a dozen paces from the twin doors, leading to the bowels of the Black Castle.

The passageway to his right ascended after a dozen paces, its broad steps rising to the rooftops above. Torches ran the lengths of both corridors, fixed into brackets along each wall and glowing brilliant upon the midnight-black stone. Only the corridor that ran directly from the throne room had windows fixed upon its higher edges. He could hear the palace steward herald his arrival to the emperor before the guard escorted him within. The throne room doors opened wider, the joints creaking under the immense weight of the porian timber from which they were constructed. General Vicon followed his escort through the entryway.

The throne room of Fera was a cavernous chamber that stretched fifty meters across and thirty abreast. Twelve pillars spiraled to the vast ceiling above, each plated in silver and two meters in width. Six pillars lined the opposing walls that ran from the doors to the throne. The floor was mirrored red stone, and the ceiling was painted like a midnight sky with jewels embedded into its dark stone. The basin torches that ran the length of the chamber bathed the ceiling with enough light to illuminate the rich adornments embedded there. Even a gargoyle like Vicon gazed in awe, as the dark stone above was alit in celestial brilliance.

The throne of Fera rested on the chamber's far end, standing alone atop a raised dais. A broad stair ran from the floor to the top of the dais some five meters above. The throne was plated in gold with an arched back and thick, wide arms. The seat alone could swallow three men, yet its occupant's bearing bespoke his terrible presence.

Emperor Tyro sat on his throne with cold, dead eyes. He was tall, dark of hair, and with a handsome face that masked his cruel nature. He wore a golden robe edged in scarlet, which draped below his knees. A reflective black crown graced his head with red-hued jewels affixed to its base. His eyes were yellow like the sun on a clear day with specks of purple across their irises.

Vicon stopped before the throne, dropped to his knees, and pressed his forehead to the floor, showing proper obeisance to the Benotrist throne. The guards did likewise, pressing their foreheads to the floor. They remained in place, awaiting Tyro to bid them rise. "Stand." Tyro spoke after a time. Vicon arose, his crimson eyes noting the dozen Imperial Elite flanking the throne. They were a mixture of men and gargoyles and clad in red tunics bearing the sigil of their post—a sun and a moon divided by a sword with a whip wound around its length.

Vicon noticed the mocking sneer of the man standing to the right of the throne. It was Morac, son of Morca and first among Tyro's Elite. He wielded the golden sword once borne by the emperor himself. 'Twas a blade that cut stone or steel with the slightest of swings or weakest of blows. 'Twas a blade that kindled vast courage in its master and struck down its foes with ease. With such a blade, Tyro had forged an empire. Morac fixed his dark-brown eyes upon Vicon, his black mane framing a chiseled face. He was lean, muscled, and strong and bore little compassion for others.

To Tyro's left stood Kriton, a gargoyle and third among the Imperial Elite. Standing nearly seventy inches, he was the tallest gargoyle most had ever seen. His eyes were always fiery red, reflective of the rage that constantly fought to surface. The curve of his fangs matched the menace of his stare. Wholly void of mercy, Kriton was the keeper of the dungeon and took wicked pleasure in the torture of his charges.

"You bring tidings of failure." Tyro's voice echoed low and dull as if it was a trivial thing, but Vicon knew better.

"My emperor." Vicon bowed his head shamefully. "I followed General Tanius in battle, obedient to his order. We entered Tuft's Gap with two hundred thousand, and I escaped with under ten thousand," Vicon said, detailing the events of the battle and how they had come undone by General Bode's tactical brilliance and Tanius's incompetence. He finished his telling with Cronus's capture and the role he played in the legions' ruination.

"And you brought this Torry prisoner to Fera?" Tyro asked.

"He and his men await your judgment in the dungeon, my emperor."

"And you hope to dull my fury upon them before it is vent on you?" He appraised Vicon with cool discernment.

"The Torry prisoners deserve your righteous fury, my emperor. As your humble servant, I take solace in your wisdom to deal them what they have earned. May their torments equal the suffering of our fallen brothers!"

"Suffer they shall, but not all debts are paid with their blood," Tyro answered. By nightfall, General Vicon's head rested upon a pike above the battlements.

*****

"What do you make of it?" Kato asked, staring curiously at the screen. Raven stood over his shoulder as Kato manned the helm.

"How many have you spotted so far?" Raven asked.

"I lost count at eighty-nine. They go on endlessly."

"From where?"

"My guess? I'd say Tenin Harbor. Most of these ships are merchant vessels flagged by every southern realm. Look." Kato expanded the current image, and the single-mast vessel came boldly into focus. The ship had a single row of heavy oars, which were withdrawn as the strong wind pressed upon its full mast, driving the vessel south. The Yatin coastline towered over the vessel below the painted evening sky. Kato tapped the screen, indicating the green flag blowing above the prow.

"That ship is a Macon merchant vessel," he said as he cycled through the previous images, bringing a dual mast vessel bearing a banner with a gold anchor upon a field of gray. "That one is Casian." He cycled the next image. "This one is Torry." He went through a dozen, noting the differing flags representing the varied realms of southern Arax. He further pointed out visible damage to several Torry merchant vessels and Yatin ships as well. They had noted the steady stream of southbound vessels all along the Yatin coast since they departed Cagan Harbor.

Raven reached over Kato's shoulder and pressed the comm switch. "Brokov!"

"Go ahead, Rav," Brokov's voice echoed from the comm.

"Prep the *Spectre* for departure."

"Where are we going?" Brokov asked.

"Tenin Harbor. We need to confirm a hunch."

*****

Cronus shuffled blindly through the corridors and winding stairways of Fera with his hands bound behind him and a coarse sack drawn over his head. The foot-length shackles allowed little slack in his measured steps. The snap of the lash whistled audibly off the stone walls as he heard one of his comrades cry out from the painful sting. He felt the cold, wet stone floor of the dungeon beneath his naked feet. As they ascended the higher levels of the castle, he could discern the drier stone floor. Their arduous climb tapered after a lengthy march. Torchlight painfully bathed his vision as a clawed black hand removed his hood. His vision cleared, finding himself amid his fellows in a single file before a large archway with a raised portcullis.

"Movesss!" a gargoyle hissed while another snapped the whip. Cronus winced as the leather bit his shoulder. The prisoners shuffled forth under the stone archway, stepping into a cavernous oval-shaped chamber that was forty meters long and twenty abreast. The archway appeared to be the only entry point, as a five-meter wall ran the circumference of the chamber. Behind the wall were rows of benches that circled the chamber. A large cupola ceiling arched overhead with gray support beams crisscrossing over black stone. A three-meter square stone block was centered in the chamber for some unknown purpose.

Cronus felt the sand floor beneath his feet. Torches lined the upper portions of the wall, bracketed into the dark stone, blinding those below to the faces staring down from above. The chamber was an arena, which was used for some dark purpose, Cronus surmised. They continued to the middle of the arena before stopping and made to face left. Cronus could vaguely discern the shadowed silhouettes positioned above before they were driven to their knees. "Headsss to the groundsss!" a deep, guttural voice boomed. "Obeisance to the emperor, in whose presence you are graced." Cronus felt the sharp-clawed fingers piercing his neck, forcing his head to the sand.

Tyro observed the captives from his royal box in the stands above. His desire to make sport of their suffering was secondary to the information he required from them. Of course, one would lead to the other, so he nodded to his minions to proceed.

Kriton regarded his emperor with a bow of his head before turning to the kneeling Torries behind him. "Liftsss yoursss headsss!" As Cronus raised his eyes, he beheld the towering gargoyle standing several paces before him. The creature stood nearly seventy inches, by far the largest of his race that Cronus had ever seen. Muscled, sinewy limbs protruded from his blood-red tunic, which bore the symbol of a sun and a moon divided by a sword and a whip, emblazoned with gold stitching. The gargoyle possessed dark-red eyes that straddled the demarcation between calmness and anger as they flickered betwixt dull red and fiery crimson.

"I amss Kriton, third among Tyro'sss Elitesss and keeper of the dungeon of Ferasss!" he spoke, menace laced in his every utterance. A terrible foreboding swept over Cronus, heightening his weary senses, as Kriton's feral gaze swept their pitiful assemblage. "Bringsss him!" Kriton commanded. Two of his minions dragged one of Cronus's men forth. The man was a little more than a boy of eighteen years named Laven Morlai. It was then that Cronus noticed two large boards crossed, driven into the sand, forming an X.

The gargoyles freed young Laven's hands from his bonds, then tied his limbs to the crossed boards, stretching his feet and hands to their utmost. His ragged garments were stripped away, exposing his quivering naked flesh. Kriton drew a dagger from his belt, its steel blade resplendent with the torchlight playing along its length. He swiftly gelded Laven, stem and root, as the boy's screams echoed off the surrounding stone walls. The Torry captives lowered their eyes, unable to further witness the savage maiming of their comrade.

"Burnsss it!" Kriton hissed as a heated brazier was brought forth. Another gargoyle removed a glowing pincer from the fire and pressed it upon Laven's gaping wound as blood pooled upon the sand at his feet. Anguished tears sprayed from Laven's desperate gray eyes as Kriton tossed his severed member upon the sand. Any hope that his torment was at an end was quickly squashed with the gargoyle's next utterance. "I have questions. You give answers, or this shall feel a mere tickle to your next punishment," Kriton snarled.

The boy wondered what information they could possibly desire that they didn't already possess. He would tell anything to spare himself further anguish. "Whatever you wish," he shamefully yielded.

"Tell me of the fire. How did it kill so many of our comrades?"

Laven hesitated, his mind trying to filter what could be revealed from what he might keep back. Kriton saw through his mental struggle and promptly acted, his clawed feet scraping the sand as he retrieved the glowing rod from the brazier. He closed upon the boy, pressing the red-hot metal into the boy's right palm, holding it there for a time as the lad's screams issued anew.

"Tellsss me!" Kriton snarled as the young Torry babbled, his voice a disjointed mixture of garbled words. Kriton pressed the iron into the boy's other palm, holding it in place till flesh melded to metal. When he pulled it free, chunks of skin came with it. The boy continued speaking, his panicked words incomprehensible. "Shutsss upsss!" Kriton grabbed his quivering face with his clawed left hand and twisted it to face his demon red eyes. "Yousss hadsss yoursss chancesss to speaksss."

"Looksss andsss learnsss!" another gargoyle hissed in Cronus's ear as he jerked his chin up, clawed fingers digging into Cronus's chin. The Torry captives were forced to watch in helpless terror for hours on end as Kriton applied his cruel ministrations to the suffering soldier. They flayed his fingers and hands, gouged his left eye, cut away his kneecaps, drove nails into his chest, burned his feet, yanked his teeth, and cut off his nose and tongue at a painfully measured pace. They were careful not to hasten their creative applications, savoring Laven's pitiful laments. When he would pass out from the pain, they would revive him until his mind allowed his heart to give out. When they were finished, they cut him down and dragged his listless corpse away.

"Bringsss another!" Kriton pointed a clawed digit toward the next Torry in line. The soldier was brought forth, his hands still bound behind him and his feet shackled. He was thrown to Kriton's feet, his panicked eyes desperately wide.

"Headsss to dirtsss, slave!" hissed one of those who brought him forth. He complied without hesitation, his heart pounding emphatically, fearful of the torment to come.

"Liftsss yoursss head!" Kriton commanded. He did so, keeping his eyes lowered, for he dared not look upon Kriton's terrible countenance. "Namesss?"

"I am… Safed Corlen," he said through quivering lips.

"Learnsss from your comrade and answer my questionsss."

"Yes." Safed nodded his agreement.

"Tell me of the fires." Safed explained General Bode's plan to the extent of what he knew of it. He detailed how they coated the gap with oil and how they set it ablaze once the gargoyle legions passed. "You liesss!" Kriton snarled. "How cansss wet grass burnsss so rapidly?"

Safed explained how the grass and oil were altered by the Earthers' magic. When asked why the Earthers aided the Torry cause, he answered that they were friends of Cronus. At this revelation, Kriton craned his neck to where the emperor sat above them. His neck then turned, his glowing eyes stopping at Cronus.

"Takesss themsss awaysss!" Kriton hissed as Cronus and his fellows were herded without, leaving Safed kneeling in the sand. "You haves two choices," Kriton said, raising two digits to emphasize the point. "You cansss suffer as Laven suffered, or you can beg the emperor to geld you and accept you in his service as a slave." Safed's eyes drew wide, unable to sort his thoughts. "Bind him to the boardsss!" Kriton snarled, impatient with Safed's indecision.

"No!" Safed pleaded desperately. "Please, I'll be your slave!" he begged.

Kriton turned, his narrowed eye slits meeting Tyro's cold stare. Tyro stood from his seat, his golden robes smoothing as he arose. "He begs servitude, my emperor," Kriton said with a deep bow.

"Then geld him and be done with it." Tyro scowled wickedly.

*****

The bluish-silver hull of the submersible glided neath the surface of the wine-dark sea, skirting the Yatin coast until the gray watchtowers of Tenin Harbor rose in the distance. Lorken raised the scope, scanning the shoreline from afar. "Transfer the image so I can see," Brokov said from the captain's chair. A clear view of Tenin manifested on the view screen, the dark green of the Tenin lowlands shadowing the ancient port city.

Spires of thick smoke drifted above the harbor. The wreckage of half-sunken vessels and listing ships littered the surrounding sea. They identified over a hundred Benotrist galleys blocking the mouth of the Yatin port. Expanding the image further revealed gargoyle encampments both north and south of the harbor. Brokov transferred the image to the bridge of the *Stenox*, which rested twenty miles southwest.

*****

Terin cast his gaze to the west, where the sun hovered above the horizon, its yellow light painted across the sea. It was the first clear night they had seen since reaching the ocean, and he yearned to see the sunset on that endless water. Looking over the port side wall of the third deck, Terin gazed in awe as he shrank before the majesty of the open sea. How insignificant he truly felt, staring at the endless expanse of ocean. The brisk evening air lifted his golden mane as he stood unfazed by the wind kissing his exposed limbs. His gray cloak billowed behind him as he faced the easterly breeze.

Leanna paused at the top of the ladder, observing Terin briefly before continuing her ascent. He seemed, at that moment, so pure and untamed, like a virgin spirit experiencing every detail of the world for the first time. "May I join you?" she asked.

He turned to her voice, extending a hand as she stepped upon the deck. "Of course."

Still holding his hand, she craned her neck, looking at the ocean all around. "What were you doing up here?" she said, bringing her blue eyes back to his.

"I find it peaceful up here." He returned his face to the setting sun, staring at the endless expanse.

"What do you see?" she asked, wondering what allure the sea held for him.

"I feel small, as if all my worries are insignificant compared to the majesty I see before me. What do you see?" he asked.

Leanna followed his gaze to the west, humoring his fascination. After a brief moment, she was struck by a memory, a memory of a face staring back at her with gentle green eyes and dark hair. It was a handsome face that reflected the passion of a noble heart, a heart captive to her own. Cronus. Her heart ached at the vision.

She saw him coming to her over calm water, standing at the prow of a vessel with the wind in his mane and his hand outstretched to hers. Her hand lifted to his, reaching desperately to feel the touch of her beloved before passing through the fading apparition. The vision shimmered, then faded to nothingness. "I see nothing." She sighed, lowering her head in profound loneliness. "Nothing."

*****

"That explains how your father got a fleet close to Molten Isle so quickly. It was because they were already off the Yatin coast," Raven remarked, scanning the Benotrist siege of Tenin through the images transmitted from the *Atlantis.*

Tosha found the vision unnerving. Her father risked much waging war against another kingdom. She thought it wiser to finish one adversary before engaging the next. Perhaps that was what the Yatins were thinking as well, which caught them by surprise. That would explain her father's legions at the gates of Tenin. Only a complete surprise could explain their deep penetration into Yatin proper so quickly. They must have caught the border forces unawares. "It is not unexpected. My father is an ambitious man," she said, concealing her doubts.

"More like cocky. He's pushing his luck by taking on two of the largest kingdoms on Arax simultaneously." Raven snorted.

"I thought cocky would be a trait you would find admirable." She smirked.

"You think I'm cocky?" He lifted an eyebrow. With her arms crossed, she gave him a knowing look. "I never boast what I can't do, and you best remember it."

"I stand corrected. You are a pillar of humility." Her smirk widened.

"If I'm so awful, why do spend all your time up here with me?" He swiveled his chair to fully face her.

She did spend an inordinate amount of time on the bridge, and he had called her on it. Why did she, she wondered. "Perhaps I find you a constant source of amusement, Raven."

"Are you saying you find my perceived arrogance amusing?"

"Well, yes, in a childlike and simpleminded way." She shrugged.

"So I'm cocky and stupid."

"Yes. I find it a common trait among all men not of my isle."

"Your isle?"

"The Federation of the Sisterhood," she further explained.

"Of course, the men on your isle aren't cocky since they spend all their time kissing your ass. What do you expect from a bunch of wimps?"

"You think you're better than them," she stated flatly.

"Yeah, but that's not sayin' a whole lot. I can't really respect a man who's been physically enslaved by a bunch of women."

"Oh yes, we poor, hapless band of females who can only assert our will on a collection of pitiful male specimen. We certainly couldn't subjugate a man so powerful as yourself."

"Damn right you can't."

"And you think you're not arrogant?" She rolled her eyes.

"That's not arrogance. That's stating fact. There's a difference, you know."

"You believe you could never be bested by a woman?"

"Listen, Princess, the only woman who ever frightened me was my paternal grandmother. When she got angry, she used to chase after us, trying to club us like baby seals. Yeesh, she was a frightening woman." He shuddered at the memory.

"A woman who frightens you. I like her already."

"If you dislike me so much, then why don't you go bug someone else?"

"I already told you. I find you amusing."

"That's because you think I'm a dummy."

She didn't understand the word but caught the meaning. "I attempted to engage your other crewmates in conversation, but Leanna feels awkward with my father responsible for her betrothed being held prisoner, Zem seems a poor conversationalist, and Argos seems overly grumpy."

"Zem is a great conversationalist as long as the conversation is about how wonderful he is. He just thinks he's better than us."

"Like you."

He gave her a look before continuing. "Argos just looks grumpy, but he is actually very happy to be here."

"Why is that?"

"Back home is a very stressful time for the Ape Empire. Ever since their victory in their revolution against the Casian Federation, the Ape tribal leaders have gathered, trying to hash out a new government. Like I always say, it's not easy being an Ape when everyone's trying to be the top banana." Raven laughed, but Tosha just stared at him, oblivious to his pun.

*****

They were herded from their cells once again, their hands bound behind them and shackles linking their feet. Shuffling along the cold, damp, rocky floor, they were led into an adjoining chamber that was ten meters abreast with jagged, uneven walls that were cut from the rocky bowels neath the Black Castle. They were knelt in a semicircle facing a corner of the chamber where another of their fellows was chained hand and foot to the bedrock, his limbs stretched to their limit as he faced his brothers in arms with festering apprehension.

His name was Clorm Margos. Cronus had known Clorm's family. His father was a blacksmith in Central City. Like Cronus, Clorm had a lady love whom he promised to wed upon his return, but now he was chained against the dungeon wall, awaiting some gruesome end.

Kriton's clawed feet scraped the rocky floor, stepping before their kneeling ranks. Blood-red eyes peered through narrowed eyelids, scanning the faces of the miserable wretches before him. His split, narrow tongue slithered over his bright lips like a serpent. "You are the commander of these mensss?" Kriton's eyes stopped at Cronus.

"I am!" Cronus affirmed in a proud, clear voice.

"The emperor has special plans for you. Your men, however, are mine to dispose of." He signaled another gargoyle forth, who brought a bucket with a broom-sized swab protruding from it. Kriton gripped the end of the swab and pulled it free, and a gelatinous liquid oozed from its tip. He ran the damp cushioned end over Clorm's limbs, leaving a thin layer of the liquid upon his skin. Kriton then sank the swab deep into the bucket, leaving thick globs of liquid pouring off its tip as he removed it again. He shoved the cushioned end of the swab into Clorm's face.

Cronus noticed, to his horror, a small ventilation shaft above Clorm's head. As understanding washed over him, he saw Kriton lift a torch from the wall and touch it to Clorm's limbs. Narrow bands of flame ignited along the Torry's arms and legs. Clorm screamed in gut-wrenching agony as Kriton turned a hateful eye to Cronus before jabbing the torch into Clorm's face. Ghastly moans echoed from Clorm's mouth as the flesh of his face burned away.

Clorm lost consciousness before the flames died away, his body shutting down from the pain. Kriton doused him with water, trying to revive him, to no avail. Kriton simply shrugged and continued by slicing away strips of flesh from his chest. He cut off Clorm's blackened nose and stuffed it in his mouth. "Comesss!" He ordered his comrades to partake.

Half a dozen gargoyles hurried forth, each cutting pieces of flesh from Clorm's listless body. "I likesss minesss cooked!" one proclaimed as he cut a piece from Clorm's thigh. Suddenly, an inhuman cry issued from Clorm's blackened lips as his body shook violently.

"He lives!" one gargoyle hissed excitedly. The others ignored his suffering and continued to pick at his flesh, avoiding vital areas to prolong their victim's agony. Clorm eventually succumbed as his fellow Torries lowered their heads and wept.

CHAPTER 14

Terin stood on the third deck, greeting the sunrise as it played off the waters of the bay. The bustling port city of Tinsay surrounded him in panoramic splendor. Tall watchtowers lined the opposing shores of the bay, guarding the mouth of the harbor. Terin saw sentries posted atop the battlements, the morning sun reflecting off their polished helms and breastplates.

Large storehouses of dark stone lined the wharves along the waterfront. Scores of circular docking piers of the Benotrist Navy jutted into the harbor proper, though most were empty with much of the navy fighting in Yatin. Straight ahead, where the Gorga River emptied into the Tinsan Bay, he descried high-domed structures with pillars rising upon their flanks. They were the city's forum and magistrate, positioned on the southern bank of the Gorga.

Opposing these stately structures on the north bank arose a massive figure cut from stone. It was a sculpture twenty meters in height in the form of a nymph with her arms pressed into the ground as if lifting her from the sea. With her head arched back and dark hair cascading below her shoulders, she was nude with endowed feminine curves crafted in pristine symmetry. Black obsidian was plated to the folds of her hair while her flesh was tinted in deep-olive hues. Two fist-sized emeralds were placed in her eye sockets, casting her beguiling gaze across the bay.

"She is called the Sea Maiden," Tosha said as she cleared the ladder to step beside him.

"Princess," Terin greeted, extending a hand to help her up.

"Thank you." She smiled coyly, her eyes running the length of him. "The statue"—she returned her eyes to the massive structure ahead—"she is called the Sea Maiden. She was crafted hundreds of years ago, commissioned by King Korbar of Old Northern Kingdom. She has greeted sailors to our shores ever since."

"Beautiful," Terin whispered.

"Yes, she is quite lovely. She has beguiled men with her wanton stare for ages, despoiling their hearts for any other, though such a fate shall not befall an attractive male like you."

Terin reddened at the comment. "It is kind of you to say, Highness, but I do prefer women of flesh over nymphs of stone."

She studied him for a time, weighing him on some internal scale. "We haven't spoken, you and I. I haven't thanked you for my rescue."

"Raven, Kato, and Argos rescued you, Princess. I aided in Princess Corry's and Princess Felicia's liberation."

"You could not have known whom each was rescuing. You are all collectively responsible for my liberation. For that, I thank you, Terin."

"You are welcome, Highness." He bowed his head.

"You are very brave and courteous. Perhaps you could instruct Raven on such courtesies," she said, for his manners were lacking.

"Do you believe he would listen?" Terin lifted a brow.

"Probably not, but since you shall be joining us on our journey to Fera, you might remind him whilst we travel."

"I shall do my best, Highness."

"Very well. Since my father and your king have foolishly gone to war one upon the other, you are in great peril while visiting the Benotrist realm. As long as you adhere to the protocols of visiting dignitaries, I shall shield you from my father's wrath."

"Thank you, Highness."

Tosha meant to step away when sunlight struck the charm hanging about his neck. She reached out, lifting the necklace from beneath his tunic, where it was concealed. She was struck by the craftmanship of the charm, the three faces carved in stone impressing her in their detail. "This is lovely, Terin. Where did you find it?"

"My father gifted it to me," he said.

"Hmm," she mused. The artist who crafted the items was uniquely skilled. "My father sculpts. He would find this of great interest."

"My father sculpts as well," Terin said, though his father rarely displayed the gift. He would make sculptures of Terin's mother when time allowed as well as other impressive works. His father would never display his works, hiding them away as if they were for his eyes only.

"Did he sculpt these?" she asked, running her fingers over the women's faces. The one in the center looked familiar, but she could not place it.

"He only claimed this one," he said, touching the one to the side, the one cast in his mother's visage.

"He is exceptional," she said. "It is a pity we are at war, for my father would enjoy your father's work. There are few to rival his artistic brilliance, but your father seems capable. Is the woman your mother?" she asked, touching the one his father carved.

"Yes."

"And the other two images? Who are they?"

"Minister Antillius says this one opposite my mother is of my grandmother. He met her long ago. He said she was named Cordela."

"You sound as if you didn't know her name."

"I didn't. My father never spoke of his kin. Neither did my mother."

"That is strange. What of the woman in the center? Do you know her?"

"No, but I guess she is my father's kin."

"She looks familiar, but I can't place it. Perhaps my father would know," she said, tucking the necklace back inside his collar.

*****

"Ow!" Raven yelped as Brokov injected the tracker into his arm.

"Stop whining, you big baby. It doesn't hurt that much," Brokov chided as they stood in the first crew cabin with Lorken and out of sight of the others. "Your turn," he said, turning to Lorken, who offered up his left arm.

A sudden jolt of pain coursed through Lorken's arm, but he refused to wince. "Didn't feel a thing." He shrugged, knowing such a lie would irritate Raven.

"Yeah? How 'bout I smash your head in the floor? Would you feel that?" Raven growled.

"Probably. I'm not as thickheaded as you."

"That's because I used to soften up your head during practice back in the academy. You were the most sacked quarterback we had in thirty years."

"I couldn't do much without a line," Lorken lamented.

"That's no excuse. I led our conference with tackles for a loss our senior year with the Jenson brothers playing in front of me. They had to be the worst defensive tackles I've ever seen. Heck, my sister could've blown them off the line. Even a dimwit like Brokov could see that."

"How would I know? I never had the time to watch your silly games. Some of us had actual fields of study that required the application of mathematics and hard science. What exactly did you two major in?" Brokov asked, with his eyes drifting to the ceiling in false contemplation. "Oh, that's right." He snapped his fingers. "Raven studied astrogeography, and it took him three semesters to locate twinkle-twinkle on an astro chart."

"We were cadet pilots. That was our primary field, book boy!" Raven growled.

"Since the first pilots in the space program were chimpanzees, I guess things haven't changed much." Brokov chuckled.

Kato's voice broke through the comm. "Rav, we're pulling into port, and it seems they have a not-so-friendly welcoming party to meet us," he said from the bridge.

"Big surprise there."

*****

They stepped out onto the stern of the first deck to the panoramic view of the mouth of Tinsay before them. Sunlight cast shadows of the upper deck on the waters before them until they turned to ascend the bridge. Benotrist war galleys shadowed their easy advance upon the central districts of the harbor. Crews in bright mail lined the upper decks of the vessels, wary of the *Stenox*'s intent. Soldiers in bronze helms and gold tunics raced along the base of the Sea Maiden, skirting the giant sculpture as the *Stenox* passed the mouth of the Gorga. Soldiers on the opposing bank mirrored their comrades' movements, racing at the base of the city forum and magistrate, their ranks dwarfed by the massive stone columns behind them.

Tosha and Terin caught Raven's eye as he stepped on the second deck. "I'd get down here before one of those idiots out there decides to put an arrow in your gut," Raven warned. They turned to his voice, staring down from the third deck.

"Those are my father's soldiers, Raven. They will not harm their princess," Tosha said confidently.

"I doubt they'd know you face-to-face, let alone at this distance. Get down before I drag you down!" She glared at him with clenched lips to bite off her anger. She crossed her arms in defiance, daring him to try.

"She might be right, Rav. Take a look." Lorken observed the warships shielding the south bank of the Gorga open a path to the magistrate building, where hundreds of soldiers paraded in disciplined ranks as if to welcome a dignitary or head of state. Scores of harbor officials dressed in flowing calnesian robes of various pastel shades stood before the ranks of soldiers.

"Pull up to the wharf where the welcoming party is," Raven commanded, stepping onto the bridge. Kato obliged, backing the stern to the stone lip of the wharf.

*****

Tosha stepped onto the wharf, the wind whipping her midnight hair across her face, as the assembled officials dropped to their knees and bowed with their foreheads to the ground. The soldiers behind them did likewise, heralding the safe return of their crown princess.

"Rise, my children!" Tosha commanded.

"Your Highness, Tinsay welcomes you," Jetar Slars, regent of Tinsay Province, greeted as he came to his feet. He wore rich scarlet robes that fell to his ankles. He was slender with braided silver hair and stood sixty inches.

"Regent Slars," Tosha stated in kind. "You were expecting me?"

"Yes, Highness. Emperor's Elite Nels Draken arrived just yester morn. He relayed the joyous news of your escape from Molten Isle before continuing on to Fera."

"Very well. I shall require the use of a dozen magantor mounts and seven guards to escort my party to Fera."

"My apologies, Highness, but we have none to give you. Most were taken with the fleets that left for Yatin while the rest have been detached for various missions over the past days."

"None? You have none to give me?" Tosha snarled, causing an apologetic Jetar to fidget nervously.

"We may have one or two to return perhaps in a day. I could send word to Laycrom to send us the mounts you require, Highness." The royal magantor stables in Laycrom housed scores of giant eagles, but it did little good sending a currier. Tosha would not wait idly in Tinsay whilst she could ride for Laycrom herself.

"I shall ride there myself!" she declared.

"If you so desire, Highness. I'll have Commander Forlit provide a suitable escort."

"See to it immediately, Regent. I plan to depart posthaste."

Raven and Lorken joined Terin on the first deck stern, observing Tosha issuing commands to the dignitaries and port officials surrounding her as if they were drones in her hive. "She's a bossy little thing, isn't she?" Raven grunted.

"Little? She's taller than most of the men out there," Terin countered.

"You're all little, Terin."

"No. You are simply a giant." Terin smiled.

"In my family, I'm one of the little ones." Raven gave him a look. "Four of my five brothers outweigh me by fifty pounds and are all taller. Of course, they don't have my good looks."

"Have you any sisters?" Terin imagined them hulking brutes with breasts and tried to shake such painful visions from his mind.

"I had two. Now I have one." Raven's dispassionate voice failed to separate him from that painful loss. Terin would ask no more.

The door to the inner section of the first deck opened as Argos and Brokov escorted Monsoon with his hands bound behind him in steel fetters. The pirate lord glared at Raven, his eyes and voice no longer pleading to turn the Earthers to his cause. They were now hate-filled for the ruin of his plans and the loss of his liberty. Raven could have shown mercy and killed him rather than visit upon him such a fate as the dungeons of Fera.

"Are you sure about this, Rav?" Brokov asked, his eyes fixed sternly upon his friend. "If Tosha's intentions are in any way hostile, we can offer no help other than vengeance."

"What's to worry about? There are only thirty thousand troops in Fera. That's only fifteen thousand apiece between me and Lorken. No problem."

Raven is going to Fera! Monsoon mused in disbelief. *Why?* He wanted to ask but thought better of it.

"Grab your bag of goodies, Lorken. Come on, sunshine. It's time we go." Raven took Monsoon by the arm and pushed him toward the wharf. Lorken slung the strap of his thick black bag over his shoulder, Terin following them off the ship.

Leanna followed Argos and Brokov to the stern as the others stepped onto the wharf. Raven passed Monsoon to Lorken and Terin, allowing them to proceed to Tosha, and he turned one last time to Leanna. She stood upon the deck, hugging her arms as she stared at him with hope-filled eyes. "We'll find him, Leanna, and bring him home," Raven said before following the others into the crowd.

*****

Yeltor found the caravan holding his prince two days ride shy of the Benotrist border. He had chanced upon several caravans of Yatin captives being herded northward since he ambushed the royal messenger and adopted the trappings of his post. With each encounter, he practiced his false identity, introducing himself as Royal Currier Veglar Sornt, a common Benotrist surname. He approached each caravan with caution, as this was a gargoyle campaign, and humans in Yatin were enemies to the Benotrist slavers driving their chattel northward. To Yeltor's surprise, the Benotrists easily believed his false tale, but their hired free swords were less trusting but deferred to their Benotrist employers.

The slavers' caravans were encumbered by the dregs bound in their coffles. The Benotrist soldiers tasked with bringing Prince Yanku to Fera were free of such impediment and moved swiftly. Yeltor happened upon them by mere chance as they were encamped off the beaten path. Unlike the slavers he had encountered, the Benotrist cavalry guarding the Yatin prince begrudgingly allowed him within their encampment. Since a poorly armed currier posed little threat, he was allowed in their midst.

He found Prince Yanku sitting in the center of the encampment with his hands bound behind him and a tether binding his right ankle to a stake driven into the ground. The boy appeared disheveled in his soiled tunic and unkempt hair that twisted about his face in tangles and sweat. His eyes stared soulless into the crackling flames of the cookfire. Yeltor wondered if the arrogant youth rightly blamed himself for his sorry state, or did he think the failure at Salamin Valley should fall upon another? Regardless, Yeltor was oath bound to protect Emperor Yangu's heir, and he would die in the attempt if necessary.

It would have to be this night, he reminded himself, for the Benotrists would not suffer his presence beyond one night, and no royal currier would attach himself to a slower-moving train. If he attempted to stay beyond one night to wait for a more opportune time to free Yanku, they would likely uncover the deceptions he carefully constructed. He would wait till the bulk of the men were bedded and strike the guards in detail, slay or disperse their mounts, and abscond with the prince.

He counted eighteen Benotrists in camp and surmised that three to five would stand post at any given time. He would have to move with stealth and haste in equal measure. The sun was kissing the horizon, slipping to the west, heralding the coming night.

Yeltor felt the prince's eyes fixed on his familiar face. He returned the stare briefly, and understanding passed between them. Yanku wisely lowered his eyes lest his captors note the look between them. Yeltor noticed a sudden shift among the Benotrists, and his hand went instinctively to his belt, where his sword normally hung. He released a cautious breath as several soldiers rushed past, indicating that he was not the source of their angst, but his relief was short-lived as a dozen riders flooded their campsite.

Several were gargoyles, including one that stood out with a heavier bulk than the others, weighing nigh 180 pounds. His demeanor was calm and calculating as his eyes swept over the assemblage, stopping on Prince Yanku's shivering form. He spoke to another rider beside him, a human with one eye and a scarred face. Their brief exchange was cut short as the riders parted, making way for an enormous man on a black ocran.

He was unlike any man Yeltor had ever seen. He was dressed in black from boot to hat. His thick trousers, boots, shirt, and jacket were as dark as a moonless night. His strange black hat had a rim that circled it. The rim bent vertically at the hat's sides and hung low over its front and back. The man's face was white like a specter expelled from its grave. Yeltor's eyes drew wide as he beheld the strange object hanging upon his hip. Another long object was slung across his back.

"Who's the boy?" the large man growled, his mere voice cowering the fellows in his group, save for the one-eyed human and the large gargoyle, who seemed diminutive beside the larger man.

"Zelo says the whelp is the Yatin crown prince," the one-eyed said, revealing the name of the gargoyle.

"A fine gift for the emperor, Thorton. Shall Neon and I return him in person?" the gargoyle Zelo said, revealing the name of the one-eyed.

"I'll have Cragor lead the others to treat with our errant general. We three will return to Fera to deliver the boy," Ben Thorton said. The sudden victories and the capture of the Yatin crown prince would surely alter the emperor's plans. Ben Thorton thought it prudent to inform the emperor of these tidings before pursuing objectives that might be detrimental to the empire.

The identity of the large man was suddenly transparent to Yeltor. He was an Earther. His bearing, clothing, and flesh bespoke a strangeness alien to Arax. He had heard rumors of their unique appearance and weapons and fanciful tales of their origin and the wonder of their vessel. The fact that one of their number was here in the service of the Benotrist emperor bode ill. If Tyro wedded his power to theirs, then what power or alliance could stand against them? If he was to save his prince, he had to act this night.

*****

Terin sat upon his pack, staring into the crackling flames of their cookfire. The late-spring night air still had the bite of a winter chill, so Terin held his cloak tight about his shoulders. He reflected on the dizzying events since the morn, when they set ashore at Tinsay. The princess wasted little time mustering her father's vassals to provide mounts and escorts and departed the harbor within an hour of their arrival. Nearly four score riders escorted their small party, their own cookfires surrounding theirs in the camp's center.

With the clear sky painted overhead, they forsook tents or pavilions and slept neath the starry night. Terin expected the princess to be housed in a grand pavilion with doting servants and rich trappings, but surprisingly, she rode with the men, wore breastplate and sword, and acted more a cavalry commander than a princess. Should anyone forget her high station, they needed only observe the thousands upon thousands of small folk, merchants, and nobles who knelt as she passed with their knees bent and heads pressed to the ground. The soldiers of her escort paid her no less in respect, each bowing in her presence lest lightning strike them down from the firmament above.

Raven snorted at the entire affair, dismissive of such ass licking, as he crudely referred to it. The looks of awe and reverence her people expressed toward Tosha contrasted sharply to the frowns of disapproval they gave Raven. Many of their escort threatened to draw their swords on Raven and Lorken for their disrespect. The princess calmly intervened, ordering her men to stand down. Terin displayed a modicum of deference toward Tosha with respectful bows of his head and addressing her by proper title. Though it was far less than the complete obeisance of her people, it went unnoticed beside the Earthers' willful ignorance of royal protocol.

The Benotrists' disdain for Raven was apparent as soon as he stepped off the ship. When the regent of Tinsay attempted to correct his lack of respect for the princess, Raven threatened to snap off the regent's manhood and shove it up his rectum. Tosha quickly intervened, assuaging Raven's ire while assuring the regent that Raven's bluster exceeded his threat. Though Raven and Tosha's interactions were amusing to a point, Terin could ill imagine how they would be received once they reached the court of Emperor Tyro.

Lorken's behavior was little better, but Tosha ignored his crude and off-color remarks, focusing her barbs and taunts for Raven. For someone who was constantly offended by the Earther's comments, she spent an inordinate amount of time in his presence. Lorken repeatedly commented that Tosha and Raven were smitten but were too stubborn to admit to it. Terin thought otherwise, as the two constantly bickered and spoke despairingly of each other.

"You can have first watch," Raven said, unfurling his bedroll on the opposite side of the fire. "Wake me when the Benotrists switch out their guards."

"If they're already standing watch, why are we—"

"They're watching out for outside threats. We need to watch them."

"If they truly mean us harm, they could easily do so when we are awake. Why—"

"If they try when we are awake, Lorken and I would wipe the floor with 'em. I don't trust our little princess. She's up to something. Don't let your guard down." Raven noticed the empty bedroll between them. "Where's Lorken?"

"He stepped away a while ago, but to where, I do not know."

"I'm here." Lorken's deep voice echoed in the dim light. "I had to piss."

"You go more than my grandfather. How many times has that been today, ten?" Raven chided.

"Just four." Lorken snorted. "You might want to go now before the trench fills up. If these fellas are anything like those Troan free swords we marched with a year ago, they're sure to make a mess of things rather quick."

"Those Troans were a little hard on the nose but were a whole lot friendlier than this bunch." Raven jerked a thumb over his shoulder.

"Yes. I'm surprised they haven't warmed up to your charming personality."

"They started it."

"Yes, but your threat to unman their local regent and to shove his member where the sun don't shine, I'm sure, had nothing to do with it." Lorken snickered.

"And he would be wise to tame his tongue before we reach Fera," Tosha said, stepping into their midst while unfurling her bedroll between Raven and Terin.

"You're sleeping here?" Raven asked.

"Where else? Did you expect me to have a grand pavilion, a full bed, and be catered to by doting servants? I am heir to two realms. I am warrior bred and raised. I have slept many times upon the ground, Raven. Do not wrongly mark me as a pampered princess. You should be honored that I allow your peasant blood in such proximity to mine."

"Maybe the open air will ease your snoring." Terin face-palmed, not believing Raven would accuse her of such.

"I don't snore!" she snarled, fixing him with a murderous glare.

Raven laid on his bedroll with his hands tucked behind his head and his feet crossed, looking far more comfortable than one should when sleeping on the ground. "I overheard the other girls on the *Stenox* commenting on it. Even Argos voiced a complaint. He could hear you in the next cabin over."

"And I heard similar complaints about your flatulence." She stood with her arms folded over her chest, staring down at him with a raised eyebrow.

"I'm sure your mother's is worse."

"Perhaps you can ask her yourself when you visit her court," she countered.

"And why would I ever visit her court?"

"Because," she said in a sultry, drawn-out voice, "when we rescue your friend, you shall escort me to Bansoch, returning me safely to my mother's court."

Raven sat bolt upright. "That was not part of our agreement!"

"Oh, I believe it is only fair considering that I am only venturing to Fera on behalf of your friend. You could at least return me to the Sisterhood. Besides, it would hardly delay your next misadventure since your ship can cross the channel in a day."

"I never wanted to come to Fera. You dragged us along. Why should I follow you back to Bansoch?"

"The objective is the release of your friend. I only advised you to join me in order to ensure his freedom. I believe you should aid my return considering the assistance I have rendered you."

"Assistance? We rescued you, remember? If anyone should be grateful, it's you."

"Gratitude? What, pray tell, do you think I have done since we disembarked? I have repeatedly stayed the hands of my escort lest they cut your throat for the insult of my person."

"You're not saving my life. You're saving theirs. If any of your soldier boys wants a piece of me, they're welcome to try. Just don't expect me to bury 'em."

And so it continued half the night, Raven and Tosha arguing without end. Eventually, Lorken and Terin forsook their campsite, setting their bedrolls beside members of their escort so they could get some sleep. Lorken wasn't even certain that Raven or Tosha noticed them leaving.

*****

He crept slowly toward the perimeter, the pale light of the crescent moon lighting his face as he drew the dagger across the sentry's throat with his left hand covering the man's mouth. Yeltor held his grip, keeping the sentry's mouth closed, easing him to the ground.

Only the thrashing of the fellow's legs echoed dully in the low grass. He waited until the body lay still before moving on. He slowly returned to his feet, fearing any sudden movement that a trained eye might catch in the dim light.

Halfway to the central campfire, he noticed a sleepy eye open as he passed. He quickly fell on the Benotrist, driving the blade of his dagger into his throat, snuffing out a scream as it issued from his mouth. Yeltor drove the blade hilt deep and wrenched it back and forth in two quick cuts, shredding the soft tissue connecting head to torso. Blood sprayed his face and tunic, casting his face in a macabre light. His head shifted back and forth, surveying the perimeter for any movement.

The stillness of the night unnerved him—no birds singing, no wind rustling the grass. Only the crackles of the waning campfire echoed dully in the air. He wished he could cut the Earther's throat, but the large ruffian was bedded too closely to his fellows. Any attempt to slice his throat without alerting his comrades was sure to fail, and if he failed, his prince was doomed.

The prince stirred as Yeltor drew near, his eyes focusing on the Elite's face as he brought a finger to his lips, warning him to silence. Yanku breathed a relieved sigh as Yeltor cut the rope binding his ankle to the post. The manacles binding his hands behind him was problematic, as Yeltor lacked the keys to undo them. Only a heavy blow would free him, and such a sound would alert the sleeping Benotrists. Nay, freeing the prince's hands would have to wait until they were in the clear. Yeltor gripped Prince Yanku's elbow, helping him to his feet.

Before they had taken their first step toward their ocran, a blinding pain washed over Yeltor, collapsing him to the ground. Yanku stared helplessly as Ben Thorton stepped from the shadows with his pistol drawn. The large gargoyle and the one-eyed man stood to either side.

"Bind his hands, Neon!" the Earther commanded.

"He lives?" one-eyed asked as he stepped forth to secure Yeltor.

"I only stunned him. He'll wake a little worse for wear, but he's alive," Ben Thorton explained, holstering his pistol as he closed on the prince and shoving the frightened youth to the ground with a palm to the chest. "All right, kid, who is he?" he said, jerking a thumb toward Yeltor's unconscious form sprawled out behind him.

The prince's voice caught in the willowy narrows of his throat, answering incoherently with quivering lips. "Agh down ghooo."

The large gargoyle stepped nigh, kneeling beside the prince and forcefully grasping his face with clawed fingers. "Speak clear, child!" Zelo moved a pointy digit over Yanku's right eye, drawing perilously close, the threat not escaping his panicked mind.

"He is my sworn protector, a…member of my…father's Elite," Yanku confessed.

"A Yatin Elite? Here?" Ben Thorton lifted a brow over a blue eye.

Another Benotrist warrior emerged at Thorton's side, a grim-faced fellow with a shaved skull and tear-shaped red tattoos descending from the corners of his eyes. "All four sentries are dead! He slit their throats."

"Efficient killer, ain't he? Wake up the clown in charge of this hapless bunch," Thorton said.

"As you command."

"And Cragor?" Thorton called him back.

"Yes, Thorton?" Cragor asked.

"Find out how many others he slew in their sleep."

*****

"Wake up!" Thorton flicked his nose. Yeltor stirred, the painful stings to his nose alerting him that something was amiss. His eyes shot open. He found himself lying upon the ground with his hands bound behind and his feet tied together. The Earther squatted beside him. It was still night, and he could see shadows moving in his periphery. Obviously, the camp was fully alerted to his failed attempt.

Pain gripped his entire left side, a deep ache that imbued each muscle and joint. "Are you ready to answer my questions, Yeltor?" Thorton asked. *He knows my name!* Yeltor froze at the revelation.

Only Yanku could have revealed such knowledge, and Yeltor wondered what torture they might have used to extract his name from the prince.

"How many friends do you have out there waiting?" Thorton asked. Yeltor regarded him carefully. It made little difference if the Earther knew the truth since no one would come to his rescue now. He cursed Yanku for not conjuring a lie that might mask who he really was. He might've claimed him to be a free sword or a common soldier, but a Yatin Elite alerted his captors to how dangerous he truly was. There would be little chance now to slip his bonds or for them to be careless in his keeping.

"I am alone," Yeltor answered with labored breath, the effects of Thorton's laser still afflicting him.

"You expect me to believe you came here alone?" Thorton growled.

"I…don't expect…anything from the likes of you. But if I weren't alone, do you believe I would be so desperate?"

"I suppose not, but I don't take needless risks. Zelo!" Thorton called the large gargoyle over, who stood a few paces away, berating the Benotrist detachment commander for his lax security.

"Yes, Thorton?" Zelo hissed lowly.

"Secure him away from his prince and guard him carefully. We'll bring him with us."

"To where?" Yeltor asked warily.

Thorton stood. "Fera," he answered. "A little time in the dungeon should loosen his tongue." Yeltor paled.

*****

The midday sun filtered through the broad leaves of the porians swaying in the breeze above, casting a patchwork of light and shadow on the trail below. The road from Tinsay to Laycrom skirted the north bank of the slow-flowing Andler. They rode apace, placing many leagues between the wharves of Tinsay and themselves. For her second day of riding, she forsook her tunic and sandals for trousers and boots. With a sword on her hip and breastplate and helm, Tosha looked more warrior than princess. When Raven commented that she would look better in a skirt, she slapped him and said that if he favored them, she would arrange for him to wear one.

At breakfast, he suggested that she join his crew after they freed Cronus rather than returning to her mother's queendom, offering her a position as his cabin girl. She hadn't spoken to him since. She could hear him even now, several riders behind her, whistling tunes from his native tongue as if he hadn't a care in the world.

"He's insufferable!" she fumed, indifferent to her surroundings.

"He's just…a little unrefined," Terin said diplomatically, struggling to balance his loyalty to Raven without triggering a further rant by Tosha. He rode beside her, his eyes following the river through the breaks in the trees.

"Unrefined?" She lifted a dark brow over a golden eye. "I haven't the words to aptly describe the man!" she hissed. "Now I have foolishly invited him to my father's court. I cannot envision a positive result from their meet. Raven around royalty is akin to a drunken moglo bull in a pottery shed."

"He doesn't mean to offend, Princess," Terin said.

"Of course, he does, and he takes great pleasure in doing so."

Terin thought it unwise to point out her idiosyncrasies that vexed Raven equally much. "I shall speak with him, Highness."

"To what end, Terin? He shan't listen. No, I have a better plan to deal with our errant acquaintance. In my mother's realm, they teach us that revenge is a delicacy to be nurtured with care and anticipation."

"What a beautiful river," Terin said, hoping to shift her foul mood to something neutral. He well noted the peaceful sounds of lapping water echoing as the river passed by. Only a thin line of porians separated them from the riverbank, Terin catching sight of the river between their thick trunks.

"That is the Andler," Tosha explained as if the name conjured a darker meaning.

"It's very scenic," Terin observed.

"It draws its name from the despotic Menotrist king Margos Andler. He claimed that his Benotrist neighbors violated terms of a treaty, a dubious claim that rallied his vassals to war in an obvious attempt to steal more lands from the Benotrists. The war culminated in Margos Andler's victory. One would believe that mercy would guide a monarch in his judgment of a conquered people on whom war was waged under a false claim. Nay, for mercy had no place in the heart of such a man.

"He gathered the Benotrists taken prisoner in the campaign, over five thousand men and boys, and ordered their arms to be stricken above their elbows to a man. Can you envision such an act? The screams of chained helpless men begging him for mercy as their arms were stretched over stumps and hacked off. The axes fell again and again for two days. Many bled to death before the hot irons could cauterize their flesh. The blood streamed into the river, discoloring its surface for days in a ghastly reddish taint.

"Margos chained the survivors neck to neck in an endless column and sent them on their way to return to their people in humiliating disgrace. They never reached their homes. They were set upon by packs of lincors on their second day in march. The lincors tore into their helpless victims as each corpse dragged on those to either side. Eventually, enough had fallen to trap the entire column, drawing even more packs of lincors upon them. Then carka birds made their claim upon the rotting flesh.

"As much of the column was along the riverbank, many pushed their heads into the water, hoping to drown and end their suffering. When word reached the Benotrist safe lands, the tribal leaders sent out a relief force to save their men. Only four hundred lived by the time the Benotrists freed them from their coffle. The stench of rotting flesh permeated the riverbank for countless days. The waters grew turbid with blood and waste, and from that day on, the Benotrists named the river the Andler for the man whose infamy stained that place. We will never forget."

"Was not your paternal grandfather a Menotrist lord, Highness?" Terin asked.

"My father was his second son, a child born from a Benotrist slave girl. His elder brother was his father's favored heir and a child of his Menotrist first wife. My father claims no kinship to his wretched sire. Speak not of it again whilst you stay in my father's realm," she reproached.

"My apologies, Highness."

"You meant no offense, Terin. I only warn you for your own safety. My father does not suffer fools who speak of his paternal lineage when he forged an empire on the bones of his father's people."

Terin reflected on the past two days of traveling through the Benotrist lands. They were greeted by the sight of thousands of Menotrist slaves working the land. They wore coarse brown tunics with corded belts. They endured in cold and heat, suffering the privations of their bonded caste. They subsisted on grains and water, wore no footwear, and endured the liberal lashings of their overseers. It was rumored that all male Menotrist slaves west of the Plate Mountains were gelded at birth. Terin believed it true when he beheld their sullen, spiritless faces before they bowed as the princess passed. The sooner he left this realm, the better.

CHAPTER 15

He soared through the firmament, his countenance contorted by the pressing wind. The hinterlands of the Feran Plain shrank below as the magantor's large wings pounded the air, driving him forth through the Benotrist sky. Terin regarded the billowy clouds above that drifted like mountainous balls of cotton just out of reach.

"Packawww!" the magantor squawked, sounding its dominion over the lands below.

"Easy, boy." Terin stroked the magantor's black-feathered neck, his voice a balm to the beast's cantankerous spirit. He spied Lorken atop his magantor mount off his bird's right wingtip while Raven trailed them a fair distance. He descried their lead guide far afield, his magantor but a dot along the horizon. Tosha raced her mount alongside Raven's, shouting to him over the wind as he nodded in kind. Terin could only discern the cordial nature of the exchange, but not the content.

He never knew what mood the two of them would be in, as they shifted rapidly between calm and rage in their interactions. Their strange relationship was a volatile balance of emotional extremes that unnerved their Benotrist escort. As the crown princess of the Benotrist Empire, Tosha was revered as divine. To look upon her unbidden was punishable by death. Their escort suffered the Earther's informality at Tosha's behest, but when Terin looked in her eye, he could see a cold fire burning neath her cool demeanor. Whenever Terin warned Raven to tread carefully around the Benotrist princess, the big Earther simply replied, "What's she gonna do, beat me up?" Lorken, however, heeded Terin's warning, ever watchful for Benotrist treachery.

Of the three of them, Lorken was quickest to master the fundamentals of riding a magantor, taking to the saddle like a second skin. Though he would never equal the skill of the bonded riders, who were trained since childhood, he had enough skill to maneuver the large avian with ease. Terin and Raven demonstrated enough skill to fly in a straight line and make slow, subtle turns. Terin reflected on the yester morn, when they entered the magantor pens at Laycrom. The stable masters patiently led them each to their assigned mounts, allowing them time to bond to the great birds. They were instructed to place their hands on the birds' beaks while staring for a time into their keen eyes. The magantor would then accept them as its rider.

Terin recalled the time he spent with Cronus on their journey to Rego when his eyes first beheld the magantors soaring overhead. How he longed to join them in the heavens, seeing the world from on high. From this place just below the clouds, he beheld the world in all its wonder. The patterned emerald squares of tended fields contrasted narrow streams that snaked through shallow vales and thick forests. The cool high air chilled his exposed flesh, lifting his hair in the breeze, trailing him like a golden flame.

Far off along the horizon, the land dimmed as if a dark curtain was drawn from the east. Tilled farms and lush forests yielded to the suffocating pestilence that lay across the landscape, endless as far as the eye could see. A trained eye could discern small black shapes moving amid the shadows, one joining another, canvassing the land in darkened dread. Realization struck him suddenly. *Gargoyles,* he thought horridly. The creatures were assembled in an endless encampment, and Terin wondered if the entirety of their savage race was gathered upon the Feran Plain. Were they gathered or spewed from whatever vile nesting ground that spawned them?

A black shape took form farther east, amid the gargoyle multitude. At first, it was but a blur in the distance. Drawing closer, it rose imperiously above the Feran Plain, presiding over the surrounding lands like a terrible lord. It was Fera, the Black Castle and first of the great fortresses constructed ages ago as bastions to withstand gargoyle invasions. Fera was centered on the flat plain like a mountain of black stone. Its outer shell was two hundred feet of vertical black stone in eight equal-length bulwarks.

The walls were smooth with tight-fitting stone and connected by massive turrets fifty meters abreast. Jagged battlements jutted in sharp angles above the outer ramparts like tortured spirits. The inner battlements mirrored the outer ramparts with eight smaller turrets twenty meters abreast connecting them at each conjoint. The walkway between the inner and outer battlements was a wide, massive corridor that circled the fortress, allowing for the mass movement of soldiers along the walls of Fera.

The walls of the inner battlements rose another fifty feet, overlooking the expansive walkways below that stretched to the outer bulwarks. The inner citadel of the fortress rose higher still with circled towers spiraling into the firmament like spear tips. The highest towers rose hundreds of feet into the air with midnight walls that swallowed the sun. The Black Castle was aptly named, a place forlorn of light and hope, casting its caliginous shadow upon the Feran Plain.

Terin's pounding heart mimicked the panic of his troubled mind. He felt the constriction tightening his chest like screws of a vice. Long ago, in the age of the old Northern Kingdom, this land was welcoming to the sons of the Middle Kingdom. Alas, those days had passed into shadow, for the Benotrists now ruled the north with their gargoyle allies. Had he erred in coming here?

He offered Raven his aid in freeing Cronus, but the Earthers did not need him to come to Fera, only to help man the *Stenox*. But Terin knew his friends were ignorant of Araxan customs and culture, and though he was ill-informed of the specific idiosyncrasies of the Benotrists, they needed his help. He felt a strong pull from his father's sword, urging him to join them in this task. Though his heart pounded in apprehension, he had to trust the will of the blade and follow his comrades to this dreadful place.

*****

Their magantors circled the highest citadels, descending with every pass, allowing the guardians of Fera full purview. Two mounts of the Imperial Magantor Squadron joined them as they drew nigh, guiding them through their approach. Their escort magantors broke away, following one of the imperial squadron to the lower platform, resting upon the roof of the inner keep. With monstrous battlements overlooking the outer keeps below them, which overlooked the inner and outer battlements of the walls of Fera, the inner keep presided over the palace proper in omnipotent splendor. The highest citadels sprouted from the roof and flanks of the great inner keep, and Terin could only stare in awe at such terrible majesty.

They set down upon the upper platform as scores of Benotrist infantry issued from the entryways of the surrounding citadels. Soldiers in copper-hued mail over black tunics flooded the rooftop of the great inner keep, parading in disciplined ranks as soon as their eyes beheld their crown princess among the arriving magantors. Handlers rushed forth to see to their mounts while slaves in brief livery surrounded Tosha, attending her.

Raven dismounted, his heavy boots pounding on the black stone as he stepped away from the large bird. He shook his head as rank upon rank of soldiers knelt before Tosha with their heads pressed to the stone floor in complete obeisance. "Let's go, sunshine!" Lorken's voice echoed behind him, the Earther pushing Monsoon's hooded form. The pirate lord stumbled blindly with his head covered and arms bound behind him. Terin kept behind his comrades, wary of his surroundings.

The four of them stood behind Tosha, awaiting her guidance. The westerly wind whipped her black hair across her face as she awaited an approaching figure in long purple robes. The figure was a plain-faced man whose countenance bespoke position and authority who suffered fools at their peril. His silver hair and aged gray eyes denoted his advancing years. Two members of the Imperial Elite flanked either side of the fellow. Both were humans wearing red tunics with the symbol of Tyro's Elite emblazoned upon their chests. The three men stopped short of the princess, prostrating themselves before her.

"Rise, Castellan Braxus," Tosha commanded.

Larus Braxus, castellan of Fera, gained his feet at the princess's command. "My princess, your father awaits you in the throne room. My men shall escort you while I"—he regarded Lorken and Raven disdainfully—"attend your companions."

"That shan't be necessary, Castellan Braxus. They shall accompany me while I treat with my father."

"As you wish, Highness." Braxus bowed, sweeping an outstretched arm toward the nearest entryway, an oval-peaked doorway at the base of a citadel.

*****

The violent pools of his golden eyes fixed upon the far end of the throne room, his calm demeanor belying the tempest within. He sat upon the massive throne, surveying the expansive chamber with cold authority. From this seat, he presided over the vast empire that spanned most of northern Arax, a testament to years of unchecked conquest. Victory upon victory marked the advent of his realm.

The union of Benotrists and gargoyles had proved their terrible potency time and again, never knowing defeat until Tuft's Mountain. Four legions were smashed at that terrible place, betrayed by his generals' incompetence as much as the enemy's cunning. Yet the enemy had unforeseen help in the name of the Earthers who accompanied his daughter. He awaited them now, uncertain with how he would deal with them. They were dangerous men who wielded strange yet powerful weapons.

Ben Thorton chronicled their strange journey across the heavens, which brought them to Arax. The Earther explained their advent in remarkable detail, revealing much on the nature of the universe that Tyro's mystics were woefully ignorant of. From what Thorton had revealed, he had a falling out with the Earther named Raven. Thorton set out on his own once they arrived on Arax, working as a mercenary until Tyro's agents recruited him into the emperor's service. Tyro found Thorton a serious, deadly, and discerning fellow, whose scowl reflected his own tortured soul.

The Earther was haunted by specters in his past, specters who were intricately linked to the Earther Raven, the very same man who aided the Torries at Tuft's Mountain and rescued his daughter at Molten Isle. Where Raven's true loyalties lay, Tyro could only surmise. If Thorton were present, he would have no doubt answered that nagging question. Fortunately for Tyro, he had discovered Raven's fondness for the Torry unit commander held captive in the dungeon.

As yet, he hadn't physically maimed the Torry captive. Instead, he ordered the mutilation of his men one by one as the miserable wretch watched helplessly at their dismemberment. Several had begged for slavery over torturous death, and Kriton obliged them, taking their manhood in exchange. Only one of Commander Kenti's men remained, a sickly, broken wretch named Marcus Elien. Kriton had a special plan for his demise, a clever, agonizing torment certain to unhinge his comrade.

If the Earther Raven was fond of the Torry captive, he would use that to his favor. Perhaps he would keep the Torry prisoner alive and untouched to ensure the Earthers' behavior lest they be tempted to aid the Torry cause a second time. Of course, the Earther was probably ignorant that he held his friend in the bowels of the dungeon. He would use this information to his advantage if the Earther proved difficult. Perhaps he should kill the Earthers immediately, for he could not be sure of their intentions. Such uncertainties were dangerous if left to fate or happenstance. Such an overt act would cause their comrades to act in kind, and he could only surmise what mischief they might cause.

The heavy doors of the throne room creaked open, pooling light from the outer corridor across the red floor of the cavernous chamber. The small group stepped within, casting long shadows across the chamber. Tosha walked briskly across the throne room, her head held high with the proud carriage of a Benotrist empress. Raven, Terin, Lorken, and Monsoon followed, the latter still hooded and stumbling as he was dragged forth. No palace steward announced their presence. No imperial guards appeared beside the throne. The vast chamber appeared empty save for the emperor and themselves.

Tosha thought it odd but not unexpected. Her father might have appeared alone, sitting upon the massive throne, but he was surrounded by unseen guardians. At the slightest command, her companions would be riddled with arrows. She took a deep breath to calm her racing heart as she beheld her father's stern countenance. She knew well the storm brewing behind those golden eyes and nervously hoped Raven would not unleash her father's wrath. Tosha stopped short of the dais, sinking to her knees, bowing with her forehead to the floor. As a visiting dignitary, Terin knelt on one knee while the Earthers stood impassively to his left, each regarding the Benotrist emperor with indifference.

"You assume much, Raven, if you dare present yourself with unbent knees." Tyro regarded him coldly.

"You know my name?" Raven asked.

"I know your name, Earther, as well as yours, Lorken. I am the emperor of the Benotrist-Gargoyle Empire. Little escapes my attention in the workings of my world," he said, speaking possessively. "The punishment for standing unbent in my esteemed presence is death."

"Since we're on a first-name basis, Tyro, I'll have to advise you that threatening me with death is punishable by death." Tosha lifted her head, craning her neck to Raven with pleading eyes, beseeching him to acquiesce.

"I haven't granted you leave to rise, daughter," Tyro warned. Tosha returned her head to the floor. Two archers stepped from behind each pillar, clad in tunics of shimmering silver, with bows drawn. Twenty-four archers with arrows notched and leveled fixed their deadly aim upon the Earthers.

Raven had drawn his pistol before the first archer stepped in the clear, aiming the barrel of his pistol in his outstretched right hand at Tyro. "I die, you die." For an eternal moment, they stared at each other, each appraising the other, studying each other's strengths, weaknesses, and fortitude. Neither would yield, as if their faces were cast in stone.

Tosha could take no more. She sprang to her feet, turning upon Raven and placing herself in his pistol's path. "Lower your weapon, Raven!" she commanded.

"Move, Tosha! He started it."

"This will not save your friend. Isn't that why you came, to save Cronus?" Her question cut deep. "Only I can save him," she added. "Only I can undo what you have just done."

Raven growled in frustration, slamming his pistol back into his holster. She sighed in relief, then turned to her father. "Father, these men saved my life. I promised them the safety of our house."

"Then you should have counseled them on the proper etiquette expected of those who treat with me."

"We're the ones who did you the favor, pal. You should be saying thank you instead of acting like an ass!" Raven growled. Terin placed a palm to his forehead, not believing that his friend just called the emperor an ass. Tosha fumed, Lorken snickered, and Tyro remained strangely quiet.

"We brought you two gifts, Emperor," Lorken interjected, figuring it best to change the focus of Raven and Tyro's discourse. "We have returned your daughter safely to your court, and we give you the life of the man responsible for her abduction." Lorken dragged Monsoon forth, forcing him to the base of the dais before removing his hood. "Monsoon!" Lorken declared, the pirate lord's eyes drawing wide as they beheld Tyro's scowling glare bearing down from above.

"Remove him!" Tyro commanded. His archers lowered their bows as several of their number stepped forth to seize the pirate lord, dragging him numbly from the throne room. "I shall speak with my daughter alone. My steward shall escort you to your chambers. I shall expect you when we dine this evening," Tyro said. They turned to leave. "Not you just yet!" Tyro called back Terin, who had started to follow Raven and Lorken to the door.

"Your Highness." Terin regarded him carefully.

"You are a Torry?" Tyro asked, finding the boy's demeanor strangely familiar.

"Yes, Highness."

"You have accompanied the Earthers to what purpose?" Raven and Lorken paused, waiting farther back for their friend.

"I have brought a message from my king." Terin removed the sealed scroll from his pouch and set it upon the floor at his feet.

"Leave it and join your friends." Terin bowed and withdrew, leaving Tosha alone with her father. Tyro regarded her as she ascended the steps of the dais before kneeling at his feet. He placed his right hand upon her bowed head. "Rise, my child." Tosha lifted her golden eyes to his, then stood as he came to his feet. They were alone in the cavernous chamber, the dim torchlight illuminating the ceiling like a midnight sky, each embedded jewel shining like a distant star.

"I have often allowed your impertinence, Tosha. Perhaps I was mistaken to do so. Never disobey me," he admonished in his eerily calm voice that unnerved better men and undid the lesser. Tosha knew he was displeased with her interference between him and Raven.

"I am sorry, Father. I did not wish either of you to perish at the other's hand."

"You assume much, child. The Earther is in no danger from my wrath at this time. But die he must."

She expected this. "There are other fates for Raven that better might serve our interests."

He lifted a brow over a curious golden eye, the purple specks in his iris sparkling in the light. "Such as?"

"Leave that to me."

"You allowed yourself to be abducted. Perhaps your confidence is misplaced."

"If you harm Raven or his friends, his comrades aboard their ship will level our harbors, sink our fleets, and destroy much of our trade."

"Perhaps their confidence is misplaced," Tyro growled.

"Their boasts are not idle threats, Father. Raven knows all too well that if you kill them, you shall rue the day."

"The man cannot go unpunished!" He ground his teeth.

"He saved my life, Father. Is that not worth forgiveness for refusing to bow in your presence?"

"Do you think me daft to risk so much over his petty insult? Nay, the man aided the Torries at Tuft's Mountain. Four legions lost to us because of his interference and his Torry friend that languishes in the dungeon."

"Cronus Kenti?" Tosha's eyes alit.

"Yes," he answered, regarding her curiously.

"Is he unharmed?" She held her breath, awaiting his answer.

"Other than the lash and hunger, the wretch is yet…untouched, though I plan on rectifying that now that I have the proper audience for his ruination. Perhaps the morrow's eve in the arena, where Captain Raven can see his friend's suffering."

"Give Commander Kenti to me, Father."

"To you? Why?"

"Leave his fate and that of the Earthers and Terin in my hands, and I shall honor my promise to you."

"Your promise," he mused audibly.

"Yes, the promise I swore to you since my childhood. To fulfill that oath, I need the Torry commander untouched."

"He must be punished. He and the Earther—"

"They shall be, Father, but in my way, not yours."

"So be it," he conceded. "Now take your leave of me. You need to bathe and change into attire more befitting a princess than a warrior. I shall see you this evening at my table. You may bring your new friends with you."

"Of course, my emperor." She smiled, placing a kiss upon his cheek before withdrawing.

Tyro descended the dais as Tosha stepped without. He snatched the sealed parchment that Terin left upon the smooth floor before retiring to his personal chambers. There was something about the boy that gnawed at him, but he couldn't place it.

*****

Terin stared out the high window with knowing dread. The royal guest apartment afforded a generous view of the endless plain stretching beyond the battlements below. The waning light of the setting sun played across his line of sight as he gazed northward. The lights of countless cookfires flickered to life as far as his eye could see. It seemed the gargoyle host occupied the entirety of the Feran Plain.

Tyro lost four legions at Tuft's Mountain and invaded Yatin with untold strength, and yet he seemed to have conjured this vast host from thin air. What hope had the Torry realms against such might? None it seemed. Even the most optimistic turn of events would fall short to turn this dark host. He could feel the power of his father's sword wash over him, driving out the ruinous despair and kindling anew his waning spirit. He needed only touch the hilt of the ancient blade for its power to restore him. He felt the clouding of his mind drawn away, affording him clear vision and awareness.

"Don't worry about all those gargoyles out there, Terin. There can't be more than a couple hundred thousand." Raven slapped him on the back, nearly jerking him from his feet. Terin smiled at the remark. Somehow, Raven always made the direst situation seem trivial. Raven came around his side, placing his left hand on the wall beside the window for support as he stared out across the endless plain.

Lorken lay upon his bed on the far side of the chamber with his hands interlocked behind his head and his bare feet crossed. His boots rested beside his bed as he stretched out on the comfortable feather mattress. "Ah, this is nice." He sighed. Raven and Terin had matching beds resting on the other walls of the chamber, each adorned with calnesian linens and thick furs. A table and chairs were centered in the chamber with a small chest at the foot of each bed.

"What is your plan?" Terin asked, shifting his gaze to Raven.

"We're gonna free Cronus and get the hell out of here."

"How?" Terin found his friend's lack of detail unsettling.

"I'll give Tosha her chance to hand him over. If not, then we'll free him ourselves."

"How?" Terin pushed further.

"How? We got guns and gizmos, and they got swords, bows, and arrows. Lorken will blow a bunch of stuff up, and I'll start shooting. You can help out by watching our backs. It's simple."

Terin did not share Raven's confidence. The peril that surrounded them was not lost on him as it seemed to be with his comrades. Between Raven's nonchalance and Lorken's apparent indifference, Terin wondered if they knew something that he did not or if they were simply crazy. "You place much faith in your guns." Terin sighed.

"There's an old saying where we come from, Terin. 'God made men, but Sam Colt made them equal,'" Lorken said with his eyes closed as he relaxed upon his bed.

"Who is Sam Colt?"

"Never mind," both Earthers said in unison.

*****

The palace steward ushered them to a vast dining hall in the bowels of the upper keep. He was a well-spoken, silver-haired fellow with an upturned nose who took an immediate dislike to Raven and Lorken, hiding his disdain with polite courtesies. He reproached their attire when he first entered their apartment to retrieve them. The princess had ordered servants to bring appropriate attire for her guests. Formal tunics of varying hues, belts, sandals, and wrist guards were brought to their chamber. Terin obliged their offer and dressed in a white calnesian tunic with his father's sword sheathed upon his left hip. Raven and Lorken said they wouldn't be caught dead in such garments. They would've said that only girls wore such things in their world but thought better of it for Terin's sake.

They waited in the outer corridor as the palace steward passed within the great hall to announce their presence before waving them on. The great hall was a vast chamber with high arches angling toward the cupola ceiling above, which rose the height of six men. Walls of black stone appeared closer than the fifty meters that separated them, casting the dark feasting hall in an ominous hue. Liberally spaced torches were bracketed along the walls, their dull flames flickering upon the dark stone.

All the tables were removed save for one. There in the chamber's center rested a table five meters in length and two in width. It was richly decorated with gold inlays winding the lengths of its legs and the arms of each chair. A crimson tablecloth was draped across its surface with richly detailed stitching of gold, azure, and forest green. Gold candlesticks ran the length of the table with plates of polished silver and goblets with rubies, sapphires, and emeralds embedded around their circumference. Guards in silver tunics and black iron helms lined the perimeter of the hall, their disciplined eyes fixed forward.

Tyro sat at the table's head, candlelight flickering off the pools of his golden eyes. His stoic expression revealed little, masking his emotions with practiced indifference. The emperor wore a scarlet robe with silver stitching edged along its collar and cuffs, coal-black hair framing his handsome face.

To Tyro's right sat a warrior with similar black hair, wearing a blood-red tunic with a symbol sewn into the chest of the garment. It was a sun and a moon divided by a sword with a whip woven along its length, the signet of Tyro's High Elite. The warrior fixed his feral brown eyes on each of them in turn, taking their measure with a dismissive sneer.

There were four chairs along the opposing lengths of the table and one on each end. The other chairs were empty save for the emperor and his arrogant companion. "Be seated." Tyro waved an open hand to the chairs lining either side. Lorken skirted the table, taking the chair beside the sneering man. Raven and Terin sat in the middle chairs on the opposite side with Raven directly across Lorken.

"Who's Mr. Personality?" Raven grunted, jerking his chin toward the fellow to Tyro's right.

"This"—Tyro regarded the man fondly—"is Morac, son of Morca and first among the Imperial Elite." He left unsaid that the young man was his ward and the only child of his friend and founder of the Benotrist revolution, Morca. With Morca's death in the early years of their revolt, Tyro ascended to lead the floundering rebels and placed the infant son of his dead friend in his household.

Though Morca led the Benotrist revolt at its founding, it was Tyro who reorganized its fledging ranks, reformed its chain of command, and forged the vital alliance with the gargoyles that led to ultimate victory. Tyro chose leaders based upon merit over bloodline, enabling the ablest of his commanders to ascend through the ranks. Morac was the only member of the High Elite whose bloodline suggested otherwise, but the man was so placed upon the merits of his sword.

"I know of you, Earther," Morac sneered, "a castaway spit upon our shores from the firmament above, cast down for your forsaken honor. Now you take up the call of a free sword and pirate. I find your presence at this esteemed table an offense to the imperial throne."

"Don't take it personally, little fella. A lot of people find me offensive. But that's the advantage of being me, because I don't give a damn," Raven said, dismissing Morac's remark. The Benotrist warrior glared daggers at Raven while Terin bit off a smile.

No sooner had Raven finished speaking than the palace steward ushered two men into the great hall. The first was a slender, sharp-faced fellow whose hair matched the silver of the steward. He was introduced as Jarkush Mol, the commander of the garrison of Fera. He wore his uniform black tunic sans armor. The second man possessed a nondescript face with pale-blue eyes and sand-colored hair. His stone countenance revealed nothing, masking his emotions behind strong mental shields. His tunic was simple gray, and he bore no adornments.

Only when he was introduced as Luzzo Korun did Raven and Lorken regard the man more carefully. The infamous inquisitor of the Benotrist Empire and fourth among Tyro's High Elite, Luzzo Korun's ill repute shook the core of the bravest souls. Seeing him in person dulled his terrible reputation.

The evil ones always look like boring librarians, Raven reminded himself. The limit of Luzzo Korun's depravity was boundless. He was rumored to allow his victims to unwittingly eat their own children. Most were driven to madness once the truth was revealed. Looking into those cold, dead eyes, Raven believed the story true.

Both men abased themselves before their emperor before taking their seats across from each other at the table's other end. The next to enter the great hall was a gargoyle dressed in a gold tunic and silver robes that conformed around his cumbersome wings. His countenance was of serene calm, most unusual for one of its species. Its usual vibrant, fiery eyes were dull and contemplative. He did not kneel to the emperor as his clawed feet scraped the stone floor, making his way to the seat on the emperor's left. His ebony skin drew taut over his sharp cheekbones and nose, framing his face like scales of obsidian. He was Regula, Tyro's second and grand chieftain of the gargoyle peoples.

There were yet two empty chairs, one beside Lorken and the one at the table's end opposite Tyro. Tosha entered next. Her coal-black hair was drawn up in a tight coiffure. She wore a shimmering turquoise gown that religiously followed the contours of her curves. She glided across the floor like ice on a wet stone. She bowed to her father, seating herself at the end of the table, facing the emperor. She smiled briefly at Lorken and Terin while ignoring Raven completely.

Six slaves followed Tosha into the chamber, five female and one male, all dressed in brief livery with silver collars fastened about their necks. They knelt several paces behind her with their heads pressed to the floor and arms outstretched in absolute obeisance. Terin noticed that each of the slaves was diminutive in stature and slight of build, none exceeding fifty-six inches in height or eighty pounds in weight. Each was exceptionally beautiful, even the lone male.

He recalled mention of the Benotrists' practice of breeding the comeliest and daintiest of slaves for house servants, further reducing the risk of rebellion in their households. The misery of the slaves' lives was only limited by the cruel imaginations of their masters. These slaves were Tosha's personal body servants, who attended her needs whenever she resided at Fera, and as such were shielded from the abuse suffered by other palace slaves. As the personal slaves of the princess, each was chaste, and the male remained uncut, as he was designated as suitable to sire slaves of a proper build and stature.

Other male servants brought tables into the great hall and multiple trays filled with steaming meat, fresh fruits, warm breads, and pitchers of wine. The palace steward hurried those slaves from the hall as Tosha snapped her fingers. Her slaves quietly rose and served the meal to the emperor's table. One of the female servants carried a small tray of bread while another served it to each guest. Two of the female slaves carried the larger tray of meat as another served it while the male followed last, pouring wine into each goblet. As princess of the realm, Tosha was served first, whereas her father, as host, would be served last.

Lorken and Raven shared a look as Lorken was served first. Lorken discretely removed a vial from his trouser pocket and poured its clear liquid onto his food. After several moments of no reaction, he knew the food was untainted and nodded to Raven that it was safe to eat. When the serving girl placed a uniform portion of meat on Raven's plate, he gave her a disapproving scowl.

"Here. Give me those," he said, not unkindly, lifting the tongs from her hand, heaping extra portions of roast moglo on his plate.

"What are you doing?" Tosha glared at him.

"Eating," he replied, stuffing a thick piece of moglo in his mouth while the others waited patiently for all to be served before partaking.

"You are expected to wait," Terin whispered, leaning close.

"For what?"

"For the emperor, knave!" Morac growled, pounding his fist upon the table as the male slave attempted to fill his goblet. The wine spilled upon the table, running off its side and onto Morac's lap.

"Master, forgive me!" The slave cowered.

"Fool!" Morac kicked his chair back, coming to his feet, striking the slave across his face. The slave cringed, instinctively raising his arm to block the blow, but his flailing limb grazed Morac's cheek. The guests drew eerily silent as the blood drained from the servant's face. He quickly fell to his knees, prostrating himself before the Benotrist Elite. "You dare…" Morac's anger strangled his words as his right hand went to his sword hilt.

"I see you can make a slave cry. How about you try it on someone a little bigger?" Raven challenged.

"This is not your concern, Earther."

"Leave the girl alone, or I'll break your neck myself," Raven snarled.

"This slave is a male, you ignorant oaf!"

"A male? You're kidding, right?" Raven said. *Hell, they all look like women.* He shook his head.

"Morac." Tyro's voice was but an utterance, calmly lifting an open palm to stay Morac's hand.

"As you command," Morac said, his eyes fixed sternly on the prostrate slave at his feet. "Guards, remove this wretch. I'll see to his punishment when I finish here."

"Alen is my slave, Morac. I shall see to his correction," Tosha reproached.

"As is your right, Princess," Morac yielded as the guards dragged the slave away.

"Why not just kill him now and be done with it?" Raven asked.

"Kill him?" Morac said with incredulity. "And why, pray tell, should we afford him such reward?"

"Reward?" Terin asked.

"Death is the only reward a slave can attain. We grant no such mercies. Nay, we shall claim either his eyes or manhood. He is no longer fit to sire slaves. We would not wish his rebellious nature passed on to our proceeding generation of servants. Defiance is an unworthy trait in slaves," Morac explained.

"Enough. Let us partake." Tyro motioned Morac to retake his seat as the meal continued.

Terin suddenly lost much of his appetite, his thoughts lingering on the slave dragged from their midst. What wretched existence must the slave have endured in this place. Would such be the fate of his countrymen if Tyro won? He was ever mindful of the price of failure during his visit to this dark realm. He felt Tyro's eyes upon him more than once, regarding him curiously. Equally unnerving was the gargoyle Regula, who seemed out of sorts whenever Terin looked his way, as if Terin was afflicted with a plague. The sooner he left this land, the better.

After a time, Tyro set his utensils down, turning his attention to Raven. "What am I to do with you, Captain Raven?"

"What do you mean?"

"Consider. You saved my daughter, which tips the scales of mercy to your favor. Then you destroy one of my galleys, which, in turn, tilts the scales to the other direction. Such is the paradox that is you."

"So Tosha told you about the ship?"

"She did not speak of it. My last guest, however, told of it and much else concerning you and your crew." Tyro almost smiled. Almost. His eyes shifted from Raven to another as the last guest entered the great hall. Nels Draken strode across the chamber dressed in crisscrossed leather trousers and tan shirt. The sword dangling from his left hip seemed his only weapon. A mirthful look adorned his scarred face as he beheld his old acquaintance.

"You keep poor company, Tyro. I judge a man by the friends he keeps. Draken reminds me of something nasty that sticks to the bottom of your boot that won't scrape off."

"I, too, judge men by the company they keep," Tyro countered.

"Raven and Lorken, what a splendid surprise." Draken smiled falsely, taking the last empty chair beside Lorken. "How fortunate that my arrival preceded yours lest I miss this festive gathering."

"You made good time, Nels. I figured you'd stay in Yatin, herding women and raping livestock," Raven said.

"How wondrous for your wit to lighten these halls, old friend. Your skilled tongue is wasted at sea. You have a mastery of oratory that rivals the bards of old."

"And you got as much brains as this moglo roast," Raven growled.

"What reward has brought you all the way to the Black Castle?" Draken mused, ignoring Raven's insult. "It would not be gold, for that could be easily delivered to you."

"Who said I came for a reward? Maybe we rescued Tosha on good faith and are merely returning her safely to dear old dad over here." Raven jerked a thumb toward the emperor.

"I doubt you are so generous with your time or life, Raven. I know well why you are here." Tyro regarded him.

"You do?" Raven asked with his mouth full, chewing his food.

"I do."

"Then give me what I want, and I'll be on my way."

"For such a reward to be granted, it must be earned."

"I saved your daughter's life. What more do you want?"

"I shall only grant your request if you prove worthy."

"How?"

"You must defeat the champion of Fera. Gorga, come hither!" Tyro ordered.

A well-muscled guard stepped from the shadows. He was dark of hair with chiseled bare torso and legs. He wore only a skirt wrapped around his waist. Leather straps crossed his chest with swords descending from either side of the straps, just above his hips. He shared the name of the great river that fed the Tinsan Bay. Blue laser illuminated the chamber as the Feran champion crumpled to the floor, a hole burned through his forehead. The emperor's guards scrambled to react as several dinner guests attempted to hide beneath the table.

"There. He's defeated," Raven said, holstering his pistol. "Now you can grant my request."

"You murder my champion and expect a reward!" Tyro erupted.

"You were supposed to challenge him and his comrades in the Pit, Raven, you and four other challengers against the champions of Fera," Tosha reproached him.

"Bring your champions here. I'll kill them all now and be done with it."

"You must meet them in the Pit sans your weapon. Only bladed weapons are allowed in contest. Unless you are craven?" Morac said.

"I could always take what I want," Raven challenged. Morac's hand went to his sword's hilt as Raven stood with pistol drawn. Morac's golden sword alit as if cast in flame, illuminating the hall in ethereal brilliance as he faced Raven's pistol leveled at his head.

Terin stood, leaning toward Raven's ear. "Raven, this is folly," he pleaded.

"We were fools to come here. They'll never give us what we want," Raven growled.

Tosha quietly stood and skirted the table, coming to Raven's side. "Put it away, Raven. There is no trickery afoot. If you do as I ask, Cronus will forever be safe from my father's reach."

"You expect me to believe that?"

"Yes. I told you that only I could save Cronus. Defeat the Feran champions and I can do so."

Raven holstered his pistol. "All right, Tosha. We'll do it your way." Everyone at the table released a measured breath save Lorken, who merely shrugged, though his right hand lingered on his pistol's grip throughout.

"Tosha, escort your friend to his chambers. I believe he has overtaxed himself," Tyro ordered.

"Of course, Father." Tosha bowed.

"One more thing," Raven said. "That slave you dragged out of here tonight, I want him with me in the Pit. If he wins, he goes free."

"No, Raven!" Tosha pleaded. "Alen is a chamber slave and unsuited to combat. You need strong partners at your side."

"Done," Tyro conceded. "If he lives and you win, he goes free."

"Agreed," Raven said.

CHAPTER 16

"Do you take me for a fool?" he growled with his back to her as he stared out the portal of his chamber, the moon bathing his face with its celestial light as he rested his left hand on the wall beside the portal.

"Nay, you are no fool, Raven," Tosha said, touching a hand gently to his shoulder.

"You're wrong. I've been a fool since that day I found you in that cell. I should've just turned around and left instead of falling under the trance of your beauty," he said, fixing her in his eyes over his shoulder.

"My beauty?" She lifted a brow, amused by the remark.

"Don't let it go to your head. I've dated many beautiful women back on Earth."

"Dated?"

"Dating is like a courtship. Of course, I never had many second dates. They always found me offensive for some reason."

"I can't imagine why." She laughed. "You certainly demonstrated a level of civility, as my father can attest."

"Yeah, he's a real charmer. He must've been a barrel of laughs when you were a kid."

"My father is a demanding man." Her smile eased.

"I'll say. I've been here one day and he's already arranged my funeral. What a guy."

"He has not arranged your death. He has offered you the only way to free your friend by Benotrist law. Cronus has grievously wounded our cause. My father cannot simply release him as a reward to my rescuer. You have to earn his freedom."

"Earn his freedom? Tosha, I know nothing of bladed weapons."

"Which was why I arranged four master swordsmen to fight beside you until you foolishly named my body servant as one of your number. Displacing an expert blade with a hapless slave was foolish." She sighed in exasperation.

"And leave that kid to your father's mercy? I wouldn't do that to a dog, let alone a boy."

"A dog?"

"A dog. You know, four legs, a tail, and barks. Never mind."

"Ah, another quaint reference from your world, of which we poor Araxans are woefully ignorant. Do you ever tire of such jests?"

"Do ever tire of your games, Tosha?"

"My games?" She folded her arms over her breasts and leaned away.

"I could ask you what you're really up to, but I doubt you'll tell me. You lured me here for a purpose, and it has nothing to do with Cronus."

"Why would I do so?" She narrowed her eyes.

"Either to kill us or have us kill someone you want dead or some other reason I can't..."

She stepped near, pressing her lips fiercely to his with savage hunger. The stiff hesitancy of his lips quickly softened, receptive to the warmth of her touch. He gripped her shoulders, forcing her head back as he held her below him, devouring her with his kiss. He held her there for an eternal moment before returning her to her feet, breathless and panting. "I would never lead you or your friends to their death. I hope you each live for a long time," she said with glazed eyes.

"That's good, Tosha, because if I die in the Pit, the *Stenox* will flatten your father's ports."

"So you constantly remind me. If somehow you do succumb to ill fortune, how would your friends on the *Stenox* even know?" she asked, moving to exit his chamber, Terin and Lorken waiting to enter.

"Magic," he said cryptically.

*****

"Are you sure about this, Rav?" Lorken asked.

"Yeah." He sighed, growing weary of the topic.

"You could die in the arena. You know nothing of swords, so that leaves you with your brawn and their mercy. The former won't carry you through, and I doubt the latter has any place with this bunch," Lorken argued. Terin paced nervously before the window of their chamber as starlight filtered through the portal. If Raven died on the morrow, what chance had they of escaping this dreadful place?

"It doesn't matter," Raven said tiredly.

"Doesn't matter?" Lorken asked.

"Look, either they free Cronus this way, or they don't. If this is a trap, then we have their answer."

"Then what?" Lorken asked.

"If it looks like I'm going to bite it, then start shooting. You'll be up in the stands, so you can toss me my pistol, and we'll fight our way free."

"How long do we last before our weapons are drained or a stray arrow or errant blade finds a home in our backs? We won't make it, Rav. Look, I don't mind sticking our necks out to fetch Cronus, but I'd at least like a fighting chance."

"Either the deck is stacked in our favor or against, but we won't know until we're in the arena."

"Why would it be in our favor?" Lorken asked.

"Tosha," Raven answered.

"Tosha? You trust her?" Lorken said incredulously.

"She's up to something, but my gut tells me she profits if I win in the arena."

"Profits? How?"

"I haven't figured that part out yet."

"So we're trusting your gut. I'd rather trust our guns unless you suddenly become a master swordsman."

"Take my sword," Terin blurted.

"That's nice of you to offer, Terin, but I…" Raven stopped mid-sentence, his eyes drawn to the glowing blade that Terin drew forth. Terin held it aloft, the light of the moon illuminating a bluish glow along its length. Terin offered him the hilt. Raven lifted the weapon from Terin's outstretched arm, a surge of power coursing his veins, spreading from his right palm throughout his body. The blade felt weightless yet spoke to him, whispering its untold power. He felt he could cleave the world in two with one swing. How had they not seen this sword before with its current majesty?

"I knew you were well-schooled in swordsmanship, but I never saw your blade with that bluish glow to it," Lorken said, transfixed by the blade's mystical beauty.

"My father gifted the sword to me the night before I departed for Rego. He has borne it since he discovered it during the Sadden Wars. I am led by the will of the blade more so than it is led by me. That instinct led me to follow you to this cursed place, and I struggled to know why. Now it is clear. I came so that you might wield its power for a time in order to save Cronus."

*****

The palace steward escorted them into the arena after their morning meal. They were surprised by the size of the vast oval-shaped chamber with its high-domed ceiling and sand-covered floor. Raven unbuckled his holster, handing it to Lorken before removing his jacket and handing it to Terin. Terin extended his sword to Raven but was interrupted by the steward. "Your sword must be placed atop the block before the challenge is commenced," the fellow stated in a nasally, proper tone.

The block the steward referred to was an eight-feet-tall block with three-meter sides that was centered in the arena. The steward went on to explain that all the combatants' weapons were placed atop the massive block, forcing each side to fight hand to hand until one of their comrades could climb atop the block and retrieve their weapons.

"All of the weapons are placed up there?" Lorken asked, pointing at the block. Its smooth sides made any ascent difficult, and he wondered how often men actually attained the summit before they bashed one another's brains in, in hand-to-hand combat.

"All of the weapons are so placed, as I have thus explained. The first to ascend may claim any or all weapons as he so chooses. Most toss them to their comrades below, ensuring their victory. Victory is achieved when each member of the opposing side is either killed or subdued," the steward continued.

"Subdued?" Terin asked.

"Not all combatants are slain. Some either submit or are subdued," the steward answered, his voice laced with condescension.

"And what fate awaits those who are defeated?" Terin pushed.

"They are bound to the throne, their fate decided by the emperor or empress. Those fortunate are sent to border garrisons to serve out their days in obscurity."

"What of the unfortunate ones or those not of Benotrist blood?" Terin asked.

"Any not of our native blood may be claimed as chattel by the emperor's house."

Lorken exchanged a knowing look with Raven. Tosha's motive seemed all too obvious, but if she believed that he would submit, then she was oblivious to what he intended. It was now clear they would have to fight their way to freedom. A sudden realization struck Raven as he returned Terin's sword. "I've an idea. Keep your sword," Raven said before Terin could inquire.

"But, Raven, how do—" Terin started to protest.

"Your sword is too valuable to be out of our hands at any time. Besides, I have a better idea," Raven whispered as he leaned close.

A score of palace guards poured into the arena with spear tips raised as they formed a protective perimeter, circling the three friends and the palace steward. They were followed by the richly adorned princess. Tosha stepped nigh, a scarlet calnesian gown gracing her curved silhouette. Her long gown split at its sides as it reached her knees, revealing the toned curvature of her calves with the crossed straps of her sandals that ran north of her ankles. Her long, voluminous hair was bound above her head in a coiffure with a thin silver tiara nestled above her brow.

She presented an unguarded smile as she approached. "Raven," she greeted, her eyes running the length of his statuesque form. "You look almost defenseless without your pistol strapped to your thigh." She smiled lasciviously, rolling her tongue.

"Almost," he emphasized, crossing his arms over his chest. "Anything else you'd like to tell me about this game, Tosha?"

"Game? This is no game, Raven. Many great warriors have perished here in the sand, warriors far deadlier than you."

"Don't bet on it."

"It is but a warning, one that I do not wish you to take lightly."

"Don't worry about me, Princess. You just have Cronus ready when I win this thing."

"As I promised you, regardless of the result of your challenge, Cronus shall live a long, healthy life."

"And free once I win," Raven added.

"It is time. Lorken and Terin shall accompany me to the royal box." Tosha regarded them. She turned, stepping away, the hem of her gown swirling about her ankles.

*****

The champions of Fera paraded along the circumference of the arena for the benefit and purview of the crowd. They were dressed uniformly in pleated black kilts that hung almost to their knees. They wore black-booted sandals that ran halfway up their calves and leather straps that crossed their chest and back. There were three Benotrist humans and two gargoyles among the champions. The gargoyles' wings were bound to their backs with heavy-knotted cords. It would be difficult for their comrades to untie them before being overcome by their challengers.

Their leader was a Benotrist human named Vorgun, who stood at sixty-six inches with a toned musculature and sharp, discerning blue eyes that surveyed the arena with deadly calm. He was second among them until Raven slew their leader, Gorga. He eyed the Earther with contempt as they circled behind him before posting on the arena's eastern end.

The other challengers had yet to present themselves, but the champions basked in the glory of their renown as the emperor appraised them from his royal box along the arena's north face. The princess sat at his right, and Lord Regula, his left. The Earther's two comrades sat to the princess's right, and Vorgun acknowledged them before regarding the three challengers who entered the arena to stand beside the Earther.

Posted to Vorgun's right were his gargoyle comrades, Laslitz and Kregnisk. They fixed their terrible crimson eyes upon their foes, their fangs glistening brightly in the torch-lit chamber. To Vorgun's left stood his Benotrist comrades, Farlin and Corliss. Each was two inches shy of his stature but skilled swordsmen nonetheless. Corliss was their strongest jumper, and to him would fall the task of climbing the stone block to retrieve their weapons while the others held the challengers at bay.

"We shall see how dangerous your Earther is without his weapons," Tyro said, observing the combatants aligned on the opposing ends of the arena. Tosha sat beside her father, her stoic face masking her anxiety. Golden eyes stared impassive through long dark lashes, observing Raven's interaction with his three team members. Two of his comrades were human and a third a gargoyle, whose wings were similarly bound as the two on the opposing side.

"Who are they?" Lorken asked in her other ear, regarding the three warriors.

"They are Raven's fellow challengers. The taller human is named Korge. He is a palace guard," she said, indicating a lanky, long-faced fellow with dirt-colored hair. "The other human is Tellis, a unit commander in the Eighth Legion. The gargoyle is Scarliss, a soldier in the Fifth Legion." All three of the challengers were bare of chest, clad only in pleated white kilts and thin-soled sandals. They appeared to be in a heated argument with Raven, and he seemed to be speaking sharply to them and repeatedly poking each of them in the chest.

"Is he fighting with his own men?" Terin asked in alarm.

"Why not? He argues with us all the time." Lorken shrugged. Tosha released an irritable sigh.

"It seems Captain Raven and his fellow challengers have differing strategies. Perhaps they shall come to blows before the contest can commence." Morac smirked, leaning back in his seat behind the emperor.

A score of palace guards entered the arena, escorting the last combatant, a rail-thin slave dressed uniformly in a pleated white kilt and sandals. The guards escorted him to his comrades before departing the arena, the heavy doors closing as they stepped without. Raven towered over the Benotrists and gargoyles, but Tosha's slave seemed but a child standing before the large Earther. Alen's shy gaze slowly lifted, appraising Raven's massive form. The Earther was three times his mass, his thick arms larger than Alen's legs. The slave pissed himself when Raven spoke.

Tosha could not hear what Raven told her errant slave, but the boy looked half frozen in trepidation until Raven snapped his fingers in front of Alen's face. After a short exchange, the boy nodded, comprehending what Raven wanted him to do.

"This should be interesting." Morac's mocking sneer echoed behind them. "This is a far more entertaining fate for your slave than the punishment I envisioned, Princess."

"I doubt my champions will fritter their energy on the slave until the others are dealt with. Does your Earther know the rules?" Tyro asked.

"He knows," she answered assuredly, masking her misgivings with a calm veneer.

"What strategy is most commonly used?" Lorken asked of her.

"Usually, whoever can ascend the block to retrieve their weapons wins the battle. The abilities to run and leap are paramount to victory."

Tyro rose from his seat to address the privileged crowd circling the arena, seated safely behind the five-meter wall that ran the circumference of the oval-shaped chamber. Gray support beams crisscrossed the black stone of the cupola ceiling, the light of the torch basins illuminating along their lengths. "To the victors, glory. To the survivors, life. To the vanquished, justice!" His deep voice rang audibly through the chamber. Tyro held a red scarf in his outstretched right fist. His hand opened, the scarlet cloth dropping freely, fluttering through its descent, and the opposing lines of warriors sprang forth at the allotted signal.

Raven ran toward the stone block, keeping Tosha's slave close to his side. The gargoyle Scarliss ran ahead to the north side of the block while the humans Korge and Tellis circled south to counter the approaching champions. The champions of Fera ran swiftly from the east end of the pit. The human Farlin ran straight for the block as his fellow Benotrist Corliss followed close behind. Their leader, the Benotrist Vorgun, circled to the north side of the block while the gargoyles Laslitz and Kregnisk angled south.

Farlin stopped two meters shy of the block and dropped to his hands and knees as Corliss jumped upon his back, using the added height to leap upon the block. Corliss's hands caught the edge of the block. He started pulling himself up as Farlin regained his feet, following Vorgun to the north.

Tyro's bemused look gave way to alarm as Raven stopped at the opposing side of the block, hoisted the slave boy Alen, and threw him atop the stone square. Audible gasps escaped the lips of the crowd as the slave crossed the top of the stone block and stepped on Corliss's fingers, whose tenuous hold on the opposing ledge gave way.

The gargoyle Scarliss stopped as he cleared the corner of the block, his feet embedding in the loose sand floor as the Benotrist champion Vorgun cleared the opposite corner. Scarliss's split tongue slithered over his bright lips, collecting the slather that oozed from his curved fangs. The Benotrist warrior fixed his steel-blue eyes on the gargoyle challenger. Before Scarliss took another step, a second champion stepped beside Vorgun, the Benotrist Farlin. Emboldened by the reinforcement, Vorgun moved swiftly, stepping to Scarliss's left while Farlin stepped to his right in order to attack the gargoyle challenger from both sides simultaneously.

Before Farlin could close on Scarliss, he sensed a shadow in his periphery. He turned to his left as Raven burst around the corner of the stone square, barreling toward him at a full run. Farlin crouched low to receive the Earther's impact. Raven tackled the Benotrist, driving his smaller frame into the sand. Farlin's lungs compressed under Raven's massive weight. Raven straddled the wheezing fellow, smashing his fist into Farlin's face before grasping his head and twisting it in an unnatural angle. The snap of Farlin's neck echoed distinctly over the sounds of battle, causing bile to rise in the throats of the onlookers who had cheered for the stricken champion. Vorgun backed a step, unsettled by this unexpected turn, his eyes shifting between Scarliss and Raven.

"Alen!" Raven shouted to the slave boy, who stood on shaky feet atop the block.

"Yes, master?" the boy nervously answered.

"Start chucking down some stuff. And I ain't your damned master!" Alen first dropped a longsword into the sand at Raven's feet. He snatched it up, tossing it toward Scarliss. "Fangs, take it and finish him!" Raven commanded. Scarliss snarled at the nickname Fangs, which Raven had referred to him as when they first spoke before the contest, but he was happy to receive the weapon, catching the hilt in midair. He turned, closing on Vorgun, who retreated, his back pressed against the north wall of the pit.

Raven turned as a large rectangular shield dropped at his feet, spraying sand on his pant legs. He grabbed the shield with both hands, gripping its sides, wielding it like a club and not for its intended purpose. Before Alen could give the Earther a better weapon, Raven circled the northeast corner of the stone square, where he found the Benotrist Corliss struggling to attain the ledge above.

Corliss's eyes drew wide as the large Earther closed upon him and bashed him with the shield. Corliss lifted his arms to block the blow, his right arm snapping as the impact drove him into the ground. Raven stood over the fallen champion, bashing him several more times with the shield for good measure, breaking his left arm and right leg before leaving him broken in the sand.

Raven shifted his attention to Vorgun, who had somehow managed to elude Scarliss and fled along the wall of the pit. Raven ran to cut his retreat as Scarliss approached from the west. Tyro's scowl matched the intensity of the crowd's disbelief as Vorgun backed into Raven to escape Scarliss's blade. The sound of a thousand gasps followed as Raven scooped him into the air upside down and drove his head into the ground. Raven left Vorgun's limp body lying upon the sand, his head bent in an unnatural angle, while Scarliss drove his sword into his still flesh to be sure of him.

"All right, Fangs, go help the others!" Raven said, catching his breath. The gargoyle grunted, giving Raven a toothsome snarl before passing on. Raven caught sight of Scarliss as the gargoyle joined his comrades on the arena's southern end. "Alen, toss me a sword this time!" Raven shouted as he stepped toward the block.

"Here, master." The boy dropped another longsword into the sand at his feet.

"I'm not your damned master!" Raven growled, picking up the blade. The battle was ended before Raven had taken a step, as Scarliss had struck down Laslitz from behind, thus freeing Korge to join Tellis in subduing Kregnisk.

"Well, that's what happens when you let a football player loose on a soccer field," Lorken thought aloud as the emperor's box was gripped in silence. Among the Benotrists, Tosha's smile stood out among the sea of scowls. She shared a knowing glance with her father, who sat stone-faced as Raven strode across the arena's sand floor, stopping below the emperor's box. He dropped his sword in the sand as Lorken tossed him his pistol belt.

"I did my part. How 'bout you do yours?" Raven directed his question to Tyro while fastening his belt, tying down his holster to his right thigh.

"You have done well, Raven." Tosha smiled sweetly, almost too sweetly, Raven thought. "The emperor agrees to your terms. We shall reconvene after a brief respite in the great hall of the inner keep, where all our brave challengers shall receive their due merit. If you desire a bath or refreshment, the steward shall see to such," she said in a singsong voice that raised his suspicion.

"Where's Cronus?" Raven growled, weary of her games.

"Mind your tongue, Earther. You shall receive your just due!" Tyro growled.

Raven and Tyro glared at each other for an eternal moment, unnerving those who observed helplessly around them. Each contemplated sacrificing their own life to ensure the death of the other but eventually succumbed to their better angels. Attendants flooded the arena, tending to the wounded Corliss and Kregnisk while removing the bodies of the fallen Vorgun, Laslitz, and Farlin. The slave boy Alen was called forth and knelt before the emperor's box with his head to the sand in complete obeisance.

"It seems you've made a new friend. He may join you and the others in your chamber until you are called for," Tosha said before rising to leave.

*****

She closed her eyes as she slipped neath the warm surface of the steaming pool. She lingered in the soothing liquid, allowing the water to soak her hair. Her head broke the frothy surface, where she rested the back of her head upon the curved black granite lip of the pool. The small pool's water was fed by aqueducts that ran from vast cisterns built into the upper hold of the inner keep. The cisterns were filled by rainwater collected from the palace roof. Scores of large cisterns throughout Fera supplied fresh water to the palace and the large garrison stationed therein. Even in times of drought, the palace could rely on the vast underground springs upon which the great fortress was built. Fresh springs were surrounded by solid rock, which supported the massive walls and structure of Fera.

The late-afternoon sun shone through the windows that lined the south and west walls of the chamber. Diaphanous curtains hued in scarlet and sand filtered the waning sunlight, casting their varied shades across the chamber. A dozen handmaids lined the ebony walls, waiting upon their mistress should she have need of them. Tosha savored the emollient caress of the soothing bath, relishing its tranquil charm, which eased the ache in her muscles. The arduous journey from Tinsay on ocran, then on magantor mounts left her muscles knotted and sore.

She lifted a finger, summoning a servant girl. The girl quickly knelt, offering her mistress a goblet of wine. Tosha sipped the sweet nectar, lazily running her left hand through the froth, her mind adrift in thought. Her carefully laid plans were coming to fruition. Her thoughts centered on Raven.

His performance in the Pit exceeded her expectations. He simply overwhelmed her father's champions with brute force. It was certainly a novel approach. He was uncouth, disrespectful, and bombastic, but she knew him well enough to know his foolishness to be a clever act. His cunning was only dimmed by his arrogance. That arrogance would play nicely into her hands.

Soon, her promise to her father would be fulfilled. She took another sip of wine, contemplating the night to come. *Tonight, Raven,* she mused, a knowing smile playing across her lips. His fate was sealed the moment he agreed to escort her to Fera. She wondered if he could feel the walls close around him. Tosha set her goblet upon the granite floor and turned her back, summoning another servant girl to massage her shoulders.

*****

He shivered uncontrollably, beset by a sudden chill that coursed his flesh. The night before, they provided him a thick gray blanket and a triple ration of porridge. He first refused their generosity when Marcus was not afforded similar reward, but they forced him to accept their gifts or have Marcus suffer for his defiance. The food was plentiful but bland.

He lost himself in the warmth of the blanket. He had spent countless nights curled in a ball to warm his fevered body. The cold of his damp cell and the fetters binding his hands and feet impaired his ability to retain heat. For days, they ignored his famished body and shivering flesh. Why would they intervene on his behalf now? The question was answered by Kriton's remark that the emperor had something special planned for him. Kriton was still free to abuse his hapless captive and planned a thorough flogging for Cronus until the princess ordered that Cronus be untouched. Whatever she intended was not as severe as what her father planned.

Cronus and Marcus were all that remained of their once proud unit. The others suffered terribly at Kriton's hands. Their tortured screams haunted the dark corridors of the black dungeon. Beylar was flayed over several days, his anguish and torment the products of

Kriton's cruelest inclinations. Forbiss was stretched to his utmost, his joints dislodged as they pressed hot irons to his flesh. They applied the glowing pincers in a slow, measured pace to prolong his suffering. Tarlan, Toran, and Geornon begged for the mercy of slavery, and the others witnessed their emasculation.

The process continued apace, Kriton dragging Cronus's men from their dank cells for torture or slavery until only Marcus and Cronus remained. When they gifted Cronus his improved ration and blanket, Kriton ordered Marcus removed from their cell. Cronus stood helpless behind the bars of his cell as Marcus was hung by his arms in the outer corridor.

Kriton's red eyes blazed, returning Cronus's stare as he stripped Marcus of his tunic and undergarment. He drew a double-bladed dagger, running it across Marcus's bare chest, drawing a line of blood. Kriton ran his split tongue along the length of the blade, savoring the taste of human blood. Marcus winced with the shallow cut. Kriton continued to slice the Torry's flesh with small, superficial cuts.

"Beg me for slavery, and I shall grant mercy," Kriton hissed in Marcus's ear. Marcus closed his eyes, refusing to answer. "So be itsss!" Kriton snarled as Marcus's screams rent the still air.

*****

"Turn around, Alen," Lorken said.

"Yes, master." Alen meekly complied.

"We're not your masters, Alen. You're free now," Lorken said, placing a small tubular device to the collar that circled Alen's throat, the distinctive sound of a metallic pop echoing in the chamber.

A strange sensation coursed Alen's spine as the symbol of his bondage slipped from his neck. There were moments in one's life that symbolized a profound change that defined the meaning of that life forevermore. When the cool air kissed his neck, Alen's transformative moment came to pass. He held no illusion of his eventual fate, knowing well his poor chance of escaping this cursed realm. But for this glorious moment, he was free. The lives of slaves were a cruel mix of prolonged drudgery and bursts of abject terror and abuse.

"Free," he whispered, repeating Lorken's utterance while touching his neck.

"Free," Terin reaffirmed, placing a comforting hand upon Alen's shoulder. The former slave stiffened at his touch as if expecting to be chastised but conditioned not to flinch from such punishment. His shoulders eased once realizing Terin's intent.

"Jumpy little thing, isn't he?" Raven muttered from across their chamber while trying to operate Lorken's structure analyzer.

"I'm surprised he's as cognizant as he is considering the psychological damage he has suffered through the years," Lorken said.

"Well, he's free now," Raven said, continuing to fumble with Lorken's device.

"Free until we leave. Then all bets are off. I doubt Tyro will suffer a freed Menotrist slave in his presence," Lorken said.

"Then he should come with us," Terin argued.

"We have enough on our plate without added baggage," Lorken countered.

"Aw, bring him along. He doesn't weigh that much. Heck, I've had craps bigger than him," Raven said, continuing to struggle with the analyzer as he shook it, held it to his ear, and twisted it upside down while grunting his frustration.

"All right. Then he'll have to share a mount with someone," Lorken relented as he closed on Raven, snatching the analyzer from his hand. "Give me that before you break it."

Alen stood numbly, indifferent to their offer to bring him along, not believing that any of them would escape the Black Castle. His mistress and masters had spent a lifetime breaking his spirit, driving out any hope of freedom. Could he now muster the courage needed to simply follow these men to freedom, or did the chains that had bound his limbs bound his heart as well?

He touched his neck, again savoring the cool air upon his liberated flesh. He clenched his chest, feeling the mending of his heart, the renewing of his spirit, and the glorious birth of a man rising from the ash of slavery. He vowed then to not fritter his one chance at freedom. "Where you lead, I shall follow!" he declared with a strangely assertive voice.

"We welcome your company, Alen." Terin gifted a smile, again placing his hand upon Alen's shoulder.

"There. You see how easy it is?" Lorken's voice echoed from across the chamber as he activated the structural analyzer.

A three-dimensional image sprang from the device, startling Alen as it floated upon the air like a glowing apparition. Fear quickly turned to recognition as Alen suddenly comprehended the image floating before him. "The palace," he said in awe.

"A map of Fera, yes," Lorken confirmed as a three-dimensional schematic of the Black Castle took shape before their eyes.

"Wizardry!" Alen gasped.

"Not quite." Lorken frowned, studying the living map. Every detail of the palace was detailed in hues of emerald and gray while every humanoid form was represented in glowing shades of red and gold. At this scale, the humanoid forms were but faint shadows until Lorken expanded select points of the palace. The humanoid forms grew exponentially, revealing the position of every soldier, citizen, and slave present in the palace.

"So where is he?" Raven asked impatiently.

"My guess is, right there." Lorken indicated the subterranean region of the palace, five levels below the surface.

"Why there?" Raven asked.

"The prisoner in that cell is the only captive that matches Cronus's stature. No other prisoner on any level exceeds sixty-six inches."

"Hey, kid, come here," Raven said, summoning Alen closer. Alen swallowed past the lump in his throat before stepping near. "Are you familiar with this region of the castle?" Raven asked. Alen closed his eyes and nodded affirm as memories of that foul place resurfaced painfully in his mind. Palace slaves were often ordered to the dungeon to watch the tortures and mutilations of captives. It was an overt reminder of what awaited disobedient slaves. "Good. You're gonna take us there," Raven said.

"P-pl-please," Alen's trembling lips pleaded, his eyes shooting open. "Do not venture there. It is a fool's errand."

"Our friend is there, and we ain't leaving him!" Raven growled.

"You…you…you do not wish to see what awaits us there," Alen said, pleading desperately.

"Whatever is there doesn't want to see us coming. You better stop being afraid of gargoyles and Benotrists and start fearing us. We're a lot scarier," Raven said.

"Gentlemen, the emperor awaits you," the palace steward echoed from the outer corridor, as Raven deactivated the analyzer and stuffed it in his jacket pocket. The moment of truth was at hand. If Tosha failed to produce Cronus, they would rescue him themselves and leave destruction in their wake.

*****

The palace steward ushered them into the great hall, where they had dined the evening last. Basin torches lined the circumference of the vast chamber, their flickering flames pooling across the mirrored stone. The large table centered in the chamber was removed, replaced by a golden fountain with a silver torch rising from its center. The emperor stood regally beside the fountain, adorned in layered robes of gold, scarlet, and gray. His dark hair spilled below his crown.

Scores of richly dressed courtesans circled the fountain at a distance. The women were dressed in shimmering calnesian gowns while the men wore pastel tunics of emerald and crimson. Raven spotted Nels Draken posted in their midst, dressed similarly as the august host who surrounded him. Morac stood along the opposite wall. He noted several others of Tyro's Elite dispersed among the high-born dignitaries.

He spied Tosha approach her father, dressed in a gossamer ivory gown that followed the contours of her curves before pooling at her feet. Her ebony hair rolled freely below her shoulders, trailing her as she glided along the mirror stone floor. The chamber was eerily calm, silent as a long-sealed tomb.

Tosha stopped a pace before her father, dropping to her knees and bowing her head slightly, allowing him to place his right hand gently upon her head. She arose as he removed his hand. Tosha's golden eyes swept the assemblage, finding Raven, who returned her stare with his steel gaze. Come, she commanded wordlessly with her hand outstretched, beckoning him hither.

"What is all this?" Lorken whispered in his ear.

"Damned if I know," Raven uttered.

"Where's Cronus?" Lorken wondered.

"I guess we'll find out," Raven said, taking a step before Lorken caught his shoulder.

"Where are you going?"

"To get Cronus even if I have to drag her to the dungeon to get him."

Raven left his comrades at the chamber's edge. The echo of his heavy boots pounding on the floor was magnified in the eerie silence that hung in the chamber. Tosha received him with her outstretched hand, intertwining her fingers with his. She placed the first fingers of her other hand over his opening lips, warning him to silence. "Shh," she whispered, the smile on her lips reaching her eyes in a strangely euphoric manner that raised the hairs on his neck.

Tyro lifted a goblet from the fountain's lip, smoky fumes rolling off its liquid surface. The goblet was cast in pure gold with silver edged along its lip and base. Countless gems of varying hues aligned along its surface, sparkling brightly in the ambient light. Tyro dipped the goblet into the foggy mist, collecting the mysterious liquid in his cup. He lifted the goblet to his lips, partaking of its content before offering it to Tosha. The princess received the goblet with awed reverence, sipping carefully, her eyes observing Raven's confusion over the lip of the goblet. She swallowed the rich wine, then presented the goblet to him.

"Drink," she commanded softly.

"What is it?" He made a face, dumbfounded by the strange ceremony.

"Wine, Raven, the sweetest of wines." She hoped to assuage his misgiving.

"No!" Alen whispered despondently, horror transfixing his face as his eyes beheld the unfolding drama.

"What vexes you?" Terin whispered.

Before Alen could verbalize the true meaning of the ceremony, Raven drank, emptying the goblet. Tyro took the goblet and set it aside before placing Raven's hand in Tosha's. The gathered assemblage knelt, their heads bowed in deep reverence. Alen knelt in kind while Lorken and Terin backed a step, observing the strange ritual with misgiving.

"Come," Tosha commanded softly. "All shall be explained," she said, leading Raven from the chamber.

*****

Moonlight shone through the open windows, illuminating the chamber in celestial light. The evening breeze rippled the gossamer curtains of ivory and scarlet, billowing their translucent folds like ghostly apparitions. She led him across the dark stone floor, the heat of the hearth warming her flank as she passed, its glowing embers melding with the moonlight illuminating the chamber. Arches hued in alabaster and sand circled the room, angling to the center of the domed ceiling. Raven paused at the hearth, where twin statues were posted on either side. Each was a head taller than him, cast in female form with ivory flesh, gowns of bronze, hair of obsidian, and sapphire eyes.

"They are my grandmothers," Tosha said, answering his unasked question. "This is my paternal grandmother." She indicated the sculpture on the left. "Her name was Ledemma."

"She's beautiful," Raven said, taken by the artist's mastery.

"She was beloved by my grandfather, who took her to his bed, favoring her above his first wife. The other is my maternal grandmother, Queen Theresa, first guardian of the Sisterhood."

"Who made them?"

"My father. He gifted them to me on my fifth birth celebration, crafted by his own hand."

"Your father can sculpt?"

"Among his other many talents," she said proudly. "The statue of his mother he forged from memory, for she died long before my birth."

"He has a perfect memory," he stated, his eyes drifting from the statue to Tosha, who stepped toward a large, voluminous bed centered in the chamber. Rich calnesian sheets the color of the sun peeked below thick furs layered above. Tosha stood beside the bed, slowly sliding her gown from her shoulders, allowing it to pool at her feet. She loosened the strings holding her undergarments in place, and they slipped freely from her toned form.

"You should be honored, Raven."

"How so?"

"Other than my father, you are the only male to ever enter my personal chamber."

"Where's Cronus?" He dismissed her remark.

"He is being brought to your friends as we speak."

"Then why are we here?" he asked, stepping closer.

"Because we are going to give each other one last favor." She removed his jacket, a flirtatious smile playing across her lips.

Raven's heart pounded emphatically at the sight of her, nearly bursting from his chest. She stood beautifully before him, her natural form unencumbered by raiment or position. Raven had desired her since the day he first set eyes upon her, and there she was, offering what he so longed for. She stepped into his chest, working his shirt free of his belt and stripping it over his head as his lips crushed hers. She returned his caress, running her fingers through his short hair and down his back, her nails digging along his flesh.

He scooped her into his arms, her warm flesh melding with his own, setting her upon the thick furs. She fumbled with his pistol belt, frantically undoing the buckle. She freed it from his waist and tossed it over the side of the bed. His boots followed one after the other, then the belt of his trousers. She rolled atop him, disrobing his remaining garments as she savaged his chest with her teeth and lips, placing her claim. He rested his hands behind his head, observing her with a bemused grin. "Are you laughing at me?" She ceased her ministration, the pools of her golden eyes glaring through her narrowed stare.

He reached out to her, pinching her lips close between his finger and thumb. "Shut up." He smiled, flipping her on her back in a fluid movement, his lips devouring hers as she feigned resistance. Her flesh tingled neath his dominion, captive to an alien vulnerability. She was warrior born and bred, the daughter of two royal lines, yet she felt helplessly feminine in his arms.

Her teeth clenched at their joining, pleasure washing away the pain of her sundered maidenhood. Tosha's back arched severely, responsive to the euphoria cascading her flesh. Raven paused, running the fingers of his right hand along her cheek.

"Beautiful," he whispered.

Her eyes shot wide as she gripped his jaw. "Don't stop!" she snarled.

"I didn't plan to." He shrugged.

*****

Lorken and Terin waited in the great hall, their backs to the wall, observing the festivities with a wary eye. After Alen revealed the meaning of the strange ceremony, Lorken thought he would give Raven a little time to escape Tosha's clutches before taking action on his own, but Raven's time was running thin. Lorken could ill imagine what suffering his friend might be enduring.

*****

She shuddered, biting the urge to shout her pleasure. She collapsed atop him, breathless and spent, her head resting upon his thick chest. He flipped her on her back, continuing apace to completion. Raven rolled on his side, attempting to climb out of bed till Tosha touched a hand to his shoulder.

"Are you leaving?"

"Aren't we done?"

"No!" she scolded, climbing back atop him, pushing on his chest and forcing him down. She shook her head at his audacity. His bedside manner required refinement. Obviously, the women he courted failed to train him properly, but she would see to his correction. "Stay!" she softly commanded as she slipped off the bed. She fetched a wine pitcher from a table along the near wall, filling two silver goblets, returning to the bed with one in each hand. "To your victory and Cronus's safekeeping." She offered him a goblet while sipping from her own.

"Speaking of Cronus—"

"He awaits you. Finish your wine, and I shall take you to him. I am certain he is as eager to depart Fera as you are, but I still insist that you escort me to Bansoch."

"All right, but we're dropping you off on a pier. I'm not stepping foot on that feminist-infested isle," he growled before draining his goblet. His eyes slightly widened, suddenly cognizant of her true intent, a devious smile playing across her lips as his eyes grew heavy.

"Sleep well, my love," she whispered as his head fell back and his body went limp. She ran her fingers over his muscled chest, relishing her conquest. She quickly cleaned and donned a fresh tunic and sandals before stepping into the outer corridor, where four of her personal guard awaited.

"Princess," they greeted as they knelt.

"Rise," she said, annoyed with such pleasantries. "My consort is fast asleep upon my bed. Bind him, burn his clothing, and bring him before my father!" she commanded.

"As you command, Highness." They bowed as she stepped gingerly away, sore from her sundered maidenhood.

"Chain him well!" she emphasized, dreading Raven's response if he somehow slipped his bonds. Her father demanded Raven be brought before him to answer for his offenses to the crown. She expected no less than a thorough flogging before he and Cronus were handed over to her. They would return with her to her mother's queendom and live out their days as captives of the Sisterhood. She planned to offer Cronus to Leanna if she was willing to reside on the isle as a citizen of her mother's realm. It was the only way her father would agree to releasing the Torry prisoner into her custody.

*****

"What do we do now?" Terin whispered as they remained along the side of the great hall. Lorken shook his head, uncertain of their next move. Alen stood at his opposite shoulder, his downcast eyes stealing furtive glances at the austere assemblage as if awaiting the roof to collapse upon them at any moment. Alen had revealed the meaning of the strange ceremony but moments ago. The sharing of the goblet offered by a woman's father represented marital union in the Benotrist tradition. Raven's victory in the pit was a requirement to prove his worthiness as a royal consort to a Benotrist princess. That was the true reason Tosha urged him to partake, not for Cronus's liberty.

Lorken doubted if Raven had yet surmised what he had done. His friend was rather obtuse when it came to the fairer sex. *Fairer sex,* Lorken mused. That term certainly didn't apply to Tosha. *Does she truly believe she could keep Raven as her consort?* Lorken would have laughed at such a notion if the situation weren't so dire. He would not rest easy until Raven returned, but there was little sign of him thus far.

Tyro surveyed the festive chamber from his throne resting upon a raised dais on the chamber's opposite wall, facing the arched entryway. A lesser throne rested to his right. The guests danced and mingled as slaves hurried to and fro with platters of steaming food, fruits, and goblets of wine. Lorken noticed Morac standing post along the opposing wall, observing them with a wary eye. Draken stood nearer the entrance, smiling every so often in their direction with a mirthless grin. Other members of Tyro's Elite were dispersed among the crowd, each observing them with furtive stares. Lorken discreetly shifted his right hand, resting it upon the grip of his holstered pistol.

The crowd suddenly stirred as Tosha entered the great hall. She strode purposefully across the mirrored stone floor, head held high as she approached her father. She knelt before the dais with measured grace before he directed her to the lesser throne to his right.

"It is done, Father," she said quietly for his ear alone as she sat her throne.

"And his friends' reprisals? Are you certain you can stay their hand?" he asked, warily observing Lorken along the wall to their left, staring back at him with deadly intent.

"The lives of Raven and Cronus shall stay their wrath if I guarantee their safety as wards of the Sisterhood as well as affording Lorken and Terin safe passage to the *Stenox*."

"After I have been afforded just measure," he snarled. Raven would suffer for his repeated insults to the emperor.

"Other than scarring his back, you promised no permanent damage to his person, Father," she reminded him.

"Yes, child. I know well my promise, as you know yours."

"I am fulfilling my promise now, Father."

"Nay. Until you bear me a male heir, your promise is unfulfilled."

"And for that, I need a healthy consort," she reminded him.

"That only requires certain functions of his anatomy to remain intact. There are countless others he can suffer without and still plant his seed. You and he would do well to remember that."

Lorken had taken a step forward, ready to challenge Tosha on Raven's whereabouts, when his eyes shifted to a sizable procession entering the great hall. A gargoyle of above-average stature and a man with one eye entered the hall, each flanking a large man wearing a black Stetson and clad similarly to Raven and himself. The blood drained from Lorken's face as he beheld Ben Thorton, their fellow Earther and former comrade.

"Welcome, Thorton, second among my Imperial Elite!" Tyro's deep voice echoed from his dais, heralding Ben Thorton's arrival, a declaration intended for Lorken to stay his hand.

CHAPTER 17

Ben Thorton strode across the great keep like an ill wind, the palace courtesans parting as the large Earther approached the throne with Zelo and Neon on either flank. He cast a wary eye to Lorken, who stood statue still along the wall off his right. Terin stood at Lorken's side, his eyes fixed on the stranger before them, the sixth Earther. His large build fell between Lorken and Raven, though his complexion was akin to Brokov's extreme white hue.

He wore the same black jacket, shirt, and trousers that Raven and Lorken wore, but the similarity ended there. He wore a strange black hat with a wide rim that bent low in front and aft but upward at its sides. His cold blue eyes bespoke a tormented soul, devoid of the human spark. Terin could ill conceive how this man was Raven's friend.

The courtesans in the great hall granted him a wide berth, backing cautiously away as he stopped at the base of the dais. Zelo and Neon knelt as Ben Thorton stood unbent before the throne. Like Raven and Lorken, Thorton knelt to no one. That was his one condition before entering Tyro's service, and the emperor had obliged.

"He fights for Tyro?" Terin whispered, a cold dread washing over him.

"It would appear so," Lorken grunted, taken aback by this unforeseen turn of events.

"But he is your friend," Terin bemoaned.

"We are his friends, but I don't think he is ours." Lorken sighed.

"Welcome, Thorton." Tyro's voice reverberated off the black stone walls. Thorton arrived at Fera just after Raven's stand in the arena, but Tyro waited until the most opportune time for him to present himself. With Raven neutralized, he needed only stay Lorken's hand.

"Emperor, we have returned prematurely from the Yatin Campaign due to fortuitous events at the front. General Yonig has sent the first prize of his conquest of Yatin. Bring them forth!" Thorton commanded, and six men escorted two bound prisoners, kneeling them before the throne, forcing their heads to the floor. Thorton stepped to his left, half facing the prisoners and the throne while keeping Lorken to his fore.

"The boy is Yanku, crown prince of Yatin," Thorton said, nudging the kneeling prisoner nearest him with the toe of his boot. "The other one is named Yeltor, a sworn sword of the Yatin Elite. Yonig caught the boy after the whelp led a cavalry charge blindly into his ranks. We captured the Elite when he attempted to free his prince."

The Yatin crown prince! Tyro mused elatedly. He lifted a finger, signaling Thorton to raise the prisoner's head. Thorton grabbed the boy by the scruff of the neck, raising his terror-filled eyes to the emperor. "Look at me, child!" Tyro commanded as the boy tried shifting away, his watered eyes lifting to Tyro's. "That's better, boy. You shouldn't be afraid of me, child. I mean only to lift your burdens." He smiled falsely, rising from his throne and descending the dais.

"We have already lifted the burden of your crown. See how lighter your head feels? The decisions of the realm no longer weigh upon your spirit, aging you beyond your tender years. Perhaps we should lift other burdens that weigh needless upon your young mind. Luzzo, I believe your unique talents might benefit our young guest."

"Of course, my emperor," Luzzo Korun said, stepping from the crowd. Luzzo Korun's nondescript face betrayed little of the man, matching his cold pale-blue eyes. He was the former keeper of the dungeon before passing the title and knowledge to the gargoyle Kriton. Fourth among Tyro's Elite, Luzzo Korun's fell deeds were known throughout the world. His very name conjured the darkest of possibilities.

Yanku was dragged to the center of the hall and secured to a metal rack that was moved into position. A horizontal bar rested two meters from the floor, fastened to two vertical posts at either end. A second horizontal bar paralleled the other, resting one foot from the floor. His hands were stretched to their utmost and secured along the length of the upper bar while his legs were similarly secured below. The boy's raiment was cut away, exposing his nakedness to the curious onlookers, as Luzzo Korun circled the frightened prince.

Yeltor's attempt to rise was poorly met, Thorton's boot pushing his head to the floor. It did not go unnoticed by Tyro, who smiled wickedly. "Loyal to the end, Yatin. You are the sworn sword to your emperor and his heirs. You needn't concern yourself with Yanku, for in a short while, he will no longer be Yangu's heir."

"Kill me before my prince!" Yeltor begged.

"Kill you?" Tyro said with pained humor. "I don't grant such mercies. You and your prince shall serve my empire until old age takes you. You may proceed, Korun." Yanku's screams rent the air under the cruel ministration of Luzzo Korun.

"What are they doing to him?" Terin winced.

"Not sure. It ain't good, whatever it is," Lorken said.

"They're emasculating him," Alen answered, turning away.

Lorken had seen enough. "Where's Raven?" he asked boldly as he stepped forth, his eyes fixed on Thorton's. Luzzo Korun stilled as the congregants shifted their eyes to Lorken. Tosha pursed her lips, regarding the Earther carefully.

"Your friend shall soon be joining us, my dear Lorken," Tyro answered him. "As you can witness, I enjoy the company of your kind, as your friend Thorton can attest." Lorken snorted, dismissive of such claims. There was little to be gained in fighting until they brought Raven to him.

Ben Thorton circled Yeltor's kneeling form, stopping halfway between Lorken and the throne. "It's been a long time, Lorken." Ben's face was stone.

"Nearly three years, Ben. You don't belong here. You belong with us. Raven's your best friend."

"No." He shook his head sadly. "Our friendship died with her."

"That wasn't his fault, Ben. You know that," Lorken pleaded.

"He made his choice," Thorton said with a dead voice.

"He was given a lousy hand, and you begrudge the result?" Lorken shook his head.

"A lousy hand or no, he could've still saved her."

Tosha listened intently as she descended the dais, stepping to Thorton's side. "Saved who?" she asked.

"It is of no concern to you, Princess," Thorton growled, stepping away.

"Raven is with Cronus, Lorken. You needn't fret. They shall both join us shortly," she said, assuaging his concern.

"He better be for your sake, Tosha," Lorken said, backing a step.

Tyro nodded, giving Luzzo Korun leave to continue.

*****

Marcus hung limply by his chained wrists, his throat raw from screaming. Kriton circled his emaciated captive, running his dagger over Marcus's skin ever so slightly. He bled him dry, every small cut adding its measure. Cronus watched helpless, chained to the floor of his cell as he gazed through the grill of his door. Marcus's entire body was covered with a thousand cuts, each oozing blood in a methodical, macabre pace. Lines of blood ran cheek to cheek under and over Marcus's nose. His lips were sliced open, and his eyebrows had been cut away. Scores of cuts covered his chest and arms. Blood smeared across his abdomen, groin, and back. Hundreds of slashes ran the length of each leg. The skin of each toe was pulled back as he teetered gingerly on the heels of his feet.

Like a lanzar weary of toying with its prey, Kriton decided to quicken the dance. He cut deeper below the skin along Marcus's torso before ripping flesh and skin over his chest, exposing several ribs to the naked eye. Marcus's screams rent the fetid air as Cronus struggled to keep his eyes on his friend, granting what encouragement his eyes might lend.

Kriton smashed Marcus's ribs with the handle of his dagger, where they adjoined the sternum, cracking several freely away before taking them in hand and snapping them back. Marcus's screams heightened to inhuman octaves before he fainted from the pain.

Kriton snarled, his eyes glowing feral crimson at the Torry's weakness, denying him the pleasure of his agony. Overcome with his bloodlust not sated, Kriton drove his dagger into Marcus's heart.

"Take me, monster!" Cronus shouted through gritted teeth. "I am all that is left. Finish me if you have the courage." His only hope for a merciful death was through Kriton's unfettered rage. Only in anger might he grant what he wouldn't when calm. Any death was a welcome respite from this living hell, Leanna forgive him for thinking so. Even nightmares were a kindness to escape this wretched existence.

Kriton's eyes blazed like embers, fixing Cronus in their gaze. They were alone in the dungeon with no others able to check Kriton's rage. The gargoyle unlocked the door to Cronus's cell and slammed it open, its hinge straining under the weight. He raised his dagger, ready to drive it into Cronus's heart as the Torry looked up from his knees with his chest offered up to receive the hoped-for blow. Cronus kept his shackled hands passively in his lap. Kriton's lips retracted, revealing the full menace of his glistening fangs with slaver dripping from their points.

"Ugh!" he screeched, fighting the desire to drive the dagger into Cronus's heart. The emperor wanted this one alive, he reminded himself. He lowered the dagger, the fire in his eyes slightly abating. "Clever human." He snorted. "The emperor has plans for you, and I shall not despoil his purpose." Kriton spoke clear, his voice void of its usual guttural accent. He bent down, unlocking the chain that fastened Cronus's shackles to the floor, before hauling him to his feet and into the outer corridor.

Kriton held him close, twisting his head to face Marcus's lifeless eyes. "See!" he snarled. "Your death shall not be as gently done," he whispered harshly in his ear, his foul spittle spraying the left side of Cronus's face. "You have escaped my dungeon each night in your sleep, yet your dreams betray you, human. A name you speak while you sleep, a name precious to you, no doubt—Leanna," he said, emphasizing slowly, the word rolling off his split tongue in wicked amusement. Cronus stiffened, his mind awash in dread. He betrayed his love, his sweet Leanna, in his dreams, offering up her name to this wretched creature. Her name was soiled on those foul lips. How dare he speak it?

"Your war is lost, Torry. You shall live to see its end, laboring without death until all that you honor is ripped away. I shall fetch your Leanna and bring her before your eyes. You will watch as I despoil her virtue and eat of her flesh as she begs you to help her."

As Cronus dismissed Kriton's threat as mere banter, the gargoyle drove home his point. "If you doubt me, Cronus, know this. Your comrades revealed much that you are woefully ignorant. They gave me a name and place. Celen is your betrothed family name, and Central City is her home. I will find her once it has fallen to our legions."

"No!" Cronus screamed desperately through the tender narrows of his throat. He reached his head back, biting into Kriton's neck, tearing a chunk of flesh with his teeth before the gargoyle broke free of his grasp.

Kriton screeched demonically, his eyes ablaze, grasping Cronus's throat in the digits of his clawed left hand, digging their jagged tips into his flesh. "Argh!" he screamed, his eyes aglow with bloodlust, intent on finishing Cronus, the emperor be damned.

A strange numbness swept Cronus's throat as Kriton's jaw slackened. The gargoyle's eyes drew mysteriously dull. Kriton toppled over, causing Cronus to lose balance as he, too, fell to the floor, the numbness in his throat weakening as Kriton's hand fell away. He heard the pounding of heavy feet striking the floor, drawing near. Whoever it was, they had prevented Kriton from killing him, a servant to the emperor, no doubt. He lay there upon the cold floor, staring hopelessly at the ceiling, as a strangely familiar face came into his view.

"You look terrible," the voice said. Cronus looked up at Raven's face, the big Earther shaking his head, appraising Cronus's poor condition. Cronus struggled to form words. "Come on, buddy. Snap out of it." Raven snapped his fingers in front of Cronus's bewildered face as he knelt by his side. He removed the cylinder-shaped metal distorter from his jacket pocket and pressed it to the shackles binding Cronus's hands and feet. The distinctive sound of a metallic pop echoed through the chamber as Cronus's shackles fell away.

"Raven?" he could barely whisper, his eyes unblinkingly fixed on his friend lest the vision fade and the nightmare return.

"Yeah, it's me. I had to use a paralysis setting when I shot your buddy in case I hit you by mistake." He regarded Kriton's listless form. "I left a trail of bodies on my way down here, and we'll have to make another trail on our way up." Raven helped him to his feet.

Cronus teetered unsteadily, his malnourished body shaking from hunger and cold. His mind ignored his suffering as he stared at his friend. *How?* he thought disbelievingly. *How is this possible?* He forced his eyes to close to test the vision before him, though fearing it would dissipate once he opened them. When he opened them, Raven was still there. Cronus threw his arms around his friend's neck and hugged him tightly.

*****

A short time before, the four guards had deftly entered the princess's private chamber, stepping quietly so as not to awaken the slumbering Earther before they secured him in irons. The dim light of embers from the glowing hearth cast their faint shadows across the chamber. Blue laser spewed behind them, striking each a mortal blow in quick succession as Raven's naked form stepped from the shadows.

He had recognized the taste of the Fleacen sleeping potion that Tosha had slipped into his wine, for it was from the vial she had kept on her person since their arrival at the palace. Lorken had identified it with his analyzer during Raven's fight in the arena. Fortunately for Raven, Earthers were immune to its effects.

Raven quickly donned his clothes and retrieved Lorken's structural analyzer from his jacket pocket, sweeping the outer corridor before stepping without. A guard stood post at the end of the outer corridor, his eyes fixed forward, oblivious that he was being observed. Raven remained in the shadow of the entrance of Tosha's bedchamber, taking careful aim. Laser flashed, illuminating the corridor in a burst of azure. The guard slumped to the floor, brains spilling from his punctured skull.

Raven moved swiftly along the corridor, sweeping the analyzer through the passageway running perpendicular to the one he was traversing, spying two guards posted intermittently on opposing walls. He passed over the slain guard, stopping at the corner of the adjoining corridor. The guard posted on the right was ten yards farther afield than the one on the left. Laser burst through the passageway, first striking the guard farther away, his body crumpling as the nearer guard stepped forth, providing Raven a clearer view. Several blasts followed, striking head, chest, and neck. The guard's spear dropped from his slackened grip as he tumbled backward, his iron helm clanging off the stone floor.

"Damn noisy armor!" Raven growled as he swept the adjoining corridors, relieved that no one was startled by the clanging metal. He could only surmise that Lorken and Terin were compromised as well, and if he wanted to rescue Cronus, he would have to do so now, then work his way back up to save the others. Sweeping the analyzer through the lower levels, it charted his course to the dungeon. "It's gonna be a long night." He sighed, lamenting the descent and length of the outlined path.

*****

Raven and Cronus retraced Raven's path through the lower levels of the dungeon, stepping over the scattered corpses of slain guards, soldiers, or habitants of those nether regions. No one had discovered Raven's handiwork on these lower reaches, as they were most recent, but a sweep of the levels above indicated a stirring of activity.

"How many did you kill on your descent?" Cronus's hoarse voice asked as he struggled to keep pace. He could barely stand without shaking. He leaned weakly against the jagged stone wall as Raven stopped short of the stairwell that spiraled to their right.

"I lost count," Raven whispered, putting a finger to his lips to quiet his friend before firing several blasts up the stairwell. Two human bodies tumbled down the stone steps, their limbs sprawled out upon the floor at Raven's feet. He dragged them clear of the entryway, tossing them aside with one hand like sacks of linen.

Cronus could only imagine the true answer to his question, as his friend was often prone to disregard the extraordinary as trivial. He surmised that Raven killed scores on his way to the dungeon. "How did you find me? How"—he coughed, his body shaking from the fever coursing his flesh—"how did you know I was here?"

"All we knew was that you were captured and taken north. The rest was just a guess."

"Thank you." Cronus nearly wept but was bereft of tears.

"Forget about it. I owe you a couple," Raven said, remembering the day Cronus saved his life from an angry mob and the day Cronus's brother died in his care.

"If I die, tell Leanna—"

"You ain't dying after we came all this way. Whatever you gotta say, you can tell her yourself. She's back on the *Stenox*, waiting for you."

"She awaits me?" He nearly wept, as all the dreams he dared not hope for were coming true.

"Of course, she's waiting for you. What did you expect? She loves you. I don't know how you landed her, you lucky dog, but she's been crying her eyes out ever since Terin told her of your capture."

"Terin survived the battle?" Cronus smiled weakly. He had often pondered Terin's fate, as he only knew of their victory and not the extent of their casualties.

"Survived? Hell, the kid's with Lorken at the top of the castle."

"What? Terin is here?"

"Yes. He insisted on coming to help rescue you. The boy's pretty handy with that fancy sword of his. Arsenc would've come too, but he's still favoring his leg. He's back on the ship with Leanna." Cronus was dumbstruck, humbled by his friends' bravery and affection. Raven noticed the stubborn tears squeezing from his friend's eyes. "Face it. Everybody loves you, pal. Besides, it's about time we rescued you for a change."

They ascended the stairwell, pausing at the top as Raven swept the analyzer through the stone wall, surveying the adjoining corridor. "What is that?" Cronus asked.

"One of Brokov's gizmos. Lorken's better at using it than I am." Raven shook it as the image shifted between fuzzy and clear.

"What does it do?"

"It sees through walls and highlights living things so I know what's waiting for us and where." Cronus leaned close, observing the image projected from the device. The length of the corridor ahead was revealed in stark detail in a clear emerald tint. His curious eyes drew wide as three humanoid forms in reddish hues materialized farther afield in an adjoining corridor. He could see their silhouettes moving apace with swords drawn. "They're still a way off. Come on," Raven said, stepping from the stairwell and onto the subterranean level.

Cronus was greeted by a dimly lit corridor cut from the bedrock below the castle. Though this was several levels above where he was held, he was struck by its morbid ambience. It was as if he was traversing an ancient tomb. Torches bracketed to the rough stone wall lighted their path, outlining the length of the passageway. They stepped over the corpses of several gargoyles, whose blood pooled along the floor, sticking to Cronus's bare feet as he passed. The corridor opened wide to either side, revealing a large armory with hundreds of blades, bows, and armor stacked in racks with large bellows feeding braziers that lit the massive chamber.

A score of bodies were strewn across the floor, an even mix of gargoyles and humans. The bodies of several smiths lay near the braziers, each felled as they were tending their craft. One still held a hammer clutched in his hand. Bodies of gargoyles littered the chamber, their corpses bent in unnatural angles, each felled by laser fire during Raven's descent.

"You slew this many?" Cronus coughed.

"Yeah. It was a rough trip getting to you. But don't worry, there are plenty more where they came from. The castle is surrounded by them."

A thousand questions came to mind. *How did Raven come here? Who else awaited them above and where? What was his plan to escape once the entire garrison was alerted to them?* Cronus mused. Too tired to contemplate the answers, he merely put one foot before the other, struggling with the task at hand. "Wait, Raven." He coughed, stepping toward the rack before lifting a shortsword from its slot. He ran a finger along the blade, testing its sharpness to his satisfaction. "I'd take a larger sword if I could wield it, but for now, this shall suffice," he said before snatching a cloak from a fallen Benotrist.

The three soldiers made their way along the corridor, moving at a quick pace as they examined each chamber they crossed with cursory glances before passing on. Their corridor ended ahead, where the adjoining passageway broke south. Raven stepped into their path, laser fire erupting from his pistol in quick succession, the three soldiers falling in swift order. He closed on their prone forms, sending additional blasts to each of their skulls to be sure of them before he and Cronus passed on.

"Crap!" Raven growled as he scanned the level above.

"What troubles you?" Cronus asked.

"Up ahead is the only way out of here, but on the floor above, there are at least fifty soldiers closing fast on our exit."

"They are above us?"

"Yeah," Raven said, sweeping the device behind and up, above where they had just come. The next level was the ground level, and their options would broaden, as there were several exits on that level, but there was only one avenue of escape for the subterranean levels. The soldiers were closing on the same stairway that they required to attain the next level. Unlike the pirate fortress, these floors were too thick for his pistol to blast. "I've got an idea." Raven removed another fist-sized device from his jacket pocket. He stripped a thin material from its back side, exposing an adhesive coating along its face. "If I lift you, can you stick this on the ceiling?"

*****

The Benotrist soldiers ran apace, traversing the lit wide corridor. Their commander ordered them to secure the dungeon since the trail of corpses they discovered led to or from that direction. The smaller patrols sent to investigate had not returned. They traversed the central corridor at the base of the palace, its black stone walls set wide enough for a troop to march twelve abreast. The stairwell ahead rested at the conjoint of four passageways that ran to each corner of the inner palace. The lead flax commander spied a shadow pass before the entrance of the stairwell.

Boom! It was a low, dull, yet distinctive sound, akin to a distant clap of thunder. *Crack!* Fissures spread beneath their feet as the floor shattered before giving way. The fore ranks dropped from sight, falling to the floor below amid the debris of crashing stone. A score of soldiers littered the floor below, their twisted limbs and broken bones intermingled with black and gray rubble. Nearly half were dead, and the rest were broken in some measure. The force of the collapse snuffed out most of the torches on the lower level as the survivors peered upward through the crater's opening to their fellows above, who had recovered and stared back through the gaping hole.

Flashes of laser spewed from the stairwell ahead, streaming freely into the rear ranks who escaped the floor's collapse. Several were struck unawares as they peered over the edge of the fractured floor, laser fire piercing their torsos, sending them over the edge and onto those strewn below. Others dropped where they stood, the searing pain piercing their flesh. Some fled, some died, and many lifted their shields in vain as Raven's volley streamed through the corridor. A commander of flax slumped to the floor, his back resting against the wall, his dimming eyes following two figures bursting from the stairwell ahead, running toward an adjoining corridor, laser fire streaming from their shadowed forms until they disappeared beyond the corner.

"Back away!" the commander shouted with his dying breath. "They are escaping along the north corridor!" The few survivors gained their feet and withdrew to obey his command. The path ahead was cut off from the crater in the floor, so doubling back would cost them precious time, but their quarry had a long journey if they planned to escape the bowels of the fortress.

They ran through the passageways that zigged and zagged along the ground level, Cronus struggling to keep pace on quivering legs. A sentry stood post along the wall ahead, turning his head as blue laser pierced his skull. "Come on, Cronus. We have to hurry!" Raven panted as they raced past the lifeless corpse. *We're in trouble if I'm the fast one.* Raven lamented Cronus's slow pace. Though Raven was larger and stronger than any Araxan human, he was also much slower. That Cronus failed to keep pace, revealing the extent of his physical deterioration.

The corridor spilled into a large, open chamber. Raven and Cronus held their position as they swept the way ahead for threats. Half-dozen men loitered throughout the chamber, attending varied tasks. Raven doubted they were soldiers, but one could never be certain. Their intended route of travel led through the center of this chamber to the stairwell on the opposing wall. Several passageways converged upon this large chamber from varying angles. Had Raven not used a muffled charge to bring down the floor, this chamber would have been flooded with soldiers. So far, the carnage he had wrought had not reached this place.

The passageway jutting right led to the outer palace and was blocked by a closed portcullis. Every exit leading to the outer reaches of Fera was heavily guarded and blocked. The alarm must have been raised once the first bodies were discovered at some point on his descent. He came down on the opposite side of the inner fortress, leaving a trail of corpses in his wake.

"It might be quicker if we just run for the stairwell," Raven said.

"Wait." Cronus jerked his chin to the mouth of the passageway off their left, where the faint sounds of shouting men grew louder.

"We don't have time for this. Run!" Raven growled as they raced across the chamber with his pistol leveled on the passageway in question. Crossing the chamber, they drew the curious stares of those loitering there.

"That's them!" shouted men emerging from another passageway.

Raven shifted his aim as soldiers in gray mail issued from the mouth of a corridor to the right of the one Raven had trained his pistol on. Raven fired into their midst as he ran, his hurried shots striking more fear than flesh as archers loosed their arrows. They reached the stairwell, stepping within as arrows struck where they had been. Raven aimed his pistol blindly around the corner, spraying laser fire as arrows whizzed by the entrance, bouncing harmlessly off the walls.

"Do you have any more of those charges?" Cronus coughed.

Raven shook his head. "I have one, but it might collapse the stairway, and we'll need it farther up."

*****

They had reached the second landing before their pursuers started firing arrows up the stairwell. Raven stopped every few steps, spraying laser fire below to stay their pursuit. One fellow leaned into his field of fire to take better aim before blue laser took him full in the chest. The sound of his fallen helm rang as it clanged off the stair.

The sound of sandals slapping stone echoed above as a flax-sized patrol descended from above to investigate the disturbance below. Knowing only speed and violence of action would save them, Raven and Cronus threw themselves into the path of the descending flax. Blue laser met startled faces before they took note of the two men in their path. A score of laser blasts spewed in half as many seconds, many piercing multiple targets, as the guards were serried in close ranks along the stair.

Breastplates melted as the intense light passed through, searing flesh, creating cavities in their wake. The fortunate died swiftly with imploded skulls or severed hearts and throats. The less fortunate screamed with vapors issuing from burnt flesh, blood flowing through the cavities of vaporized innards.

Raven and Cronus jumped back as a corpse tumbled down the stair, nearly knocking them from their feet. Raven recovered as he spied the two most rear guards unscathed and turning to flee. He took one in the base of his spine, the fellow crumpling on useless legs. The second blast struck the second guard in his leg before he disappeared up the stair. "Crap!" he growled as the fellow slipped from his line of sight.

Cronus wasted little time stepping among the fallen, sticking his sword tip into any who lingered. He stepped carefully between the corpses strewn upon the wide stone stair. They quickly ascended as arrows flew up from whence they came. Raven fired as they went, spewing laser down the stairway as they passed the archway leading to the third level of the inner palace. They noted the trail of blood leading through the archway—left by the one Raven wounded, no doubt. They bypassed that level and continued their ascent with scores of Benotrists at their heels.

*****

Tosha observed as they dragged the Yatin prince from the great hall with cool indifference. The ruined prince returned the mocking stares of her father's vassals with the dull, broken eyes of a shattered spirit. He was gelded, chained, and beaten, relegated to a servile existence. He would be tended by Tyro's healers to ensure his survival in order to serve as a living mockery of the Royal House of Yatin.

As soon as Yanku was removed, Tyro's guests clamored for further entertainment. The pitiful screams of a pampered princeling whetted their appetite for more difficult game: the debasement of a Yatin Elite. Yeltor was dragged to the metal rack that his prince was affixed to. He uttered not a word or protest as they secured his limbs, nor would he until they brutalized him to good measure. All men broke eventually, and so would he. But all he had left was honor, and he would surrender it grudgingly.

Tosha observed the Yatin Elite curiously, wondering how long before he begged for mercy. He seemed sturdier than most with discerning dark eyes that denoted his hard seasoning. She found the cruelty unnecessary, but her father recalled the brutal treatment visited upon his mother's people and meant to return the favor. The Yatins were no exception, turning a blind eye to the Menotrists' cruelty.

"My emperor." Luzzo Korun bent at the waist, bowing before the throne. "Shall I geld the prisoner before his admonishment or after?"

"The night is young, and I wish to savor its fullness. We shan't take his manhood unless he begs for you to do so," Tyro said dryly.

Tosha knew full well that her father's joyless face masked an inner glee. After they finished making sport of the Yatin Elite, then it would be Raven's turn to suffer for her father's amusement. He would be brought forth to be chastised for his offenses to the throne.

He would be bound naked to the rack, then flogged with forty lashes before being handed over to her. She pleaded leniency for her consort, but her father refused. He would have his pound of flesh, her consort be damned.

She wondered if Raven would ever forgive her, but did it truly matter? He would be hers regardless. The life of a royal consort was not an unkind fate, though Raven would think it so. She pondered her mother's reaction when she returned to Bansoch with Raven in tow or Raven's when he was presented to her mother's court. Of course, Raven's demeanor would be much changed by then, tempered by chains and the lash. It might take years to fully break him.

Men were like pets, needing a firm hand to bring them to heel. She wondered how many years she would have to keep him chained before he accepted his place. Their children should assuage his anger, and he would have his friend Cronus's company, though he would be bound to Leanna, as Raven would be to her. It was a far gentler fate for Cronus than the cruel ministrations of Luzzo Korun. And of course, Lorken and Terin would be granted safe passage.

As Tosha pondered these matters, something felt amiss. Her guards should have brought Raven to the great hall by now. She summoned the nearest guard, sending him to investigate their delay.

*****

They stepped without, forsaking the north stairway at the seventh level before tossing their last charge down the stair as they left. They raced along the adjoining passageway, crashing stone echoing in their wake. Laser fire caught sentries unaware, dropping them where they stood as they traversed the dimly lit corridors, making their way to the lift that rested near the center of the keep. Laser fire dropped the four soldiers guarding the platform. Cronus slashed the ropes holding the counterweight. The wide-set wooden platform lifted suddenly, nearly knocking them from their feet as it sped through its ascent.

"You look like crap." Raven coughed, catching his breath.

Cronus panted beside him, exhausted and spent, his gaunt cheekbones seeming thin enough to break his skin. "Yes. I believe you said that already." Cronus smiled. Though he felt drained and looked worse, the spark in his eyes reflected the hope that sprang anew in his heart. "How did you come to this awful place?"

"We were invited."

"By whom?"

Raven paused before answering. "Princess Tosha."

"The princess?" Cronus coughed again, lifting a curious brow.

"Yeah."

"How did you come to know the Benotrist princess? I didn't think you kept such company." Cronus grinned.

"You know me, Cronus. I'm used to dealing with treacherous lowlifes."

"Are you comparing the Benotrist princess to the riffraff that you so often associate with?"

"No. She's worse."

"Worse?"

"What do you call a woman who slips you a sleep drug after taking you to her bed? If she had her way, I'd be dead now or worse. Even lowlifes have better bedside manners."

"You bedded the princess?" Cronus coughed, not believing his ears. Of course, knowing Raven, it wasn't really surprising.

"It's a long story. This is where we get off," Raven said as the lift slowed, granting him reprieve from having to respond. The sentries posted to guard the lift were caught unaware, Raven dropping them in quick succession.

*****

Yeltor hung on the rack for some time before the first lash fell, his cold eyes fixed on the Earther who had brought him to this place. He could see Ben Thorton standing below the throne, returning his stare with apparent indifference. The Earther actually appeared bored with his suffering and directed his interest to the other Earther standing along the wall to Yeltor's right.

The second Earther was an even stranger sight with very dark skin and broader nose. Neither seemed overly fond of the other, but the fact that both were armed and in Tyro's court denoted their Benotrist loyalties. The whistle of the whip brought him back from his drifting thoughts. The scream caught in his throat as if he was dipped in frigid water, the boiled leather tip stripping his flesh.

"We should do something," Terin pleaded as the madness of his blade beckoned him to act.

"We wait for Raven," Lorken whispered, clearly agitated by the prisoner's treatment and their friend's absence. He had never imagined people to be as cruel as the Benotrists. They were truly worthy allies of the gargoyles.

Tyro sensed Terin's discomfiture, no doubt empathetic toward the Yatin's degradation and anxious concerning Raven's mysterious absence. He was shielded from Tyro's wrath by Tosha and the cover of diplomacy. Something about the boy felt off, gnawing at his brain, as if he had seen him before but couldn't remember where. Tyro reflected on the scroll the boy had presented him on behalf of his king.

The Torry monarch hoped to parlay his victory at Tuft's Mountain for peace coupled with Torry dominion of the Wid River Valley and Rego. Such bold claims could only be answered with blood, and answer it he should with rivers of Torry blood and mountains of Torry skulls, a testament for all of Arax for the price of defiance. He had ordered his palace steward to give the boy his reply, a rolled parchment with the Benotrist royal seal. Terin had received the parchment and tucked it into a satchel slung over his shoulder. Strangely, both the boy and Lorken carried pouches over their shoulders.

Tyro eagerly awaited Raven's arrival with joyous anticipation, anxious to see the Earther being dragged into the great hall, chained and broken as Luzzo Korun administered the lash. He had planned on taking the Earther's gun hand as payment for his many affronts, but Tosha insisted he be kept whole. He would be merely whipped, knelt before the throne, then handed over to Tosha. He was an insolent cur but would likely sire a strong male heir, which Tosha would surrender to her father. Tyro would have preferred that Tosha choose Thorton to beget his heir, but he had need of Thorton's services, as her consort would have to reside within the confines of the Sisterhood.

"Continue, Korun!" Tyro commanded as the lash fell a second time. Yeltor stiffened neath Luzzo Korun's cruel ministration, a second welt rising across his naked back, blood oozing along its length. The gargoyles in attendance licked the slaver from their lips as the delicious sight of human blood teased their insatiable hunger.

Blue laser streamed from the arched entryway, piercing the skull of Luzzo Korun, his pale, dead eyes drawing wide as he crumpled to the floor. Hands went to hilts as every eye followed the source of the azure light. Thorton's pistol cleared leather, fixing his sight to the source.

"I wouldn't do it, Ben," Raven said, standing at the entrance with his pistol leveled on his former friend as the congregants beheld him with shock and disdain.

"Nobody moves, or your boss man gets it!" Lorken added, his pistol trained on Tyro.

"Stay your blades!" Tyro ordered, his eyes ablaze in barely restrained rage.

Tosha paled, her carefully laid plans turning to ash before her eyes. She sat on her throne, frozen in place. Morac snarled, struggling to keep his hand from drawing his sword. Terin's smile transitioned to unadulterated joy as he beheld Cronus standing post behind Raven, straddling the entrance and guarding Raven's back. He was gaunt, half naked, and well-used, but he was alive.

"Let's go," Lorken ordered his comrades. Alen lingered, frozen in place, until Lorken snatched his tunic collar in his free hand, shoving him toward the exit while keeping Tyro in his sights. They made their way swiftly to the door, the torchlight casting their shadows across the reflective stone floor.

Terin paused midway, his hand drawn by the mystical power bound in his blade. He drew forth the sword, azure light glowing brightly along the blade as he strode toward the bound Yatin prisoner. Stepping over the corpse of Luzzo Korun, he struck Yeltor's bindings, the blow cutting the chains fastened to the rack like thin parchment, freeing him. He collapsed in Terin's arms before gaining his feet. Yeltor turned, his eyes fixed on Terin's blue, wondering in disbelief at this turn of events.

"This is your only chance. Come," Terin said, backing toward the entrance as Tyro, Morac, and the gathered host stared slack-jawed at the weapon in his hands. Understanding washed over Tyro, suddenly cognizant of the nature of Terin's blade. Tosha also knew all too well what Terin wielded. There were secrets of the Sisterhood that she was sworn to protect, even from her mighty sire.

"Wait!" Tosha interjected, returning her focus to Raven. She stood, descended the dais, and stepped nigh, passing between the guests gathered on either side of her path to the entrance. She stopped midway at Thorton's side. "Lower your weapon, Ben." She touched his shoulder. Thorton snorted derisively before relenting and holstering his pistol.

She continued on, skirting the rack and Luzzo's still form, stopping several paces from Raven and his comrades. "Yield and we shall grant Terin and Lorken safe passage. Cronus and you, however, shall accompany me to Bansoch, where he shall suffer a far gentler captivity than in my father's dungeon. Lower your weapon!"

"I don't think so."

"There is no escape," she countered.

"We'll see about that."

"Then go! Make haste! I am certain you shall navigate our northern regions whether by magantor or ocran. Do not be deterred by the scant forces my father has assembled about the palace," she mocked.

"Reverse psychology doesn't work on backward thinking, Tosha," Lorken said before Raven waved him on.

"Get them going!" Raven ordered, keeping his pistol trained on the congregants in the great hall, especially Thorton. Lorken gave him a knowing look before pushing their motley group through the entrance. Yeltor paused briefly at Raven's side, nodding his head in gratitude before passing on. Cronus was well met by Terin, who clasped his arm firmly with moist eyes. Alen lingered briefly, uncertain and weighed with apprehension, until Lorken snatched his tunic and tossed him into the outer corridor. Lorken stepped without, and Raven stood alone.

*****

Lorken burst into the outer corridor, nearly tripping on a guard's corpse lying just outside the great hall. The wide outer passageway was well-lit with a high-arched ceiling that ran north to south, intersecting with adjoining corridors perpendicular to their path. The bodies of a dozen guards stretched along the southern end of the corridor, blood pooling neath their prone, listless forms. Another passageway ran straight ahead from the entrance to the great hall, wider still, nearly five meters abreast, its walls shaded in distinct alabaster and richly lit. "Cover the rear and keep them moving," Lorken told Terin before taking the lead, guiding them down the ivory-hued corridor.

There was so much Terin wanted to say to Cronus, but time only afforded them a knowing glance. Cronus fell in behind Lorken, his trembling legs taxed with exertion and malnourishment. He gripped his shortsword with uncanny strength for one so poorly used. Cronus was emaciated, gaunt, and covered in welts, bruises, and scars. His hair was tangled and matted, but his eyes sparkled with life and with hope renewed like cool water on parched lips.

Yeltor followed, strangely coherent despite not knowing any of the fellows in his midst. What he did know was, they were his enemy's enemy and the only hope he had of escaping this foul realm. His limbs were stiff from days of bondage and ill use. He was nearly as naked as Cronus with only the skirt of his tunic encircling his waist. He snatched a sword from the nearest corpse and followed Cronus.

Though healthy, Alen was afflicted with a far more crippling wound. His conditioned servitude rendered him mentally impotent and indecisive. "Grab that sword and come!" Terin ordered, shaking the former slave from his numb indecision. Alen obeyed immediately, snatching the shortsword that lay near the body of another slain guard. Whether he reacted to Terin's command or followed the instinct to survive, Terin could only surmise.

Looking at the number of guards littering the length of the corridor, Terin marveled at Raven's handiwork and wondered how such carnage went unnoticed by any within the great hall. Lorken led the others swiftly along the corridor, stopping at the base of a narrow, winding stairwell. He quickly removed a small, fist-sized device from his pack and affixed it upon the wall at the base of the stair. "Come on!" he ordered as they rushed up the stairwell.

Attaining the level above, they stepped without, passing under the stone archway of the stairwell. Half a score of guards in black tunics and gray mail were drawn to their shadowed forms emerging from the stair. Blue laser spewed from Lorken's pistol, striking several in quick succession as the others fanned out on either side of him. Their jaws slackened as they beheld Lorken's deadly magic. Cronus and Terin were unmoved, each well-accustomed to the Earthers' prowess.

Terin swept around Lorken's left, driven by the will of his father's sword. The stairwell was set at a corner where two corridors joined. Terin wasted little time closing on the nearest guard, who first met him with curious, determined eyes. Terin split the fellow's upraised blade and followed through with a savage thrust to the fellow's chest, splitting his mail like stale bread. The man's eyes transitioned to abject terror in that brief second between the splitting of his blade and the mortal blow that followed.

Terin swiftly retracted the blade, moving on with economy of motion. Bright bursts of blue passed over either shoulder, striking targets further afield as he closed on the nearest foe. He swung down upon his opponent's blade, the blow splitting the northern steel before taking the guard's wrists. The guard stared with terror-filled eyes as his hands fell away. Terin followed with a side swing, halving his foe.

He felt the others close on his heel, his eyes sweeping the corridor ahead for threats. Dim torchlight poorly illuminated the still forms of fallen guards along the length of the dark corridor. Terin caught his breath as the madness of the blade abated, bringing him back to the present.

Cronus marveled at Terin's swordsmanship and the luminous glow of azure light emitting along the length of his sword. He recalled when he last beheld its magnificence that night along the Wid River after the Costelin raid. Then, Terin's use of the weapon was clumsy and unnatural compared to now, as he was becoming one with the blade.

"Go!" Lorken's voice broke their distraction as he ushered them away from the stairwell. At a dozen paces, he removed a palm-sized device from his jacket pocket and pressed the gray switch on the side of the device. *Boom!* The stairwell behind him exploded, stone shattering as heavy blocks broke free, raining vertically down the stair tower. Other explosions thundered in succession, reverberating throughout the palace. The floors shook violently neath their feet as a deafening concussion passed through the corridors of the inner palace.

*****

Moments before, a hundred pairs of eyes stared back at him, intent on his destruction, save one. Tosha stood brazenly before him, her countenance betraying little of the turmoil within. She appraised him with her discerning gold eyes. He could never tell what she was thinking, but whatever it was, it wasn't good. His sister had a pet cat that looked at him that way, always looking at him with a superior air as if he was a moron. How he hated that cat. It was the same look that Tosha gave him more often than not.

He still wondered what her plan was. If she wanted to kill him, she had no shortage of opportunities. If capture was her intent, for what purpose? Any act against either him or Lorken would bring the *Stenox*'s wrath down upon her. And why, of all things, did she take him to bed? Why grant him her maidenhood, only to betray him immediately after?

"So long, Princess." He smiled wanly, backing a step.

"I can't protect you if you do this!" she said. *Protect me?* Raven thought, scrunching his face at the oddity of her comment. "Drop your weapon and kneel, and I will guarantee your life and that of your friends'."

"I'll only kneel when you're on all fours in front of me," he said. She gave him a murderous glare. He turned his attention to Ben Thorton, who stood past her right shoulder. "You don't belong here, Ben. You belong with us, with your family," Raven pleaded with a heavy heart.

"We aren't family, Raven, not anymore," Ben growled.

"Is that how you see it?"

"No. It was your choice, not mine."

Boom! The explosion rocked the great hall, taking them unawares, dust flooding the outer corridor. Other explosions echoed in quick succession, collapsing several passageways around the inner keep. Many of the guests and courtesans were knocked from their feet, disoriented and dazed. Others felt that death was calling them home. Others thought it an earthquake.

Tosha stumbled briefly, nearly losing her feet, before steadying herself. Bringing the chamber back into focus, she noticed Raven was missing. "After him!" she shouted, ordering her father's men to take chase. "I want him alive!"

"Bring me their heads, all of them!" Tyro commanded, standing from his throne. "Morac!" Tyro called his chief Elite, drawing him toward the dais as the others flooded the exit.

"My emperor," Morac said, stepping nigh.

"Take the secret entrance and secure the magantor platforms."

"Do you believe they are going to the roof?"

"Either up or down. I would guess up. If it is down, then no amount of luck shall avail them."

✳✳✳✳✳

He raced into the outer corridor, banking right as powdered rock permeated the air. Lorken collapsed the nearest stairwell, giving the others a head start. Raven would take a longer route, however, drawing out their pursuers to give Lorken's group the time needed to find and prepare their magantors for a hasty depart. Raven panted heavily, turning left at the next corridor as arrows whizzed in his wake. He removed the analyzer from his jacket, sweeping the way ahead as he ran. The image grew fuzzy in his shaking hand, but he could ill afford to stop. A guard turned into his path from an adjoining corridor with blade raised. Raven cut him down, running past his bleeding corpse as the sound of his pursuers echoed in his wake. At the next turn, he raced up a wide stair as arrows whistled, striking the stone wall where he had just been.

*****

Fifty miles off the northern Benotrist coast, the *Stenox* waited, gentle ocean waves lapping its hull with the eastern wind rippling the dark surface of the northern sea. Kato sat by the console in the engineering room with Brokov and Leanna hovering over either shoulder as he expanded the live image sent from the transmitter affixed to Lorken's structural analyzer.

"Why are they separating again?" Leanna asked, unable to mask the worry in her voice.

"There could be any number of reasons," Brokov said somberly.

They had observed their friends' movement throughout the night through Lorken's device, as the trackers they embedded in Raven and Lorken only fixed their location on a digital map sans definition of their surroundings. Brokov silently cursed himself for not planting a similar tracker in Terin but trusted his comrades to keep the boy close. They had observed Raven separating from the crowded chamber in the company of one other earlier in the evening, where he engaged in some sort of intimate encounter before setting off on his own.

They followed his movements to the base of the fortress, where he fetched another and returned to the others, where they separated again. Curiously, Lorken left the crowded chamber in the company of four others while Raven lingered. Brokov feared they were both compromised until he received signals of explosions throughout the upper reaches of the castle. Lorken's group ascended rapidly as

Raven's signal sped in the opposite direction, also making his way to the higher reaches of Fera. That was when the signal faded to black.

"What's wrong? Where are they?" Leanna cried. Kato adjusted the console's settings but to no avail, as only the two markers representing Raven and Lorken remained on the screen. The information only revealed their location in distance and direction sans the detailed surroundings that the analyzer provided. They were effectively blind to what was now transpiring hundreds of miles away atop the Black Castle. All they knew was that Raven and Lorken were still alive, and nothing else.

*****

"Crap!" Raven growled, futilely shaking the analyzer, hoping brute force would fix the damage he had rendered when he dropped it turning the last corner. He stood in the middle of the well-lit wide corridor, his brain struggling to conjure a solution. Desperate, he removed his comm and hailed Lorken. "Lorken!"

*****

They panted heavily, racing up the wide steps, where they were met by half a score of descending guards. Lorken fired into their close ranks, dropping several in rapid order. Terin drove headlong into their ranks, his sword glowing as it danced in his hands, splitting blades, shields, and flesh. Yeltor struggled to keep pace with the young Torry, unable to match the madness of the blade with his weakened body, but managed to take one guard, protecting Terin's flank to his utmost. Cronus and Alen lingered farther back, one crippled by malnourishment and the other by fear.

"Who are you?" Yeltor asked of him as Terin finished the last Benotrist, sending his severed head tumbling down the stair.

"Terin," he answered as his eyes refocused, "Terin Caleph. And you?"

"I am Yeltor of the Yatin Elite." He nodded, his eyes betraying the deep gratitude that his firm countenance did not. When he had time to ponder why two Torries, a slave, and a strange pair of Earthers were there at the Black Castle and helping him escape, he doubted he would believe it if not seeing with his own eyes. Of course, he doubted any of them would live long enough to tell their tale or reflect on such things.

The top of the stair opened up to a spacious conjoint of the three corridors adjoining the entrance to the throne room, where the massive statue of a man and gargoyle twisted into a foul grotesquerie. The guards posted along the perimeter of the statue closed ranks with spears leveled in unison at their approach. Lorken took steady aim, his laser fire quickly unnerving their trained discipline, their fellows dropping in swift, methodical order. Terin raced along the dark stone floor, angling for the break in the line that Lorken's laser had rendered. The others followed in his wake.

Yeltor parried a spear thrust as Lorken's laser pierced the shield of another, passing through the bearer's chest. Cronus fended off another guard while Alen retrieved a fallen spear, thrusting it toward Cronus's attacker. Terin circled to his left, skirting the massive statue as he split blades and limbs with unnatural swiftness, coming full circle behind the guards aligned right of the statue. Lorken cursed Terin's foolhardiness as he again crossed his line of fire, forcing him to check his aim. Within moments, even these guards had been cut down when Lorken heard his comm go off.

"Lorken!"

Visibly irritated, Lorken removed his comm from his jacket pocket. "We're a little busy, Rav. What is it?"

"The analyzer is malfunctioning. How do I restart it?"

"Why would it malfunction? Did you break it?" Lorken growled, knowing full well that any malfunction was user error or the likely result of Raven's clumsiness.

"No, I didn't break it. It just stopped working!" Raven's voice was too indignant, confirming Lorken's suspicion.

"You dropped it, didn't you?"

"How do I fix it?" Raven ignored the accusation, desperate to get it working.

"I need to see it. Where are you?"

"Two levels up from where we started. Where do I go from here?"

"Make your way…" Lorken tried to finish, but he heard Raven curse, followed by the distinct sound of laser fire and men shouting. "Idiot," Lorken growled under his breath.

*****

Raven fired over his shoulder as he ran with scores of soldiers flooding the corridor in his wake. The passageway ahead intersected another, and he lacked the luxury of a careful crossing. Liberally set torches illuminated the black stone corridor, highlighting himself and his foes. As Raven drew near, several guards stepped into his path from the adjoining passageway, drawn by the sounds of the soldiers pursuing him. He barely had time to shift his aim, spraying a hasty volley into their midst, striking three with fatal blows to their chests and necks while dropping a fourth with a blast to the knee.

Raven lowered his shoulder, ramming into another, who braced himself with his shield. Raven slammed into the upraised shield, sending the guard sailing far afield on the unforgiving floor. Raven kept his feet, rushing past the stunned guard as arrows loosed behind him. He reached the end of the corridor, passing under the archway to the stairwell as arrows flew, some missing by a breath as he passed within. He stepped to his left, behind the safety of fat stone.

Arrows poured through the archway like heavy rain as Raven began his ascent. Before taking a third step, Raven stumbled as blue laser blasted through the stairwell's thick wall, striking where he stood but a moment before. He gained his feet and hurried up the stair.

*****

"Which way?" Yeltor asked, stripping the cloak and shield from a slain guard. They stood below the towering statue before the throne room. The corridor running straight from the massive doors of the throne room led to the lower magantor platforms while the passageway opposite the direction from whence they had come led to the higher platforms that they landed upon when they first arrived.

"That way!" Terin said, indicating the latter. The open roof was but one floor above. Lorken took one last glance at the grotesque statue, the macabre physical union of man and gargoyle forms, and lifted the muzzle of his pistol to the crotch of the form, where the creature was well-apportioned. Carefully aimed laser fire cut away the enlarged male genitalia, sending it smashing into the floor. A steady stream of deftly placed laser fire followed, leaving a roughly shaped female form in its wake. Cronus shook his head and smiled as he tugged Lorken's jacket to hasten their exit.

*****

Raven struggled to catch his breath as he emerged from the east stairwell on the throne room level, racing toward the central stairwell, which Lorken and the others had already ascended to the open roof above. He could see a group of guards closing on the stairwell from the direction of the throne room. He fired into their midst, scattering their group and retarding their advance as he passed within the stairwell. Once within, he shifted his fire upon his pursuers who had followed him from the east stairwell. They broke from the east stairwell, issuing through the entryway and flooding the corridor.

The sounds of shouting men, clanging swords, and armored sandals echoed through the passageway. Only Raven's laser fire stayed their pursuit while Thorton's return fire dulled Raven's zeal to tarry in his flight. Flashes of laser fire streamed in each direction, bathing the corridor in deadly light. Raven wasted little time shooting one last volley before ascending the stair, Thorton's return fire riddling the stair entryway.

"Lorken, cover me once I clear!" he barked into the comm as the concussion of crumbling stone shook the comm from his left hand.

"Copy!" Lorken's voice issued from the comm as it slipped from his grasp, striking the first step of the stair. Before Raven could snatch it from the floor, falling rock crashed all around it, smashing the small device. Raven reached through the rubble, retrieving the pieces of the shattered comm., cursing his misfortune. The comm was reduced to a useless trinket.

*****

Moments before.

Terin was met by a clear, starlit sky as he stepped without onto the open walkway of the palace roof. The blade of his silver sword illuminated bright azure as he stepped into the clear light of the waxing moon. The powerful, luminous glow turned night into day, illuminating the walkway in otherworldly brilliance. The others followed on his heels, Yeltor the second to step onto the walkway followed by Alen and Cronus while Lorken covered their rear. They moved swiftly across the walkway as the cool night breeze swirled amid these highest battlements.

The upper magantor platforms were set north, northeast, and northwest of the central stairwell. Each was connected to an open central-roofed turret just north of the central stairwell. They found the turret strangely unguarded. Despite the thousands of gargoyles surrounding the palace with their cookfires stretching to the horizon, forming a mirror image to the myriad of stars above, one could not help but feel alone upon these high walkways that ran along the roof of the inner keep, a feeling akin to walking among the heavens.

"The magantors we arrived with are on the north platform. You can get them ready while I cover Raven!" Lorken shouted over the wind as he took up position within the central turret, fixing his aim on the stairwell entrance whence they came. Terin nodded in kind, moving swiftly along the north-running walkway, his father's sword heralding their advent like a young star bursting to life.

Soldiers in gray mail and black tunics issued from the central stairwell with shields raised and swords leveled. Lorken fired into their midst, cutting them down like ripened wheat. They quickly abandoned their advance, forsaking the open walkways for the safety of the stairwell, Lorken's laser following them through their retreat. Once the last of the survivors passed within, Lorken sprayed the arched entryway, striking several who congregated at the opening. A higher setting of his laser could easily bring down the stairwell, but Raven still had need of it if he hoped to escape.

Only the towering citadels that spiraled into the firmament around them offered access to the magantor platforms, but each was heavily garrisoned with entry points far below the throne room level, which would require Raven to backtrack without losing his way. With Thorton close on his heels and the palace flooded with soldiers, Raven's only hope of reaching them was the central stairwell.

"Lorken, cover me once I clear!" Raven's voice echoed from the comm.

"Received!" Lorken answered. "Where are you?" he asked, but the comm went dead.

Lorken kept his pistol trained on the entryway, taking aim at any target that presented itself. One Benotrist reared his head, stealing a glance around the curved stone, and Lorken took him between the eyes. The fellow's body slipped to the floor, littering the entry before being dragged away from behind by his comrades to clear the path. If Raven was near, he would have to cut his way through those guarding the stair.

The sounds of shouting suddenly echoed from the bowels of the serried chamber. Lorken held his fire as the stairwell became alit with flashes of azure light from below. The screams of desperate men issued from the spiraling chamber as the flashes grew closer and brighter, illuminating the stairwell in deathly light. Several Benotrists burst through the archway sans shield or sword, desperate to flee the destruction trailing below. Lorken dropped them in quick succession.

"Hold your fire!" Raven's voice echoed as he cleared the stairwell. Lorken covered the entryway as Raven ran between the corpses littering the walkway, nearly slipping on the blood-soaked stone.

*****

Terin raced along the walkway, passing under the slanted rooftop of the north magantor platform. The center of the platform was a stone circle ten meters abreast with a half dozen magantor stalls branching outward in a half circle opposite the entry point. The platform extended beyond each stall with a flat perch, from which each great avian could take flight.

"The emperor has not granted you leave, Terin." The voice stopped Terin in place. Terin gripped his sword tightly with both hands, holding it guardedly before him as the figure emerged from the shadow of his magantor stall. Terin backed a step as the man stepped into the torchlight. The black hair and sneering grin belonging to none other than Morac.

"How—"

"How did I reach these great heights before you? Very simple. I climbed." Yeltor, Alen, and Cronus came to his side, but Morac paid them no heed. "Very clever of your Earther friends to destroy most of the stairways to the upper platforms, but they could not have known of the ladders built into the outer walls that run from here to the great hall." Morac smiled falsely, his gaze drifting to the sword in Terin's hands. "I see you bring a wondrous gift, a sword that befits an Imperial Elite. Perhaps I shall gift it to one of my worthy comrades."

"Or keep it for yourself if you dare take it," Terin warned, lifting it ever slightly toward his foe.

Morac's smile grew ominously genuine as he drew his own sword, a golden blade that bore a dull-reddish glow. "I have no need of a lesser blade."

Terin's blue eyes drew wide as Morac rushed to meet him, barely blocking the vicious blow. Morac's sword burst with fiery light as it touched Terin's blade, the force of the blow driving Terin back a step as Morac came at him again. Yeltor stepped off line, attempting to take Morac from his left, but the Benotrist Elite pivoted, splitting Yeltor's blade before turning to block Terin's counterstrike.

Cronus planned to circle opposite Yeltor but caught himself as a strange sensation coursed his flesh. Craning his neck, he was met by two crimson eyes glowing like embers staring down upon him from the rafters above. Torchlight played off lucent ebony flesh and ivory-hued fangs curving over blood-red lips. "Kriton," Cronus whispered in recognition as the creature sprang. He barely lifted his sword in time as the weight of the blow drove him back, sprawling him to the floor.

*****

"Collapse the stairwell!" Raven shouted as he closed on the turret where Lorken waited. "Ben's right behind me."

Before Lorken could adjust his pistol's power setting, arrows whizzed overhead. He turned, catching sight of Benotrist archers positioned upon the northwest and northeast platforms with columns of swordsmen closing from each direction. "Oh, come on!" Lorken grunted in disbelief, wondering how this could get any worse. When blue laser spewed from the stairwell in his direction, things became heatedly worse. Fortunately, it was an errant shot, hastily fired as Thorton took up position in the central stairwell.

Raven dived as he rushed onto the central turret, his knees and elbows painfully meeting the unforgiving stone floor as he dodged arrows and laser fire. His eyes caught sight of Lorken crouched below the curved low wall to his right. "Well, this sucks!" he complained.

"This was your bright idea, Rav. Nice family you married into, by the way." Lorken snorted.

"Married?" Raven gave him a look.

"That little ceremony your girlfriend had you take part in wasn't a cocktail party, pal."

Understanding washed over him, confusion giving way to disbelief. "Then why is she trying to kill me?"

"Maybe she figured out that you're a lousy husband," Lorken said, crawling toward the walkway to the northwest platform. Peering around the corner, he could see the wall of shields fast approaching. He took aim, spraying laser fire into their serried column. Raven followed his cue, crawling toward the walkway entrance to the northeast platform.

"Like fish in a barrel!" Raven said, his laser tearing into the approaching column. Each pull of the trigger dropped several ranks as the intense beams passed through their victims and those standing behind them in the laser's path. At the current settings, it could pass through a dozen men before stopping. The bodies on either walkway were piling up like cord wood. "I'll keep his head down. You blast 'em!" Raven shouted as they ceased their fire on their respective walkways. Lorken nodded, adjusting his pistol's setting. They rose in unison from the opposing sides of the turret, training their aim on the central stairwell.

Thorton jumped back from the entrance as Raven's laser swept the archway. He knew what would follow. Wasting no time, he quickly descended the stairwell, pushing men aside who blocked his path as the roof gave way.

*****

Morac's blade flickered betwixt crimson and gold, igniting in otherworldly radiance as he drove Terin across the platform. Terin forsook all his father's teachings, yielding to the will of the silver blade, which guided his hand with every block and thrust. His blade's azure brilliance radiated exponentially where touching Morac's golden sword, lighting his wavering countenance as he yielded ground to Morac's blade.

Across the platform, Kriton closed upon Cronus, who lay sprawled upon the floor. Wasting little motion, he prepared to thrust his blade into whatever flesh Cronus offered him. He had followed him from the dungeon, where Raven's blow rendered him unconscious. Though briefly stunned, he was able to follow them through the trail of corpses they left in their wake. Once he surmised their direction of travel, he flew to the upper battlements, where he joined Morac.

He sensed something amiss as he prepared to finish Cronus. He turned as Yeltor came upon him with his broken blade, attempting to drive its jagged edge into his back. Kriton swung, nearly taking the Yatin's head, Yeltor ducking below the blade's path.

Alen's eyes were transfixed upon the struggle before him, freezing him in place. The emphatic beating of his heart deafened his ears. He was sorely afraid, but to do nothing meant certain death or worse. He felt his body moving independent of his will as he stepped to Kriton's back side and thrust his blade. Kriton shifted suddenly, the blade piercing his left wing. Dark blood issued from the gaping wound as his hateful scream pained their ears. Kriton was distracted long enough for Cronus to gain his feet.

Caught between Alen and Cronus, he was unprepared as Yeltor struck his sword arm with his broken blade. The jagged edge cut deep into the muscle of his upper arm, causing his grip to falter. His feral eyes drew wide and dull as his blade slipped from his grasp. He backed away, turned, and sped through the nearest magantor stall, skirting the great beast within as he passed onto the outer platform. His wings spread, his clawed feet scraping the outer stone lip of the edge, soaring into the darkness and beyond their reach.

Morac's eyes alit with euphoric glee as he felt Terin's sword waning. One more well-placed blow might separate it from his weakening grip. Terin held on with all the strength he could muster as Morac pressed, backing him into a magantor pen. The flash of the blades unnerved the mammoth avian as they passed beside its closed right wing, its clawed feet shuffling left to the length of its tether.

Morac's glancing blow slid along Terin's blade, striking the magantor's hind quarter. The bird thrashed violently, nearly knocking them over as it came briefly between them. The magantor's scream rang over the ramparts with violent discord. Morac released his fury upon the beast, running his blade along its neck, silencing its screams, the blow nearly cutting head from body. The bird's body dropped to the floor, its head dangling from its neck. Morac wasted little time circling the dead beast, again closing on Terin, who backed onto the exposed outer lip of the platform.

The outer platform that extended beyond each magantor pen was a curved, flat landing perch without walls or cover. There were six in all in each of the three platforms of the upper keep, each hanging over the lower battlements some twenty meters below. The outer lips of each magantor stall formed a half circle akin to the petal of a giant flower. Morac pressed his advantage, driving Terin to the edge of the stone lip, mere inches from a perilous drop. Moonlight played ominously off Morac's face, casting his countenance in a ghastly scowl.

Terin could yield no more ground as he stood upon the precipice, yet Morac's unforgiving blade radiated power he could not stay. No longer within the shadow of the magantor pen, the moonlight that shone upon Morac's face in turn bathed Terin's sword with its celestial light. The light of the moon strengthened the azure of Terin's sword, igniting along its length like light bursting from a star, awakening its ancient power.

Terin met Morac's blow, the force nearly knocking the Benotrist from his feet as he stumbled back, his eyes transfixed in uncertainty and apprehension. Terin surrendered to the will of his sword, stepping forth to press his advantage and strike again. Morac barely lifted his blade in time, the blow driving him farther back as the fiery glow of his own sword began to falter. It was Morac who now struggled to hold ground as he felt graver danger approaching from behind.

He pivoted, catching Cronus's blade before it struck his unprotected flesh, shattering the Torry's sword from hilt to tip before turning back to meet Terin's blow. The distraction weakened his focus and loosened his grip enough for the weight of Terin's blow to knock the fiery blade from his grasp as his hand reached out desperately, grasping the necklace about Terin's throat. Terin was jerking free of his grasp to position his sword for the kill when the necklace came loose in Morac's grasp. Panic gripped Morac's heart as his eyes followed his sword gliding through the night air over the lip of the platform before dropping to the battlements below.

Morac broke away. Knowing any delay would mean his death, he ran to the edge, leaping over the side onto the adjoining platform, his body soaring over open air before landing upon the unforgiving stone lip, clearing the two meters that separated the outer platforms. Wasting little time, he leaped to the next platform where the stone ladder built into the side of the upper keep's outer wall would carry him whence he came with Terin's necklace his only reward for his effort.

Yeltor, who had been at Cronus's side, rushed off to pursue the fleeing Benotrist, quickly searching the adjoining magantor stalls before discovering the hidden ladder. Standing upon the precipice, he gazed down as Morac descended to the battlements below. He lowered his sword in resignation, the same sword that Kriton had dropped but moments before. Yeltor hoped to deliver to his emperor the head of Morac to appease his failure to save his prince. Alas, he would return empty-handed, if he returned at all.

Terin sighed in relief, exhausted from his engagement and thankful for Cronus's timely intervention. His friend shared a knowing smile, overcome by emotion. "We must hurry!" Alen's voice called to them from the center of the platform.

*****

"Cover!" Lorken shouted.

"Move!" Raven answered, holding position midway between the turret and the north platform, spewing laser fire to either of the other platforms as Lorken withdrew from the turret. Lorken crouch-walked at a brisk pace, keeping his head below the low stone rampart that ran the length of the walkway. He moved a dozen paces beyond Raven, taking position to cover his friend's withdraw.

"I got you covered!"

"Moving!" Raven shouted.

"Move!" Lorken answered as Raven moved past him. Lorken caught sight of a palace bowman about to loose an arrow neath the northwest platform. Blue laser streamed across the open air, taking the fellow in the chest. Lorken shifted aim, watching the bowman drop as the arrow struck the rampart near his head.

"Packaww!" The deafening screech of a magantor pierced the night air as arrows rained upon them. Lorken ducked below the jagged rampart of the walkway as the large war bird drew nigh. Blue laser swept along the sternum of the beast, spilling its innards as it tumbled from the sky, throwing its riders through its descent. Blood splattered across Lorken's back as Raven shifted his aim to other magantors farther afield.

"Yuck!" Lorken bemoaned the slick fluid running off his jacket, pooling upon the stone beneath his feet. He quickly turned as a half score of magantors drew from the west. Laser fire streamed from his right where Raven stood near the entrance of the north platform before Lorken joined his laser fire to his. Terrible screams issued from the beaks of the stricken avian, matching the terror in their riders' eyes as many were thrown to their death, their bodies breaking upon the jagged ramparts below. Half the mounts broke away, speeding to safety, their brethren succumbing to the Earthers' deadly volley.

"Move!" Raven shouted over the wind and din, shifting his fire from magantors to the bowmen positioned upon the other platforms and back again. Lorken ran apace, forsaking the safety of crouching low as he sprinted along the walkway through the portal ahead. Once within, he was greeted by the sight of Terin aiding the others in bonding to their mounts. Terin was currently in the stall farthest left, aiding Yeltor in preparing his mount. Alen and Cronus waited in the adjoining pen, sharing a mount with Cronus holding the reins as they sat in the saddle.

"We're out of time, Terin!" Lorken barked, making his way to the second pen from the right, where the magantor he arrived upon was saddled and waiting.

"Go!" Terin ordered, nodding an encouragement to Yeltor while racing across the platform to his own mount. Yeltor eased the bird onto the outer lip of the platform, took a breath, and issued the command Terin had instructed. The bird's powerful legs burst into the air, its wings fanning gracefully as it glided off the high perch and over the battlements below. Terin followed, trailing Yeltor eastward over the Feran Plain.

"Hurry up, Rav!" Lorken shouted after failing to reach him on the comm.

"Go!" He could faintly hear Raven's voice from the walkway without.

"Go, Cronus!" Lorken commanded, his mount slipping from the perch, its wings pounding the air with powerful, even strokes. Cronus followed in kind, the wind slapping his face, his stomach lifting with their descent. Alen shut his eyes, clinging to Cronus's back, their magantor sweeping over the outer battlements before lifting into the clear night sky.

*****

Raven's eyes swept east to west and the sky above. Archers on opposing platforms fired arrows sporadically as their infantry held back, fearful of the devastation wrought among their fellows. He could hear the sounds of shifting rubble in the ruined stairwell as those buried there and trapped below struggled to ascend. He could follow Lorken's deadly blast with another, finishing those in the stairwell for good, but if Thorton lived, he did not desire to kill him. He only wished to stay his friend's hand and hoped the crashing stairwell had not harmed him. *Why did you join up with this bunch, Ben?* he thought bitterly.

Once the enemy magantors were out of view, Raven broke from his position, bursting into the platform and finding his magantor saddled and waiting in the stall farthest right. Holstering his pistol, he untied the bird from its hitch and climbed aboard. The great avian strutted onto the outer platform and over the edge, sweeping over the battlements and beyond before turning sharply east, following his friends into the waiting night.

*****

Tosha followed Thorton through the opening of the stairwell, climbing over the rubble-strewn wreckage as Raven sped from sight. She cursed her ill fortune. If only the potion she slipped him had taken effect, all this would have been avoided. She would have allowed Terin and Lorken safe passage and had Raven and Cronus under her protection, where their safety would stay the Earthers' hands. Now it was all to ruin. She cursed her father's soldiers for trying to kill her prey, for she wanted them alive, a point she emphasized to Thorton, who preceded her onto the walkway.

Thorton removed his rifle, which was slung across his back, as he stepped within the turret where Lorken and Raven had wrought such destruction. Lifting the weapon to his shoulder, he leaned over the low wall of the turret, facing the east night sky as he pressed the Scope Up button on the weapon. The top of the weapon that rested above the trigger guard opened. A narrow tubular scope arose from the rifle's inner workings, providing him a clear view of the eastern sky and the retreating magantors.

"Can you strike them from this distance?" Tosha asked, standing at his elbow.

"For a few more moments at least," he said.

"I want them alive!" she cautioned.

"Then I'll just slow them down."

*****

Emerald light streamed through the firmament in dazzling brilliance, passing from the upper battlements in measured bursts. Raven urged his magantor eastward as green laser swept over the beast's left wing, unnerving the bird. He shifted his flight, diving to a lower elevation above the plain. The second laser blast struck true, piercing the left wing near the tip. The magantor released a painful squeal, nearly throwing Raven from its back. The third blast struck its hind quarters, and a fourth crippled its right leg.

Thorton shifted his aim to the magantor farther afield. Green laser struck true, striking several precise hits along the length of its right wing. Cronus quickly recovered, steadying his wounded mount as he continued east through the moonlit sky. They pushed on, their mounts struggling to keep pace, keeping Lorken in sight. After a time, Cronus released a breath, relief washing over him. Even the bite of the cool wind upon his face and naked limbs could not dull the euphoria and relief washing over him. He was free.

*****

"That should slow them," Thorton said, lowering his rifle. Tosha gazed eastward, her eyes narrowed in quiet rage. She would pursue them to the ends of Arax if need be, her father be damned, and when she found Raven, he would rue the day he was born.

EPILOGUE

He turned once again, circling back to his slower comrades. Lorken felt the chill of the night air seeping into his bones, wondering how his Araxan comrades endured it dressed only in tunics and cloaks. The waning light of the full moon shone off the large black wings of his magantor as they pounded the air with powerful thrusts. He cursed his misfortune for losing sight of Terin and Yeltor when he first circled back to check on their slower comrades. He swept the sky with his pistol's night scope to no avail. He tried raising Raven on the comm with equal futility, wondering if Raven turned his off. "Or lost it!" Lorken snorted to himself.

Even in the dark, Lorken could see that Raven's mount was favoring a wing, the magantor growing weaker with every thrust of its wings, drifting ever lower. Raven shouted over the wind, his words muffled in the night air. Lorken could see him point to the forests ahead, signaling his plan to set down. Cronus and Alen followed, struggling to maneuver their mount throughout their midnight trek. Lorken thought they would have to double them up, as neither was bonded to their mount, but the beast strangely accepted them, though their control was minimal at best.

Raven found a small clearing a few hundred meters within the forest, a perfect place to set down and still provide ample concealment from Benotrist magantors that would be searching for them. The magantors outstretched their powerful talons, imprinting into the dew-soaked grass, save for Raven's mount, whose right leg nearly buckled under the strain. Towering torbin trees encircled them, moisture dripping from their flush emerald needles, reminding Lorken of North American evergreens. They each landed in kind before tethering their mounts to the sturdiest boughs or trunks they could find.

"What's wrong with your comm, Rav?" Lorken asked as he finished tying off his mount.

"It's broken," he said while examining his magantor's wing and belly, where Thorton's laser grazed the beast.

"How bad is it?" Lorken asked.

"Not good. He's lost a lot of blood. I'm going to have to cauterize the wound."

"I meant the comm."

"Oh, here." Raven fished the parts from his jacket pocket, placing them in Lorken's hand.

"What happened? Did an elephant sit on it?" Lorken snorted.

"It was crushed under falling rock after it fell from my hand!" Raven shot back.

"How did it fall from your hand? Did a ghost spook you?"

"You try talking in that thing while Thorton's blasting the walls of the stairway that you're standing in. It ain't much fun, I can tell you."

"It's not fun fixing all the things you break either," Lorken grumbled. His own comm was now useless until they came in range of the *Stenox*. They were ill-suited for long-range communication without satellites to bounce their signals.

"Oh, I forgot," Raven said, fishing the structural analyzer from his other pocket, setting it in Lorken's other hand. "Maybe you can tinker with that while you're at it."

"I knew you broke it when you complained that it malfunctioned. What did you do to it, shoot it by mistake?"

Cronus's painful cough drew their attention as he and Alen dismounted. His tunic was little more than a rag that covered his loins and little else. The black cloak he had taken from a dead Benotrist swallowed his emaciated form. They could hear Cronus's teeth chatter in the brisk predawn air. Alen fared little better, wearing a thin cloak over threadbare tunic. Cronus knelt beside his magantor, examining its damaged right wing. 'Twas a miracle the beast kept as good a pace as it did with such a grievous injury. Dried blood caked its slate-gray feathers along the length of the wing. Enough blood was lost to dampen the bird's restless spirit, and if Cronus pushed any harder, the beast would soon drop dead.

A gray light struck the great avian in the breast, keeling it over. Cronus craned his neck over his right shoulder, finding Lorken with his pistol drawn. "Don't worry. It's only stunned," he said, answering Cronus's questioning look while holstering his pistol. Raven's mount was similarly afflicted, lying upon its side as if dead but merely asleep like Cronus's.

"Why?" Alen asked with rising panic.

"They're going to seal the magantors' wounds. I wouldn't recommend doing so on one that is awake," Cronus said, answering him after gaining his feet, drawing Alen aside as Lorken went to work with his pistol.

Lorken bathed the wounds with yellow light, the burn sealing the sundered flesh, Raven tending his mount with equal care. They removed the saddles from each beast and fished a spade from the saddle pack. Raven dug, collecting a good-sized pile of rocks, then heated the stones with his pistol.

"Get warm, fellas." Raven motioned Cronus and Alen to gather around the glowing rocks. With the dawn breaking through the trees to the east, the stones provided warmth without the smoke that would betray their location.

"Here. Eat up," Lorken said, handing each of them strips of dried douri, which he carried in his pack. Raven had set the stones within the tree line, keeping their crimson-hued glow concealed from above. They constructed makeshift bedrolls from their saddle packs, setting them around the heated stones.

"We'll sleep during the day while the birds rest. It'll be safer if we travel at night," Lorken said.

"What of Terin?" Cronus asked.

"If we were to become separated, he was to make his way south to Rego, though we repeatedly told him to stay close," Raven growled his displeasure.

"That other fella didn't know the importance of keeping a tight formation. He sped off as fast as his mount would allow, and Terin kept pace, trying to slow him down. That's when we lost sight of each other," Lorken explained.

"How far off do you think he is?" Cronus asked, worried for his young friend.

"Hell, he could be anywhere," snorted Raven.

"Hopefully, he made haste once he realized our separation. He and the Yatin have two healthy mounts going for them. Their safety now rests in their speed. If they head straight for Rego, I doubt the Benotrists will catch 'em," Lorken said, trying to assuage Cronus's worry.

"Don't worry. The kid can take care of himself. He can cut anything with that sword of his," Raven said.

"Not anything." Alen sighed.

"What do you mean?" Lorken didn't like the way he said that. Alen relayed the wonders of Morac's golden blade, which cut steel like thin parchment and glowed fiery red in the sunlight.

*****

They continued east until the rising sun broke upon their countenance, soaring over the endless stretch of forest for a good measure before the breaking dawn, placing many leagues between themselves and the Black Castle. They had lost sight of their comrades hours past, and Terin feared for their safety. There was little he could do now except make his way home.

Flying in the full light of day was a risky venture, so they needed to set down. He pointed to a clearing below, along the western banks of a narrow riverbend. Yeltor nodded, understanding his intent. They set down, each struggling with the commands to properly maneuver the large avian. They were as likely to perish in mishandling their mounts as they were by enemy blades or bows. If they encountered an enemy magantor patrol, they would suffer certain death considering their feeble skills in handling the great birds.

They set down in the clearing of the thick forest. Unfortunately, their magantor packs were not provisioned with tack or bedrolls, making the day ahead a cold and hungry affair unless they could improvise. Terin shivered just looking at Yeltor's bare torso with his tunic torn to his waist and a cloak tied around his shoulders. He recalled the severe beating Yeltor had received before their escape. The man's face betrayed no sense of pain or self-pity, just grim determination.

Yeltor searched the saddle packs for anything of use, finding spare saddle straps, a water pouch, a bow and quiver, a sack of magantor feed, and a grooming brush. Opening the sack, he scooped a handful of feed in his hand and shoved it into his mouth. He was fed only enough to be kept alive these past days but never enough to sate his hunger. He washed down the bland grains with a swig of water before sitting on the ground, leaning his back against a thick porian, exhausted and spent.

Terin joined him, sitting at the base of a tree beside him with his legs outstretched atop layers of dead leaves carpeting the forest floor. Long branches stretched overhead, from the barest of stems to the thickest boughs nearer the treetops, their broad leaves shielding the sky above.

"Forgive my failings in keeping with your friends. I did not know," Yeltor apologized.

"You could not have known of our plans and contingencies. We had little time to offer you more than rudimentary commands to handle the magantor. It is a miracle you took off at all, let alone come as far as we did. You could not have known of the others' position. I trust Raven and Lorken to survive without my meager assistance."

"Meager assistance?" Yeltor shook his head at Terin's humility. "You fought bravely, my friend. I sit a free man because of you, and because of me, you are now separated from your friends."

Terin sighed, uncomfortable with Yeltor's praise. "It was the will of my sword that urged me to strike your bonds. It was not for naught that our paths crossed, Yeltor. It was also the will of the blade that I kept pace with you even if it separated me from my friends."

"And here we are." Yeltor sighed tiredly, waving an open hand to the barren wilds surrounding them.

"What should we do?" Terin asked wearily, leaning his head back against the tree's trunk, his hair catching in its jagged bark.

"We rest by day, fly at night. They'll be searching for us east and south, believing us bound for Torry North. Where were your friends heading?" Yeltor asked, his eyes closed from exhaustion.

"We were to go east before breaking north, where their ship would meet us along the coast."

"How?" Yeltor's tired eyes remained closed. "Where did their ship intend to meet them, and how did they expect to navigate this foul land?"

"They have powers I cannot explain. All they need to do is reach the coast, and their ship will find them. Alas, I have no such means for them to find me. If separated, I was to make my way to Torry North," Terin explained. He wondered about his friends' whereabouts, plagued by visions of their capture or death. Were he and Yeltor the only ones to escape? If so, then this entire venture was for naught. The thought of his friends suffering in Fera's dungeon haunted his thoughts.

"Their wizardry seems limitless." Yeltor sighed, his eyes still closed as sleep began to place its claim. It felt so soothing to merely sit without his hands bound or running for his life. Even the weight of his failures would not cloud his weary mind this day. His curiosity with his comrade's tale and Earther friends could not vie with his utter exhaustion. No sooner had the words escaped his lips than sleep overtook him.

Terin was not as fortunate, his brain tortured with worry. Did his friends escape? Did any fall in flight? Would Cronus survive the exposure in this unforgiving wilderness? He looked so weak when he last saw him, a mere shadow of his former glory. Terin could ill imagine what he had suffered. He lingered awake for a time, huddled in the chill of the night upon the forest floor before succumbing.

*****

They slept until midday, stiff but better rested. Terin woke first, exploring their surroundings and circling back every few minutes to see if Yeltor had awoken. The small clearing where they had set down was surrounded by porian, lupec, torenta, and torbin trees. He gathered torenta nuts as he went. They would have to suffice until they placed many more miles between themselves and the Black Castle. Hunting game before then would be for naught, for they could ill afford the time or risk a fire that would surely draw the enemy upon them. The surrounding forest was easily traversed with tall trunks and high branches that blocked sunlight to vegetation below, allowing Terin to see far in each direction.

Yeltor fed their mounts and checked the saddle straps for tears and tightened their slack. Many a rider met their end from broken saddles, riding the useless leather to the ground as their war birds flew away. Loose saddles were nearly as deadly, twisting to either side, spilling their riders if they were caught unawares. It took years to fully train a magantor rider, but they had no such luxury. As a Yatin Elite, Yeltor had some training, but Terin was hopelessly unprepared. They would be best served avoiding contact with the enemy patrols at all cost.

"Where should we go?" Terin asked, coming to his side, his arms full of nuts.

"I plan to wait until the sun hangs just above the horizon and follow the direction of the setting sun. You are welcome to join me," Yeltor offered, testing the straps of Terin's mount.

"That direction takes us back toward Fera." Terin liked that not at all.

"South of Fera, yes, but they shouldn't be looking for us there. They will press hard east and south, not expecting us to double back. I mean to return to Telfer and then Mosar to relay the news of my prince to our emperor." Yeltor expected the news to be ill received, wondering what fate awaited him for his failure.

Terin thought for a time on whether to follow Yeltor or to break off on his own. Reason suggested the latter, uncertain of the wisdom of trusting his sword's fate once in the keeping of the Yatin realm. The Yatins were age-old enemies of the Torry realms, but would they follow reason when faced with a greater foe? Only a fool would trust them not to try to seize his sword for their own, but Terin's instincts cried out to follow the Yatin Elite. "I will follow you to your realm as far as Telfer."

Yeltor regarded Terin for a moment, surprised by the boy's trust. The Torries had been enemies of his people for as long as he could remember, yet this Torry and his comrades saved his life, risking their own to do so. After suffering the cruelties of the Gargoyle race, the Yatins and Torries' ancient feud seemed petty in compare. "I vow that no harm shall come to you by Yatin hands, my friend. I so swear upon my blood," Yeltor avowed, his dark-brown eyes staring intently in Terin's blue as he placed his hands upon the young Torry's shoulders.

"I hope our peoples can unite against our common foe." Terin sighed.

"They can if we show them the way."

*****

Hours hence. They could not see the magantor scouts passing overhead, heading south and west. They could only hear their squawks echoing above the trees as they passed. By dusk, they again gained the heavens, keeping south of the setting sun, speeding through the crisp summer air with nary an enemy magantor in sight.

*****

The dim light played poorly off the dark walls of the quiet sanctum. It was a dark and windowless chamber with a single basin torch opposite the doorway. Tyro sat at the head of a triangular-shaped table with four chairs to either side, each facing him with guarded apprehension. His fair countenance masked the tempest beneath, waiting to spring upon any poor counsel. He had dismissed the palace steward and his commanders of rank, leaving Morac, Regula, Kriton, Draken, and Tosha seated at the table.

Tyro sat through his commanders' briefings with cool indifference as they reported the loss of life and extensive damage to the castle. Hundreds of guards were slain in the melee, including Luzzo Korun, fourth among Tyro's High Elite. The damnable Earthers devastated the palace, blasting entire towers to rubble, slaying hundreds of highly trained guards, and defacing the massive sculpture at the throne room's entrance. Guards could be replaced and the castle repaired, but his humiliation could not go unpunished. They would suffer for their insolence.

After receiving the reports, Tyro dismissed his commanders and conferred with his highest Elite. Ben Thorton entered the sanctum, taking his seat among the others as Tyro's golden eyes regarded him. "What have you?" the emperor asked.

"They fled east—five birds and six riders with the Torry prisoner and the princess's body slave sharing a mount. I wounded that magantor along with Raven's. I doubt they'll make it far without stopping," Ben answered.

"East." Tyro sighed, stroking his long fingers over his chin.

"They're being clever. Expect them to double back or turn sharply north or south to their ship or Torry North," Nels Draken surmised.

"The *Stenox* could appear anywhere along our coast. Once far enough east, they will likely break north at whichever angle they find advantageous," Tosha conceded.

"We must send out our scouts immediately before they slip from sight!" Morac growled, his body battle worn from his duel with Terin.

"I doubt they'll see anything in the air. Knowing Raven, I expect them to bed down in the day and travel at night," Thorton explained. Though his black clothing was coated in gray dust from the crashing stairwell, he appeared unharmed. Kriton was less fortunate with his wing and arm bandaged.

"I want them found, all of them," Tyro emphasized. "It falls to you, my Elite, that I entrust this task. But not you, Morac. I have another path for you to follow. And, Thorton, I wish for you to continue with the task I sent you west before the distraction of the Yatin prince. You others have a moon's turn to find them. If not, then I shall place a bounty so large upon their heads they would turn on each other to claim it. No bounty shall be placed on Caleph, however. I want him found by us and no other. The retrieval of his sword is paramount. The others you may kill on sight, though I would prefer them alive."

"Father, I need Raven alive," Tosha said firmly.

"If possible, then it shall be so, but he must pay for his crimes," Tyro warned.

"I shall see to his punishment," she affirmed.

"You sound as if you'll be hunting him yourself," Thorton said.

"I shall, and I shall be certain to find him."

"If you find him, you may see to his chastisement. However, if my Elite find him alive, I shall claim his hands as recompense," Tyro said dryly. Tosha swallowed a gasp, refusing to betray the leanings of her heart. Tyro could see the veiled anguish in the gold of her eyes. The Earther did not need hands for the role appointed him. In fact, there were many functions of nature he needed not possess to fulfill his role of consort.

"And if I find him?" she asked.

"Then you may spare or shave whichever portions of his flesh as you like." Tosha nodded, her father's offer forcing her urgency to find him first. Tyro regarded her briefly before catching sight of an object Morac toyed with in his fingers. "What is that?"

"I claimed this from Caleph during our duel," Morac offered, tossing the necklace upon the table. Tyro's eyes narrowed suspiciously, lifting the charm into his shaking hands. How did the boy come to possess this?

"Terin's necklace," Tosha recalled, recognizing the unique artistry.

"Where did he find this?" Tyro asked curiously, his golden eyes lifting to Tosha for the answer.

"His father gifted it to him," she answered, disturbed by the strange look in her father's eyes.

"His father?" he asked darkly.

"Yes. One of the carvings is of his mother, crafted by his father's hand," she said, taken aback by her father's interest.

"He claims his father carved each of these?" Tyro challenged.

"No, his father only carved the one. The one opposite his mother is of his grandmother. The one in the center is unknown," she explained, unnerved by her father's behavior.

"His grandmother?" Tyro almost growled.

"Yes, or so Minister Antillius claims. Her name is Corella—no, Cordela," she corrected herself. "She is long dead now, or so Antillius claims."

The silence in the chamber grew unbearable with Tyro staring at the necklace, his mind elsewhere. "I want him alive and untouched."

Thus ends book 1 of the Chronicles of Arax: of War and Heroes. The adventure continues with book 2: The Siege of Corell.

APPENDIX A

Chronology of Araxan History

–502	Fall of Old Kingdom.
	Deaths of King Kal and Queen Celenia.
	Rise of the traitor realms.
	Gargoyles emerge from Mote Mountains and Nameless Hills.
–497	Corvar Dynasty expands from Gorga River to Reguh River.
–493	Verunium Federation conquers upper Veneba and Tur River Valley.
	Nonn tribes sweep over Lone Hills to Rocky Coast.
–490	Sargoan Kingdom conquers upper Muva; King Sagus builds capital at Faust.
–480	Varabis the Cruel raids southeastern coast and sacks Carig, renaming the port in his namesake.
–471	Remnants of Old Kingdom build settlements along the Lower Nila.
–400	Gargoyles expand to Western Plate and crush Vayon tribes, driving them into the Upper Nila.
–390	Remnants of Old Kingdom are driven from the Lower Nila by Vayon tribes.

–384	Remnants of Old Kingdom settle along the northern shore of Lake Monata and build the sanctuary of Tarelia, sheltered by the Arian Hills.
–314	Ape tribes withdraw to Ape Hills.
–230	Gargoyles expand into Eastern Plate.
–197	Battle of Castara; General Zuvo repels gargoyle invasion along the upper Veneba.
–150	Gargoyles destroy Vayon tribes along the Upper Nila.
–130	Gargoyles expand to Eastern Cress.
–111	Gargoyles defeat Corvar army along the Reguh.
–73	Gargoyles cross the Cress and raid Sargoan settlements along the Muva.
–63	Battle of Tevara. Gargoyles crush Ionian tribes along the Stlen.
–59	Gargoyles expand to Lone Hills, checked by Nonn tribes.
–43	Gargoyles raid Western Ape Hills, driven off by General Gour.
–31	Tarelian expedition drives gargoyles from the Stlen. General Pelen crushes gargoyle army at the conjoint of the Stlen and Javo Rivers. Javo was renamed Pelen.
–23	Fall of Corvar Dynasty. Death of King Fabis. Levotrist tribes sack Laycoris.
–15	Gargoyles crush Verunium Army along the Upper Tur. Verunium Federation fractures.
0	Jenaii fleet reach the mouth of the Elaris and establish port of El-Tova. El Ebiorn becomes first lord of the birdmen.

117   Smiths of Tarelia complete the Sword of the Sun. Council gifts the golden sword to General Clorvis Cal. General Cal leads new expedition north of the Mote Mountains.

120   Clorvis Cal founds Northern Kingdom and establishes capital at Laycrom.

122   King Clorvis Cal begins construction of Fera, the Black Castle.

159   Death of Cal. His son Seres Cal assumes the throne.

187   Smiths of Tarelia forge Swords of the Moon and gift the first Sword of the Moon to General Zar Zaronan, who leads Tarelian expedition to the Pelen Valley.

197   General Zar expands Tarelian hold along the Pelen and Stlen and founds Middle Kingdom, uniting the tribes and minor kingdoms south of the Plate. He builds the capital city of Central City.

205   Battle of Cular north of the Lone Hills. King Zar crushes gargoyle army.

212   Ape tribes drive Kregarins from Torn Valley.

213   Soch Federation establishes slave ports of Tenin and Tinsay and expands raids along the Gorga, Tenia, and Muva.

237   Smiths of Tarelia forge first Sword of the Stars. Council of Tarelia gifts the sword to General Telfa, who leads expedition to the Upper Muva and establishes Western Kingdom.

242   King Corell assumes throne of Middle Kingdom and begins construction of the White Castle.

243   Jenaii complete El-Orva, the Blue Castle. Tarelian council gifts second Sword of the Stars to Zeltar king Eustice II. Zeltar begins construction of Nonn, the Yellow Castle.

251   Tarelian emissaries and engineers journey to Ape tribes and help begin construction of Gregok, the Green Castle.

253   King Culnar Cal defeats Soch Federation at Tinsan Bay and drives them off the northern coast.

256   The kingdom of Cagia is founded at the mouth of the Nila.

258   King Culnar Cal expands Northern Kingdom to the Reguh.

301   Western Kingdom drives Soch Federation from Tenin.

King Telfer begins construction of the Purple Castle.

325   Tarelian general Melida and her sister Telisa are gifted two Swords of the Stars and lead expedition to North Isle.

326   General Melida slays Soch king Vagar at the port of Soch.

Fall of Soch Federation.

The port is named the Bane of Soch and eventually shortened to Bansoch.

Melida leads the slave revolt.

Soch Federation is outnumbered by their female slaves by one hundred to one.

Melida establishes the Federation of the Sisterhood.

Massacre of Soch masters throughout the Isle.

Melida is named queen and first guardian of the Sisterhood.

331   Tarelian council gifts fifth and sixth Sword of the Stars to Generals Vatar and Nisin, who lead an expedition north of Veneba.

337   Battle of Tur Valley.

King Sargos Cal leads Northern Kingdom
to aid Generals Vatar and Nisin, and
they defeat the gargoyle horde.

General Vatar falls in battle.

General Nisin is named the king of
Eastern Kingdom and gifts the sword of
Vatar to Prince Sartos Cal of the Northern
Kingdom for their aid in battle.

339	King Nisin begins construction of the Red Castle.
351	Fera, the Black Castle, is completed.
380	Nonn, the Yellow Castle, is completed. It is later named simply Non.
390	Western Kingdom moves its capital to Tenin.
406	Telfer, the Purple Castle, is completed. Western Kingdom expands its realm into the Cress foothills.
415	Gregok, the Green Castle, is completed. Ape tribes agree to share command of fortress and form the Council of Chieftains.
431	Plague strikes Varabis.
437	Ports of Teris and Coven wage war of control for Casian Sea.
441	Corell, the White Castle, is completed.
453	Tarelian colonists build port of Sawyer.
470	Naybin tribes cross the Naiba and slay Zeltos king Eustice VII at the Battle of Der. The Sword of the Stars is taken.
471	King El Elen leads Jenaii army across the Elaris to aid Zeltar. Naybin chieftain Plou ambushes Jenaii in the Serren Forest. Jenaii withdraw. Defenders yield the Fortress of Non. Naybins declare Plou the first king of Nayboria.

500	Gargoyle horde sweeps from the Lone Hills, cross the Upper Monata, and invade the Jenaii Kingdom.
	Naybin Army, led by Pou II, cross the Elaris.
	Zar II leads Middle Kingdom Army to aid the Jenaii, breaking the siege of El-Orva.
	Plou II is slain in battle.
	Sword of the Stars is passed to his son, Prince Plou III.
	Naybins withdraw across the Elaris.
	Gargoyle horde is crushed.
503	Middle Kingdom and Jenaii armies aid local tribes and clear gargoyles from the Lone Hills.
512	Teris and Coven wage second war for control of Casian Sea.
	The war ends with a truce and the Treaty of Casian Alliance.
513	Gargoyles spill out of the Cress Mountains and siege Telfer.
	Death of King Telfin II.
	Prince Telfin III rallies Western Kingdom and breaks siege of Telfer.
	Gargoyles withdraw.
518–520	Western Kingdom and Northern Kingdom expel gargoyles from the Cress Mountains and destroy nesting grounds.
	Gargoyles withdraw to Mote and Plate Mountains.
	King Telfin III is slain in the Vorun Gap.
	The Sword of the Stars is lost.
525	Plague strikes Tarelia.
522–526	Tatin, Yatin, and Maltin barbarians swarm southwestern coast of Arax.

Tatins siege Cagan. Yatins seize Faust and advance up the Muva. Maltins settle by the lower Monata River and assail Sawyer.

Tatins are driven off.

527   Gargoyles invade Middle Kingdom.

Siege of Corell.

King El Evur breaks siege and drives gargoyles back to the Plate.

Maltin Army crosses Lake Monata and sack Tarelia.

The ancient holdfast is destroyed.

The library of Tarelia is burned.

528   Maltins siege Sawyer.

King Corell IV and King El Evur lead Middle Kingdom and Jenaii hosts to lift siege.

The Maltins are crushed.

530   In the Battle of Muva, Yatin king Mosar slays Western king Telfer V.

Yatins invade upper half of the kingdom.

Fall of Tenin.

Western Kingdom falls.

Yatin general Mosar named first emperor of Yatin.

540   Nisin, the Red Castle, is completed.

543   Kingdom of Cesa allies with Null consortium and fortifies coastal defenses against Maltin barbarians, who still dwell north and east along the Maconan heartland.

551   Ruling families establish Troan city state.

563   Gargoyles siege Nisin.

King Netso II repels invaders.

Gargoyles break upon the ramparts and withdraw to the Plate.

574   King Clorvis V calls for King Corell VI and King Netso to join in alliance to expel gargoyles from their last holdfasts along the Mote and Plate Mountains. Each agree to the Feran Alliance, the last great crusade to expel the gargoyles from Arax.

575   King Clorvis V and King Corell VI drive gargoyles from the Wid River Valley.

King Netso clears the Plate foothills from Veneba to the Reguh.

King El Oberan joins the Feran Alliance and leads Jenaii battlegroups into the Middle Kingdom.

Jenaii and the Middle Kingdom drive gargoyles deep into the Plate Mountains.

576   Prince Clorvis VI is ambushed by Menotrist tribes east of the Mote Mountains. The Sword of the Stars gifted by the Eastern Kingdom is lost with him.

King Clorvis V abandons Plate Campaign to expel Menotrists from his realm.

577   Yatin king Mosun II crosses the Rolun Gap and invades the Middle Kingdom.

Siege of Central City.

King Corell VI abandons Plate Campaign to lift the siege.

Battle of Turlis ends Yatin invasion.

Death of Mosun II and King Corell VI.

The Sisterhood's fleet sacks Tenin harbor, frees thousands of female slaves, burns Yatin fleet, and seizes the imperial treasury.

Yatins sue for peace with the Middle Kingdom and the Sisterhood.

Nayborians invade Jenaii Kingdom.

Prince Zar V is crowned king of the Middle
Kingdom and leads Torry Army to Jenaii's defense.

El Oberan abandons Plate Campaign
and joins Zar V in Jenaii campaign.

In the Battle of Etavorun, the Naybins are crushed.

Zar V sacks Plou, and the forces of Naybins submit.

Jenaii seize Non.

578   King Netso falls in the battle of the Western Plate.

The Sword of the Stars is lost.

Gargoyles rout Eastern Kingdom army
and swarm the upper Tur Valley.

579   King Zar V weds Queen Melina of the Sisterhood,
the first marriage of the monarchies.

581   Queen Melina III births twins, Prince Zar
VI and Princess Melina II. Zar VI is named
heir to the Middle Kingdom, and Melina II
is named crown princess of the Sisterhood.

583   Tro Harbor is sacked by Venotrist tribes.
Venotrists migrate north along the Veneba.

603   Gargoyles siege Nisin.

The Eastern Kingdom calls for aid to Northern
Kingdom. King Clorvis V ignores their pleas,
driven mad by the death of his son, Clorvis VI.

Benotrist tribes seize the Upper Reguh.

604   Venotrists ambush Nisin's relief army and settle in the Eastern Kingdom. Gargoyles fail to
sack Nisin and withdraw to the Upper Plate.
The Eastern Kingdom is greatly reduced.

630   Menotrist tribes invade the Middle Kingdom.

King Zar VI falls in battle.

Prince Cot assumes the throne and drives
Menotrists beyond Tuft's Mountain.

631   King Cot defeats Menotrists at the Winding River.

641   Venotrists sack Nisin. The palace falls
in one night through trickery.
Fall of the Eastern Kingdom.

648   Northern Kingdom repels Venotrists at the Reguh.

652   Gargoyles massacre Menotrists
near Mote Mountains.

660–663   Menotrists migrate into the Northern Kingdom.

King Clorvin crushes Menotrist tribes and
drives them into the northern Cress Mountains.
Clorvin the Cruel slaughters thousands of prisoners, hanging them upon crossed boards along
his borders, including women and children.

674   Gargoyles advance to the Nameless Mountains and
slaughter thousands of Benotrists, Venotrists, and
Menotrists. Clorvin the Cruel ignores their plight,
allowing gargoyles to purge inferior peoples.

704   Queen Velima II leads the Sisterhood's fleet into
the Bay of Faust and destroys the Yatin fleet.

Yatin prince Yagnar is captured and enslaved
by the Council of Guardians. Queen
Velima II claims him as slave consort.

Yatins sue for peace.

The Sisterhood's trade routes along
the western sea board are secure.

711   The Sword of the Sun is stolen. The
Northern Kingdom searches the Nameless
Mountains and Mote foothills to no avail.

The Northern Kingdom begins to fade.

821   Gargoyles invade the Middle Kingdom.

King Corell VI and Jenaii king El Enor
drive gargoyles back across the Plate.

Naybins seize Non and slaughter Jenaii's garrison.
Naybin's restoration.

	Jenaii withdraws across the Elaris.
841	King Vanlar is ambushed at Pharna.
	The Sword of the Moon is lost.
	The Middle Kingdom begins to fade.
871	Menotrists seize Laycrom.
	Garrison of Fera dwindles.
	Death of King Clorvis XII.
	The Northern Kingdom shatters into a dozen separate regencies.
872	King Vantor II receives great prophecy of the lost sword of the Middle Kingdom and gathers the Tarelian faithful from the fallen kingdoms to Corell.
	The Middle Kingdom endures.
899	Cagia expands borders.
	King Orvonus weds the princess of Tuk.
	Union of both kingdoms into greater Cagia.
920	Port West joins the Casian League.
931	Bacel and Notsu repel Venotrist invasion. King Vanlar III leads the Middle Kingdom to their aid.
1004	Plague sweeps Central City. Sixty percent perish in its wake.
1014	Yatins invade Cagia. Storm destroys half of the Yatin fleet. Emperor Yagun II sees the storm as an ill omen and withdraws.
1036	Menotrists expand westward and seize Tinsay.
	Menotrists name Maglar king of Menot Kingdom and gain dominion of all lands from the northern coast to the Cress foothills and Tinsay to Laycrom.
1041	Eastern Menotrists seize Fera.
	Last of the Northern Kingdom's regencies falls.

Eastern Menotrists name Malan first King of East Menot and gain dominion of all lands from Fera to Mordicay and the Reguh and Morga River Valleys.

Drive Benotrists into Plate foothills and eastward into the Vale of Nisa.

1049–1059	Venotrists repel Benotrist incursion.

Benotrist tribes migrate along the Plate and settle in the gap between Mote and Plate Mountains, an arduous trek known as the Trail of Woes.

1099–1101	Gargoyles gather great host in Central Plate and invade the Middle Kingdom.

Siege of Corell.

King Cot V and King El Evore crush gargoyles at the Battle of Besos.

1115–1117	Naybins seize Barbeario.

Varabin and Casian mercenaries lead revolt.

The bloody streets are heralded in song.

Casian League cuts Naybin sea routes.

Jenaii threatens invasion.

Naybins withdraw claim upon Barbeario.

1241	Menot Armada assails Bansoch. The Sisterhood crushes invasion. Thousands of Menot sailors are enslaved.
1259	Gargoyles recover strength and sweep across the northern plains.

Venotrists lose control of Tur Valley.

Pagan is sacked and burned.

1290	Menotrists seize undermanned Nisin.
1305	The Middle Kingdom extends east-west road from Corell to Notsu.
1386	Cesa wars with Fleace. Battle of Iotia.

	Fleace gains control over greater Maconia.
1409–1415	Gargoyles invade Reguh Valley.
	East Menot seeks alliance with West Menot.
	Union of Fera and Laycrom is sealed with the marriage of Menot crown prince Matan II and East Menot princess Alleria.
	Greater Menot union drives gargoyles from Reguh Valley.
1425	Matan II ascends the throne of Menot and seeks union with western Menotrist tribes who hold Greater Nisa and the Red Castle.
1431	Union of all Menotrist kingdoms under Matan II.
1440	Gargoyles again invade the Middle Kingdom.
	Siege of Corell.
	King Toria and El Elon, lord of the birdmen, lift siege and drive gargoyles back to the Plate.
1453	Gargoyles swarm out of Mote and Plate Mountains.
	Benotrists flee Gargoyle hordes and enter western Menot at the invite of Menotrist king Matan III to settle lands between Fera and the Nameless Mountains.
	Benotrists ae betrayed by Menotrist host. Their leaders are slain, and their people are reduced to serfdom.
1477	Yatins cross the Rolun Gap and seize Turlis.
	War of the Middle Kingdom and Yatin.
	King Toria II is slain at the Nila.
	Turlis ceded to the Yatin Empire.
	Prince Torry ascends the throne at the age of twelve.
1484	Yatins cross the Yagan swamps and advance to Cagan Harbor.

1485	King Torry declares war upon Yatin, seizes Turlis in one night, aligns with the kingdoms of Zulon and Teso, drives Yatins from the Nila Valley, relieves Tuk, and smashes Yatin host before the walls of Cagan.
1486	King Torry weds the princess Galena of Cagia, joining their kingdoms.
	Old Cagia becomes Torry South, and the Middle Kingdom is renamed Torry North.
	Zulon and Teso control Nila between the Torry realms.
1517	Milito, Krakita, and Morito join the Casian League and establish the Plutocratic Federation, controlling trade routes from the Rocky Shores to Linkortus.
1525	Casian Federation seizes Torn and expands control along the Ape Coast.
1542–1576	Benotrist population swells.
	Menotrists relocate one hundred thousand serfs along the northwestern coast.
	Benotrists revolt over mistreatment. The revolt is put down by Menot king Margos Andler.
	Five thousand disfigured prisoners perish along the northern branch of the Gorga River, renamed the Andler.
1605–1650	The Middle Kingdom expands magantor cavalry and begins clearing lower Plate of gargoyle raiders.
1685	Union of Fleace, Cesa, and Null.
	Mortun is named regent of the Macon Empire.
	Macons control all lands south of Monata River, between Torry South and the Jenaii kingdoms. Only Sawyer blocks their full access to Lake Monata.
1701	Macons assail Sawyer.

	Siege is lifted by King Torry III and Jenaii king El Ellon.
1783	Torry king Lorn I expels gargoyles from Wid River.
	Colonists flock to the fertile valley.
1830	Birth of Tyro.
1848	Birth of Jonas Caleph
1853–1864	Benotrist revolution lead by Morca.
	Tyro finds the Sword of the Sun. He unifies gargoyles and Benotrists.
	Birth of Morac. Death of Morca.
	Tyro overthrows Menotrist kingdom and is named emperor of Benotrist-Gargoyle Empire.
	Benotrist Empire expands from Tinsay to Nisin.
	Gargoyles establish secure nesting grounds across Benotrist Empire and grow in great numbers.
	Tyro searches in vain for his wife and child.
1863–1866	Sadden Wars.
	Gargoyles are driven north of the Plate.
	Trade routes are secured between Torry North and South.
	Yatins are expelled from Nila Valley.
	Jonas Caleph finds the Sword of the Moon and leads charge of Celti Flats.
	Prince Lore assumes throne of Torry realms.
1866	Princess Letha of the Sisterhood weds Tyro.
	Birth of Cronus Kenti.
1867	Birth of Lorn II.
1868	Birth of Tosha.
	Letha revokes marriage to Tyro.
1872	Birth of Princess Corry.
1873	Birth of Terin Caleph.
1882	Tyro forms alliance with Naybin emperor Lichu.

1887	Earthers arrive on Arax.
1889	Revolution in the Ape Empire.
	General Matuzak expels merchant bureaucracy and despot Ape chieftains.
1891	Battle of Tuft's Mountain.
	Thus begins the Great War.

APPENDIX B

Armies of Arax

Torry Armies

Army	Based	Commander	Size (1 telnic = 1,000)
1st	Cagan	Lewins	twenty telnics
2nd	Central City	Fonis	twenty telnics
3rd	Central City	Bode	twenty telnics
4rth	Cagan	Korath	twenty telnics
5th	Corell	Morton	twenty telnics

Large Garrisons

Cropus	Torgus Vantel	five telnics
Corell	Nevias	ten telnics
Central City	Torvin	five telnics
Cagan	Telanus	five telnics

Cavalry

1st	Central City	Tevlin	five hundred mounts
2nd	Central City	Connly	five hundred mounts (1,500 reserves)
3rd	western border	Meborn	five hundred mounts
4th	Cagan	Avliam	five hundred mounts (300 reserves)

Navy

1st	Cagan	Kilan (grand admiral)	sixty galleys
2nd	Cagan	Horikor	fifty galleys
3rd	Cagan	Liman	thirty galleys
4th	Cagan	Nylo	forty galleys
5th	Cagan	Morita	twenty galleys

Benotrist-Gargoyle Armies

Legion	Based	Commander	Size
1st (gargoyle)	Tinsay	Yonig	fifty telnics
2nd (gargoyle)	Tinsay	Torab	fifty telnics
3rd (gargoyle)	Tinsay	Yonig	fifty telnics
4th (gargoyle)	Fera	Tuvukk	fifty telnics
5th (gargoyle)	Fera	Concaka	fifty telnics
6th (gargoyle)	Fera	Maglakk	fifty telnics
7th (gargoyle)	Fera	Vaginak	fifty telnics
8th (Benotrist)	Nisin	Vlesnivolk	fifty telnics
9th (Benotrist)	Mordicay	Marcinia	fifty telnics
10th (Benotrist)	Pagan	Gavis	fifty telnics
11th (Benotrist)	Nisin	Felinaius	fifty telnics
12th (gargoyle)	eastern border	Krakeni	fifty telnics
13th (Benotrist)	Laycrom	Trinapolis	fifty telnics
14th (gargoyle)	Laycrom	Trimopolak	fifty telnics
15th (gargoyle)	southern border	Vicon	fifty telnics

16th (gargoyle)	southern border	Tombin	fifty telnics
17th (gargoyle)	southern border	Tanius	fifty telnics
18th (gargoyle)	southern border	Marcisis	fifty telnics

Garrison Forces

Based	Size
Fera	thirty telnics (Benotrist)
Nisin	twenty telnics (Benotrist)
Pagan	ten telnics (Benotrist)
Mordicay	ten telnics (Benotrist)
Tinsay	twenty telnics (Benotrist)
Laycrom	twenty telnics (Benotrist)
Border posts	ten telnics Benotrist)
	ten telnics (gargoyle)

Benotrist Navy

Fleet	Based	Admiral	Size
1st	Mordicay	Plesnivolk	50 galleys
2nd	Tinsay	Kruson	30 galleys
3rd	Pagan	Elto (grand admiral)	80 galleys
4th	Pagan	Pinota	50 galleys
5th	Tinsay	Mulsen	120 galleys
6th	Pagan	Silniw	50 galleys
7th	Tinsay	Onab	50 galleys
8th	Tinsay	Zelitov	50 galleys

Yatin Armies

Army	Based	Commander	Size (telnics)
1st	Mosar	Yoria	twenty-five
2nd	eastern border	Yitia	twenty-five
3rd	southern border	Jutol	fifteen
4th	Tenin	Teminas	ten

Garrison Forces

Mosar	Yakue	ten
Telfer	Morue	forty
Tenin	Yanis	twenty-five

Yatin Cavalry

Army	Based	Commander	Size (mounts)
1st	Telfer	Yebbit	seven hundred
2nd	Mosar	Cornyana	eight hundred

Yatin Navy

Fleet	Based	Admiral	Size
1st	Tenin	Pilian	thirty galleys
2nd	Tenin	Morily (grand admiral)	thirty galleys
3rd	Faust	Horician	forty galleys

Jenaii Armies

Battle Group	Based	Commander	Size
1st	El-Orva	El Tuvo	twenty telnics
2nd	El-Orva	Ev Evorn	twenty telnics
3rd	El Tova	En Elon	twenty telnics
Garrison Forces			
El-Orva	El Orta	fifteen telnics	
El Tova	En Vor	five telnics	

Jenaii Navy

Fleet	Based	Admiral	Size
1st	El Tova	En Atar	twenty galleys
2nd	El Tova	En Ovir	twenty galleys
3rd	El Tova	En Toshin	twenty galleys

Naybin Armies

Army	Based	Commander	Size
1st	northern border	Duloc	ten telnics
2nd	Plou	Rorin	ten telnics
3rd	Non	Corivan	ten telnics
4th	western border	Cuss	ten telnics

Garrison Forces

	Plou	Cestes	five telnics
	Non	Rasin	seven telnics
	Naiba	Tesra	three telnics
	border posts		five telnics

Naybin Navy

Fleet	Based	Admiral	Size
1st	Naiba	Gustub	ten galleys
2nd	Naiba	Galton	ten galleys

Macon Empire Armies

Army	Based	Commander	Size
1st	Fleace	Noivi	ten telnics
2nd	northern border	Vecious	fifteen telnics
3rd	western border	Ciyon	ten telnics
4th	Null	Farin	eight telnics

Garrison Forces

	Fleace	Novin	five telnics
	Cesa	Clyvo	five telnics

Macon Navy

Fleet	Based	Admiral	Size
1st	Cesa	Goren	twenty galleys
2nd	Null	Vulet	twenty galleys
3rd	Eastern Coast	Talmet	twenty galleys
4th	Western Coast	Gara	twenty galleys

Ape Empire
Armies

Army	Based	Commander	Size
1st	Gregok	Cragok	twenty telnics
2nd	Torn	Mocvoran	twenty telnics
3rd	Talon Pass	Vorklit	ten telnics
4th	Northern Coast	Matuzon	ten telnics
5th	Southern Coast	Vonzin	ten telnics

Garrison Forces

Based	Size
Gregok	ten telnics
Torn	ten telnics
Talon Pass	ten telnics

Ape Navy

Fleet	Based	Admiral	Size
1st	Torn	Zorgon	sixty galleys
2nd	Torn	Vornam	forty galleys

*Casian
Federation
Armies*

Army	Based	Commander	Size
1st	Coven	Gidvia	twelve telnics
2nd	Milito	Motchi	twelve telnics
3rd	Teris	Elke	seven telnics

Garrison Forces

Based	Size
Milito	three telnics
Coven	four telnics
Port West	three telnics
Teris	three telnics

Casian Navy

Fleet	Based	Admiral	Size
1st	Coven	Voelin	one hundred
2nd	Milito	Gylan	eighty
3rd	Port West	Gydar	sixty
4th	Teris	Eltar	sixty

*Federation of
the Sisterhood
Armies*

Army	Based	Commander	Size
1st	Bansoch	Na	twenty telnics
2nd	Fela	Vola	twenty telnics
3rd	southern border	Mial	twenty telnics

Garrison Forces

Bansoch		ten telnics
Fela		ten telnics

*Federation of
the Sisterhood
Navy*

Fleet	Based	Admiral	Size
1st	Bansoch	Nyla	120 galleys
2nd	Bansoch	Carel	80 galleys
3rd	Southern Coast	Daila	50 galleys

Teso Armies

1st Army	southeast-ern border	Hovel	four telnics
2nd Army	Central Teso	Velen	two telnics

Zulon Armies

1st Army	northern border	Zarento	two telnics
2nd Army	western border	Zubarro	three telnics

*City State
Armies*

Sawyer	five telnics	one hundred cavalry
Rego	five telnics	one hundred cavalry
Notsu	seven telnics	two hundred cavalry
Bacel	eight telnics	one hundred cavalry
Barbeario	eight telnics	

Bedo	ten telnics	one hundred cavalry	forty galleys
Tro Harbor	ten telnics	fifty cavalry	fifty galleys
Varabis	five telnics		thirty galleys

BENOTORIS
ANDLER RIVER
LAYCROM
MORGA RIVER
TINSAY
GORGA RIVER
FERA
MOTE MOUNTAINS
TUSS RIVER
COT RIVER
FEDERATION
OF THE
SISTERHOOD
FELA
BANSOCH
VORUN GAP
TENIN
TELFER
RULON GAP
REGO
NILA
STLEN RIVER
PE
TENIA RIVER
YATIN
MUVA RIVER
CENT
CIT
FAUST
MOSAR
EMPIRE
TURLIS
YAGAN MARSHES
ZULON
RIVER
TESO
LAKE MONATA
TOK NILA
TORRY
SOUTH
MONATA RIVER
SAWYER
CAGAN
FLEACE
MACON
CLEV RIVER
CESA
NULL
EMPIRE
CHIHAN ISLE

EMPIRE
PAGAN
TUR RIVER
BEDO
CORPI
REGUH RIVER
NISIN
TERSE
LATE MTS
LAKE VENEBA
CROP
BACEL
BESOS
NOTSU
FLEN RIVER
TRO
CORELL
TORRY
KREGARIN ISLE
LEN RIVER
LONE HILLS
RAL NORTH
TALON PASS
APE
TORN
GREGOK
EMPIRE
TORN RIVER
JENAII
EL ORVA
BARBEARIO
NON
PLOU
NAIBA RIVER
ELARIS RIVER
NAYBORIA
EL TOVA
ENORUCTA
MIKUS
VARABIS
LINKORTIS
ROCKY SHORE
CASIAN SEA
MILITO
TERIS
COVEN
PORT WEST
CASIAN LEAGUE

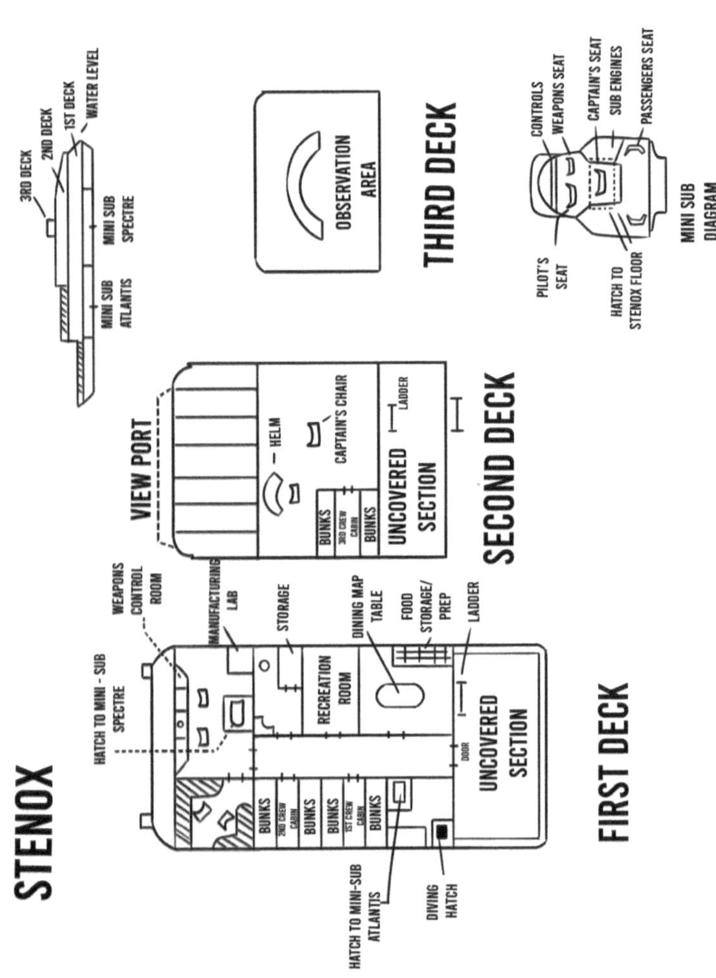
STENOX
3RD DECK
2ND DECK
1ST DECK
WATER LEVEL
MINI SUB SPECTRE
MINI SUB ATLANTIS
OBSERVATION AREA
THIRD DECK
CONTROLS
WEAPONS SEAT
CAPTAIN'S SEAT
SUB ENGINES
PASSENGERS SEAT
PILOT'S SEAT
HATCH TO STENOX FLOOR
MINI SUB DIAGRAM
VIEW PORT
HELM
CAPTAIN'S CHAIR
BUNKS
3RD CREW CABIN
BUNKS
UNCOVERED SECTION
LADDER
SECOND DECK
WEAPONS CONTROL ROOM
MANUFACTURING LAB
STORAGE
DINING MAP TABLE
FOOD STORAGE/ PREP
LADDER
HATCH TO MINI - SUB SPECTRE
RECREATION ROOM
UNCOVERED SECTION
DOOR
BUNKS
2ND CREW CABIN
BUNKS
1ST CREW CABIN
BUNKS
HATCH TO MINI-SUB ATLANTIS
DIVING HATCH
FIRST DECK

Other Books Available by Author:

Free Born saga
    Free Born
    Elysia

Chronicles of Arax
    Book one: Of War And Heroes
    Book two: The Siege of Corell
    Book three: The Battle of Yatin
    Book four: The Making of a King

ABOUT THE AUTHOR

Ben Sanford grew up in Western New York. He spent almost twenty years as an air marshal, traveling across the United States and many parts of the world, meeting people from a broad range of cultures and backgrounds. It was from these thousands of interactions that he drew inspiration for the characters in his books. He currently resides in Maryland with his family.